SACRED FIRE

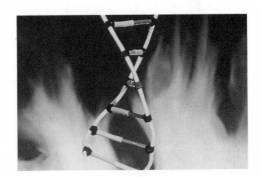

SACRED FIRE

ISI BELLER

Arcade Publishing · New York

FIRST NORTH AMERICAN EDITION

The characters and events in this book are fictitious. Any similarity to real persons, living or dead, is coincidental and not intended by the author.

ISBN 1-55970-226-5
Library of Congress Catalog Card Number 94-9936
Library of Congress Cataloging-in-Publication information is available.

Published in the United States of America by Arcade Publishing, Inc., New York
Distributed by Little, Brown and Company

10   9   8   7   6   5   4   3   2   1

BP

Designed by API

PRINTED IN THE UNITED STATES OF AMERICA

Acknowledgments

I would like to thank Dr. Sam Merrick of the Center for Special Studies at New York Hospital and Joan Aichner of Danville, Virginia, for their technical assistance. My thanks also go to my friends at Arcade, Dick Seaver and Jeannette Seaver. I am especially grateful to Tim Bent for his editorial insight.

SACRED FIRE

Prologue

The surveillance vehicle coasted silently down the dirt road until it came to a stop under a pine tree.

Annabelle Weaver looked through the rear window down to the cabin, whose front, nestled against the cliffs about a hundred yards below, was just within her line of vision. She could see part of a timbered roof. She could also see that the only access was from the front. Large rocks stood sentry next to the door and, combined with the fact that the structure was perched over the water, gave the cabin a look of nearly fortresslike invincibility. Behind it, Lake Tahoe shimmered in the sun, and behind Lake Tahoe the white-capped Toiyabe Mountains stood in stark profile against the deep azure of the sky.

So this was Paul Verne's little hideaway.

"Rocky Roost," she said to no one in particular. "A good name for this place."

Annabelle turned to Robert Kane, who was sitting in front of the control panel inside the van and wearing a headset. His eyes were glued to a screen.

"Well, how's the reception?"

The agent from the Federal Bureau of Biological Supervision grunted with satisfaction and played with a few switches.

"Good, boss. The static's gone. It was caused by an electrical transformer at King's Beach."

"When this is over, John goes back for retraining," replied Annabelle dryly. "He almost botched everything. No excuse. Now make sure everyone's in position."

Kane mumbled something into his headset and scratched the shaved crown of his scalp. The inside of the van glowed from the lights on the control panel.

"Everyone's in position," he said at last, leaning back in his chair.

"All we can do now is wait. Just hope we don't have to spend a week here," he added.

"No need to worry about that," sneered Annabelle, sliding into the chair next to his. She poured herself a carbonated Cocaid® and drained the glass. Then, euphoric at the prospect that the drug would soon be moving along her bloodstream, she added, "Let me see what you've got."

Kane fingered some keys, and a line of monitors lit up, one after the other. Each one showed the interior of the house below from a different angle.

"The cameras will follow them the moment they walk in," he explained. "That's the living room, the kitchen. There's the kid's room. And look, these are the important ones — the master bedroom from four different angles. The cameras use infrared light and are equipped with a zoom. Everything gets recorded automatically. Take my word for it," Kane concluded, "we're ready for them."

"You're absolutely positive there's no chance he'll spot the cameras?" asked Annabelle, her tone as hard as stone.

"They're as small as a pinhead. He'd have to know exactly where to look. And they've been in place for a month, so I — "

Annabelle cut him off. "With Verne, anything can happen. OK, then. What about the other rooms?"

"Everything's covered, even the bathrooms," said Kane, swallowing.

"Fine. It's out of our hands. We wait."

The boat — a sloop composed entirely of plastic and wood so that no radar could detect it — glided toward the dock and with a light thud struck the rubber protectors. Standing at the helm, Paul Verne watched Clara jump lightly onto the dock and secure the lines. He felt his throat tighten.

"Hey, Paul, snap out of it," she chided when she saw he was staring. Then she smiled. "Julia and I are hungry."

"I'm coming, I'm coming," Verne replied. "You know, we were lucky that old couple didn't see us out there. That's the last time we go out like that. I think they're watching us."

"No one saw anything, Paul, trust me," said Clara, her voice suddenly serious. "Julia was below, and anyway — "

She made a gesture of helplessness and turned away so that he wouldn't see the tears that were filling her eyes.

They had a twenty-four-hour respite. Then, Verne knew, Herakles would come for Julia, and he and Clara wouldn't see her again until her third birthday. After that, thanks to help from the Network, Julia would be adopted by a family. If everything went smoothly, Paul and Clara might be able to visit her.

Verne went below into the tiny cabin. His four-month-old daughter was lying awake in her basket. He lifted her into his arms and, despite her squirming, managed to cover her with the blanket.

Clutching this odd little bundle against his chest, he leapt onto the dock and hurriedly climbed the wooden stairs that led to the house.

Clara followed him, glancing behind her from time to time.

"That's them," said Kane.

Lights appeared on the control panel. The trap was closing.

"We've got them," said Annabelle, exulting, watching the couple on the screen go into their house. "Two years, Kane. Do you understand that? I have been waiting almost *two years* for this. That's when I first heard about Joseph Milner's letter. Now turn up the volume. I don't want to miss a thing."

In the kitchen Clara handed Verne the bottle. Julia began sucking greedily on it.

"She's got your appetite," mused her father.

"Oh, who knows. My appetite, your intelligence . . . what will any of that matter in three years?"

"She's a wonderful little girl. The best thing that's happened to us. We should be grateful, Clara. Just think of all those millions of people who can't — "

"I do think of them, but it doesn't help . . . Let's go to bed," she added brusquely and left the kitchen.

"Oh my God! Would you look at them!" Kane was nearly shouting.

"Hey, calm down," Annabelle replied. She herself was feeling very composed. "You haven't seen anything yet. We're still missing the most essential thing of all for Promised Land to be a complete success."

"You think they'll really do it?"

"Let's just say I know how these things go," she murmured smugly. Kane gave her a look of disbelief.

"Come on, Kane. Women have always known more than men about those things. And not just because of the implant you all have . . . or at least are supposed to have," she added, taking her attention back to the screen.

She saw Julia's parents putting their child in her crib.

"Give me a close-up on Clara Hastings. I want to see this."

The camera framed the young woman at the moment she was bending over tenderly to kiss her child good night.

"How unbelievably revolting!" gasped Annabelle.

Out on the deck off the bedroom, Paul Verne read — for the third time — the same sentence out of the book he was holding. It was written by Kess Sherman, the former leader of the Southern California Network who was now rotting in an Arizona prison, where he had been for about a year. It was a miracle Clara had managed to find the book.

Verne's mind wandered, and he let the book fall to his lap. His eyes followed the path of a falcon circling far above. The sun had just set behind Barker's Peak, and the first lights from Homewood were appearing on the far side of the lake.

The smallest noise made him jump. He knew that nothing had changed since they had gotten Herakles's message — that everything was still on for tomorrow night. But he was worried.

He got up, paced the deck, and went back inside the dark bedroom.

"Don't turn on the light," Clara murmured. "Come lie down next to me."

"OK, here we go," said Annabelle triumphantly. "Now you'll really get to see something. This is it."

Kane didn't respond. He was too engrossed in the images on the monitor.

Verne held Clara in his arms. She embraced him back as tightly as he held her and covered his face with tear-moistened kisses. He was overwhelmed by the desire to melt into her.

"That clinches it!" Annabelle whooped. "The great Paul Verne won't be able to talk his way out of this one. The whole damn country's going to see this! Get everything, Kane. I don't want a detail left out. It's not every day you're going to see something like this. Not if I have anything to do with it."

Kane was still staring glassy-eyed at the screen.

"OK, we've got plenty. That'll do, Kane. Kane? Hey, Kane! Damn it, snap out of it! Tell everyone to stay alert. Now do it!"

Kane shook off his stupor and mumbled something into the microphone.

Some inexplicable distraction was keeping Verne from giving in to the desire he felt surging inside him. Clara was nude, straddling him.

A steady rattle came from deep in her throat, like pebbles drawn back by a receding wave. He was no longer watching her face in the shadows, or listening to the slow dissipation of her ecstasy.

"Shhh!" he hissed suddenly, grabbing Clara's wrists.

"What? What is it? It must be Julia — "

"No. Listen."

A low purr was coming through the open window. A motor.

"A boat just landed at the dock. Get dressed. Hurry," he added, pushing her away almost roughly.

"It's a boat," said Kane, who had just gotten the message over the intercom.

Annabelle hesitated.

"We've got everything we need. Send them in now," urged Kane.

"No," she replied. "Maybe it's someone from the Network. Let's find out why they're here first. No one's going anywhere."

Carrying his rifle, Verne sprinted to the back door. Then he froze and listened hard. He heard footsteps move fast up the outer staircase. When he estimated they had reached the door, he backed away from it as he undid the safety.

Someone knocked: two long, three short, one long. Verne half closed his eyes and exhaled raggedly in relief. It was the Network.

He opened the door.

"Herakles!" he cried, taking into his arms the looming figure standing there. "But, what — "

"So, how're you lovebirds doing?" said Herakles, loudly interrupting Verne's question and hugging him back affectionately.

Verne felt something being slipped into his pocket.

"Read it in the cellar," Herakles whispered quickly in his ear.

Verne felt as if his chest had just been pierced with something sharp. He wanted to speak but found no breath.

"Where's the rest of your little family?" asked Herakles, smiling broadly and looking around. His voice was still very loud.

Clara appeared, holding Julia. She stopped when she saw Herakles.

"Herakles! What are — "

The big man went to her and kissed her swiftly on the mouth, leaving her momentarily voiceless.

"I just wanted to surprise you," he said jovially. "I thought I'd come spend a few days at Rocky Roost. Plenty of time for us to catch up."

He turned to Verne:

"Hey, Paul, don't you think this calls for a little something from your wine cellar? I could use a pick-me-up."

"Can you believe those bastards?" Annabelle exclaimed. "They're going to drink alcohol! Who do they think they are? Worshipers? Wait a minute. What did he mean about a cellar? Kane, what he's talking about?"

"Um, I dunno. There's no cellar indicated on the floorplan."

"I don't like this. I do *not* like this." Annabelle was drumming her fingernails on the console. "Another minute and we go in."

Down in the cellar, which Verne had dug the moment he set up shop at Rocky Roost, he read the note Herakles had slipped him.

FROM: FBBS CENTRAL HEADQUARTERS.
ROCKY ROOST UNDER SURVEILLANCE. ANNABELLE WEAVER. OVER A MONTH. REMOTE CONTROL VIDEOS THROUGHOUT. HOUSE SURROUNDED. IMMEDIATE EXECUTION OF CALYPSO. BACKUP PLAN: LONG MARCH. MERCURY

Verne reopened the trapdoor hidden beneath the stairwell.

"Where in *hell* is his voice coming from?" snapped Annabelle. Her nerves were starting to fray. She was madly scanning the monitors for Verne. "Don't you have a zoom on this thing? What's he saying? Goddamn it, Kane!"

Verne's amplified voice filled the inside of the van.

"He's calling them," said Kane.

"What do you mean, calling them? Calling them from fucking where? We're going in. Now!"

Herakles went first through the underground passage, head bowed, holding Julia in one arm. In the other he had a flashlight. Clara was right behind him, breathing heavily. Verne, carrying the rifle, brought up the rear.

The end of the tunnel was lit up.

"Shit," hissed Herakles, "they're using searchlights."

He handed the child to Clara, signaled that she was not to move, and moved cautiously toward the exit. He was back several seconds later.

"We've got a slim chance. The searchlights are all pointed at the house. The dock isn't lit. We'll have to run."

He reached out for Julia. Clara pulled back instinctively.

6 /

"Be reasonable," he told her softly.

Herakles adjusted the blanket around the child, took a deep breath, and sprinted out of the cave.

For a moment there was nothing. From the reflection of the spotlights on the water, the dock was visible from a hundred feet away.

Then there were cries.

"They've seen us," shouted Verne, right behind Herakles. "I'll cover you."

They were flooded with light.

Verne threw himself on his stomach and fired several bursts.

The sound of something shattering. A light went out. A startled scream. Verne turned and saw Herakles jump into the boat with Julia. Clara had only a few feet to go.

Verne got up and ran toward her, hunched over. Bullets hissed by his ears. Suddenly he stumbled on a rock and went sprawling facedown.

He raised his head. Clara had stopped and was motioning frantically at him.

"Jump on board for Christ's sake!" he yelled.

She hesitated. There was a gunshot. A stain appeared on her white blouse. In one motion her mouth opened and she tumbled off the dock into the water.

Verne raised himself and ran like a madman, screaming her name. He dove off the dock into the dark water.

When he came to the surface he heard the boat speeding off. Julia was safe.

Fighting back panic, he dove again to look for Clara.

He bumped into her inanimate body. With a violent effort he managed to grab the back of her blouse and haul her up to the surface.

Holding her head out of the water, he swam on his back. He had one goal: to reach the small stream just beyond the breakwater where the *Aleph* was waiting.

A sob rose in his throat, and he had to fight off an irrepressible desire to let go, to sink, with Clara, into the boundless obscurity of the night.

Part I

Eighteen months earlier

Chapter 1

1

"Dr. Verne?"

Paul Verne wheeled around. "Yes?"

The man paused, as if gathering strength. The accent was slightly Germanic, but what immediately struck Verne was the cadaverous pallor of the stranger standing before him. His eyes made it look as if he were suffering from a severe thyroid condition. He was tall; his thin, graying blond hair was meticulously combed over to one side. He was dressed in a gray flannel suit that looked dapper and dated. His emaciated neck didn't even touch the collar of his shirt, which was done up with a dandy's purple bow tie.

Verne's clinical eye diagnosed the final stages of Spermatic Fever: febrile expression, pallor, emaciation, motor instability, trembling.

The man began to scratch furiously at the crown of his head.

"What can I do for you?" Verne asked, realizing that he had been examining the man in silence. "I'm a little pressed for time. I have to go to a lecture in" — he glanced at his watch — "about three minutes and . . ."

He stopped, struck by the sweetness of the man's smile.

"I'll only use up one of your precious minutes, Dr. Verne. I am from Austria."

"From Austria."

"Yes, from Vienna. I have news of Dr. Joseph Milner."

Verne felt the blood draining from his face.

"You know him?" he finally managed to ask.

The man glanced around with a pained expression.

The cavernous first floor of the United Nations bustled with the usual cosmopolitan crowd. No one seemed to be paying any attention to them.

"Why don't we go somewhere else," Verne said quietly. "The question is where? Are you with a delegation?"

"The Austrian delegation." The man began to cough.

"Let's try the cafeteria."

"That won't be necessary, Dr. Verne. I only have one thing to say. I did not know Dr. Milner personally."

"You *did not* know . . ."

The man inhaled deeply and slowly, as if taking in air for the first time — or the last. Verne knew the man would live for only a few more weeks.

"Dr. Milner is dead," wheezed the stranger abruptly.

Verne froze.

"He has killed himself. Nine days ago his body was found. He'd ingested pills."

"Dead?" stammered Verne. "Joseph Milner is dead?"

The stranger seemed to take no notice of Verne's distress. He said nothing.

"What are you talking about? He took pills?"

"That is correct. Pills. He committed suicide."

"But — but no one has said anything. Nothing. I haven't — are you sure?"

"Unfortunately, I am. The news will be picked up by the media when the news blackout is lifted. Authorities are conducting an investigation." The stranger timidly touched Verne's arm. "I am terribly sorry," he added.

Verne was too stunned to notice the sympathy.

"This investigation — " he said finally, then stopped. "What is your name?"

"Karl Schiele. I am the new secretary of the Austrian delegation. I am also a member of Socrates," he added quickly and quietly, glancing around him again.

"Of what?"

"Socrates. Surely you must . . ."

"Yes, of course. Socrates. Thank you. I think I should be going. Maybe you'll understand . . . Where can I find you?"

"Here. For as long as I am granted life."

"Well, good-bye. I'll — I'll contact you."

Verne walked toward the exit feeling as if he were moving through a fog.

"Take me to Penn Station," Verne ordered the taxi driver.

"Bapré, man. First you say airport. Now you are wanting Penn Station."

"Just do it, please."

"OK, OK."

The taxi driver found an exit and headed back toward Manhattan.

Something was telling Verne to take a train. He knew it was crazy. Cross-country trains would be absurdly slow. If he caught a sonic he could be back in San Francisco in under an hour; the train would take days. There would be delays at every state border. But he wanted delays; he wanted time. The idea of sharing Joe's death with anyone — even with Melissa — seemed impossible. He didn't even know what his feelings were, just that they were being sifted through the screen of his intuition, his sixth sense. Paul Verne's intuition was a gift that those who knew him knew enough to respect.

He wanted, most of all, to be alone — to measure his grief and to reflect in lonely meditation on the man who, despite their falling out, had been his teacher and his friend. There would be time later to feel guilty about this selfishness.

Four days to get back to San Francisco by train. Four days of solitude. He would call Melissa from the train. The Institute could survive without him for a few days.

Verne settled deeper into the seat of the cab.

2

"I think maybe the freeway would be better," suggested Clara Hastings in as breezy a tone as she could manage through her nervousness. She tightened her hold on her purse.

The driver was a man in his sixties. His milky blue eyes watched her in the rearview mirror. He hadn't stopped chewing gum from the moment he'd picked her up on Sunset. He accelerated to keep his place in line at the intersection of Venice Boulevard.

Clara let out an exasperated sigh. She was well aware that men didn't like to talk with a woman they didn't know. But these days a woman couldn't even ask for the time from a man without getting snubbed. Even Wes, her oldest friend, had acted more coolly toward her than usual. Half an hour earlier, when he carefully slipped her the letter in the menu at Le Dome, he'd avoided eye contact, as if hiding something. No words of encouragement.

Clara ran her hand through her hair, which, contrary to the latest fashion of buzz-cuts, fell freely about her shoulders. Her brown eyes were only lightly made up and the light Indian-cotton blouse she wore emphasized her slender white neck.

She looked at the traffic in despair. There was little chance she would make her flight. She'd have to catch the subsonic instead, and that would mean a tedious three-hour trip to New York. The whole effort would be a waste of time if she missed the Network contact at Kennedy. She wouldn't even have time to call Wes as they'd agreed. Everything was getting screwed up.

With deliberate clumsiness, she opened her purse and dumped the contents on the floor of the cab.

The driver snickered and stuffed a fresh piece of Cocaid gum in his mouth.

Clara leaned forward, found the envelope Wes had given her, and slipped it behind the lining of her purse. She made sure it fell to the bottom. Then she stuffed the other contents back inside. The hiding place wouldn't stand up to a serious search, she knew, but it was the best she could do for now.

She straightened up, noticing with irritation that the driver had been watching her steadily.

"I'll pay double if you get me to the airport in less than half an hour," she said to him.

"I'm going as fast as I can," he replied, as if he were enjoying himself. They were the first words he had spoken. "Maybe you should go on foot," he added. "Money won't help."

The light changed.

The driver accelerated and headed off into Baldwin Hills, where abandoned gas pumps stood like petrified trees. This was where La Cienega left Culver City and for a mile and a half resembled a real freeway — until it hit traffic at Inglewood.

The vehicle picked up speed. Clara felt sweat beading on her forehead. Nerves, probably. For the first time since she'd gotten into the cab, she noticed the clear plastic yarmulke the driver wore on his head.

"Are you Jewish?" she asked in a friendly voice.

"What's it to you?"

"Oh, well, I just saw your yarmulke and — "

"It's regulation."

The man reached up and touched it with his stubby fingers. "Been wearing it since Rabbi Horowitz signed the deal with the FBBS. Me, I could care less that it's plastic. I got nothing to do with the NJO. You know about them?"

"Excuse me?"

"The New Jewish Organization."

"Oh. No."

"They're all in prison. And a lot of good that does anyone."

The traffic moved in four lanes, heading south.

The driver swerved slightly to avoid a car pushing in from the left. Now he was talking nonstop.

While he regaled her in great detail about the conflicts between the various Jewish communities, Clara recalled a scene she had witnessed on Wilshire Boulevard. Three young men walking arm-in-arm handing out flyers, fully aware of the effect their opaque yarmulkes had on the passersby. People turned and whispered. Most refused to take a leaflet. Then, suddenly, sirens everywhere. Two police vehicles screeched to a halt at the curb. The police pushed the men around and handcuffed them roughly; the men had offered no resistance.

The taxi headed down the hill toward Inglewood.

Clara saw a plane take off over Venice. The airport couldn't be far. Maybe she would make her flight after all.

"Hey, what's going on here?" the driver exclaimed suddenly.

A high-speed police helicopter thundered overhead. It moved ahead of them, did a U-turn, and hung in the air. The driver turned off the ignition.

"Why are you turning it off?" asked Clara.

"Where's to go? Take a look around. Everything's backed up all the way to the Centinela traffic light. Hey, look! They're coming down right in the middle of the intersection! Must be after someone. I'd forget about making your flight. We're gonna be here for a while."

The driver got out of the car. Clara followed him. "I'm going to take your advice and walk," she said, holding out a hundred-dollar bill. He made no effort to make change. Instead he opened the trunk, then watched impassively while she pulled her suitcase out of the cab and started walking in the opposite direction from the airport.

3

The train whistled and slowed as it rounded a bend. Paul Verne saw a sign indicating that work was being done on the track.

He got up.

When they heard the train approaching, the workers straightened their backs and the steam shovel drivers paused. The raw color of freshly dug earth contrasted with the grayish snow that stretched to the horizon, all the way to the outline of the Allegheny Mountains.

In their bright orange work coats the workers looked like an honor guard at a military funeral. The rhythmic vibrations of the train accentuated the black mood that Verne had found himself slipping into with a certain morbid pleasure.

He waved, a little tentatively, to a worker leaning on the handle of a pickax who was following him with his eyes. No response. That was when he noticed a uniform with a weapon balanced on his hip. Work patrol. The hostility of the convicts was palpable. He imagined that the other travelers were pressing their noses against the windows gawking, like people at a zoo.

The bleak winter landscape began moving by more quickly.

Verne sat down again on the bed, which, along with the foldaway table, was the only furniture in his first-class, single-occupancy compartment. Paul Verne looked about forty years old. Tall, with slightly graying temples and dark eyes set deeply beneath bushy eyebrows, he wore a baggy, academic-looking corduroy jacket with the leather elbow-patches that had recently become fashionable again in certain circles. An occasional nervous gesture betrayed inner tensions and contradicted his outward look of detached calm.

He wished the trip would never end. Four days of solitude would not be enough time to sort through his thoughts. Perhaps it was time to distance himself from the Reiss Institute in Marin County, at which, for the last twelve years, he had served as director of research. And do what? He knew exactly what. Go to France. He had been thinking about France more and more, and about returning to Colmar, the Alsatian town of his birth. The death of Joseph Milner lent an urgency to his nostalgia, and thoughts that he usually relegated to the back of his mind were, more and more, refusing to stay there.

He got up, went into the cramped bathroom, and looked at his reflection in the mirror above the sink. The room was moving, and not just from the action of the train. He felt dizzy. He focused on his reflection to calm himself.

It was precisely at moments like these that Melissa would accuse him of closing her out of his thoughts. His aloofness could provoke an anxiety attack in her that might last for days. Lately, when he retreated into the privacy of his thoughts, she would respond with a stream of sarcasm. It was as if she couldn't help herself. "There it is again, ladies and gentlemen," she would begin, "Paul Verne's world-famous *inner look*. A moment of silence, if you please!"

Verne splashed some water on his face and returned to the compartment.

Dizziness was turning into nausea.

He picked up a scientific quarterly he had left on the bed, determined to finish reading the article on retroviruses. He soon found himself staring at the nail of his left index finger. Little by little, he was slipping into daydream.

When preoccupied or under pressure, Verne would spend hours concentrating on that fingernail; it was slightly different than the other nails. Careful nosological examination led him to conclude that in shape the nail was cuneiform, as opposed to the rest, which were ovoid. When he was young, the singularity of the fingernail had been a source of embarrassment, even shame. He had always been careful to keep it folded into his hand or in his pocket. His mother told him he had inherited it from his grandfather and that it was nothing to be ashamed about. His grandfather was the man in the photograph that had always occupied a place of prominence on her dressing table. A man with a long white beard. He died somewhere in Poland, long before.

Verne was suddenly aware of a stinging sensation in his fingertips.

He tried to get up. His muscles wouldn't respond. With strange lucidity, he realized he was losing consciousness.

His head slumped forward at the precise moment that the door of his compartment slowly opened.

4

Kess Sherman leaned over the railing of his terrace.

He felt a stab of hunger. Each time he got bad news he got hungry. Danger whetted the appetite. The amphetamines that the Network doctor had prescribed for him six months ago did nothing but give him insomnia. Another enduring side effect of the ASP; implantation may have crushed some cerebral knot.

Conceived by scientists at the National Institutes of Health in Bethesda, the Anti-Sex Program, or ASP, as it was generally referred to, had become a constant companion for all men. Its development had originally been instigated per a directive from the Surgeon General, who, along with the Pentagon, was concerned that peace-keeping units returning from countries where AIDS was totally out of control would infect the home population.

The standard mechanisms for protecting citizens from carriers of HIV — identity cards, quarantining, tattooing, all adopted fairly early on (Germany in particular was innovative) — had proven ineffective. Many Americans were initially suspicious of the ASP, though just as many said it could prove invaluable — at least until some method of solving the puzzle of the HIV's mutative capacities was found.

An inch in circumference, a fraction of an inch in thickness, the new device was implanted below the skin of the man's scalp, roughly at the level of the tonsure — the crown of the scalp that during the Middle Ages monks shaved as a symbol of their renunciation of worldly pleasures.

Two microscopic wires connected the ASP to the neurological zones governing sexual activity. One of the wires — having been threaded through the cranium and the brain tissue — dipped down between the two cerebral hemispheres toward the base of the fourth ventricle of the hypothalamus, where the inhibitors of sexual activity are located. The other ran along the axis of the vertebral column to the critical second vertebra, where it was fused to the spinal cord.

The idea was very simple: the instant the ASP's electronic receiver discerned the beginnings of sexual stimulation from the vertebral electrode, it emitted a charge directly into the central cerebral inhibitor through the intracerebral electrode. The erection was forestalled.

Unfortunately, electronic castration also produced a few side effects, most of them caused by the exceptional density of the regulatory knots in the hypothalamus. Because it couldn't pinpoint its target, the current spilled over into other areas, creating sleeplessness, nervousness, nausea, muscle ache, depression, or insatiable hunger. But those ailments notwithstanding, the ASP did what it was supposed to do. The wearer was no longer troubled by sexual arousal. The side effects could be dealt with through intensive neurological and psychotherapeutic treatments.

However, a practical problem slowed the diffusion of this ingenious apparatus. Implantation required surgery, and this posed difficulties. The army needed thousands, even hundreds of thousands, of the implants. There was a mad rush among researchers around the world to refine the process and find a method of implantation that would not require surgery.

The first improvement obviated the microscopic wires. Medical researchers discovered that it was possible to stimulate the inhibitors in the hypothalamus by means of a laser beam. This was a tremendous step forward because: one, the beam was far more precise than the electrode; two, it didn't require actual contact. Soon the apparatus could directly measure the intracerebral potential induced by erections, meaning it was no longer necessary to lodge the electrode in the vertebra.

This required a larger source of power than before — a considerably larger source. Researchers found that a photoelectric cell did the trick. The ASP had its source. Hence why implantees had their head tonsured: to help the solar batteries recharge. For the same reason, men were forbidden to wear any manner of headgear not made of transparent material.

The government warned that unofficial removal of the ASP could be lethal. Each implant contained a particular code, and if a surgeon didn't know that code he was sure to cause extensive brain damage. The penalties if you were caught for attempting to disconnect the ASP were fierce.

ASP wearers were closely monitored. They had to undergo ASP Supervision on a regular basis so that the device could be checked.

There had been some scattered protest at first, the occasional demonstration organized by idealists and civil libertarians. They were as much disturbed by the complexity of the surgery required as by the abrogation of individual rights it entailed. Even if sex could never be safe enough, weren't there other methods? The consensus, however, was that any soldier infected by the virus should be forced to undergo implantation.

Indeed there was soon vigorous lobbying to have ASPs implanted in anyone with HIV — convicts, for example. But initially there was enough resistance to the idea that for a short time the number of implants were limited.

Then came Spermatic Fever — Sacred Fire. Suddenly there was no doubt: the ASP should serve as a frontline defense against the destruction of the race. Blood wasn't the primary danger; sperm was. All transmission of sperm had to be stopped. Condoms weren't nearly enough protection. Vasectomies were often reversible — and back-alley physicians willing to do the operation for a price would inevitably arise. The ASP seemed to offer the best method of ensuring abstinence; it was backed up by impotence. All men were required to carry the "roof spider," as some now called it. Getting "bitten" or "bugged" was more than a mere patriotic duty; patriotic or not, you had to have the implant. Male sexuality was but a small price to pay to save the life of the nation.

Whenever he thought about everything the Government had asked — forced — citizens to believe blindly and without reservation, Sherman felt bile rise in his throat. He believed that the ASP was far more than simply an effective way of preventing the transmission of sperm. It was a symbol of mind control, repression, and resignation. The cure turned out to be more maleficent than the disease: it was killing off any effort to find another way of dealing with the epidemic, a way that might preserve a few civil liberties — and spare human dignity.

A year earlier, a surgeon in the Network had succeeded in removing Sherman's ASP, but disconnection had done little to alleviate his polyphagia: Sherman was always hungry. As for his sexual appetite, it had never returned. He was beginning to believe that the effects of the ASP, even one that had been unplugged, were permanent.

Close by on his left stood the ruins of the Chateau Marmont, the last of the luxury hotels rebuilt in the last century, destroyed in the same earthquake that leveled much of the city. The large studios took advantage of the disaster to move their operations a comfortable distance away from the San Andreas Fault.

A native of Los Angeles, Sherman had become something of a celebrity because of a novel he had written a dozen years earlier — an epic about the decline and fall of a great American city. Ever since the Fuchs Amendment had gone into effect he had not written a single line. All energies were directed toward the great struggle.

Sherman scratched his tonsure — a nervous habit many men had acquired. Wesley Marshall had stopped by half an hour earlier to inform him that his meeting with Clara Hastings had gone according to plan. She had Milner's letter.

The Southern California Network chief was now waiting to learn whether Clara had caught the sonic, and while he was waiting he mused over the idea of bringing Paul Verne into the resistance fold. It would be an extraordinary coup, but Sherman thought it unlikely. A member of the Biosociology Commission joining the Network? A very long shot.

He went back inside the house. The spacious living room was in a pitiful state. Paint was chipping, the carpet was threadbare, and the couch sagged. Small feathers and wisps of down floated everywhere. At the far end of the room stood a giant floor-to-ceiling cage, and inside were doves, dozens of them. There was a commotion of wings the moment Sherman entered.

Making sure that the doors to the terrace were completely closed, Sherman walked over to the cage and opened it. Suddenly there were doves everywhere, coo-cooing and shuddering, lining the curtain rods and perching on lampshades. One landed on his shoulder just as the phone beeped.

"Hector? Finally. So? . . . What? Well, sweet Jesus, man, what happened to it? Keep checking around the registration counter. If it doesn't arrive, send a message to Pollux. He can pass it along to Troy. Let me know if anything changes."

Sherman clicked off. If the FBBS picked up Clara Hastings, it was very likely they would trace everything back to him. He had already begun to suspect his house was wired, even though he had done an exhaustive search and for years had avoided buying new appliances.

He was seething. What a waste of time, he thought. The whole thing. For starters, using names from Greek mythology was hopelessly corny, an embarrassment really. All they did was make Networkers sound like bumbling amateurs. Peter Alexos had started it. Proposed it at the first meeting of the National Resistance Council — years ago, a year to the day before the election of President Gray.

Sherman went into the kitchen, which, like the living room, was in unbelievable disarray.

He took a chicken thigh out of the refrigerator and poured a glass of fruit Cocaid, one of the cocaine-laced beverages available on the open market (to counteract the ASP's side effects) since the Supreme Court confirmed the constitutionality of the Fuchs Amendment. A light hum would do him good, even though the Network doctor had solemnly and emphatically warned him not to drink it while he was also taking amphetamines.

He went back into the living room and collapsed in a chair.

The dove was still perched on his shoulder. Sherman put a piece of chicken on his tongue and turned his head. The bird took it delicately in its beak.

5

Paul was holding his father's hand.

He was very excited. The heavy door closed behind him with a thunderous noise. Verne senior was smiling and leading him forward, but Paul was afraid. It was very dark. He wanted someone to turn on a light.

"Come, Paul. You'll see." His father was trying to coax him onward.

"Papa, please turn on a light. I can't see anything." That's what Paul wanted to say, but he couldn't find his voice.

Terrified, the child followed him in the darkness. How could Papa see anything? And Monsieur Steiner, the curator. Where was he?

His father was speaking.

"Today, I am taking you to see the *Retable*."

That was it. Today was Paul's birthday, and his mother was waiting for them back at the house.

A shaft of light appeared on the stone floor.

Paul saw his father's tight smile. His upper lip was chapped and cracked, and his eyes were bright with a fervency that the child couldn't understand.

What was so important about coming here?

Then his fear disappeared. There was light. He dropped his father's hand, ran ahead of him, and pushed open the door. Two spotlights blinded him.

He turned and gave a terrified cry.

There was his father, hanging, a soiled and shredded cloth draped around his loins, his body covered with sores, his arms extended, and his hands open in frozen agony. In his horror, the boy saw that the body was strangely contorted: the legs and lower body pointed in one direction, the torso and head pointed in the other. His father was staring, unblinking, a frozen smile on his lips.

Paul began running toward him. He ran into something with numbing force and was thrown on his back. An invisible glass partition separated them.

He sprang to his feet, his mouth open wide to scream, but the cry stuck in his throat. All he could do was stare helplessly at this painting of his father.

Paul Verne's eyes blinked open.

He was lying sprawled between his compartment and the corridor — chest in one, legs in the other. The door was pinned against his back.

In a daze, Verne undid his tie — it felt like a hangman's noose — and crawled to his knees. A wave of nausea overwhelmed him and he vomited bile. He noted that the pattern on the rug resembled the wounds he had seen covering the naked body of his father in the dream.

He slowly got up by gripping the door handle with both hands. The corridor was empty. His coat and shirt were splattered with vomit. His head was pulsating with waves of pain. He felt that at any moment he might pass out again.

Night had fallen. In the twilight, Verne saw that his compartment had been ransacked. Papers were spread out on the floor, his suitcase was opened, and his clothes were strewn everywhere. Someone had turned over the mattress on the bed.

He closed the door, sat on the bed, and stared at the mess.

Not only had they searched through his things, they had taken no pains to conceal it. What had made him pass out like that? He had eaten nothing since he left New York, had drunk only some bottled water he bought at Penn Station, yet he knew beyond a doubt that he was suffering the side effects of chemical intoxication.

Verne rose stiffly off the bed and started to gather up his papers. Everything was there. Even his money hadn't been touched. Whoever did this was clearly looking for something specific. But what? He had nothing to hide.

He went into the bathroom to wash up and comb his hair. Afterward he took off his jacket and put a sweater over his soiled shirt. Then he went out into the corridor, carefully locking the door behind him, and walked a little woozily in the direction of the dining car.

At the end of the first-class corridor was the conductor's cabin; the door was ajar. A uniformed man was sitting at a small table that served as his desk. He raised his head when Verne appeared.

"I see you're up, Dr. Verne. Can I get you anything?"

Verne glared at him.

"You're not the same conductor who started in New York."

"What do you mean?" replied the man with a smile. "Of course I am."

"No — you're not. The other man was much older."

The conductor stood up.

"Dr. Verne, why don't you go to the dining car and get a bite to eat? You look like you could use something."

"Thanks, but I'm not hungry. I think I'll just get some coffee."

He headed off, then turned, hesitating.

"You didn't see anything in the corridor a little earlier?"

"No, sir, not a thing."

Verne looked at him, then nodded, and turned away.

6

Compared to La Cienega Boulevard, Hillsdale Street was a veritable oasis of peace. The modest bungalows of Inglewood spread everywhere behind badly parched front yards.

Clara walked briskly, constantly glancing behind her. The noise from the traffic jam grew fainter.

There was no way of knowing whether she was the one the police were after, but the Network's instructions had been clear: in case of even the smallest doubt, hightail it. The stakes were too high. Clara thought again about the letter hidden in the lining of her purse. Wes had said it was very important. He had made things clear without being explicit. There would be no hope for leniency if she were found with that letter.

She had asked Wes what Paul Verne had to do with the Network, but he had only shrugged in response. He may not know any more about her mission than she did. There was a rumor Wes had had his ASP disconnected. She wondered if it were true.

Strange how things turned out. Here she was, a Bio, risking the best years of her life to fight against the Fuchs Amendment. Yet she wouldn't have changed her place for the world. The last two years had meant everything to her.

Clara had been born in Los Angeles, at the first Center for Applied Eugenics to open in the United States. At six months — although Bios' official age of adoption was three — she had been adopted by the owners of a Santa Monica supermarket. Adoption was still open in those days. Sacred Fire had only just begun its rampage, and her adoptive parents had heeded the increasingly urgent advice of federal agencies trying to convince couples not to have children by natural procreation. Would-be parents were encouraged to adopt a child produced through the safe selection process used by the Gamete Conservation centers — a "Bio," in other words.

Artificial gestation, which the Fuchs Amendment had made mandatory, was an extraordinary scientific feat. An Australian team headed by Dr. Kelvin Fast first accomplished it. It wasn't long before eugenic centers using Fast's discovery were springing up everywhere. Soon they were generally acknowledged as the only way of defeating the contagion spread by cellular and placental means.

Clara was one of the first Bios to come out of the CAE in Los Angeles. She was eight when her adoptive parents died within several months of each other; it turned out that her father had contracted SF during a trip to Hawaii. Clara was raised by her aunt. She used her modest inheritance to get a degree in fine arts from UCLA; she wanted to become a photographer.

The older members of Clara's generation were Uteros — womb-carried — and she had quickly sensed that they looked on her as a sort of alien. Some Uteros blamed Bios for the tragic fate of an entire generation.

Clara refused to join in the campus struggles that more and more frequently pitted Bios and Uteros against each other. The notion that her identity was defined solely by the modality of her conception was beyond her comprehension. Other Bios had begun to form clubs, wear the same clothes, and adopt their own slang.

Refusing to join their community, Clara was rejected by the Bios, having already been rejected by the Uteros. The paradoxical effect was to reinforce her conviction that nothing could justify the unshaded simplicity of the hatred. During these difficult years, she had had one friend, a black Utero named Wes Marshall. He seemed to understand her feelings of alienation.

It was Wes who had introduced her to the the underground movement fighting the Fuchs Amendment. She became an eager adherent.

Of course, she had already heard of the Network. There were routine announcements on the news about the arrest of men and women for refusing to comply with Fuchs. They were accused of the worst sort of moral turpitude and were suspected of being affiliated with the Worshipers of the Sacred Fire, who, under the pretext of a pseudo-humanitarian lingo, actually advocated accelerating the progress of the disease by apocalyptic orgies, so that the new Messianic Age would arrive all the more quickly.

But Clara had carefully read the tracts distributed secretly by students associated with the Network, and her conclusions brought her to sympathize with the activist wing. She was hardly surprised later to discover that the only person for whom she felt any affection was already a member.

The organization was perfectly sealed off. For more than a year after Clara joined, she knew only Wes and two other members. Her job consisted primarily of carrying messages from one end of Los Angeles to another. She had often complained to Wes that she was not being allowed to do enough to help the cause.

Today was changing all that.

The voice behind her nearly made her jump out of her skin.

"Shouldn't be hurrying like you are. The heat'll make you sick."

A young black woman came out of the shadows on the veranda of a house, followed by a young girl.

Clara stopped, took a tissue out of her purse, and mopped the sweat off her brow.

"You're right. But I don't know what else to do. I've got to be at the airport in half an hour. If I don't, I'll miss my flight."

"That's not a good enough reason," replied the woman. "One plane more or less can't mean that much. Anyway, you're going in the wrong direction."

"I know. But La Cienega is backed up. The police are setting up a roadblock. That's why I got out of my cab."

"The police?"

Clara panicked. Had she said too much?

"If you go on foot, it will take you at least an hour. The only way you're going to make . . . Madison?" — she turned to the little girl — "be a good girl and go see if Ted is home. Maybe he can drive her to the airport."

The girl ran off.

"My name is Jael. Come and drink a glass of ice water."

With a sigh of relief, Clara sat down in an old wicker chair.

Jael came back with the water.

"Drink it down. It'll do you good."

"Your daughter is pretty," Clara said after she had greedily drunk the contents of the glass. "Did you adopt her nearby?"

"I got her at the CAE center in Santa Monica," Jael said, sitting down. "You know? The one on Pico Boulevard? They made me take a bunch of tests. It was three months before they finally told me I could have a girl. I wanted a boy. But now that I have Madison, I'm content. She's smart. Here she comes with Ted."

An elderly man, his hair white but his smile fully toothed, approached them. He announced with some ceremony that he would be delighted to drive her to the airport if she could pay for fuel.

Clara gratefully accepted. She thanked Madison and Jael, said good-bye, and climbed into the front seat of Ted's antique car.

"We ought to be there in about fifteen minutes," said Ted, grinding the ancient gear mechanism.

"Where is it you're goin'?" Ted asked, abruptly breaking the silence. He was driving with surprising dexterity through a maze of nearly empty side streets bordered by endless and seemingly deserted suburban lawns.

"To New York. I'm going to visit my family," Clara replied.

"It's been a long time since I was in a plane. A long time. About the time of the Vietnam War. Do you know anything about that?

"Sure. I think we lost it."

Ted burst into laughter and ended up in a coughing fit.

"Excuse me — I used to smoke a little too much," he said finally, tears in his eyes. "Yes, we probably did lose it. I was just a kid, but my daddy used to go on about it." He looked over at Clara. "So. You're goin' to see your family. I hope I'm not botherin' you. It's just that I don't often get a chance to talk with a woman."

"Oh no, you're not bothering me. I'm not a conformist."

Ted gave her a searching look.

"You a Bio?" he asked.

This took Clara by surprise. Few posed the question in such a straightforward way. Years of education had taught her never to bring up the subject of origins.

"You see, conformist or not — all the same," Ted continued. "Far's I'm concerned, I never wore this ASP without it bothering me."

"You're being pretty bold," Clara said with a small laugh.

"No I'm not, young lady. I know you. Well, I can guess anyway. Just look at how you're dressed. No ballooners. No ponytail. Normal hair, you know? No makeup under the eyes. That's rare at your age. None of my business, but if you don't want to attract attention — "

"Why wouldn't I want to attract attention?" Clara replied testily, suddenly on her guard.

"Hey, it's just talk."

He accelerated and the car came out on Century Boulevard. On both sides of the streets were the huge international hotels.

"Yes, I am a Bio." Clara couldn't keep her voice as steady as she would have wanted.

"You must have been one of the first. Back when everything started. Sacred Fire, all this damned sexual infection. You know, all that is nothin' compared to what they've been cookin' up, the feds and the uniforms. My daughter would be alive today if they hadn't driven her to suicide after they arrested her for being pregnant."

He turned toward Clara. There was rage in his kind eyes.

"I've got nothin' against you, young lady. Nothin' against Bios. We all got to live, and life, however it comes, is sacred. But you will never know what joy there is in holdin' someone in your arms. And that's the worst sin of all. War, misery, death — we could put up with anything. Because there was always love. You remember that."

They had arrived at the airport. Ted pulled up in front of the terminal. Clara had never heard a strange man talk about love before. She rummaged through her purse, pulled out a bill, and gave it to him.

He wished her a good trip and stuck out his hand. Caught off guard by the man's archaic straightforwardness and manners, Clara shook his hand awkwardly. He burst into laughter, delighted at having forced her to engage in a ritual that had so long ago gone out of style.

7

The door to the dining car slammed shut behind Verne. Faces turned and stared at him.

The bar was at the far end. To get there he had to pass several tables aligned along the length of the car. The neon sconces gave off a soft light. The sweet, heavy odor of hashish filled the air.

Verne saw a group of three women with razor-cut hair. One was smoking a small pipe.

A middle-aged woman wearing balloon pants bound tightly around the ankles was perched on a stool at the bar. Standing behind the bar was a woman wearing a shiny gray cocktail dress. She was drying glasses and putting them on racks.

Everyone went back to their conversations. It was Women's Hour. Separation of the sexes in bars and restaurants had become a common practice.

But Verne was determined to find some coffee.

He walked up to the bar and put in his order. Without bothering to glance in his direction, the bartender told him that there wasn't any. Verne saw the steaming pot sitting behind the counter and without changing expression repeated his request, expecting the same rebuff. He was surprised when the woman on the stool interceded on his behalf.

"Oh, give him his coffee. Then maybe he'll get out."

"Don't tell me what to do," replied the bartender, irritated. "Unless all these ladies present — "

The end of her sentence hung in the air as she indicated the three young women who were smoking.

"Give him some coffee — for the sake of his mother's joker," said the youngest, a teenager sporting a long pigtail on top of her otherwise shaved head.

Everyone laughed.

Verne didn't flinch. "Joker" was an expression popular among some Bios to designate the uterus of a woman who had carried a child. He was in fact born from a uterus, a "joker." So (judging from her age) was the woman who had come to his defense. He wondered if the young Bio who had spoken realized that by insulting him she had also insulted the woman. Probably the least of her worries. That he was a man and a Utero was more than enough to justify her response.

The bartender, still impassive, poured him some coffee. In the general silence, Verne drank it in quick gulps, concealing his pleasure. Then he put a twenty on the counter. It was taken in silence.

Verne wanted to thank her, but she had already turned back to her conversation. Instead he made a small gesture of recognition to the woman to whom he owed the coffee. She made no sign in return. He moved toward the exit.

He felt a slight lift when he noticed that the teenager, the one who had made reference to his mother's uterus, avoided looking at him.

8

In her office overlooking Pennsylvania Avenue, Annabelle Weaver, senior assistant to Claudia Lombard, director of the Federal Bureau of Biological Supervision, hadn't stopped fidgeting since her little chat an hour earlier with Special Agent Robert Kane, dispatched to Los Angeles to take charge of the Milner case.

Kane had learned that Wesley Marshall had left Le Dome restaurant at 2:35 P.M., gotten on his motorcycle, and driven to Sunset View Drive, location of the residence of Kess Sherman. Thanks to the ultra-mikes hidden in the house, Kane knew that Marshall had passed Milner's letter on to someone named Agony.

"Agony? What do you mean, 'Agony?' " Annabelle cried, exasperated. "Haven't you caught on yet, Kane? It's *Antigone!*"

"Boss, we could hardly hear anything."

"And why not?"

"Because of the pigeons."

"Pigeons? What in hell are you talking about?"

"Sherman's got pigeons in his apartment, I swear it. They were making one apocalyptic racket."

Annabelle would have burst out laughing had Kane's imbecilic incompetence not put her in a particularly delicate position with her boss. Claudia Lombard suffered no fools and never more than one mistake. Kane hadn't even succeeded in spotting Antigone before the message was transmitted to her. In public!

As soon as she realized his mistake, Annabelle had moved heaven and earth to find the messenger. The police had stopped hundreds of cars on the road to the airport. She had gone through the list of flights for New York, searched passengers under the pretext of looking for an unlicensed heroin trafficker. All in vain.

"You delayed the plane's departure, I hope," Weaver had asked Kane.

"No way. Senator Wyatt was on the same flight," Kane had answered.

Having failed to uncover Antigone, Annabelle knew she had to keep an even closer watch on Verne than before. So far that had proven disappointing: a search through his train compartment had turned up nothing. There were risks involved in detaining an HPO (High Public Official). By this time Verne couldn't be far from Pittsburgh. What in God's name had inspired him to take a train home rather than fly? It didn't make sense. Only locals and retirees with time on their hands took trains. Not a distinguished member of the Commission. Weaver knew she would have to get everything straightened out — fast — before Lombard got personally involved.

Thirty-eight years old, Annabelle Weaver looked ten years younger. Tall, well-built, blond hair in a crew cut. The trace of eyeliner on her lower eyelid brought out the striking clarity of her eyes. She wore a short-sleeved jacket over an open beige blouse, balloon pants bound tightly at the ankles, and flats decorated with transparent half-moons so that you could see part of her glittered toes. Not long after she was hired by Claudia Lombard, Annabelle became aware that Lombard was attracted to her. She had calculatedly decided to use that power to advance her career.

She glanced at her watch: six P.M. From the fifth floor of the Hoover Building, which housed both the FBI and the FBBS, she looked distractedly at the Capitol dome towering over the lower section of Pennsylvania Avenue. At this very moment, she knew, Claudia Lombard was in a meeting with FBI director Howard Black.

Black's career was the envy of many. His close friendship with President Hughes meant he had regular contact with the White House — to the displeasure of Attorney General Harris Taylor, who was, in principle at least, Black's superior. Hours after confirmation came of President Gray's death, and only minutes after taking the oath of office, President Hughes had nominated Black as FBI chief. A Congress in shock had quickly approved him.

Elizabeth Hughes had been on Nathan Gray's Republican ticket, distinguishing herself in the way she had gone after the Democrats for the moral laxity and spinelessness with which they were dealing with Sacred Fire. She spearheaded the drive to adopt the more draconian recommendations made by Senator Larry Fuchs of North Carolina.

After the Gray-Hughes ticket was elected, Vice President Hughes had taken over directorship of the Commission on Biosociology, generally referred to simply as the Commission, created as an advisory panel by the previous Democratic administration and now endowed with considerably greater powers.

Once the Fuchs Amendment was ruled constitutional, it provided the Commission with broad policy-making responsibilities in dealing with all aspects of Sacred Fire. Right after being sworn in, the new president had given Black — up to that point merely an assistant attorney general — the power to create a branch of the FBI that would bypass the Commission in the execution of its directives. The Federal Bureau of Biological Supervision came into being.

The FBBS was empowered to ensure that the Fuchs Amendment was followed to the letter, and in particular the provision worded as follows: Male residents of the United States of America shall be implanted with the cerebral Anti-Sex Program known as the ASP, until such time as a cure for the disease Sacred Fire, or Spermatic Fever, has been discovered and the entire population is rendered safe from infection.

Howard had appointed FBI agent Claudia Lombard to lead the FBBS, but he remained closely involved in day-to-day operations.

There was a loud buzz. Annabelle flinched. Her secretary was telling her that the director was back. She checked her makeup, took a deep breath, then headed for Lombard's office.

9

The airport was teeming. Clara directed her steps toward the electronic arrival/departure board. A blinking red dot informed her that the sonic for New York was preparing for immediate departure from gate 12. There was a slim chance, if she hurried.

Suddenly, she was nearly knocked off her feet by someone who seemed to come out of nowhere. She lost her balance and dropped her purse. The man who had collided with her was wearing coveralls. He stammered an apology, and then, as if it were the most natural thing to do, picked up Clara's purse, grabbed her suitcase, and started moving off at a good clip.

Sputtering with outrage, Clara ran after him and caught up right at the moment he was opening a door behind the arrival/departure board.

"What do you think you're — "

"Go in," he said in a low voice. "Quickly. You're being watched."

He nudged her toward the door.

Clara found herself in a storeroom packed with cleaning equipment — waxers, vacuums, buckets, and mops. The man closed the door carefully and wordlessly began undressing.

She watched without even thinking of turning away. He rolled the coveralls into a ball and threw them under a table. He was now in a uniform, which Clara recognized immediately as belonging to the Air Police. She glanced nervously at the door.

"Don't worry. My name's Lobell. Achilles sent me," said the policeman, adjusting his holster.

He put on his regulation hat with exposed crown. He saw Clara staring at his belt.

"Are you really a uniform?" she asked him.

"Yes, I'm really a uniform. Time to move."

He pulled a heavily charged key chain out of his pocket and began walking briskly, carrying Clara's suitcase toward a door at the far end of the storeroom.

They entered an immense room lit by a skylight in which baggage handlers were pulling luggage off a conveyor belt. No one paid any attention to them.

Threading between the traffic of baggage carts, they trotted toward an exit that opened on the runway.

"I'm putting you on a WA flight," Lobell told her over the din. "No chance of catching the sonic flight. Way too risky anyway."

Clara was struggling to keep pace with him. One of the workers, a woman, was wiping her pallid face with a handkerchief. Lobell saw Clara staring at her.

"The airlines get them from a list given to us by the Post-Cure Commission," he said. "Supposedly because their Sacred Fire is in remission. The truth is they'll all be gone in three months."

Clara knew that these people had to work in order to defray the cost of the treatments given to them by charitable organizations. They paid with their last remaining months of health.

The airport runways stretched out of sight. The planes parked on either side of the building, to which they were attached by passenger loading docks like gigantic parasites.

"If someone stops you and asks you something, say nothing," Lobell told her. "Let me do the talking, OK?"

Clara nodded.

A beep emanated from his belt. Lobell unhooked his walkie-talkie and listened.

"They're looking for you," he said as he reattached it. "But we're in luck."

"In luck?" Clara repeated, nearly trotting to keep pace.

"They don't know your identity. They also haven't got clearance to hold back departures."

They approached the jet with its two ramps — one for passengers, the other, beneath it, for luggage. From another direction came the high whine of turbos gearing up. The sonic flight that Clara was to have been on. They began climbing the ladder that led up to the ramps.

10

The conductor was out. His cabin door was open, however, and the light was on.

Verne walked in, then closed and locked the door behind him.

Sitting on the desk were a pile of ticket stubs, a Thermos, and a copy of the *Post*.

The lead article summarized announcements made at a press conference the night before by the spokesperson for the Commission. The article enumerated the usual sorts of announcements and recommendations: increasing government support for the Special Hospitals designed to treat SF; new measures to coordinate public and private research laboratories; nomination of yet another director at the National Institutes of Health; proposals that would force the states to devote a third of their budget to dealing with the epidemic; and so on.

No mention whatever of the speech Verne had given before the Commission at the last general meeting.

He had proposed that young boys be given a choice between having the ASP implantation or undergoing a neurosurgical operation, the advantage of the latter being to free them of the intrusive meddling of the FBBS in their lives. Justice Department representative Jelawny Paulwell had objected to this, arguing that all the choice did was make the job of the police even more complicated than it already was. Verne was chided for entertaining what were termed "outdated humanist preoccupations."

Verne put the newspaper back on the desk and looked around the compartment. Something shiny and metallic in the wastebasket attracted his attention. He rummaged through it and found what he was looking for. It was an ordinary-looking aerosol container, quite obviously empty, about the same size as a can of shaving cream. Nothing was written on it. A clear plastic tube, a few inches long and very small in diameter, extended from the end of it. Verne sniffed the tube and immediately recognized the noisome odor of fluothane.

He had discovered the cause of his fainting spell. Someone had found a way of introducing it into the climate control mechanism for his cabin.

Verne put the can in plain view on the conductor's desk and left the compartment.

He headed back in the direction of the dining car and found a phone. He punched in his code.

A woman's voice answered.

"Melissa?"

"Paul! Where are you calling from?" She sounded very relieved. "You were supposed to be back this afternoon. Were you held up at the U.N.?"

"No, I . . . Melissa, listen. I'm not coming home right away."

"What do you mean? Everyone at the Institute will be waiting for you tomorrow morning, and — "

"I know. Melissa, you're going to have to do without me for a few days."

"Paul, what's going on? Why all the mystery?"

"I'm on a train."

"A *train?* To San Francisco? You're kidding!"

"I needed a little time to myself," replied Verne wearily. "I need to think over some things. To be alone. Do you understand?"

"OK, fine. You need to be alone. I still don't see why you couldn't have let Reiss know."

"Melissa, you're not listening. Stop obsessing about the Institute."

"Now *that's* a switch," said Melissa with sarcasm. "*You're* telling *me* not to obsess? I've always been the one who's been telling you to ease up."

"Joe died," said Verne, his voice cracking.

"What?"

Verne cleared his throat. "Joe Milner's dead."

"Oh, Paul," said Melissa after a long silence. "When did you hear?"

"At the U.N., this morning. From a member of the Austrian delegation."

"From . . . natural causes? I mean . . ."

"We'll talk about it Tuesday."

"Shall I pick you up?"

"No. Don't bother. I'll come right home. See you Tuesday. I love you."

Verne was about to hang up.

"Paul?" Melissa interjected quickly. "Wait. Paul . . ."

"Yes?"

"You are . . . coming back, aren't you?"

Paul paused. "Yes, Melissa. I am coming back. I simply need some time to think."

Before she could comment, he was gone.

When he passed the conductor's cabin, Verne saw that someone had closed the door.

Chapter 2

1

A blanket of fog unfolding from the north advanced like a gigantic, slow-motion wave of foam. Soon the golden light of the setting sun disappeared, and it was as if the house were plunged into soapy water. The clarity of the interior of the house contrasted with the impression of unreality Melissa felt as she looked out the large bay windows of the living room. The silhouettes of the wild conifers made them seem like a patrol of petrified shadows.

She got up off the leather couch, where she had just finished talking with Paul, and used the remote to raise the heating control and illumination level. The temperature outdoors would soon be dropping by ten degrees. Tobias, an Irish setter, was in the garden, barking, keeping at bay the coyotes and foxes who made nightly forays on the property, irresistibly drawn by the hens Melissa insisted on keeping.

She opened the door and called him. He arrived noisily, heading straight for the steps dividing the living room from the kitchen, which was where his food dish was.

"OK, OK. Keep your collar on, Toby."

She took a bag of dog food from the cabinet and filled his dish.

"Your master isn't coming tonight," she said, watching him launch into his dinner with sloppy enthusiasm.

"So you can share my room again. That should make you happy, right?"

Melissa glanced at the groceries she had bought at a supermarket in San Rafael on her way back from the Institute. Her appetite was nearly gone. She took out an apple, bit into it, and leaned her elbows on the breakfast bar, which overlooked the living room. When it was clear, there was a sweeping view of the length of Tomales Bay, which stretched for fifteen miles between the mainland and Point Reyes National Park.

Joseph Milner drifted across her consciousness. The last time she had seen him was at Zack's, in Sausalito, nine years ago almost to the day. Joe had broken off their friendship after Paul publicly voiced his agreement with the new politics of the Biosociology Commission.

Two months of total silence followed. They periodically called Joe, but there was never any answer. Then Melissa had left a message begging him to join them on the terrace at Zack's, the restaurant at which the three of them had spent so many wonderful hours.

They were the first to arrive. Paul asked Carlos to let them know when Joe arrived. If he ever did — they weren't at all sure he would show. It was likely he would simply ignore this latest attempt at reconciliation.

They waited in the shady corner that was Joe's favorite. The old man had once joked that the days on the plains of Silesia, his gentle euphemism for Auschwitz, had made him overly sensitive to exposure.

Joe Milner rarely mentioned his childhood days in the concentration camp. In fact, this luminary in the world of molecular biology, perhaps the most important scientist of the last decades, talked very little about his past. From some mutual friends Melissa had learned that he had lost both parents and his only brother in the camps. After the war, he went back to Vienna to live with his younger sister, miraculously spared her family's fate by a Catholic couple who had hidden her. Later she had to be put into a psychiatric clinic.

Joe mentioned her only once. One night, when the three of them were having dinner in Inverness, he rather abruptly announced the death of Esther Milner. He had tried to sound matter-of-fact, but Melissa recalled the strain in his voice. His sister was his last living relative.

They had waited at Zack's that night, and the appointed hour had come and gone. No Joe. Paul killed time by throwing pretzels into the air and watching the sea gulls catch them in full flight. It was a glorious day. San Francisco Bay shone as bright as a mirror. On the horizon, the city's skyscrapers seemed to melt together into the blue intensity of the sky.

Joe finally did arrive — trailed by Carlos, gesticulating his apologies for having had no time to forewarn them. Paul got up so quickly that he knocked over his chair.

Milner looked as if he had aged. His fine white hair, his pallor, the crumpled sports jacket hanging off his sagging frame. He went straight to Melissa.

"I'm just passing through," he said, embracing her. Then he

whispered, "Take very good care of Paul. He may be the best hope we have."

He turned to Paul, who was standing motionless, paralyzed by emotion, and took his former protegé's hand in his. They looked at each other without speaking for a long moment. Time seemed to stand still.

Then Joe's face lit up. "Farewell, old friend. I'll miss you. *Auf Wiedersehen.*"

Milner had turned and walked out by the way he came. Why hadn't they run after him?

They learned not long after that Milner had gone back to live in Vienna.

Night fell on Inverness.

Climbing the steps to her bedroom, Melissa thought about what Milner had said to her. Had she taken care of Paul? She couldn't be sure. The thought upset her so much she stumbled and had to grab the rail to keep from falling backward.

2

Clara nearly skidded on one of the narrow metallic steps. She caught herself at the same moment she saw Lobell open the cargo door and disappear through it with her suitcase.

She started to follow him when the sound of voices stopped her.

"What do you mean she disappeared in baggage? What are you carrying?"

Clara climbed higher up the ladder and hugged the stairs closely. A hand grabbed the strap of the door below her and closed it. The voices stopped. She was seized by panic. Alone, wanted by every airport uniform, and clinging to a ladder twenty-five feet above the pavement.

A small insistent noise finally got her attention.

"Psssst. Psssst."

Clara turned and nearly cried out in surprise.

Through the tiny side window on the pilot's side she could see a man motioning to her. The ladder was positioned near the flight cabin. She strained to hear what he was saying.

"Come aboard . . . gone."

"Aboard?" was all she could manage.

"Hurry."

That she heard. "I'm coming in!" she cried, climbing rapidly up the ladder to the passenger ramp. The door opened. A flight attendant welcomed her with a smile and directed her to the flight deck.

"Sit there," said a man at the controls, pointing to a seat behind him. "And put on your seat belt. We'll talk after takeoff. My name is Lyndon. This is my copilot, Captain Michaela Church."

"Hello," said the copilot, tipping her hat courteously, then returning to her checklist.

Clara sat down and sighed deeply. The sudden relief exhausted her. Clara let herself sink into a sweet lethargy, soothed by the voice she heard talking to the control tower.

The plane began to move.

She was asleep by the time the plane rose above the Pacific.

3

Claudia Lucia Lombard had been nominated to become director of the FBBS shortly after its creation. Howard Black had chosen her from among dozens of superior officers in the FBI, probably because she was one of the first women to have climbed so high in the Bureau's ranks. And her political contacts were strong.

Following her confirmation, Director Black had told her that the fate of the country rested on her shoulders. He made his point with limpid clarity: either the Fuchs Amendment halted the spread of SF and stabilized the country's declining population, or the United States would be caught in an endless spiral of death and desolation, like so many other countries in the world. This was the time of trial for the American soul.

Claudia Lombard was deeply impressed with the gravity of her mission. Under her iron rule, the FBBS rapidly took on such importance that it was now feared by some of the most powerful figures in the administration.

Besides her ardent devotion to the two Siamese cats she returned home to every night in Georgetown, Claudia Lombard, mid-forties, unattached, nursed a secret (so she thought) but consuming passion for Annabelle Weaver. She had first met Annabelle at a tedious dinner party and had immediately been taken with the ease with which the young woman — whose whole career had been in the FBI — had handled herself with even the most seasoned veterans of the administration. She was a perfect choice to serve as her senior assistant.

Since then, Lombard had been possessed by one idea: to invite Annabelle to her house for a weekend. But her assistant had always found a pretext for refusing: a tennis game with some important contact on the Rock Creek Park courts, a play with a source at the Kennedy Center. The FBBS director was reasonably sure her protégée was having an affair with a young secretary from the State Department. The idea was almost too disturbing to entertain. Lombard wondered if she should have Annabelle's movements monitored.

When Annabelle entered her office, Lombard's attention was ostensibly absorbed by a folder she was holding. She made the young woman wait for a few minutes.

When she looked up and saw again the striking beauty of her assistant, all it did was darken her mood.

"Come closer," Lombard ordered in a metallic voice.

Annabelle, far from unconscious of the effect she had on her boss, moved forward slowly. Her face had a determined expression.

"You shouldn't wear so much eyeliner. It doesn't go with your features," said Lombard.

Annabelle gave her a knowing look.

"Anyway . . . that's what *I* think. Sit down," she added, pointing to a couch and two easy chairs around a coffee table.

In the window behind them, the illuminated dome of the Capitol was half obscured by fog.

"What lovely flowers," said Annabelle, settling herself on the couch facing the director.

"They are pretty, aren't they?" Lombard replied, unable to hide the feeling of pleasure that Annabelle's words gave her.

"Annabelle, tell me about this Joseph Milner letter. What happened in Los Angeles?"

Trying hard to conceal her alarm, Annabelle told Lombard about the screwup, subtly suggesting that it was Kane's fault. As for Paul Verne, for some mysterious reason he had left the U.N. and gotten on a train. His compartment had been thoroughly searched, but nothing of importance had turned up.

"Nothing?" replied Lombard, eyebrows arching. "Well, my dear, I'm beginning to wonder if I shouldn't hand over the operation to someone else."

"But Claudia," said Annabelle defensively, "Kane was the one who — "

"Kane is *your* responsibility. Operatives make mistakes when they're unsure of their orders. You haven't been firm enough."

Annabelle lowered her eyes. Lombard exulted.

"In the next two days, I want you to find out who this Network courier is and how she plans to get in touch with Verne. If you can't do that, arrest her before she meets him. The contents of that letter should at least be enough to incriminate the celebrated Dr. Verne. But be careful. You must be absolutely sure of what you're doing. If you're not absolutely sure, do nothing. Just keep an eye on him. The last thing I want is to stir up trouble with the Commission. You've got an operative on the train?"

"Yes. A new agent gets on at every border crossing. I'm staying at the office all weekend to remain in direct contact."

"What about Kess Sherman?"

"We're on him day and night."

Lombard got up, took a few steps, and then turned toward Weaver.

"Annabelle," she began in a voice considerably softer, "to follow the operation, you need only be near a Bureau coder. Staying in the office for the whole weekend wouldn't be necessary. Am I right?" Annabelle thought she sounded almost coy.

"Well, I would actually prefer to be home," she replied. "But I wouldn't be able to stay in contact with the other agents involved. I haven't got the equipment on my own phone. Unless . . ."

"Unless?"

". . . unless you would be so gracious as to let me be a guest at your home, Claudia. You have everything, and that way I could take full advantage of your proximity . . ."

Annabelle let the phrase hang in suspense. Her face was animated with concern, as if she had asked too large a favor.

Lombard felt a deep sense of triumph. She knew that Annabelle's submission — so sudden — was tied to the problems she was having with the Milner case. But that didn't mean she was any less willing to take advantage of the situation.

"All right," Lombard said finally, "I'll expect you tomorrow morning at ten."

Weaver thanked her, rose. The faint ironic glint had returned to her expression.

Along with the desire, Lombard felt the same disquiet she always felt whenever Annabelle Weaver looked at her.

4

With his customary slightly excessive caution, Kess Sherman drove down Olympic Boulevard.

Since the Great Shake, as it was called now that it was part of myth and song, downtown had become almost entirely deserted. The large banks and financial concerns had long since moved to the western part of the city. The skyscrapers were now inhabited by small-time ped-dlers and black marketeers. Most of the people jostling in these old buildings were Hispanic, Asian, and African — the last wave before the closing of the gates.

Sherman passed beneath the Pasadena Highway and turned down Broadway. He pulled into a parking garage and bought a ticket from an enormous man in a glass booth whose eyes never left the video screen attached to the wall.

The meeting was set for 6 P.M. sharp on the corner of Broadway and 9th Street, in front of the parking garage. Someone would make contact.

Leaning against the wall of a building, his hands buried in the pockets of his crumpled trousers, a combed cotton coat draped over his shoulders, Sherman watched the people on the sidewalk. A hashish dealer was hawking his wares. Sherman wondered how much it could be worth now that usage — but not the sale — had been legalized. A whole variety of Cocaid products, on the other hand, could be had just about anywhere. Alcohol had been outlawed when it was discovered that it compromised the effectiveness of the ASP. Consumption by women, however, was fairly common, although most now favored the Cocaids.

The biggest difference these days, Sherman thought as he observed a prostitute solicit a woman, was that one so rarely saw any mixed couples even just out walking together. Relations between the sexes had deteriorated to that point. And men seemed to care less and less about their appearance. Hats were outlawed, of course, and wearing them was a serious offense. Golf visors, crownless baseball hats, were popular, to keep the sun from blistering the face — like the ones the uniforms strolling in front of him were wearing.

Sherman checked the time. Six-thirty. He walked to the edge of the sidewalk, knowing that he was probably being observed from a win-dow. This meeting with Michael Engelhardt intrigued him. What, he wondered, would a notorious Mafia capo want to do with the Network? It was a question Sherman had asked himself at least a hundred times over the last few hours.

"Don't turn around," said a male voice. "Cross Broadway, turn right, walk down to number 812. Someone will find you."

Sherman followed the instructions.

Once he'd reached the other side of the street he risked a quick glance over his shoulder. The crowds made it impossible for him to know who had spoken.

Sherman walked two blocks and stopped in front of 812, a building of about twenty stories that had seen better days. Under the filth you could still see floral patterns and bright mosaics. The front door was plated with metal, however, and looked new.

He was suddenly seized by the arm and unceremoniously pulled through the small door that had suddenly opened in front of him. The door then slammed shut behind him.

He found himself in an entryway lit by colored halogen bulbs.

Two men were standing above him.

"What is this? A kidnapping? I need to call my lawyer!" said Sherman, trying to conceal his surprise in humor. "Hey! What are you guys wearing?"

He pointed at their fedoras. Behind them other fedoras were hanging on a coatrack. The sight, for some reason, made Sherman giddy with laughter. He was nearly in hysterics when they frisked him for weapons.

"I've got to tell you guys, you look great. Really. Do you carry violin cases?"

When they had finished searching him, one of the men signaled to Sherman, who had regained his composure, to follow him into the elevator. The other — equally expressionless — took up a position in front of the door.

The elevator began moving. Sherman noticed there were no floor indicators and that a pencil-tip-size camera eye had leveled its gaze right on him.

The door hissed open. A man stood before them. His face was disfigured by a large scar.

"Mr. Kess Sherman. Follow me, please."

These were the first words anyone had spoken to Sherman.

The elevator had opened directly into a large room. Seated in overstuffed easy chairs were men dressed in exactly the same fashion as the others — suit and black tie, light blue dress shirt, and fedora — all watching a hockey game.

Sherman's escort led the way past the men, who barely bothered to look up, to large mahogany double doors at the far end of the room. A light blinked. The doors opened.

The office they entered was nearly as large as the room they had gone through. Sitting in an oversize genuine leather desk chair was a bald man in a bathrobe holding a cigar and watching a screen.

Sherman was face to face with the celebrated Michael Engelhardt, the head of the West Coast Syndicate.

"Have a seat, Mr. Sherman. I'll be with you in a minute," he said, running his eyes over Sherman from head to toe. "You want a scotch? Help yourself. No? Surprised? You like hockey?"

Sherman sat in the chair Engelhardt had indicated and admired the bottles of alcohol positioned in soldierly fashion on the sideboard. Brand names from days gone by. He didn't know why exactly, but Engelhardt's expression made him feel uneasy. It took something special to repress Sherman's normally irrepressible high spirits.

"Not particularly. I prefer basketball. But don't let me interrupt."

Several minutes went by. Then Engelhardt touched a control and the screen went black and receded. He swiveled toward Sherman.

"The Kings are going to take this one, no question. That means a lot to me. Drink?"

"Nothing for me, thanks," replied Sherman. "Not because of the ASP. It's been disconnected for three months," he added breezily. "I'm just not a drinker."

"I take your confession as a sign of confidence, my friend. But you're wrong. About the alcohol, I mean."

He poured himself a couple of fingers' worth. Sherman glanced around at the office.

"Not bad, hey?" said Engelhardt. "This," he announced expansively, as if surveying it for the first time, "is my office." He took a slug of the scotch and smacked his tongue. Then, with great serenity, he lit his cigar, watching Sherman all the while. Sherman realized what he found unsettling about the man. Engelhardt's eyes were different colors — one was blue and the other brown. It was hard to know which one to fix on.

"You saw my men's hats?" asked Engelhardt.

"I did indeed."

"Of course they take them off when they go out. Provocation isn't good for business. But here, in my place, no exception made. You gotta wear a hat."

"At the risk of being fired?"

"You bet. Here's the point — it's their responsibility not to put themselves in any situation where they'd have to take them off. They seem to have caught on. No uniform's ever made it through my door. Not officially, anyways." He gave Sherman an elaborate wink.

Sherman was as amused as he was impressed.

"I've got to hand it to you, Mr. Engelhardt. No, I really mean it," he added, noticing Engelhardt's features had suddenly hardened, sensing derision. "History shows us that no restriction can't be circumvented by some maneuver or another."

"Like your ASP, for example," said the mafioso with a twinkle.

"Exactly. Like my ASP. I'll tell you who disconnected it in case you're interested."

"Jeff!" called Engelhardt.

The door opened. Scarface came in.

"Jeff, bring in the box."

Jeff disappeared and then immediately reappeared, carrying what looked like a ring box.

"Show Mr. Sherman our little jewel."

Jeff opened the box and handed it to Sherman, who immediately recognized the tiny apparatus sitting on the velvet.

"Know what that is?" asked Engelhardt.

"An ASP. But I don't know what you're getting at."

"He doesn't know what I'm getting at," Engelhardt repeated to his bodyguard.

The two men smiled conspiratorially.

"This is not a true ASP," said Engelhardt, leaning forward, savoring every syllable. "Its a Non-Operational ASP, a NOX, a fake ASP. FBBS can't tell 'em apart." He sat back in triumph.

Sherman looked at Engelhardt in silence. He was incredulous. An undetectable phony ASP? That was why the guy could drink alcohol. If what he said was true this would offer one of the first real methods of escaping the feds.

"Do you know what you're saying?" asked Sherman. "I mean, does this thing really work?"

"It works," said Engelhardt with an enigmatic smile. "Today, with a little clever knife work, you can get debugged without making too big a mess. You know what I'm talking about. The problem is finding a fake ASP to put in its place. One that carries the code, the signature. Any FBBS idiot could tell the difference. But with this little jewel, which can reproduce the original code, you can't. You saw me drink. I've been drinking as much as I want for six months now, and without any sign of a discharge. Maybe one day I'll tell you how it was perfected."

Sherman reached over to take the box from Jeff, who looked at his boss before letting go of it. Engelhardt signaled his OK.

Sherman stared at the NOX, fascinated. This wondrous little device could prove a vital weapon for the Network. No, not vital, he thought. Invaluable. Earthshaking.

5

Verne was awake.

Having first made sure the lock on his compartment door was secure, he turned off the heat and closed the air vent. Then he slid under the covers fully clothed. He shivered, despite being covered by two blankets. The caffeine combined with the sleeping tablet had left him overwrought. He felt as if his body was caught in a free-fall, plunging downward, and that at any moment he would hit the ground. He was alert to the smallest sound.

For an hour, he tossed and turned in a half-sleep. The train began to slow. They must be coming to a city.

Which city? Colmar!

He was seized by panic. He fought the crazy but overwhelming impression that he was a child again, and that the train was taking him home from vacation. Home to Colmar.

The train was coming into the station. The brakes hissed. Verne knew he would have to hurry. Colmar was only a three-minute stop — and his parents would be waiting for him on the platform. But he couldn't move. He imagined his parents, frantic with worry because they didn't see him get off the train.

The Omnivoice system activated.

"PITTSburgh. Five-minute stop. PITTSburgh."

Verne's chest heaved in a silent scream. That helped. Now he could move.

He wasn't sure his legs were strong enough to bear his weight, so he moved gingerly. Shifting his weight toward the window, he found the control that raised the blind. Foggy light from the platform flooded the compartment.

Through the fog, Verne could make out the commotion of passengers getting on and off the train. He lowered the blind and gulped down some water. He stretched out on the bed, folding his hands behind his head.

Verne was surprised with himself. He hadn't dreamed about his childhood for years, yet now, in a matter of only several hours, he had had two nightmares and both were rooted in that time of his life. It must be related to this archaic method of traveling.

The Retable at Issenheim. His father venerated that medieval triptych, Grunewald's masterpiece, pride of the Unterlinden Museum, a Dominican monastery located in the heart of Colmar.

His father had dreamed of going to the Ecole des Beaux Arts in Paris. But instead he became a civil servant and indulged his passion for art by initiating his only son into the cult of medieval painting. Paul always got exhibition catalogs and art books from his father on his birthday. He had every book on Grunewald's *Retable* ever published.

Not only was the *Retable* Colmar's centerpiece, but it was Henri Verne's primal reference point. And not because of its religious significance (its three panels depicted the crucifixion and scenes from the life of Jesus and the saints). What drove his passion was the painter's artistic technique. Raised in the faith, Henri was a free thinker. Religion, he thought, was little more than a collection of superstitions. He teased his Jewish wife when she tried to keep traditions alive by going to synagogue on holy days.

On the eve of Paul's sixth birthday his father announced, quite solemnly, that he was going to take his son to see the work. He thought the boy was at the age at which he might begin to appreciate its sublime beauty. Verne could recall his trembling fear when he saw Christ on the cross in the chapel of the ancient monastery, his body covered with sores and bleeding wounds. He had forced himself to stare at the painting. The precocious Paul was in his own agony worrying whether he could produce the admiration his father seemed to expect of him.

Verne senior seemed not to guess at his son's inner conflict, and the memory of that first hypocrisy had settled in Verne's memory. It was weighted with the additional memory of his father, who was not an emotional man, taking him in his arms after they emerged from the convent and hugging him effusively.

The noises from the platform faded. A whistle sounded; the train started slowly to move.

Verne drifted off to sleep convinced that somehow *The Retable at Issenheim* would continue to play a part in his life.

6

They had been circling Long Island for over half an hour. Clara had woken as they approached the lights of New York, which cut a brilliant, jagged line along the ink-black stretch of the Atlantic.

Captain Lyndon pointed out a few of the constellations. If things continued as they were, he told Clara, soon no one would be able even to see the night sky toward which, since its beginnings, humanity had directed its gaze. The countless satellites that spun through the atmosphere looked like stars moving in a confusion of directions. The magisterial immobility of the celestial bodies, enduring symbols and inspiration for those whose thoughts drifted toward infinity, was a thing of the past. Only space travelers had a chance to see the view terrestrials had lost sight of. For Captain Lyndon, that was more significant than any of the other events of the last one hundred years.

Clara was moved. This was the second time in a matter of only several hours that she had talked with such friendly intimacy to a man. The captain asked her how long she had known his good friend Lieutenant Lobell. She had tried to find a way of recounting her adventure without implicating the Air Police officer. Lyndon interrupted her.

"The less I know, the better for all of us. I'm just glad I could be of service."

He pointed out an orange streak plummeting down toward the lights of the airport.

"A military jet," he said. "Those bastards always get to land first."

The copilot exchanged a few words with the control tower.

"We're going in," she said, thumb pointing down.

Fascinated by all the dials and displays, Clara watched the movements of the two pilots while they began to ease the jet downward.

She wondered how she would get by the New York Border Police. Lieutenant Lobell hadn't mentioned anything about a contact. Whoever had been waiting for the sonic from L.A. must have reported back to the Network that Antigone had missed her flight. Apart from Lobell, who by now had probably been picked up by FBBS agents, no one knew that she had managed to catch another flight. She was sure the NYBP were going to be more rigorous than the Air Police.

The runway lights formed two luminous lines extending to the horizon. The plane hung suspended above them for what seemed an interminable amount of time.

The shock of the wheels touching down made Clara jump. Snow was whipping past, barely visible as faint white streaks. The end of the runway, indicated by three horizontal lines of red lights, was speeding toward them. The copilot reversed the controls. Motors roared in response and the jet slowed. They turned off onto a taxi strip bordered by blue lights that led toward the brightly illuminated terminal.

"This is where we part company," said Captain Lyndon. "The attendant is waiting for you in the passenger cabin."

Clara stood up and extended her hand. "Thank you."

Taken aback by the young woman's gesture, the captain shook it awkwardly.

"I'm sorry I can't do more," he said. "You see, we have to pass through police checkpoints as well."

Clara waved her hand and left the flight cabin. While the plane rolled toward its docking point, she sat next to the attendant. Fear made her mind go blank. These were her last minutes of freedom.

She was one of the first off the plane. Tightening her arm around her bag, she walked through the reception lounge and headed straight for the border checkpoint. She was fighting despair. There would be no way around it: either she would get through or she would be arrested. Her fate waited for her at the end of the carpeted corridor.

She came out into a large area divided into two zones by a continuous line of sentry boxes. A double gate channeled the passengers into lines.

She didn't have long to wait. A large female uniform pointed to her. Clara handed over her passcard.

The agent inserted the card into a terminal. Her face changed expression as she read what came up on the screen.

"One moment," she said, and ran her hand over a console.

Clara felt blood draining from her body.

A male in civilian clothes materialized.

"Detective, I believe you've been expecting her," the agent told him.

"This way, please," he said to Clara.

Trapped. All the exits were guarded. Clara followed the man, grimly determined to make a break the first chance she got.

She noticed that the cuff of his oversize trousers was slightly frayed. Why, she asked herself, did she always focus on insignificant details during moments of crisis?

Clara was led into an office. The detective produced her suitcase.

"Yours?" he asked.

Stunned, Clara recognized that it was.

"Yes, but how did it get here? I was sure I'd lost it in L.A. or that someone had stolen it and so I . . . was about to fill out a claim report on it."

The man appeared to ignore her.

"It was addressed to us by someone on a sonic flight from Honolulu making an exceptional stopover in Los Angeles. There's a letter with it," he added tonelessly, handing her an envelope. "Now, if you would please sign for it, we will remand this property to your custody."

He pushed a signing screen toward her.

"May I go?" she asked after signing it, trying to keep her smile in place.

"Everything seems in order," said the detective, handing her back her passcard. "Next time, take better care of your belongings."

Clara left the office carrying her luggage. Her legs wobbly, she headed for the exit under the watchful eye of a police officer.

In the reception lounge, she went to the women's room. She locked herself in one of the stalls, then opened the letter.

Dear Ms. Hastings,

I'm sorry I didn't have the time to assist you. I was called away for an emergency. I saw that you had forgotten your suitcase. Luckily, I was able to find a way to send it by separate courier. If you need anything at Kennedy, code in 63–14 on any of the phones in the airport and you'll be in direct contact with a colleague. He doesn't get to work until 6 in the morning, so you'll have to wait until then.

> Good luck.
> Yours sincerely,
> Lieutenant Lobell

Clara closed her eyes in relief. Not only was she free, but she was still in contact with the Network.

She got up, put her suitcase on top of the commode, and took out her coat. She propped it against the stall partition, set her wrist alarm for six A.M., and settled herself as comfortably as she could.

Several minutes later, sitting on the commode and leaning against the partition, her hands balled up and pressed tightly against her chest, she was asleep.

7

Sherman was ecstatic. The partnership Engelhardt was proposing with the Network seemed to him a magnificent opportunity. It wouldn't be the first time a resistance movement had allied itself with the Mafia.

He imagined the horizons of possibility the Non-Operational ASP would open to men across the country, Networkers or otherwise. For the majority of them, to be rid of the humiliating contraption was a hopeless dream. The NOX put it within reach. The anti-Fuchs movement would spread like wildfire. The mighty FBBS would be reduced to insignificance. Sherman decided he would make contact with the Network's National Council immediately.

Exiting the elevator, he found himself back in the building's foyer. Bodyguards were positioned on either side of the door.

An alarm whined.

"Stay where you are," one of the men ordered, punching in some numbers on a wall unit.

"Wait here," he said after switching off.

Sherman shrugged and walked over to the coatrack where the fedoras hung.

"Mind if I try one on?" he asked, taking one down.

Without waiting for a reply, Sherman put it on his head and went over to a mirror to take a look.

"You know? Mr. Engelhardt knows what he's doing," he said, smiling at his reflection. "Headwear is so much more than just a matter of vanity."

The elevator doors suddenly hissed open and Jeff appeared. His expression was impassive as he deftly snatched the hat Sherman was wearing and put it back on a peg. Then he turned to one of the bodyguards.

"Get the vehicle and wait for us in back," he told him.

The man nodded once, removed his hat, and disappeared through a door.

Watching Jeff, Sherman noticed that the scar that slashed across his face, from his left eye to his chin, gave him a perpetually sardonic look.

"What's up?" Sherman asked him. "Trouble?"

"You were followed," Jeff replied. "And very smoothly. Probably FBBS. We only spotted them by accident. Good thing we left someone down in the parking garage where you parked. The boss is not happy about this, Mr. Sherman. He doesn't like it when outsiders stick their nose in our business. He asked me to tell you that this is your responsibility. He'll only be back in touch if your organization gets clear."

Sherman tried to take in the news. If he had been followed that meant the Network was under surveillance, perhaps even infiltrated. A disaster. He had to contact Wesley Marshall before it was too late. The Network would have to put an emergency plan into effect, and the leadership would have to disappear into the woodwork. Just when it had found a powerful new weapon.

The man who had gone for the car reappeared and announced that the coast was clear. Jeff hung his hat on the peg and signaled Sherman to follow him.

A limo was waiting in the alley behind the building. It was getting dark. There was garbage blowing around. Jeff and Sherman got in the back; the bodyguard got behind the controls.

"Head toward Watts," Jeff told the driver.

The car shot off and emerged on Hill Street, then veered north on 7th Street. Sherman gripped the armrests, knuckles white. They flew through an intersection, leaving behind a cacophony of horns.

"Scared, Mr. Sherman?" asked Jeff, enjoying Sherman's discomfort. "Don't sweat. Nick here is an ace. Right, Nick?"

Nick snickered grimly while barely managing to avoid a car pulling out of a parking place.

"This ought be fun," he said. "We're being dogged."

Sherman and Jeff looked around. Behind them was a police unit, lights flashing.

"Just wait till we hit Central," said Nick, accelerating. "Then let's see if you can keep up. Fucking uniforms."

The car rocketed across Main Street. A truck coming the other way smashed through a storefront trying to avoid a collision. But the police car, sirens screaming, was keeping up.

Unperturbed, Jeff took an antique cigarette case out of his pocket and offered one to Sherman. Sherman shook his head. Dope smoke filled the cabin.

Jeff burst out laughing. The car suddenly veered to the left on Central Avenue. Sherman hurtled into Jeff, who nearly swallowed his joint.

"Now let's see what we've got," said Nick from the front. "Let's kick out the jams."

A turbo roared to life and the car seemed to lift off the ground. Within seconds, it was slicing down the middle of the road at racing speed. Cars were spilling onto the sidewalk to avoid the juggernaut.

"Let me the hell out of here!" yelled Sherman, now in full panic.

"No can do." Jeff's laughing fit had shrunk to a chuckle. "We're going too fast."

"Now we're gonna beat those beefheads!" yelled Nick.

He hit the controls to avoid smashing head-on into a car turning onto the Santa Monica Freeway. The limo skidded and went under the bridge sideways. Nick spun the controls in the direction of the spin, regained control, and set the car straight. Jeff and Sherman looked behind them. The police vehicle was farther behind.

"Left on Adams," barked Jeff.

The car braked violently and spun completely around. Sherman had a second's look at two police units barricading the road.

Then the windshield exploded.

Sherman threw himself on the floor and held his head in his hands. He felt the car taking off again. Nick was swearing wildly. It sounded as if he were speaking in tongues. Gun flashes. Sherman risked a look. Jeff was kneeling on the seat firing his weapon out the rear windshield.

Sherman was about to yell that it wouldn't do any good when Jeff collapsed gasping in Sherman's arms, smeared with blood. A bullet had cut through his neck. His eyes grew still.

Everything seemed to be happening at once — there was a crash, air-filling noise, air bags popping. The world turned upside down.

Finally, almost miraculously, there was silence. Stunned but alert, Sherman crawled out the back window. His left thigh throbbed with pain. He heard the sirens behind him. The vehicle's wheels were still spinning. Nick lay unconscious against the controls, his knees pressed against his chin, his face hidden in the billowy whiteness of the air bag.

Sherman leaned over and checked for a pulse. It was faint.

"Well, you beat 'em all," he mumbled.

In front of him was a dark alley between two buildings. Groaning from the pain in his leg, Sherman managed to hobble off into the night.

8

Omnivoice musical tones jolted Verne out of a deep sleep.

"Beaver Falls. Border stop. Disembarkation mandatory."

Verne turned on his night-light. Half past midnight. The train had left Pittsburgh only an hour before. He sat shivering on the bed. His head still hurt, and his mouth tasted like soggy ashes.

He got up, picked up his coat, and after checking the gauge on the apparatus on the inside pocket, turned the heat up to maximum.

The corridor was empty, but a state uniform stood at the far end of the car. His insignia was of the Pennsylvania Border Patrol.

"Cold part of the world," Verne said to him as he passed.

"You're telling me," replied the uniform. "We've been waiting for you. This train's behind schedule."

At the other end of the platform was a trailer, lit up by spotlights. The Pennsylvania and Ohio state flags waved side by side.

Two state police agents wearing winter suits and shoulder holsters were directing the passengers through an automatic door that made a whining sound as it closed. An icy blast blew a cloud of snow dust, which sparkled in the light.

"You can't stand there," a voice said to Verne. "Please keep moving."

Verne headed down the platform and toward the door marked PASS-CARD CHECKPOINT.

It was hot inside. Verne shut off the heating device in his coat. He was in a long room. At either end were tables, a state banner draped over them. Terminals sat on each table, and behind them a checkpoint agent. After going through one checkpoint, the passengers crossed a yellow line in the middle of the room, symbolizing the border, and went on to the second checkpoint. The line painted on the floor extended up the walls and across the ceiling.

Verne took his place on the Pennsylvania side of the line. Ahead of him was a woman holding a boy's hand. The two checkpoints were separated by thirty feet or so, and from either side, uniforms watched the drowsy passengers moving through. The silence was punctuated only by an occasional cough or a sneeze.

Verne took off his coat and draped it over his arm. The room was stifling. A faint smell of disinfectant hovered. The travelers sagged and looked oppressed. Verne recalled that when William Penn had given his name to this state in the seventeenth century, he had dedicated it to all of the earth's persecuted peoples. More outdated humanist pre-occupations.

As the passengers crossed the border to form a second line in front of the Ohio desk, the men were asked to go into an adjacent room for ASP Supervision, while the women were allowed to proceed directly. After several minutes the men exited by another door and joined the line with the women.

The boy ahead of Verne kept fidgeting and turning around. He could not have been more than twelve. Verne smiled at him and put his hand reassuringly on the boy's back. The guard signaled to his mother to approach. She took two magnetized passcards from her purse; the agent put them through the terminal.

Verne's attention wandered but was brought back by raised voices. A dispute had broken out.

"I'm asking you to wait for your son on the other side," said a domineering voice. "Your son must go through the ASP checkpoint like every other male. No exceptions."

The woman looked at Verne in desperation. She then leaned toward her son and whispered something in his ear. As they moved off toward the Ohio side, she kept looking at him, until he disappeared behind the door.

When it was his turn, Verne handed over his passcard. The agent saw immediately that it bore the federal seal of government service.

"Excuse me, sir, but you should have told us you were carrying a Public Official passcard," the agent told him, returning it without putting it through the terminal. "You may go directly through."

"I'd rather undergo AS, just like everyone else," Verne replied stiffly.

The agent motioned to the uniformed officer, who approached them.

"Problem?" asked the officer.

"This gentleman is carrying an HPO passcard, but he still wants to go through the AS monitor," the agent explained, looking embarrassed. "I've told him that he didn't need to."

Just then there was a cry. The boy came running out of the ASP checkpoint.

"Mom! They say I can't go through!"

His mother, who in the meantime had crossed over into Ohio, let out a scream and ran toward her son. She was stopped.

"David!"

She broke into sobs and collapsed in a heap. Everyone in the room was staring.

"Let him go," said Verne to the officer. "I'll vouch for him."

The officer went into the checkpoint.

Mother and son were being held on opposite sides of the yellow line. Their sobs were the only sounds in the heavy silence. Everyone was waiting for the officer to come back out. After a few minutes, he did.

"I'm sorry," he said to Verne in a voice intended for everyone to hear. "His ASP isn't working. He'll have to go to Pittsburgh for verification. He'll be able to meet with his mother in a day or two — once everything is in order. She can wait for him at the FBBS headquarters in Canton."

"Can't she at least stay with him?" asked Verne.

The officer shrugged. "Against regulations. My Ohio colleagues will take good care of her. They'll give her instructions."

The boy was dragged away. His mother's sobbing continued.

"This is barbaric," Verne said through clenched teeth.

"You make the laws, sir," said the agent at the terminal.

Verne was directed to the AS checkpoint. In a small room, a technician wearing a white jacket sat on a raised stool before a terminal. He held a magnetic sensor.

Verne was reminded that some hospitals were starting to use electroshock treatment again. He wondered why he'd never thought of the analogy before.

He inclined his body forward so that the technician could scan his head.

9

Two A.M. A high beep sounded in the apartment on M Street where Annabelle Weaver was lying in the arms of Mary Peale. They had just finished their lovemaking and were starting to drift off to sleep.

Disengaging herself from Mary's arms, Annabelle jumped up and found her Bureau phone. She took it out to the living room.

"I was just about to give up," said the voice on the line. "Kane here. There's a problem. We lost Sherman."

"Damn it to hell, Kane!" cursed Annabelle, instantly enraged. "What went wrong?"

Kane recounted the story of the high-speed chase through the streets of Los Angeles following Sherman's visit with Michael Engelhardt.

"Engelhardt? You mean the Mafia capo?"

"That was the big surprise of the evening. It was Engelhardt's men who picked up on us. Just by luck we saw Engelhardt's car pull out behind their hideout. I had the place surrounded, because I knew that — "

"Quit congratulating yourself, Kane. So far this is one big fuckup," Annabelle snapped. "Then what happened?"

"They ran head-on into a police barricade. The two men accompanying Sherman were found. One's dead. The other's in a coma."

"Sherman?"

"Vanished. We know he was in the car at the time of the accident, so he must be hurt. He can't have gone far. I've sealed off the neighborhood. I'll call when there's news."

"After ten tomorrow, call me at the boss's place."

"At her private residence? Is that what you mean?"

Annabelle took a deep breath. "That is exactly what I mean. At her home. And Kane? You'd better call with good news. Lombard's patience is already razor thin about all this."

"OK. Don't worry — we'll find him. By the way, we may have something on the courier carrying Milner's letter."

"Explain."

"Has to do with a suitcase. We think. I'll keep you posted."

Kane was gone.

What was the Network doing flirting with the Mafia? The stage was getting crowded, Annabelle thought. When the Network was only a bunch of bumbling idealists dispensing quaint-sounding ACLU dogma, things were a lot simpler for the FBBS. Routine work. The Mafia? A whole different story. Those people were a force to be reckoned with. She wondered if she ought to say something to Lombard. No. Best to wait until Kane found Sherman. Bringing Sherman in was becoming urgent. She went back into the bedroom.

Sitting on the edge of the bed, Annabelle pondered the implications of what Kane had told her. Mary turned over on her back, still asleep. The light filtering through the window made her skin seem more pale. Moaning, then smacking her lips, Mary unfolded a leg and spread out her arms. Annabelle's look lingered on her body. She wondered if Mary was faking sleep.

Annabelle leaned over to examine closely the sleeping figure. The idea of not giving in right away to the temptation to stroke the smooth skin gave her indescribable pleasure. She drew her face near Mary's and inhaled the musky scent in the recess behind her ear. Her eyes rested on her slightly asymmetrical breasts. The erect nipples were standing in invitation.

An image of taking both breasts in her mouth at one time came to her. Since she had first met Mary, the impossibility of that feat, and the impossibility of repressing the desire for it, sharpened even further Annabelle's insatiable appetite for this woman.

Impatience was becoming ache. It was painful, yet she lived in fear that she wouldn't again feel that sweet yearning; when it came back she welcomed it like a lost friend.

A delicate line of downy hair carried Annabelle's eyes to the soft triangle, slightly hidden under the blanket of shadow that moved to the rhythm of Mary's breathing.

/ 57

The younger woman moved her leg and pressed it against the other, as if to escape the devouring regard of her mistress. Annabelle could not resist any longer. She plunged her face between Mary's thighs, found her moistened sex, and began to lick delicately but imperiously.

Mary moaned and, slowly, opened her thighs, shifting to meet the embrace. When she seized Annabelle's head to guide her caresses, her ravisher felt orgasm overcome her in triumph.

Chapter 3

1

The light from the ceiling of the airport terminal descended like a giant parachute. Surrounding the main hall were enormous glass barriers designed to protect the passengers from the frigid air.

Clara shivered and buttoned her collar. The temperature was well below what was comfortable. She had awakened several times during the night because her teeth were chattering.

At six in the morning most of the offices were still closed. A group of sullen-looking passengers were beginning to line up in front of the check-in counter. They looked at Clara in silence.

After a moment's hesitation, she began walking briskly across the sparkling immensity of the terminal, resisting the urge to break into a run.

She reached the other side with a great sense of relief. There was a bank of phones, each separated by a faux-tapestry barrier, and she took refuge in the last one. Then she removed Lieutenant Lobell's letter from her pocket and pushed in the numbers 63-14. A male voice answered.

"This is Antigone," Clara whispered a little hoarsely. "I'm calling on behalf of —"

"I know who you are," a male voice broke in. "They want you to make it on your own to the Metropolitan Museum, which opens at ten. You'll be met in the nineteenth-century room on the second floor. Do you know who Manet is?"

"You mean the painter?"

"Correct. Now listen carefully. In the museum there's a painting by Manet called *Young Woman in the Costume of an Espada*. Be there at exactly ten-thirty A.M. Someone'll come up to you and ask, 'Do you like Dutch still lifes?' and you'll answer, 'Yes, but I prefer the Impressionists.' That's all there is to it. Now repeat it."

Clara repeated it.

"Good luck," said the voice.

Clara walked in the direction of the exit feeling much better. Not only was she free, she was in contact with the Network. She also had plenty of time.

It was still dark. An icy wind swept over the parking lot stretching out in front of the terminal. Bundled up in her coat and hood, she waited near the New York shuttle stop along with three other people. No one spoke.

A uniform approached the group. Clara tensed. He looked everyone over, then stationed himself a few feet away. Finally the shuttle arrived.

Clara went to the back and sat by the window, glancing up at the other passengers who climbed aboard at various terminals. She soon dozed off.

She woke with a start. The shuttle had just gone into the Queens tunnel. She looked at her watch display. Ten to eight.

While she was asleep a woman holding a bundle on her lap had taken the seat next to hers. Clara looked out the window. The yellow lights inside the tunnel mottled the snow on the passing cars and made them look camouflaged.

They entered Manhattan. The buildings were hidden behind a thick curtain of snow, which was already concealing the sidewalks.

The shuttle turned up 38th Street and pulled to a stop in front of the new East Side Terminal.

Clara took a taxi up to the Plaza on Central Park South. First she was going to eat a big, leisurely breakfast.

At 9:45, breakfasted, feeling refreshed, Clara walked up Fifth Avenue toward the Metropolitan Museum. It had stopped snowing. Around her the towers of Manhattan loomed over the bare trees.

Clara walked smartly; for the first time since she had started carrying Milner's letter, the weight of anxiety she had been carrying with it lifted. Even her suitcase seemed light. All she felt was the pleasure of the exercise and youthful elation at the way the frigid air pinched her face. It was a welcome contrast to the smothering smog-heat of L.A.

A homeless man muffled in rags stopped to watch her pass. He interpreted her smile as a signal of sympathy and smiled back.

At 10 A.M. on the dot Clara climbed the monumental front steps of the Met. The huge main hall was deserted. She bought her ticket and dropped her bag off at the coat check. A guard watched her with detached curiosity as she mounted the marble stairway.

On the first floor, she walked the length of a narrow room filled with antique pianos. She stopped in front of an upright with intricately patterned woodwork. The lid was open. Without thinking, she placed her index finger over one of the yellowed ivory keys and pushed down. The resonating sound it produced startled her. She hurried out of the room, the note still echoing behind her.

Now she was in a long corridor that sloped gently upward for about fifty feet and ended in what looked like a halo of bright light. Clara saw that her approach was being watched by a figure at the far end. Suddenly uneasy, she slowed her pace. Her anxiety sharpened. The figure watching her was — floating? She couldn't believe her eyes. He was sitting, quite literally, on air. It was all she could do not to turn around and retrace her steps. Slowly she realized that the play of light and perspective had made a figure in a painting look as if he were alive. She nearly laughed out loud at herself.

The figure — a gypsy holding a guitar, sitting on a bench — was in the middle of a group of three paintings. One of the others she immediately recognized as *Young Woman in the Costume of an Espada*.

Clara had no idea what an "Espada" was supposed to look like. What she saw was a young woman dressed like a toreador holding a sword aloft. Clara stood back to get a better look. In the foreground, the young woman stood in profile, holding the sword in her right hand and a bullfighter's cape in her left. Her clothes were dark: a waist-length jacket, knee breeches, and white silk stockings. A wide-brimmed black hat rested on a pink scarf knotted behind her head, like a gypsy. She was supposed to be festive — a rich girl cross-dressing for a bit of fun — but her expression was as serious as it would have been for a formal sitting. She was standing in an arena, whose retaining wall was lightly sketched. You could make out some shadowy figures of people. In the background, painted in a way that made it seem intentionally distorted and painterly — like the studio backdrop it probably was — a picador was leveling his lance at a bull.

The painting intrigued Clara. She had never heard of a female toreador before. The casual way in which the young woman held the sword seemed inappropriate for someone about to gore an animal.

There was also something vaguely obscene about the way the weapon poked out over the cape, which itself seemed like a frilly woman's dress. It was all a sort of parody of virility, Clara thought.

She drew back one more step to get an even better look.

"If you'd only stop moving for another minute, I'll be finished," said a voice behind her.

Clara turned to see a young woman standing behind an easel a few feet away, smiling.

"I beg your pardon," said Clara.

"I was taking advantage of your absorption in that painting to do a sketch," said the girl. "I thought it was such a great scene. There. I'm finished. Do you like Dutch still lifes?"

Disconcerted, Clara struggled for a moment to find the proper response.

"Yes, but I prefer the Impressionists."

The girl smiled and began putting away her easel.

"The password was my idea," she said ingenuously. "I told my aunt we should use it. That's who we're going to see now."

Her equipment under her arm, she headed for the exit. Clara followed, wishing she could have had another minute to look at the other Manets.

2

The darkness was barely attenuated by the feeble light of the stars. Sherman made his way slowly and painfully, one hand against the wall to steady himself. Each step was agony to his left thigh. Soon he would be able to go no farther.

Torn between the desire to get away from the scene of the accident as quickly as possible and the need to stop and rest, he lunged forward and ran straight into something blocking the passage. There was a loud noise and he fell flat on the ground.

A ray of light pierced the blackness.

"Who's there?" cried a voice.

Sherman raised his head. He saw he was lying among garbage and junk behind an apartment building. The garbage can he had run into had fallen over on its side and spewed out its contents. The light went out.

Gritting his teeth, Sherman managed to get himself into an upright position and prop his back against the wall. The police had probably surrounded the whole neighborhood. He concentrated and listened but heard nothing except a distant rumble from Central Avenue. He had noticed for the last few minutes that the fingers on his left hand were sticky. He fumbled for a pocket-light. His hand was covered with blood. He rubbed his arm and felt a shooting pain. The sleeve of his coat was torn several inches above his biceps.

The wounds were worse than he'd thought. Probably had left an easy trail for someone to follow. Why his leg was causing him such pain he didn't know. There was no wound — maybe he'd broken something.

Sherman put his injured hand in his coat pocket and pushed himself up. He had to contact Wesley — Polynices — before he was arrested.

Using his good hand for balance, he began moving forward again. The left leg was now completely stiff, and any progress took heroic effort.

Suddenly he came up against another wall, perpendicular to the one he had been following. He stepped sideways. Yet another wall. Then a smooth and cold surface, a contrast to the roughness of the others. A door. Fumbling, he found a doorknob. His heart pounding, he slowly turned it. The door opened noiselessly. Sherman went in and closed it behind him.

A dim light from an exit sign showed he was in a garage in which two trucks were parked. The smell of oil blended with a sweeter odor Sherman couldn't immediately place. He limped over to the first truck. Without hesitating he hauled himself up to unfasten the latch, opened the door to peer in, then lost his balance and fell headfirst into the back of the truck. But instead of hitting the floor with a jolt, he landed in something soft. The sweet odor he'd noticed when he first came in filled his nostrils.

Relief revived his spirits. Sherman turned on his pocket-light. Bundles of furs — he had literally stumbled upon an illegal shipment. The sale of animal furs on American soil had been banned for years. The wearing of fur, on the other hand, was permitted so long as the coat's provenance could be verified. In some circles, having one of these rare commodities was considered the height of snobbery. Fox, seal, and mink — they were all worth their weight in gold and nourished a very lucrative black-market traffic run by gangs who specialized in them.

Sherman found some loose rags and hastily fashioned a bandage that, with the help of his teeth, he managed to knot around his wounded arm. Then he lay back among the furs. It would be easier to call Wesley in a few hours. If the police hadn't found him by then. He willed his body to relax and let his mind wander.

Images of the whole tragicomic car chase came floating back to him. When had the uniforms spotted him? Scarface Jeff must have been right. It had to be the FBBS. Sherman knew the price he would pay if they picked him up: twenty years in a reeducation facility, maybe longer. Just when Engelhardt had offered him a way of breaking the ASP stranglehold.

Ever since the removal of his roof spider, the idea that he could once again have sexual relations had aroused his curiosity, but so far nothing else. Finding a partner would not be easy. That familiar ache that had accompanied him since his wife Jane's death reawakened in his chest.

He remembered the happiness he'd felt when he first held her in his arms. Their life had seemed so charmed. Then came Sacred Fire. Unlike many of their friends, he and Jane still planned to have a child. A hedge against life, he told those who accused him of ignoring the consequences. Jane agreed. She would wait for him to finish his novel. She contracted SF at the hospital where she worked as a nurse. Probably from a cut. The fever had taken her away in almost no time. She died several days before his book was published.

A door slammed, and Sherman was jolted out of his reverie. Unable to raise himself, he hid as best he could under a bundle of furs. Women's voices. Three of them. One spoke with a heavy accent. What were they saying? Something about the route. Compadres? He couldn't make it out.

"Sergeant Elipas said he'd let us through," one voice said. "Anyway, they're not after us. They're looking for some Network man who was in a car accident. I told him that you'd be in the truck. He thought that was funny. He said, 'I only hope she remembers I didn't use it as an excuse to impound the cargo.' "

"Let him try," replied the woman with the accent. "You'd think we didn't pay him enough, that little worm. *Vamos!* Hey, Annetta, close the doors after we leave. Wait for us back at the apartment."

Sherman heard the women climb into the cab of the truck. The truck began to move.

He tried to wedge himself in as best he could, but every bump sent a blinding pain through his thigh. His whole left side was paralyzed. Even if he'd had the chance, he wouldn't have the strength to get out.

The brakes hissed, and the truck came to a sudden stop.

"That you, Loca?" a man's voice called.

"It's me, little man," replied the accented one.

"OK. The Sergeant said you'd be coming. You're lucky, you know. We're after a bigger fish. Otherwise no way we'd let you through."

"Want to bet?" replied the woman.

"All right, get moving."

The truck began moving again. Sherman heard the women laughing and exclaiming.

Loca. Then Sherman remembered. Loca! He had fallen into the hands of a gang leader. Las Virginas. The savagery of these gangs of women was legendary. They ruled whole sections of East Los Angeles. From the Mafia to a street gang. What a night.

The truck kept making turns, obviously following back roads and side streets. He periodically heard them talking, but couldn't make out what they were saying.

Then the brakes squealed. The truck came to a hard stop. Sherman groaned as much from hopelessness as from pain. He wouldn't have the time to explain what he was doing there before they skinned him alive.

"Take Eagle Street," cried a woman's voice. "They're waiting for you down on Lorena!"

The truck veered sharply. Sherman was thrown from one side of the truck to the other. The furs absorbed some of the shock, but he had crossed his threshold of pain. He began to scream.

When the truck arrived at its destination, the Virginas found Sherman lying half-conscious among furs splotched with blood.

3

"My name is Kathy," declared the young woman as she and Clara were leaving the museum.

Clara said nothing in reply. Kathy didn't seem to take offense.

They crossed Fifth Avenue and walked north past luxury apartment buildings. It had gotten colder. The occasional passerby huffed past, bundled up beyond recognition, back bent against the wind. Funnels of fetid steam rose from the open vents on the street.

At 85th Street they turned right. At the corner of Park they went into an apartment building. An elderly uniformed doorman was sitting behind a desk. He nodded at Kathy and glanced suspiciously at Clara. With her overcoat and suitcase, she looked a bit like a cosmetic saleswoman arriving for an appointment with some rich dowager.

"A friend from Miami," said Kathy, leading Clara to the elevator.

The apartment was on the top floor. Clara waited in the hallway. The walls were decorated with antique movie posters showing *Arabian Nights* landscapes, bedouins in djellabas, camel caravans at the foot of a fortress, oases lost in the desert, prop planes passing overhead, scenes from *Lawrence of Arabia*. They were probably worth a great deal of money, Clara thought.

The room into which Kathy led her several moments later also came straight off a film set: Persian rugs, leather ottomans, gaudy lamps sitting on intricately tooled copper tables, hookahs, and all kinds of Middle Eastern bric-a-brac. The light bulbs in the antique oil lamps were tinted orange and gave off a rich amber luster.

"Come and sit near me, Antigone. That is what we are calling you, is it not?" This from a voice startlingly clear, tinged with an indefinable accent.

Kathy's aunt was sitting in an easy chair with an embroidered slipcover that matched her dress. Her white hair was gathered into a bun and held by a large pin of Japanese lacquer. She clutched the ends of a shawl in her fragile-looking hands. What most impressed Clara was the extraordinary intensity of her dark eyes.

"Sit here on this pillow," she said to Clara, pointing to a large cushion by her feet.

Clara sat.

"I hope you don't mind. I am so small I must make the most of what height I have."

Clara replied by smiling, though she did feel patronized.

"I am referred to as Hestia. All these Greek stories — that was Peter Alexos's idea. An old fool but an excellent organizer."

"Who is Peter Alexos?" asked Clara, though the name was distantly familiar.

"Not long ago a young girl like yourself would never have asked such a question," replied the old lady with a smile. "Don't be hurt. Times have changed, that's all . . . You may call me Myra. I risk nothing by telling you my real name: Myra Cornfeld. I have long been taken for an inoffensive old lady. Federal agents came to visit a couple of years ago because they knew of my old ties with the Boston Group. They departed convinced I was harmless. You have at least heard of the Boston Group, haven't you?"

"Only vaguely."

"The Boston Group was the original Network. We were — there were nine."

Clara realized she was sitting at the feet of one of the original founders of the Network.

"Peter Alexos was one of us. No one knows what became of him. There was a rumor he was living somewhere in Canada, organizing Network strategy from there. If that's true, he must not have any more time to write. For him philosophy was a way of life — I am going on, aren't I? Not very prudent on my part. But you should at least know the first meeting took place in Boston one year before the election of Gray, may he roast in hell. That day, the members of the Group made a solemn vow to go underground if Gray was elected and pushed through his programs."

The old woman passed her hand before her eyes.

"So there you are. Nine Americans, just like any others. Two are dead — Simon Bishop, a pediatrician and child psychologist, who was arrested in Chicago. He died in a prison in Dubuque. And Pamela Vogt, a journalist. She committed suicide. Since then, those nine have turned into many. And now here you are sitting at my feet. I haven't even asked you if you had a good trip. Pretty eventful, I would imagine?"

An enormous Persian cat with tawny fur emerged from beneath the chair and glared at Clara with green eyes.

"That is Maia. A name she richly deserves." Hestia laughed. "The letter you are carrying is very important. You are still carrying it, are you not?"

Clara opened her purse, felt around behind the lining, brought out the letter, and handed it to Hestia. The old woman's face took on an expression of reverence. She adjusted her bifocals, which were hanging around her neck on an elaborate silver chain, and scrutinized the envelope in close detail.

"Nothing is written on it," she said at last in a disappointed tone. "The important part is inside. I would give a great deal to read the contents."

She handed it back to Clara. "In a minute I will tell you what we are going to do to protect it better."

The old lady paused, then seemed to brighten.

"I knew the author of the letter. Joseph Milner. Have you ever heard of him?"

"Yes," replied Clara, still a little mesmerized by the unreality of the atmosphere in which she found herself.

"A scientist, a great scientist. The only one who might have gotten us out of the daily horror in which we now live. Alas, no one listened to him. He believed that nothing on earth could justify limiting individual liberties. An idealist. Intelligent people, famous people, told him he was wrong, that humanity's basic existence was at stake because of Sacred Fire. They used all kinds of lofty rhetoric to justify the unjustifiable. But I knew he was right. He thought that science had absolutely no chance of finding a cure for SF if there was no freedom of inquiry. And that we had to pay the price of that liberty, once and for all. Look at how science works in countries where there are repressive regimes. All we have really done is destroy creativity. Have you not noticed? There is no music, no poetry; no real art is being produced. There have never been so many museums, but nothing new is being created to put in them. The whole country has become a self-contained museum for soulless spectators. If we had listened to what Joseph was telling us, we might have had a chance. Now even if a cure is found, it will do nothing for us. We have gone too far. It would be like trying to raise the dead."

Clara couldn't approve of such defeatism. Nor could she understand why someone of Myra Cornfeld's experience could say such things. What was the Network for, after all? To try and change everything. Why else would people across the country risk so much?

But she kept silent. Under other circumstances, Clara might have interrupted ten times to say what she thought. But this woman exerted a strange power over her. Perhaps it was the way her face lit up the moment she'd touched Milner's letter.

Clara uncrossed and recrossed her legs.

"You don't agree," said Myra Cornfeld, smiling. "I can see that you don't. A good thing. I didn't always think this way, you know. Perhaps Milner's death has brought it on. I am sure you have in your possession the very last thing that he wrote. Anyway, enough philosophy for today. Let's talk about your mission. We are very unlucky. Paul Verne has left New York for the West Coast."

"Do you mean I've come all this way for nothing?" exclaimed Clara. It seemed unbelievable.

"Perhaps. I don't know. The latest report is that he is on a train somewhere in the middle of Ohio."

"A train?"

"It does seem incomprehensible, doesn't it? Verne left the U.N. abruptly, we're not sure why exactly, though probably Milner's death has something to do with it. That was where you were to have delivered the letter. Otherwise, we would have waited until he returned to California. But there may still be time. We need to find a way of getting you on that train."

The old woman pressed a buzzer. Her niece came into the room.

"Kathy, would you show Hermes in?"

"I will now explain what we are going to do," began Myra Cornfeld, turning to Clara.

4

Crossing the border between Ohio and Indiana was considerably simplified by the absence of an AS checkpoint. Uniforms had gotten on the train at seven A.M. that morning. Verne had heard them going by his door without stopping. They had doubtless received instructions to leave him alone.

After the mother of the detained boy had gotten off in Canton, Verne had spent a sleepless night. He finally did reopen the heating vent. He was positive they would not try anything else, now that they knew he wasn't carrying anything besides a few scientific papers. He also saw no point in trying to find out their identity. They were probably part of one of the many organizations, official or pseudo-official, that for several years had infected the land.

The train passed through Valparaiso and hurtled on toward the Chicago suburbs. Verne looked distractedly at the bleak industrial complexes. Factory smokestacks rose like immense columns, and out of them belched grayish smoke that blended into the leaden sky.

He began to remember the last part of his dream, when his father's face suddenly became Christ's, the Christ of the *Retable*. The *Retable* had long haunted his thoughts and dreams, but this was the first time his father's image had blended with it. His father, who had died ten years ago from a coronary.

The images on two of the three panels — the Virgin Mary, Mary Magdalen, and St. John — involved removing the old cloth from the dead Christ. He had asked his father one day why Grunewald had replaced the shredded cloth covering Christ's loins on the cross with a clean one for the tomb scene. His father had burst out laughing and complimented his son on his powers of observation. But he ignored the question. His father had deliberately refused to answer what young Paul thought a reasonable question. He was convinced his father's refusal was related to the subject matter. Avoiding the question was a way of avoiding discussing Christ's nakedness.

Would his life have been different had he and his father been able to talk like men with each other? Henri Verne never mentioned his sex life, and the young Paul never told him about his first experiences. It probably wouldn't have changed a thing. But perhaps it would have shortened the distance that separated them during those last years of his father's life.

The *Retable*. Again. Always coming back at a decisive point in his life, offering new questions, puzzles, clues.

It had been a topic during his first conversation with Joseph Milner.

Like so many students of his generation, Verne went to listen to the lectures given by Milner. Having finished his medical studies and completed a doctorate in molecular biology, Verne left France to finish his education in California. He planned to return a year later, to take up the directorship of the immunology lab at the Curie Institute in Paris. First he wanted to meet Milner, who was renowned for one discovery in particular.

The celebrated scientist had succeeded in cloning fragments of a DNA cell collected in cerebral tissue eight thousand years old, discovered miraculously conserved in a peat bog in Florida. Although much shrunk, it was still possible to discern from the internal structure that the tissue came from the brains of a 45-year-old woman and three 25-to-35-year-old men. The distinction between the gray matter of the cortex and the white matter was clear. The cell organization was not as discernible. However, both neuron traces and axonal fibers were very much in evidence. During the months following this discovery, scientists put a half-ounce fragment through a battery of biochemical tests that revealed the existence — the stupefying existence — of DNA, the deoxyribonucleic acid that carries genetic inheritance.

The question became, was this DNA from a human brain, or was it produced by those microorganisms that proliferate in decaying cadavers? The presence of mitochondria, enclaves containing a different DNA from that of the nucleus and existing only in multicellular organisms, confirmed that it indeed came from 8,000-year-old human gray matter. It became known familiarly as the "Maggie gene."

Once the extraordinary find was confirmed, several laboratories began to work on the remains. Milner succeeding in cloning several fragments of the DNA and multiplying them in vitro, thereby creating an entirely new scientific discipline: genetic evolution.

Milner's find also permitted him to discover, almost by chance, a gene sequence never seen before. He postulated that this sequence, whose function was unknown, might one day explain a great deal about our early ancestors. Why it had died out was a baffling mystery. Laboratories around the world worked feverishly to find an answer.

Verne's pilgrimage to San Francisco was based on his hope to meet the great man. This proved difficult, since Milner was in constant demand and traveled a good deal. But one night Verne was invited to a reception in Sausalito given by the director of a hospital. The party was noisy, so he went outside for a walk in the garden. The garden overlooked San Francisco Bay, which shimmered in the moonlight.

He was staring at the water when he was startled by a voice.

"It is a beautiful sight, is it not?"

He instantly recognized the heavy Viennese accent.

"I have never been able to understand that all of this is the same — the same moon, the same trees, the same smell of grass, and yet we are six thousand miles from Europe. You are French, am I right?" Milner asked Verne.

"Yes. From Colmar. A little village in Alsace."

"Oh yes, I know Colmar. I am from Vienna. The Danube is the sister of the Rhine, and the Rhine is no stranger to me. The two rivers form the liquid axis of Europe. Have you ever thought of that?"

"Yes — I mean, no — I mean, the two rivers do not flow in the same direction."

Milner burst out laughing.

"You are right. Still, you and I speak the same language. You speak Alsatian. Yes?"

"Um, actually, I do not."

"Pity."

Verne was embarrassed, so Milner picked up the conversation.

"I would suspect you are not having a very good time. What would you say to a walk?"

Verne readily agreed.

They walked down the hill toward the water through streets bordered by gardens. The moon was so bright it seemed almost like daytime.

Verne was in heaven. He venerated this famous little man (Milner came up only to his shoulders), dressed as he always was in a tight-fitting sweater over pants whose tailoring seemed to emphasize the roundness of his belly. He reminded Verne of pictures he had seen of Einstein. Unkempt white hair flew around a bald spot that extended down to an enormous forehead and a large nose he was continually rubbing, giving Milner a comic air accentuated by the childlike expression of his eyes.

"You like your studies?" he asked, walking briskly.

"I am very happy to be here," replied Verne, nearly jogging to keep up.

"If I may ask, what particular area of study is interesting you most?"

"HIV. The most perplexing biological problem that has faced medical science for generations, perhaps ever."

Without stopping, Milner gave his young companion a sharp look, but Verne continued.

"Vaccination solved nothing. Every time the virus mutates, thousands of people are in peril. It is an exhausting race against the clock. There must be something else we have not found." He blushed, remembering who he was talking to.

"And what is to be done, do you think?" Milner asked. "In what direction should one orient one's research?"

"We need to find an antibody that has an effect on the mutative capacities of the virus. Your current work on the origin of carcinogenic genetic sequences seems to me to hold one of the keys to the solution."

Milner stopped walking. He rubbed his nose between his thumb and the folded index finger of his left hand.

"You are doubtless correct. That is where one needs to look. We will have to talk about this further," he added, starting to walk again.

"Tell me, Paul Verne, do you know of Grunewald's *Retable* in Colmar?"

Verne stopped in his tracks.

"Yes, of course," he stammered. "Why do you ask me that?"

"Because you are from Colmar, and because it has everything to do with what is preoccupying you, my young friend. Grunewald was a member of the Order of St. Anthony. Did you know that?"

"Well — I suppose I knew, but — "

Milner interrupted, "The Antonians were a monastic order whose principal mission during the Middle Ages was to deal with rye ergotism, which was called 'Sacred Fire.' The disease spread in epidemic fashion, and those poor souls who caught it flocked to the monastery at Issenheim to pray to Saint Anthony. The Antonians knew nothing about the origins of the disease — that it was caused by mold in the rye used for making bread, acting as a sort of hallucinogen — but they had herbal remedies that alleviated its symptoms, which is why their prestige grew. The afflicted believed that they had been possessed by the devil. Many believed this was also true for syphilis when it came along in the fifteenth century. AIDS has produced the same reaction. From that point of view, it is difficult to argue that humanity has evolved very much . . . But to come back to the Sacred Fire, you really should look into the symptoms of ergotism. In many respects they resembled those of AIDS — the multiple necroses, the delirium."

They had arrived at the foot of the hill and began to head toward the waterfront. In the distance, the lights of San Francisco glittered fiercely.

For another hour they walked and talked, with increasing passion, about medicine, plagues, the *Retable*. Then suddenly Milner stopped and turned to Verne.

"Listen to me, Paul Verne. It is rare that one enjoys oneself in life. Thanks to you I have spent a most enjoyable evening. Why don't you come work for me?"

The whistle blew, and the train began to slow. The name *Hammond*, painted in bold white letters, stretched across the entire wall of a warehouse. Verne sat up and rubbed his eyes with the balls of his fists, like a child.

The evening Milner had asked him to join his lab he did not give his answer. He called Colmar the next day, but he made no mention of his plans.

"I just wanted to know how you are," he had said awkwardly to his father.

He had gone to the UCSF hospital and spent the morning with AIDS patients. That afternoon he met with Milner again. He told him he would accept the position.

5

The sound of the door slamming startled Melissa Verne. Steve Jackson came striding through the laboratory toward her. Beneath the shock of red hair his eyes were shining with rage.

"What the HELL is all this about?" he shouted. "Paul won't be here for another four days?"

"That's no reason to shout," Melissa replied wearily.

"Don't you realize the position that puts us in? Margaret Brittain is coming here at eleven. I can already guess what she's going to put in that report for Chamberlain when she goes back to Santa Barbara! What a mess!"

Melissa didn't respond. During the night she had realized that Verne had said nothing about his meeting with the lawyer of the famous financier. She had been so upset by the news of Milner's death she had forgotten to bring it up.

Steve sank into a chair and looked desperate.

"The deepest cut of all is that Brittain's going to be received by Doris Hathaway." He threw his head back and made gagging noises.

Melissa giggled. Always the ham, she thought.

"Listen, Steve, we'll get through this as best we can." She forced herself to adopt a tone of assurance. "How about if she came to your ward? Do you have some patient you could introduce her to? Someone who won't make too much of an impression, you know what I mean?"

Steve seemed to contemplate this. He swung his head forward and rested his chin in the palm of his hand. His white lab coat made him look even more adolescent. For perhaps the hundredth time, she wondered why she hadn't given in to his advances years earlier. Life would have been much simpler. She smiled and shook her head.

"Melissa, stop making fun of me. I'm telling you that Paul's absence affects me deeply." He blinked his eyes.

"I'm not making fun of you."

"You know what? I'm never sure where I stand with you." He gave her a look of exaggerated melancholy. Then his features regained their composure. "But let's see. This morning I have an appointment with a young teacher. Maybe he'll do. But Doris Hathaway? She'll never do. She'll take advantage of Paul's absence to kidnap Brittain. She'll bad-mouth him all over the place. She's been spoiling to do that for a long time."

The hostility between Verne and Hathaway, who was vice president of the Reiss Institute, dated back to its beginnings. He cared only about therapeutic results; she saw only the bottom line. Their battles sent shock waves throughout the Institute, clearly dividing it into two camps: scientists on the one hand, administrators on the other.

The financial situation of the privately funded Institute had worsened because of the steady rise in nonpaying SF patients admitted to the treatment center. Verne was told that the Institute would close if he didn't change his ways, yet he adamantly refused to admit only patients with the resources to pay for treatments, arguing that the state's Special Hospitals were designed for patients with modest incomes.

But now Verne had to face the facts. Money was getting tighter. He had finally resolved to seek the aid of Jerome Chamberlain, a wealthy member of the board of directors. Chamberlain had asked Margaret Brittain, his head legal counsel, to write him a report about the Institute before committing any funds.

Meanwhile, Doris Hathaway was ready and waiting to take full advantage of Verne's difficulties in order to seize control. And she was about to meet with Chamberlain's proxy.

"What if *we* kidnap Margaret Brittain?" exclaimed Melissa suddenly.

Steve's look of incredulity was genuine. "What? How? Sweet and Holy John of the Apocalypse, Melissa, what a nutball idea."

"Listen, I have a plan and it might just work." Melissa suddenly became very animated. "What time is it? Ten-fifteen? Okay, this is what you're going to do — take the ambulance and position it at the front gate. Then open the hood. Take Lorraine with you — she's pretty wily and can give you a hand. As soon as Brittain arrives, beep me. Put yourself smack in the middle of the street if you have to. The important thing is not to let her get by you. She'll be driving something flashy. Get it?" Steve nodded. "Good. She knows who you are and will offer you a ride. Once you're in the car tell her that you were coming back from an emergency call."

"But I haven't done that since I was an intern!"

"So what? She won't know that."

"A chief of medicine going on an emergency call? That's a little unbelievable, don't you think?" replied Steve, trying to sound ruffled.

"Soothe your ego another day."

Steve thought over the proposal in silence.

"All right," he said. "But on one condition — that you invite me over for dinner."

"I'll do whatever you want — except anything that upsets your ASP—"

"What makes you think I've still got one?"

"You old scaredy-cat! You wouldn't take such a risk. Now get going. We're almost out of time."

Steve's playful tone troubled Melissa just a little. She wondered if the big baby really had found a way of getting himself debugged.

"Say everything goes as you plan," said Steve, jumping out of his chair. "Then what do I do?"

"You tell her Paul had organized a reception in her honor at the hospital but was suddenly called away to Washington."

"Is he in Washington?"

"No, but I'm the only one who knows where he is."

Steve looked as if he were about to ask something.

"I'll explain later," she added hurriedly. "This just might work, you know. Bring Brittain in through the emergency room. Doris will probably be waiting for her in her office. I'm sure her secretary will be out prowling for Brittain at the main entrance. In the meantime I'll let everyone know what's going on."

"It's worth a shot," agreed Steve, looking at Melissa with open admiration. "At least it'll be fun."

Steve called his office.

"This is Dr. Jackson. Would you tell my secretary that I won't be able to meet with Mr. Simmons for another three-quarters of an hour? Yes, Simmons. Right, thanks."

He snapped the phone shut.

"We'll make this work," said Steve, grinning broadly. "Melissa, you're some woman. But then I always knew that."

He left the room. Melissa watched him go and felt a wave of tenderness wash over her.

Steve Jackson's ward occupied nearly the entire northern wing of the building. Melissa walked briskly down the long corridor. The walls were painted light yellow and the floors shone in the reflection of the bright lights. The corridor was lined with rooms filled with patients.

She headed toward the nurses' station, pausing to say hello to a group of orderlies she passed on the way.

Cindy Pryce, chief of staff, was a solid, middle-aged woman with prematurely white hair and an abrupt manner that intimidated her colleagues. But Melissa knew there was no one who could match her ability to console a patient or comfort a crying nurse.

"Where's Dr. Jackson?" she asked loudly as soon as she saw Melissa. "His schedule is filled. He'll never fit everyone in."

"He'll be arriving at any minute with Margaret Brittain," replied Melissa.

"With who?"

"Listen, Cindy, today's a bit special. Dr. Jackson is going to be showing Jerome Chamberlain's lawyer around. Her name is Margaret Brittain. You know how important this is for us and — "

"Is Dr. Verne on vacation?"

"Well, no, not exactly. He was held over in — Washington."

"Can't he play politics some other day? Dr. Jackson has other business to attend to. And just what good is a lawyer around here? That's what I'd like to know!"

Melissa let Cindy in on the kidnapping scheme.

"Well, the whole thing is pretty irregular," pronounced the head nurse. A smile was playing on the corners of her mouth.

"We'll give her a coat so she can accompany the doctor on his rounds. She'll get a good long look at how things are."

"Cindy, I'm not even sure she's coming in here. But for the moment the important thing is that everyone be ready. Would you take charge of that? I'll see to the patients."

"Very good, Melissa. But this is not how things should be done, I must tell you."

Melissa headed for the elevator.

When she got to the main floor she went into the waiting area. It was packed with patients and worried family members. Her white coat attracted attention. She speeded up her pace.

In Steve's consultation room were a dozen doctors and students sitting in a semicircle facing a bed and a table on which some medical instruments were laid out.

They all rose to greet Melissa and made room for her in the front row. Thanking them, she moved to the back of the room — but first she checked with the nurse to make sure everything was ready for Chamberlain's visit.

Melissa sat down and thought about Paul. It wasn't like him to forget about a meeting, especially one so vital to the Institute's future. In fact, this was the first time he had ever done anything so reckless. Over the years she had grown to admire the determination with which he defended his work. They had encountered fierce opposition when the Institute's treatment center first opened its doors, but it soon became one of the best in the country. Paul had insisted they push ahead after a trip they had taken to visit several Special Hospitals around the country. One in particular she remembered with a shudder.

Tipton Special Hospital was located on a former army base in the San Joaquin Valley. Paul and Melissa had arranged a late-morning meeting with the director to learn about the hospital's organization. To get there, they traveled across miles of scraggly fields in the full heat of summer.

Melissa remembered that the guard at the main gate who had checked their papers wore a hat equipped with a beanie fan designed to keep the scalp cool. The tonsure opening had been cut out of course. (Since then the authorities had banned the hats, saying they interfered with the proper functioning of the ASPs.)

The Special Hospital complex was comprised of a dozen buildings two stories high, with gray walls, each bordered by a parched-looking garden of eucalyptus trees. Patients wearing light-blue gowns crowded the benches along the walls. Orange groves stretched indefinitely to the horizon. Guards played cards in the shadow of a sentry box and watched the comings and goings of the patients. It felt and looked like a prison.

They pulled up to a parking lot in front of the reception building. A woman in a white lab coat approached the car.

"Dr. Verne? Are you the Vernes?" she asked in an ebullient tone. "This *is* a great honor. My name is Dr. Smith. Joan Smith. The director's waiting for you in his office. If you'd just follow me, please . . ."

"We don't have much time," Paul told her, "and we would like to see the patients. If it isn't too inconvenient, we'll come and see the director afterward."

Dr. Smith's mouth hardened. She pointed out the building in front of them at the far end of the parking lot. Patients were going in and out the door. But what caught Paul's eye was the building next to it. An unmarked white vehicle was parked in front.

"And that building?" he'd asked.

Dr. Smith became nervous and evasive.

"I don't think there's clearance . . . I'm not sure . . . ," she stammered.

"We're going into that one," Paul informed her. "Come on, Mel."

He got out of the car and began to stride toward the building,

Melissa right behind him. Dr. Smith, taken by surprise, ran to catch up with them.

"Dr. Verne!" she cried. "Dr. Verne! You need clearance first!"

She was too late to stop them from going in.

An obese orderly sat at a desk eating a sandwich and drinking a soft drink. He lumbered to his feet when they came in, knocking over his chair.

"Hey, whoa. Where do you think — "

Paul swept past without answering and headed for the door at the far end of the vestibule. He opened it and disappeared. Melissa went after him.

It was an immense room, stiflingly hot and smelling of both disinfectant and putrescence. Beds were arranged in groups of four. Aside from two nurses, who turned abruptly when they came in, the room at first seemed deserted. Gradually, her eyes adjusting to the light, Melissa could make out human figures in the beds.

"There must be at least two hundred," Paul murmured.

He took her hand and squeezed it tightly. The room echoed with sounds — coughing and hacking, wheezing, sighing, bodies thrashing in sheets. Melissa had never seen such overcrowding.

She felt Paul tugging her arm and started to walk slowly beside him between the two lines of beds, followed by the heavy-breathing orderly. The patient in the bed closest to her was a child.

At that instant she looked at Paul. His expression revealed nothing. He was squeezing her fingers very hard.

The child appeared to be around twelve but could have been older or younger. It was impossible to tell whether it was a girl or a boy. The hair was gone, and the gray skin was covered with fever blisters. He — or she — was lying on his side, curled up in a fetal position. The dark eyes, unmoving, were enlarged by emaciation. From time to time the body was racked with a coughing fit; it sucked a corner of the sheet as if it were a lifeline.

Melissa began to move toward the child. Paul held her back.

"This child will die within the hour," he said. "Leave him alone. He is in his own world now."

They were of all colors, all ages, some covered by a sheet, others lying nearly naked on top of the bed, exhibiting all the stigmata of the disease. They were waiting for death. Few even reacted to Paul and Melissa's presence.

"We've seen enough," Paul said.

Melissa had let herself be guided to the exit. The director was waiting for them there. Melissa had a vague recollection of some kind of altercation between him and Paul, but remembered almost nothing about leaving Tipton Special Hospital. All she remembered about the drive back to Inverness was that Paul announced his intention of creating a treatment center at the Institute. A Beethoven string quartet was playing. Tomales Bay was just visible in the dying light.

Margaret Brittain entered the consultation room, trailed by Steve Jackson.

Everyone rose.

She was dressed in a stylish pink outfit. Her short coat, which went to her waist, was open to a white, transparent lace blouse that accentuated the makeup on her nipples. Her pants stopped below her knees, beneath which she wore white stockings. Her boots were the same color and showed to advantage the slenderness of her ankles. Her blond hair was buzz-cut, and she wore blue eyeliner on her lower lids. Her complexion was nearly white and gave her a high-fashion allure.

Jackson introduced her to the team and pointed out Melissa. She refused the labcoat a nurse held out to her and took her place among the first row of doctors — though not before giving Melissa a lingering look. The room went completely silent. Jackson remained standing and addressed the group:

"We will proceed as we always do whenever a new case comes to our attention. I will begin by giving you the results of the clinical exam and show you a few X rays. Then we'll give the patient in question a quick exam. I trust that each of you will find a diagnosis by the time the patient leaves. Anyone unable to arrive at a diagnosis will have to tell us why — the usual procedure," he added with a smile. "Everyone agreed?"

Melissa wondered what game Steve was playing. She had never seen him do such a song-and-dance, nor act so cavalierly about the unknown factors involved. He seemed to have forgotten about the most important moment of any clinical group consultation — when all the elements of a diagnosis have to be systematically evaluated. This unanimity he was referring to was ridiculous.

Steve continued, grinning all the while at Margaret Brittain: "Mr. A. — I won't give you his name, of course — is an only uterinean son, thirty-three years of age. A schoolteacher by training, he has had no previous medical history, apart from an appendix operation at the age of eight, and a tendency for asthma as a child, which has since disappeared. His father is retired and in good health. His mother has had some attacks of angina, for which she gets treatment. Nothing out of the ordinary, as you can see.

"Our patient had no problems with his ASP implant, or so he says. He had it regularly checked. For some time, he has had recurring rhinopharyngitis, and the resulting buccal mycosis has not responded to treatment. That's it. Any questions? Bring in the patient," said Steve, turning to the nurse.

Mr. A. came in, helped by the nurse. He was extremely pale and walked with a pronounced limp.

The nurse helped him to sit on the bed.

"For two years this man has been suffering from severe neck pains, and they have only increased in intensity. He also has frequent dizzy spells, nausea, and persistent encephalitis. Am I right, sir?"

The man took several seconds before he responded to Jackson's question. Then, with great effort, he stuttered several words.

"Y-y-y-esss, D-d-d-octor."

"You will note his difficulty in speaking," Jackson continued. "It has become worse, to the point that for several months he has been unable to work. That is why he decided to come here for a medical opinion."

Jackson picked up a reflex hammer.

"His reflexes have become highly sensitive," he continued, tapping each of the rotulian tendons in the knee.

While Steve continued the neurological examination, Melissa's anxiety grew. She wondered if the whole thing wasn't a stupid idea. She glanced at Brittain, who was listening to Steve, her face expressionless.

". . . and you will also note the deterioration of the right quadrant, as well as the parasia of the right-hand side. I will add a clinical map of the ganglia of the axillary indentation and the inguinal regions. His temperature is 101," he added, glancing at the electronic thermometer. "OK, you can get dressed now," he said to Mr. A. Then he turned to his assistant.

"We will admit him to the clinic immediately."

"B-b-b-but . . ." stammered the man.

"Please accompany him, nurse," Jackson interrupted.

Mr. A. was taken out of the room.

Steve put the X-rays his assistant had handed him on the light board.

"Look at these tomographies of the brain taken by magnetic resonance. They reveal hypodensity zones in the right and left frontal regions, as well as . . ."

Melissa was boiling with rage. If Margaret Brittain had not been present for this farce she would have left the room immediately.

"Finally, you should know that there is significant leukopenia present in the blood count. Now. The floor is open," he said to his audience, sitting down in his chair with a look of satisfaction.

Everyone began talking at once. There was no doubt that what they were dealing with was cerebral toxoplasmosis, probably indicating SF.

"My belief is that these symptoms arise from complications due to Sacred Fire," said Steve, as if unable to contain himself. "But if that is the case, we have to ask ourselves how the man could have contracted SF if at the time of implantation of his ASP he tested negative for the disease?"

The room went silent.

Steve looked over at Brittain.

"The answer is obvious. He lied to us. He has had sexual relations — passive ones, of course — with a man not fitted with an ASP. His partner is in all probability someone who has succeeded in evading the FBBS. None of that prevents us from admitting him, but — "

"Why doesn't it?" interrupted an authoritative voice.

All heads turned toward Margaret Brittain.

"Why do you feel that doesn't prevent you from admitting him?" she repeated. "If you have proof that he has broken the law, shouldn't he be handed over to the FBBS?"

Jackson turned white. He looked over nervously at Melissa, who was staring at her feet.

"I really don't think we can do that," he replied nervously. "The Hippocratic oath — "

"I am a lawyer, Dr. Jackson. Spare me your Hippocratic oath," she retorted dryly. "You haven't answered my question. I would seriously doubt that Mr. Chamberlain would be much pleased if he knew his funds were being used by this institute to treat outlaws!"

She rose.

"Now I would like to meet with Doris Hathaway," she announced.

She turned to Melissa and addressed her directly.

"Would you be so kind as to take me to see your vice president?"

"Of course," Melissa replied, getting up.

The two women passed in front of the astonished doctors and left the consulting room in silence.

6

Claudia Lombard's brick eighteenth-century Georgetown house was wired directly to the FBBS headquarters by a sophisticated remote system that permitted the director to be in constant communication with branches across the country.

Annabelle Weaver arrived at precisely ten A.M. A sullen, elderly butler showed her directly into her boss's office. He must come with the house, thought Annabelle.

Before leaving home Annabelle had left several messages at the Los Angeles office for Robert Kane. She needed an update on the Kess Sherman manhunt. As for Paul Verne, the Chicago office had informed her he was sitting in Union Station, waiting for the 2:30 train. She was told Verne had had no contact with anyone.

Annabelle was exasperated. She wanted to get in touch with Mary — who was probably still sound asleep in the warm bed she herself had left two hours earlier — but couldn't risk it. Calls from Lombard's were monitored. Annabelle felt cold hate at the thought of her boss. She resented Lombard making her hang around by the phone. It promised to be a wretched weekend.

She wandered to the window and looked out. The skies were steel gray; a few snowflakes floated onto the bare branches of the trees. An agent patrolled the sidewalk in front of the iron gate, his hands sunk in his pockets.

There was a light tap at the door. The butler appeared carrying a tray.

"Ms. Lombard has asked me to tell you that she will see you in a little while," he said archly, putting down the tray. "She asked me to bring you something to eat."

"You wouldn't have any Cocaid, would you?" Annabelle asked.

He grimaced. "Ah, no. Ms. Lombard is not fond of those beverages." Then he added: "But if you would like, I can try to find one for you."

"It's not important," said Annabelle.

"As you wish," he said, withdrawing.

Annabelle knew that Jeeves would probably immediately go and tell that bag of bones about her request. "Goddamn it all," she mumbled beneath her breath, slumping in a chair at a priceless antique desk. Lombard would think the request a provocation. Though consumption of Cocaid had been entirely legal for years, Lombard made it known she was not pleased at the idea that anybody in the Bureau indulged in it.

Annabelle glanced with disgust at the food: a watercress sandwich and a glass of mineral water. She pushed the tray away and looked around for a way to stave off boredom. Her attention was drawn to a framed photograph sitting on the desk. It was of a distinguished-looking middle-aged man giving a speech. In front of him was a cluster of microphones. Behind the podium ran banners proclaiming "Sullivan for Senator." A campaign photo. Annabelle looked closer. Beside him was a man wearing a coal-black suit. It was impossible to read his expression.

Sullivan. She'd heard the name before. Then she remembered why. There had been a scandal some years earlier. Six months after being elected, Senator Vincent Sullivan of Indiana had been found dead in his home. An inquest was ordered. The coroner had concluded it was a suicide. Some newspapers, she remembered, were skeptical about the determination.

Annabelle got up to look at some other photographs hanging along the wall. Most of them were of a younger Claudia Lombard with the same brown-haired man in the black suit in the desk photo. Their resemblance was obvious. It had to be her father. Lombard did once talk about her father. It was the only time Annabelle had seen her show any emotion.

Beneath one photograph of Sullivan, a dedication read: "To my good friend, Pete Lombardi, without whose help I never would have made it to the Senate. Your friend, Vince Sullivan."

It was a picture of father and daughter in the company of the senator and an unknown woman, standing on the shore of a lake in a mountainous region.

Annabelle's interest was aroused. What was the connection between her boss's father and Senator Sullivan? Surely that was worth a peek into Lombard's FBI file, though Annabelle knew it wouldn't be easy. Still, it might pay off. What a coup it would be to find a skeleton in the closet of the FBBS director.

A red light began flashing on the console. Annabelle pressed the decoding button.

"Weaver? Kane."

"Where have you been? I've been trying to reach you all morning!" exclaimed Annabelle.

Annabelle heard a faint tap on the line and her trained ear told her someone else had picked up — Lombard, probably from her room. The likelihood exasperated Annabelle.

"We've got a problem," Kane told her.

"I told you we would," replied Annabelle, restraining her rage with effort.

"Kess Sherman has been picked up by one of the women's gangs. They've had him since last night. Commissioner Williams is sure they are intercepting our calls on high frequencies. That's why I haven't called before now. I had to come back to the office."

"Kane, I swear if you've — "

"Calm down. We'll get him. But we'll have to go in with some muscle."

"So what are you waiting for?" Annabelle was trying not to yell.

Knowing that Lombard was listening in was too much for her. This whole fucking weekend was ridiculous.

"We're getting ready to go in," Kane went on, "but cut me some slack, will you. This is not going to be routine."

"Why the hell not?"

"We're going to have to invade a sector in which the police haven't set foot for years. They've long since ceded it to the gang armies, Las Virginas in this case. And the Virginas are armed to the teeth. Their territory is guarded like a fortress. Worse, as soon as things get started, other gangs may join in with them. Partly to show how they'd protect their turf, and partly just for a good time. This means heavy resistance by several battalions fighting building-to-building. I don't see any other way. In any case . . ."

"Say it," said Annabelle.

"You're going to have to talk to the director. If she wants us to pick him up, I'll need the green light from Washington. A call to the mayor wouldn't hurt things either. This is going to be messy."

"OK, Kane. I'll talk to the director. Call me back in an hour."

Annabelle had just signed off when the butler came in to announce that Lombard would see her. She followed him up a flight of heavily carpeted stairs. He knocked on a door for her, opened it, then moved away.

The heavy odor of dried roses floated from the room, which was stuffy. It took Annabelle a second to get her bearings. Lombard was sitting before a fireplace in which a simulated fire was crackling. Gas jets sent flames around glowing artificial logs. Facing the window was a platform bed covered with a yellow quilt on which were sprawled two Siamese cats. Annabelle had heard a great deal about those cats. A console identical to the one downstairs was sitting on the bedside table.

She had never seen Lombard looking this way — her shoulder-length hair was undone, and she was wearing a brightly colored Chinese silk dressing gown. She looks ten times older dressed like that, Annabelle said to herself, gloating inwardly. What a wreck.

"Please sit down, my dear Annabelle," said the director. She

84 /

pointed languidly to the chair next to hers. "Have you had something to eat?"

"No thanks, Claudia. I'm not very hungry."

"Well, you must make yourself at home. I'm sorry I couldn't greet you when you arrived earlier, but I had a slight headache. Billy will show you your room a little later. It's right across the hall. So, what's the news?"

"I think you know."

"Know? What do I know?"

Lombard seemed taken aback. Then she burst out laughing.

"All right. I confess. But how did you know I was listening?"

"That's not important," replied Annabelle, in a drier tone than she had intended.

Lombard ran her fingers nervously through her hair.

I got to her, thought Annabelle, becoming very satisfied with the turn of events.

"I'll have to see to — I should be able to — Well, no more about that . . . Do you have any faith in this man Kane?" Lombard added brusquely, getting back to business.

"Not overly," Annabelle answered.

"Quite right. I'm not sure he's up to the job. Kess Sherman is a pretty big fish. We need to get him to talk. Tell Kane to get in touch with Calvin Marshall. Do you know him?"

"I know who he is."

"Then perhaps I need say nothing about his skills. He happens to be in California on other business, but if it's going to get rough, he'll know what to do. I'll call the mayor of Los Angeles. She should be delighted to hear we're going to restore a little law and order out there. Tell Kane not to move a muscle until Marshall arrives. If there's going to be an operation, I want Marshall in charge of it. Kane can stay in charge for the moment, so we can see what he's made of. He is, after all, the son of Renata Kane, chairperson of the Senate Rules Committee, which means we'll have to watch how we treat him.

"Well, that's settled. I will meet you in my sitting room in half an hour. I do hope we can have a quiet afternoon together. I'll ask Billy to make us something special for dinner. Perhaps by then you'll have an appetite."

Annabelle got up and started to leave. As she passed the bed she reached out to stroke one of the cats. It hissed nastily and lashed out at her. Surprised, she let out a little scream. Lombard jumped out of her chair.

She glared at Annabelle. "What are you doing? You should never

wake a cat. You startled him. There, there, Titus, my poor pussums."
She picked up the cat and cradled him, nuzzling him affectionately.

Rubbing the bleeding scratch on the back of her hand, Annabelle
watched the pitiful spectacle: a woman of immense power showering
affection on a cat. She left without saying a word.

Chapter 4

1

"I think Doris Hathaway would be more open with you if I didn't accompany you into her office," Melissa said to Margaret Brittain.

Somehow she couldn't bring herself to feel hostility toward the lawyer. From the corner of her eye, she was admiring the ease with which Margaret Brittain crossed the waiting room, indifferent to the stares the patients were giving her. She was remembering her own discomfort when she crossed the same room an hour earlier. This time she felt shielded from the stares, just as she did every time she found herself in the company of an attractive woman.

She had felt like that sometimes with her mother. Melissa remembered going to a fashion show with her. When she was little more than a teenager. Her mother wrote a column for a fashion magazine in New York and was widely celebrated for both the elegance of her appearance and the quality of her prose. Melissa recalled the approving murmurs that greeted her mother's arrival in the couturier's salon, and the wonderful effect it had of making her feel invisible.

The two women arrived at the elevator in the Institute's main hall.

"Actually, I have absolutely no interest in meeting with Doris Hathaway," said Margaret Brittain with a nonchalance that betrayed none of the aggressiveness she had shown during the exchange with Steve. "I would rather talk with you."

"With me? My husband would be more qualified to answer your questions, and — "

"Not at all. And given that Dr. Verne isn't in San Rafael, this would be an excellent chance to get to know you. Why don't you show me around your lab?"

"My lab?" Melissa replied without enthusiasm. "Well, it's just that most of my colleagues have left for the weekend, and if you really want to see how it runs . . ."

"Just for a few minutes." Brittain's voice carried a tone of insistence. Then softened: "I would be very interested and grateful."

Melissa didn't know quite what to say. Brittain's sudden interest in her laboratory — and in her — didn't square at all with the official reasons that had brought the lawyer to the Institute. It was with Doris Hathaway that the lawyer should be meeting. The fact that she found Brittain so seductive made Melissa even more cautious.

When they reached the top floor, a guard opened an electric gate to let them in. Brittain gave a gasp of surprise. What she saw looked to the untrained eye like unbelievable confusion.

"This is the laboratory," said Melissa.

"I didn't expect it to look like this!"

"Every lab in the world looks like this. There's never enough room for all the equipment."

Following Melissa, Brittain did her best to wend through the clutter, peering curiously left and right into the side rooms. Most of the doors were wide open. Lab assistants greeted Melissa as she passed.

"Under normal conditions, we're about forty in all," Melissa explained. "The lab is grouped into blocks, depending on the kind of research being conducted. Whether it's clean or dirty."

"Clean or dirty?"

"Yes. Certain techniques can only be conducted under sterile conditions. In a minute I'll show you the lab in which SF viruses are cultivated. The 'clean zone' is the one in which you will find living cells, while the 'dirty zone' contains only subcellular cultures. This means that no living pathogenic germ can be experimented on in the dirty zone — only its molecular components, such as DNA, or various proteins. The slightest error can result in incalculable consequences. Strict organization of experiments is a basic precaution."

Brittain listened to her explanation with careful attention. This emboldened Melissa.

She went on to explain, briefly, how ultracentrifuges and radioactive counters worked before leading Brittain into a room where animal and human cells used in experiments were kept. She showed her how cultures were made in cookers using laminar flow. Constant vacuuming formed a curtain of pulsating air in front of the cooker being used and prevented the culture's escape into the room's atmosphere. She pointed out the solvent cookers, the lysophilisators, the freezers in which the cells were kept at minus 80 degrees, and the ovens.

In one room was a solitary, bearded young man with very long hair, sitting in front of a microscope. His open lab coat revealed a bulky wool turtleneck and jeans.

"This is our resident beatnik," said Melissa, introducing him to Brittain. "Don't ask me what that means, because I'm not sure. Gordon here is doing some of the most promising work in the lab. He's working on the HIV mutative gene."

"Melissa, I've told you what it means," said Gordon, without looking up from his microscope. In front of him was a large window with a view over the Institute's park. In the distance, through the trees, were the houses of San Rafael.

" 'Beatnik' was a term for people who felt life's rhythms . . . and who took life seriously," he added.

"And just what is that supposed to mean?"

Gordon looked up from the microscope. "It means people who are more interested in looking at life than at some simulation. I see life in my microscope."

He didn't bother to turn his head when the two women left.

"Strange man," Brittain commented to Melissa in the hallway.

"A bit eccentric. He's a great admirer of my husband, even though he goes to great pains to conceal it."

They went through the largest laboratory, whose "speciality was no speciality," as Melissa explained. It was the place where experiments were planned out before being subjected to the rigorous protocols of a particular research division. They also spent a few seconds in the darkroom, in which a fluorescent microscope took negatives of cells that had already been injected with fluorescein. Then they went into the "dirty" part of the laboratory.

They began by visiting the cold room, which was packed with containers of azotic liquid, agitators, test tubes, flasks with thousands of different colors, and from there into the rooms devoted to biochemistry and molecular biology, where optic density of the biological components was measured by means of spectrophotometry, total acidity by means of the pH meter, and weight using an ultrasensitive electronic balance, which measured to the thousandth of a milligram. The most critical operation consisted of decoding the molecular composition of biochemical sequences. High-performance chromatographs yielded results within split seconds.

"All of our experiments are guided by the lab's computer, which is connected with the database at the National Institutes of Health in Bethesda," Melissa explained.

"Tell me Melissa, my dear — may I use your first name?" Melissa smiled her agreement. "Yes? I'm glad," said Margaret. "A question has been nagging at me for the last few minutes, Melissa. It may be stupid, but I'd like to know where the SF viruses are. Do the workers here work with them freely? Didn't you mention there was a special room?"

"We've almost arrived there."

Melissa led Brittain up a small corridor that ran perpendicular to the corridor they had just been walking down; it came to an abrupt end at a steel door with a glass dormer window.

"This is called P3, in accordance with the international classification," said Melissa. "Look through the window."

Brittain leaned forward and peered in.

"What you're seeing is an airlock. On the other side is an identical door that leads directly into the laboratory. To gain entrance you have to undress in the airlock and put on a suit. Coming out you do the same thing, having first showered. You have to go through the disinfectant chamber before leaving. Would you like to see it?"

Brittain seemed to hesitate.

"There's no danger?"

"I suppose you could slip in the shower."

They both laughed.

"Come on, let's take a look," said Melissa. "No one's there, and this would be the perfect moment."

She pushed a button on the wall console.

"Margaret Brittain and I are going into the submarine," she said into the phone.

"OK," said a voice.

There was the sound of an electric lever being released. The door opened before them.

2

Verne wondered if choosing not to fly back to San Francisco may have been a mistake. Four days were not enough time. With sudden and terrible clarity he realized that for years now he had been denying something inside, something essential, managing to persuade himself that if he threw himself into the search for a cure to SF, that would be fulfillment enough.

Sitting in the waiting room at Union Station in Chicago, he began to imagine what would happen were he to disappear — just like that, without a trace. The Institute would survive without him. So would Melissa, for that matter.

He thought about his wife's unhappiness — not abnormal, given their years of married life. His disappearance would force her into a crisis, out of which might come some good. At least he would no longer be the focus of her frustrations. She would have to begin a new life.

Verne laughed at himself. He knew exactly what he was doing — giving in to his favorite form of self-indulgence, which consisted of imagining the effects of splitting up with Melissa exclusively from her point of view. He had absolutely no idea how he would feel. On the subject of his marriage, deep inside there was silence, a void that was sometimes filled by the moments of tenderness. He was able to imagine leaving Melissa, but also living near her — and the paradoxical result of that would be that he could believe, by her very proximity, that he wouldn't miss her. A curious credo. It had the advantage of explaining why he never felt the slightest hesitation in proclaiming that he loved his wife. Today, at this moment, he didn't miss her.

Verne glanced at his watch. The *California Zephyr* wouldn't leave for another two hours. He felt exhausted. The atmosphere in the waiting room was oppressive despite the cold. Maybe it was the overdone old-fashionedness of the decor, or the presence of the other passengers waiting for the same train. Under a large synthetic tree, a couple argued in low voices. From another corner, an elderly lady watched them with disapproval.

Deciding to walk around, Verne got up.

The temperature in the cavernous main hall was glacial. In the middle was a ticket-booth kiosk, and inside two station employees were bundled up, patting themselves to keep warm. Farther away on wooden benches arranged in a circle a few isolated passengers huddled. Towering Corinthian columns seventy-five feet high were spaced along the perimeter, supporting a glass ceiling through which came the dull glare of winter light.

Union Station took up an entire city block inside the Loop. Most of it had been built underground and was connected by grandiose staircases to Canal Street. A tunnel on the far side of the hall led down to the platforms.

Verne hesitated, wondering which way to go. He felt claustrophobic at the thought of being below ground, but he had no desire to wander out into the snow-covered streets of Chicago and doubtless get buffeted by the razor-sharp winds slicing off the lake.

At a newsstand he bought a newspaper. The front page carried the news of the death of Nobel Prize–winner Joseph Milner.

Seeing it in print was a shock. Now it had become a media event, not simply his private tragedy. He sat down to read the article.

Two weeks had gone by before Milner's body was found in his tiny apartment. The circumstances surrounding his death were still obscure; the autopsy had revealed little. According to local police, he seemed to have prepared for his death, and that fact made suicide a likely hypothesis. The press's silence was inexplicable, though the article speculated that Austrian officials had withheld details pending their investigation into the underground international organization of which Milner was one of the presumed leaders.

Then followed a brief, official obituary that recalled the scientist's vehement and early opposition to the Fuchs Amendment, an opposition most of America learned about at a meeting of the Biosociology Panel in Washington.

The meeting took place just before the triumphant election of Nathan Gray. A debate was raging among the panel members as to whether or not it should reconstitute itself as a commission and assume greater powers. The panel had been assembled by Gray's more liberal predecessor, Stanhope Dillon — the man Gray went on to defeat in the next election — along the lines of the bio-ethical advisory groups that existed in most other democratic countries. Its goal was to consider the medical, social, and moral consequences of SF and artificial gestation. These two events, though entirely different in nature, were nonetheless closely connected in their implications.

In the beginning, ethical points of view were variously represented: there was a Catholic priest, a pastor, a rabbi, an eminent philosopher, a writer, a psychiatrist, a sociologist, a political scientist, and an anthropologist. The scientists were then in a minority: a virologist, a specialist in artificial gestation, Joseph Milner, and Paul Verne, who had first discovered SF.

The panel discussions soon degenerated into bitter divisiveness, which explained why Gray encountered little opposition when he decided to turn the panel into an official branch of government. During the campaign he had pledged not to change its membership.

The meeting took place in Washington, in the ballroom of the Madison Hotel, a few hundred feet from the White House. The proposal to turn the panel into a commission had already been put forward by Senator Dale. He hoped to beat the Gray-Hughes ticket to the punch and take away a campaign issue. President Dillon had asked the senator, as a courtesy, to present the proposal before the panel itself first.

There was wide media coverage. Dale had just finished his speech before the panel, which was in plenary session, all thirteen members present. Given the explosion of SF cases at home and around the world, the federal government would have to take more severe measures in the near future. The panel needed to be given more authority and to exert more power.

Verne tended to agree with his argument, but he also found himself in sympathy with Milner, who didn't. Dale's political cynicism was exasperating. Like most political observers he was convinced that Dillon was going to lose the election. Dillon had too many political scruples about basic liberties and Bill of Rights guarantees. Verne thought highly of the old man — and had empathy for the loneliness of his positions. Stanhope Dillon didn't want to be the first chief executive to preside over the demise of the American Constitution.

Honorable though Dillon's hesitations might have been, they began to take on the appearance of weakness. Decisions had to be made. An overwhelming majority of the country agreed with the Program for Public Health of the opposition candidate — "putting health first," as he called it.

Verne felt he could no longer avoid yielding to the necessity of action, however much he despised the politics of it all, and however much he was fascinated and influenced by Milner's adamant opposition.

Milner, on the other hand, would concede nothing. He felt scientists should have nothing to do with any abrogation of the basic rights of liberty and democracy. Period. He reminded the panel of the perils of fascism. His position was exasperating because it denied a place to disagree or discuss. With idealists, thought Verne, it is all or nothing. But he admired his mentor too deeply to make his opposition open. Each time Milner raised the issue in private, Verne found a way of avoiding a collision.

In fact, since the about-face on the part of the Democratic administration, Milner hadn't cooled down. To him, it was all still a matter of advancing principles. Before the meeting in Washington, he had requested that the chairman accord him the honor of being the first to reply to Senator Dale's proposal.

Verne would have given anything not to have been in the ballroom of the Madison Hotel that day. He thought of excusing himself, but he knew that was putting off the inevitable. Better to be there when the panel faced the question for the first time. Perhaps that way he could defuse a conflict.

He remembered Milner's face when the latter rose to speak. Milner was wearing an oversize tweed jacket over a striped shirt, with a mismatched tie, making him look more than ever like a wizened child.

His glasses slid off his nose as he wrestled a sheet of crumpled paper out of his pocket.

He began by reading his speech, then stopped.

"Ladies and gentlemen, I beg you to excuse an old man," he said, "but I am finding it difficult to read what I have written. With your indulgence I would like to speak to you directly."

Scattered applause broke out among among the journalists in attendance. The press liked Milner, with his affability and keen gift for phrasing. Verne felt his uneasiness mount. He knew this time he would have to confront Milner.

Milner's voice occasionally shook with passion. He reiterated the universal principles that in his opinion should inspire all scientific research. From time to time he gave Verne a probing look. Verne tried not to make eye contact. Instead, he watched the senator, who was sitting just a few yards away and conversing in a low voice with his aide.

Verne shuddered and looked around. The station had begun to get crowded. A glance at his watch told him he had an hour to kill. He resumed reading the newspaper. An advertisement for a bra made him smile. The ad was designed to make the bra look as if it were being worn by an invisible woman. Probably an African-American woman against a black background wearing a fluorescent bra, Verne thought. That was about the limit of what was tolerated these days.

Verne was jarred out of his reverie by a sudden jolt of nauseating pain. The first signs of an ASP discharge. He jumped up and ran toward the stairs, taking them two at a time.

He stumbled forward onto the street, nearly falling in the snow.

The wind slashed though his overcoat, and he shivered violently, then felt his throat fill with bile. He bent over and vomited. He slowly straightened up and began to walk. Now the cold air felt good.

He seemed to have managed to avoid a major AD surge. But why was this happening? It felt like something besides sexual memory, which had gotten steadily weaker over the years. Verne went up the street to the corner of the station. The old Sears Tower still loomed over Jackson Boulevard. Jackson went all the way down to Lake Michigan, and for a second Verne thought about walking to the lake shore, then gave up on the idea. Not enough strength.

He leaned against one of the columns of the station, remembering when he was first implanted with the ASP. He had found to his great surprise that he adjusted to it quickly. It was even something of a relief to have the whole business of sex decided once and for all. There were more important things to worry about. Melissa had had no difficulty accepting the situation.

Another spasm of nausea overtook Verne, and he began to vomit again. A passerby came to his aid — in these times of misery it was common to see a man bent over double — but Verne waved him off. He didn't need help. At the moment the spasm had become acute, an image of Milner, his unkempt white hair flying in every direction, came back to him.

Milner's blue eyes were fixed on Verne. His smile was sad.

"And you, Paul? We have yet to hear from you. Is the distinguished discoverer of Sacred Fire ready to offer his opinion?"

The old man had finished his speech several minutes earlier. Some on the panel had already indicated how they would vote, and the result was mixed. No one went as far as Milner did. A slight majority supported Senator Dale. Some had decided to abstain until they had time to reflect on the matter.

Verne said nothing, still hoping that he wouldn't have to reveal his opposition to Milner in front of the millions of people following the discussion on World-View. Melissa was watching the proceedings with some of her friends back at Berkeley. Before he'd left, she had begged him not to make his disagreement with Milner public. But it was too late now. Milner was calling him on it.

A silence fell over the room. Verne began to state his position on the matter. Even now, he could remember word for word what he said. He had tried to avoid confrontation — but he had also prepared for it. Directing his gaze out at the audience, rather than at Milner, he said:

"The principles of scientific and medical ethics have permitted civilization to progress. No one has embraced them more fully than my mentor and friend Joseph Milner. He reminds us what we owe to those who have preceded us and passed along the mantle of their ideas. I thank him and pay homage to him.

"When science fails in its mission to light the way for humanity, the consequences have been disastrous. Civilization has borne tragic witness to what sorts of dangers follow when science goes mad. None has known that better than Dr. Milner. Nonetheless, I believe that the terrifying dilemma confronting us here today has no true precedent. Must we, in the name of principle — however noble — send millions of people to certain death, or have we the strength to compromise our greater principles in order to save the human species?

"I have been debating long and hard about how to respond to Senator Dale's proposal. It is with great sadness that I differ on this particular point with Dr. Milner. I do believe that we have to temporarily suspend individual freedoms, and in particular sexual freedoms. We have no choice but to take forceful measures to slow the course of the epidemic. We need to remember that what is at stake here is the very survival of our species.

"Now more than ever, scientists must not shrink from their responsibilities. It is crucial that they become involved at every level of the decision-making process. Their involvement will be a guarantee against any risk that a willing suspension of civil rights will degenerate into unwilling repression. And that is because scientists know exactly what is at stake with the direct cellular infection by SF, which is what is happening all around us.

"In conclusion, I believe it is necessary that this country establish a commission with broad-based powers, so that it can help free not just itself but the world of a disease of which we are only beginning to comprehend the dimensions. If the President of the United States has resolved to support Senator Dale's project, then I propose that members of this panel solemnly undertake to see to it that all the liberties, public and private, be immediately reinstated according to the Constitution as soon as a cure has been found."

Verne stopped. He knew very well that if the outcome of the vote had been in any doubt, his words would help the proposal pass. He had believed in what he'd said. But it had also seemed like an act of profound betrayal.

Milner had not moved during the speech. When order was re-established, he spoke in a voice that was surprisingly soft. The audience leaned forward in one movement to catch his words. Verne remembered them as well:

"I cannot describe my feelings to you, having just heard one of my former colleagues, without any doubt one of the most gifted researchers of his generation, take a position antithetical to the one in which I have invested my pride as a scientist. Of course, what he has said is guided by his intelligence and common sense. But, like many among us, he seems to believe that human nature can be reduced to several more or less manageable equations.

"Scientists should never be given political power of any kind. They should be subject to no influence, for all influence is coercive and will cause them to act against their higher beliefs and better judgments.

"The necessity of this is dictated by an ethical code that creates the only conditions under which science can progress. Ethics are the heart of scientific inquiry. They are as essential as the laws of materiality. Through them — and through them alone — we know that what scientists discover, and what they bring to that discovery, are indistinguishable. Who among us can say why the Sacred Fire retrovirus has appeared if we do not know what agency is responsible for SF itself? Therein lies the problem. Science is acted out upon the world, and the world acts upon science. Our philosophical, ethical, and religious codes reshape reality and transform it. That is why I am convinced that the question raised today goes far beyond personal disagreements or expressions of homage.

"In the end, pure democracy — no matter the risks — offers us the best chance we have of defeating Sacred Fire. I believe that the question raised by Dr. Verne about the necessity of temporarily restraining the functions of democracy is also a scientific question. It is inseparable from the mystery that faces us, each and every day, in our laboratories."

Milner paused, exhausted by the exertion. He removed his glasses and put them into his coat pocket. Everyone watched in silence. Then, raising his head, he added a final word:

"I would like all Americans to know that whatever the decision of this panel, I am proud and happy to have worked for the good of this great country."

He left the room with dignity.

Verne felt his tears freezing under his eyelids. He still felt a little dizzy, but the spasms seemed to be abating. He glanced up at the brilliant, crystalline sky, then went back downstairs into the train station.

3

"Can I ask you a question?" Melissa asked Margaret Brittain. "Don't feel you have to reply, but is there some personal reason behind your interest in the discovery of SF?"

"I will say a few words about my interest a little later. But right now, please, tell me what you can."

"All right. Let's sit over there." Melissa pointed to two stools at a white ceramic bench. "That way we can talk more easily."

The two women had put on laboratory coats and surgical masks to enter the "submarine," which was large, windowless, and crammed with equipment. The lighting was mercilessly bright. Halfway up one wall was a round door, a yard wide, made of bright steel; in the middle was what looked like a large steering wheel. Melissa had explained to Margaret that this was an autoclave designed to sterilize any equipment coming out of P3.

"I met Paul Verne several months before his discovery of the SF virus," she began quietly. "I'm originally from Connecticut, and that's where I went to school. Before moving to California, I worked in a lab at Yale, where I was writing a doctoral thesis on the ecology of the host-virus system and the part it plays in the outbreak of an epidemic. Host-virus system refers to the entity formed by the combination of the host, whatever it is — lettuce, a sheep, or a human being — and whatever virus is infecting it. I was convinced that one couldn't understand what an epidemic was without first understanding why one host group could be immune and another overwhelmed by infection. Do you follow me?"

"Yes."

"You may know that one of the hypotheses involving the AIDS virus was that it existed in an endemic state — possibly for centuries — among certain African tribes. It was the change in the balance of the world's ecological system that might have been the cause of the epidemic that we've been fighting for so long — the rapid changes in living conditions, the movement of populations, the speed of communications, and so forth . . . So far so good?"

"Yes, yes."

"Fine. When I learned that Dr. Milner would be working in San Francisco, I decided to join him. Milner was the panel member who took up a position in opposition to the Fuchs Amendment."

"I know who he is, Melissa."

Melissa was silent for a moment. She decided not to tell Margaret the news about his death.

"At that time he was working on the phylogenesis of viruses; Paul was working with him. I couldn't keep my eyes off Paul. For the first three months he didn't even look at me. I was in despair until I met him at Misha Oblomov's apartment."

Margaret Brittain made an abrupt gesture that nearly knocked her off the stool. She apologized profusely, embarrassed for having interrupted Melissa.

"Don't worry about it," replied Melissa, noting Margaret's nervousness. "But understand that what I'm telling you is important to the story."

"Please . . . continue."

"Misha was a mystical painter, originally from Russia. An exposition of his work once took place in New York, part of some kind of cultural exchange, and he decided to stay on in the States. He was obsessed by icons and deeply influenced by the work of Andrei Roublev, a medieval painter. Misha thought Roublev the greatest icon painter who had ever lived. He had a studio on Telegraph Hill. I often went to watch him paint. He was very popular and always sold everything he produced.

"Misha was also gay, and the remote possibility of infection terrified him. He never talked to me about his sex life, but I knew he was sexually active. I just hoped he took precautions."

"Anyway, one day when I went over to his studio I found him in a state of complete excitement. He told me that he'd just received a magnificent gift from a French friend of his. I immediately thought of Paul Verne, and I was correct. Paul had given him a book on *The Retable at Issenheim*. Do you know the work?"

"No, I'm afraid I don't. Sorry to be such a Philistine."

"I didn't know either at the time. It's a religious triptych. It comes from the same town in Alsace Paul is from, Colmar. Misha had heard about it but had never seen it, so the book was a real revelation. All he talked about was the *Retable*. It would change the way he painted, he said. He said lots of things . . . he was kind of a child. Two days later, I met Paul at Misha's studio. We left together. When Misha learned something was going on between us he was overjoyed. For months all that was really going on were long walks and some sailing. Sometimes Milner would come along. Then things went sour — "

"Go on."

"Misha had Paul and me paged one day when we were in the lab. We hadn't seen him for ten days because of an urgent grant deadline we were working under. He was waiting for us in the consulting room, pale as death. His eyes were clotted with blood, and he had a raging fever. They hospitalized him. In the weeks that followed, every form of treatment we tried had no effect whatsoever. Most dangerous was his fever. It was simply out of control. We gave him all the antipyretics we knew of, but it just wouldn't break.

"Misha also had an enormous outbreak of genital herpes, which we couldn't help him get rid of, and he was covered with blisters. He itched everywhere. He took in gallons and gallons of liquid. He also vomited anything he swallowed, and shrunk to a skeleton. His fever didn't seem to be caused by any accompanying infection or inflammation. The tests we put him through revealed nothing. We assumed he had AIDS. In Misha's case, however, we could find no infection. His blood samples seemed normal. His body was breaking down because of the fever, and it was as if the HIV was the *direct* cause of his symptoms." Melissa looked straight at Margaret. "In fact, that is exactly what it was.

"Paul worked in the lab night and day. He was desperate to find a solution. Before starting antiretroviral therapy — there were a series of treatments that, if used regularly, slowed the progress of AIDS. Unfortunately, they also had rather serious side effects. But Paul thought there was more to it. He thought that some low-level disease was at work. What else could it be? Misha underwent every exam possible. Each day I explained to him that he needed to be patient, that it was important not to hurry things. We wanted to be sure we knew what we were doing before blindly beginning some treatment that might do more harm than good.

"Then, one day, Paul had an idea that at first seemed ridiculous. He decided to do a scintigraphic test. It's a radiographic exam. You inject the patient with an antibody labeled by radioactive iodine. An antigen rises to the surface of any cell infected by a virus and is recognized by the antibody that then attaches itself. With the help of a sensitive radioactivity gauge, you can see where the infection is developing. On the screen, the zones where the infected cells are concentrated appear in red against the blue background of the body. The exam was commonly used by cancer researchers to detect sites of metastasis. With Misha, we expected to find the zones of concentration customary to someone with HIV — the lymphatic system, the cells that line the intestines, the central nervous system. To our surprise, we discovered an incredibly dense concentration of virus in his testicles.

"What had happened? We examined Misha's sperm. With AIDS, contrary to what many people used to think, the concentration of lymphocytes in the seminal fluid infected with HIV is no greater than in any other bodily liquid. Sperm is the most 'infectious' because it has the capacity to temporarily reduce the immune system of its host. After all, the whole goal of sperm is to bring about the penetration of a foreign element in the woman's body. We knew that the disease spread by the infiltration of infected lymphocytes into the sperm or blood. But with most AIDS patients the spermatozoa — the cells themselves — were untouched. In Misha's case, it didn't take long to discover that the spermatozoa were very affected; they were infected to a phenomenal degree. The virus had penetrated the nucleus of a spermatozoa as successfully as it had previously infected T4 lymphocytes. That could only mean one thing — the virus had mutated.

"We were no longer dealing with the same infecting agent. Paradoxically, this mutation — with all its consequences — is relatively small from a biological point of view. Even insignificant. After all, a spermatozoa is a cell just like any other. The virus could have mutated into any other cell in the organism. It just happened that the germinating cells were targeted by the SFV mutation!"

"Don't you think it was fate?"

"How can anyone answer a question like that? A friend calculated that the probability of this particular mutation was around one in ten billion. That's about all one can say. The tragedy of SF is that the infection is transmitted directly to the fetus by the intermediary of the spermatozoa every time the egg is fertilized. That's why we talk about it as hereditary AIDS — the line is directly affected. Once it has infected the sperm, it enters the gene pool in the same way that eye color or skin color do.

"As soon as Paul announced his discovery to the world, dozens of cases of this new type of AIDS began cropping up. In fact, the disease had been quietly spreading for several months, probably longer."

"What about Misha Oblomov?" asked Margaret, very quietly.

"The fever killed him within three months. I think he no longer wanted to live when he learned what had happened.

"Paul wanted to call the virus simply Spermatic Fever," continued Melissa. "But on the eve of his announcement at a conference on disease in Atlanta, Joe Milner suggested he call it Sacred Fire instead. That was the name some monks in the Middle Ages had given to ergotism, a disease caused by rye mold, and the epidemic of it wiped out whole populations. People believed they were possessed by the devil. Two centuries later it was the same thing with syphilis. Paul told me about Milner's idea the morning of his talk. He thought it was a little theatrical, but he had to acknowledge the parallel. He also re-membered Misha's passion for the *Retable*. Misha died an hour before Paul's speech.

"Paul began by paying homage to Misha Oblomov. Then he went on to describe the disease that had killed him. He explained clearly and concisely how HIV had mutated. He concluded by saying he would call this new disease Sacred Fire. His words cast a pall over the room. People were trying to take in the enormity of what they had just heard. It was shattering. The virus had infected the creation of life itself. There was no way of escape . . . but you know that already. That's it. Misha was cremated. His last wishes were that his ashes be scattered upon the ocean."

Melissa stopped. A long silence followed.

Then Margaret began to speak. Her voice had changed.

"Melissa, I had an only brother, three years older than I. Freddy. He was an instructor in art history at Berkeley. He lived alone for a couple of years, after his wife had left with their son to live in Oklahoma with her family. We had dinner together one evening — I hadn't seen him in months — and I noticed he couldn't keep still. He seemed sick. He'd lost weight, he was pale, his eyes had dark circles under them. I asked him all kinds of questions, and he reacted by becoming furious with me. He refused to go and see a doctor. Several weeks later, he was dead."

"Do you mean he died of — "

"He was one of the first to die of SF. At least that's what they told me. It was a terrible shock. I couldn't understand why there was so much mystery surrounding his death. But when someone finally told me the truth, I understood. Rumors about SF were everywhere. Several weeks ago I went up to Berkeley to meet with a client of Chamberlain's. I had a little time on my hands so I went to a gallery, where I ran into an old friend of Freddy's — Stephen Javitt, an English professor. He invited me for a drink. He looked a little strange. We talked a lot about Freddy, of course. He told me what someone should have told me years ago — that Freddy had gotten to know a gay artist and fallen deeply in love with him. Admitting he was gay was hard for my brother."

"And this artist — "

"Misha Oblomov. Steve explained the circumstances surrounding the discovery of SF. My brother was one of the first victims. Maybe the second. I wanted you to tell me about the man who killed Freddy."

"No one killed anyone, Margaret. That's a ridiculous idea. It was no one's fault . . ."

The phone buzzed. Melissa said a few words into it, then switched off.

"That was Dr. Jackson. He was worried about your reaction a little earlier."

"I should hope so," replied Brittain, struggling with some difficulty to regain her composure. "We have work to do. Shall we go to your office?"

While they were removing their lab coats back in the P3 vestibule, Melissa understood once more why Joseph Milner had suggested calling Spermatic Fever Sacred Fire. He knew that the disease wouldn't only attack the body; it would infect the soul.

4

Sherman was so hungry he was nauseated. An amphetamine would help. He found it strange that his thigh no longer hurt. What had the Virginas given him? It was not like them to care for an outsider, particularly a white male.

Of the female gangs that controlled most of East Los Angeles, the

Virginas had the reputation for being the most vicious. The Compadres were the only surviving male gang. Only fifteen years ago, when Sherman was working with some Chicanos on a video project, the barrios were almost exclusively male-run.

Sherman listened. Not a sound, not a sliver of light. Maybe these crazies had buried him alive. Maybe that was why he couldn't move. He had to be cool and think this through. If he were buried alive, he would have suffocated by now, right? Why in Christ's name couldn't he move?

He wanted to open his mouth to cry out, but he couldn't produce a sound. His jaw wouldn't open.

Paradoxically, the idea that he was dead but still thinking began to relax him a little. And at least he wasn't in pain. That was the most important thing. In fact, he felt nothing. But he was breathing. Air was going in and out of his lungs. And he was hungry. The staccato of footsteps brought him back to reality. Suddenly two blinding lights bore through the depths of the darkness all the way to the back of his skull. He wanted to close his eyes and move his head, but he couldn't. Helpless rage.

"Give me the syringe," said a woman's voice.

They were ripping something off his eyes.

Tears blurred his sight, but he could make out the face of a woman leaning over him.

"Hello, little man. Coming back to life?"

Sherman was beginning to feel pain in his thigh, and it was waking him up. He realized that he was upright, strapped to a plank or a stretcher. He couldn't move a muscle.

"We pumped you with curare, limp little man," said the woman standing in front of him. "To shut you up. Now we'll take care of you. Don't need to put it off. The curare's wearing off. Time to have a little fun . . ."

Slowly, Sherman's vision was returning. Before him was a woman in a sleeveless leather tunic and leather pants decorated with strange-looking symbols. Her brown hair was cropped ultrashort and formed a dark halo around her head. She was holding the tape she had just taken off Sherman's eyes and he saw that her fingers were covered with rings. At her side was a younger woman holding a syringe. Both had a rose tattoo on their left cheek.

Sherman burst out laughing at the spectacle. He couldn't help it. But then a shuddering pain in his groin turned his laughter into a howl of pain.

"What's so funny, little man?" asked the older woman. She was violently squeezing his scrotum. Sherman couldn't breathe. An eternity passed. Finally she let go. Then she left.

Gasping for breath, Sherman looked down and saw that his trousers had been cut away around his crotch. The exposed region had been completely painted red. Reflexively he tried to put his hands in front of his groin, but the straps holding his wrists kept his arms crossed. His ankles were also bound. He was facing an enormous room half-covered in darkness. There were rows of empty seats. The stage of a theater. The pain and wonder of it all made him giddy.

A slight noise attracted his attention. He turned his head and saw the young woman who had given him the injection. She was sitting on the floor in a corner of the stage, watching him with curiosity. She couldn't have been more than eighteen and had a beautiful face.

"Where are we?" asked Sherman, hoarsely.

A long pause followed until finally the young woman replied, "New York."

"Where?"

"The New York Street section. That's what we call it here. You know it?"

"No, but I've heard of the Virginas."

"That's who we are."

"What's going to happen now?" Sherman felt the pain in his thigh grow more acute. He wondered how long it would be before he collapsed and sagged in the straps. He needed to piss.

"What happens is what happens to any man who gets too close," she answered.

"Why have my pants been cut?"

"For the sacrifice," she said simply.

"What sacrifice?"

"You'll see."

"When?"

"Tonight. Maybe tomorrow night. Depends on Loca. They used to show movies here. Now we have shows."

"At least could you get me some water?"

"Against the rules."

"You mean I have to stay like this?"

"It's better. You aren't the first. You've got some visitors."

Three woman had just entered the room and were moving down the main aisle, talking among themselves. They mounted the steps to the stage.

Sherman watched them approach. Giddiness was being replaced by panic. The need to urinate was becoming overpowering. He wondered what would happen if he relieved himself in front of them. What would they do? Asking for any kind of help was hopeless.

The women observed him in silence. The girl had joined them. They were all looking at his penis. Sherman was completely alert. He flinched when one of them seized it. There was laughter. She began to sing a lullaby while dexterously caressing his member. Sherman closed his eyes. He waited for the spasms of nausea.

From painful experience he knew that even without the ASP, touching his sex could still unleash an ASP discharge. Habit was still too strong. And once it started, nothing could stop it.

"You fucking bitches, you fucking bitches, you fucking bitches," Sherman repeated over and over again.

Half-drowning in the bile in his throat, he was in the grip of a foaming rage that kept him from passing out. As soon as the discharge began, the women backed away in fascination to get a better view of his agony.

"You . . . fucking . . . *savages*," he sputtered, his whole body shaking violently and his fists clenched.

Then the spasm stopped. Blood trickled down the length of his arm. But his head was clear. Was it over? He was stunned by the brevity of the seizure.

He began to notice that the tiny feeling of euphoria that had accompanied the spasm was growing. Growing fast. Now it dominated the nausea. It was overcoming everything. What was this? Was this what was meant by AD eroticizing? An AD orgasm?

One of the women rushed forward and struck him in the face with a riding crop.

"You smell, little man. You're an ugly piece of shit," she cried, enraged by Sherman's look of blissful obliviousness. "I'm going to cut off your balls and stuff them down your throat!"

The beautiful young woman Sherman had spoken with a few minutes earlier grabbed his assailant's arm.

"Gillian, stop. Wait for the sacrifice or Loca won't be pleased," she said.

"Yeah, yeah, the sacrifice — right. He's going nowhere," she replied, breathing heavily. She spit at Sherman's feet.

They headed back up the aisle. Sherman hardly noticed they had gone. He was free-floating above the room.

Chapter 5

1

As agreed, Kane kept Annabelle informed.

"There's something else I can tell you," he added jubilantly to the news that Sherman was being held in an abandoned movie theater in East L.A. "I know what happened to the Network's courier."

"About time, Kane!"

"That suitcase? It was sent yesterday from L.A. to New York unaccompanied on a sonic out of Honolulu. Some airport uniform sent it along. Strange, no?"

"A uniform?"

"Yeah, a Lieutenant Michael Lobell. I picked him out after doing a systematic search through the luggage reports — lost baggage claims, that sort of thing. He'd personally sent it on to New York."

"Have you picked him up?"

"Yeah. He gave us a whole bullshit story about how the suitcase belonged to one of his friends, someone named Clara Hastings, a twenty-three-year-old Bio from L.A. He said he's known her for a while and was looking out for her. They hadn't seen each other for some time, and she missed her flight while they were talking. Registration was closed, so he told her he'd send her suitcase back along on the next flight. His version doesn't stand up. This has got to have something to do with Antigone. I think Lobell also works for the Network."

"You said the woman was a Bio?"

"Yeah, strange. Hard to believe that a Bio might be working for the Network. That would be a first. She's been in New York since yesterday. We should warn our people there."

Annabelle came as close as she ever had to congratulating Kane and told him to hold, then conferenced in Paul Crick, New York branch chief. They all talked about Antigone.

Before letting Kane go, Annabelle asked him to get in touch with

Calvin Marshall, the ex-Marine Lombard wanted to lead the assault on the Virginas fortress. The mayor was willing to offer whatever assistance she could.

Annabelle filled Lombard in, and added that she had instructed the New York bureau to pick up Clara Hastings. This time Annabelle didn't mention the click she'd heard on the line. Lombard asked to be kept apprised, hour by hour, of what was going on.

All Annabelle could do now was wait for a call from New York or Los Angeles. She grimly looked out across the snow-covered garden. Lombard's house gave her the creeps. The thought of spending the night a few feet away from Lombard was almost more than she could stomach. How could she get out of this trap that she herself had helped to set? No excuse presented itself.

She thought back over her conversation with Kane. Clara Hastings intrigued her greatly. A Bio in the Network. Incredible.

When Dr. Kelvin Fast first announced to the world that he had succeeded in bringing to term a child whose entire gestation had taken place in vitro in his Sydney hospital, the news had created a storm of controversy. Religious leaders and even elected officials revolted against the notion of wombless birth, denouncing it as the most diabolical enterprise ever devised. Others welcomed the advance and thought that Fast should be awarded the Nobel Prize. He was, eventually, but every religion, society, political party, ethical movement, and social organization was deeply affected and sometimes deeply scarred by the debate over his remarkable scientific feat. The nuclear family was changed forever.

At first, like many others, Annabelle didn't grasp the full implications of the news. It was a fascinating scientific and technical achievement. Then, gradually, she came to understand that Dr. Fast had provided a dazzling escape from the slavery of pregnancy and all its drains upon body and soul. Here was revenge against men who forced women to shoulder the heaviest biological burdens. Birth control was supposed to have liberated women. It hadn't. True liberation would come only when pregnancy itself was no longer a necessity. Everything else was just talk.

The great day did come, but it didn't alter what was still regarded as women's work. Responsibility for everything having to do with artificial gestation would, naturally, fall to them. Scientists, preoccupied with sexually transmitted diseases, did not yet see what role Fast's formidable discovery would play in the women's movement. But the role soon became clear.

That was why Annabelle had joined the Deliverance from Pregnancy Crusade. Founded in the days following Fast's announcement, it quickly gained popularity. Open to members of both sexes (large numbers of men supported the movement for reasons both ideological and practical), the DPC proclaimed that artificial gestation was not a freedom but a necessity of which each citizen should be aware. Extremists within the DPC formed the feminist wing, called the WDPC, believing that it was not in the movement's best interests to join forces with men (however right-minded) on an issue such as this. Had not men, through history, ultimately been responsible for pregnancy and its disastrous consequences?

While a student at Georgetown, Annabelle had joined the militant WDPC wing. She felt nothing but disdain for those women who continued to think men could help them or satisfy them sexually — during a period when doing it was still legal. In her article that appeared in *The Student Voice*, an article that made her known to her fellow students, she denounced certain women's compulsions to "fill themselves, stuff themselves, cram themselves, to allow themselves to be pinned, pumped, or penetrated . . ." Thanks to Dr. Fast's success — and even though she herself was a Utero — Annabelle's article predicted the arrival of the New Woman, who would be impervious to patriarchal influences to which a child born of man's seed couldn't help but submit. This woman, born without entangling family alliances, would finally have the ability to devote herself completely to the fulfillment of her natural gifts, which is to say "self-reliance, a just environment, control of means and ends, resistance, systematic solidarity with other women, a lifting of the burdens that thousands of years of phallocratic history had placed on their shoulders."

Annabelle was impatient to hear from New York. She wanted nothing more in the world than to meet this Clara Hastings. She hungered to know how a Bio — a Bio! — could espouse the cause of any movement that opposed the new order, with all that it had done for women. Annabelle thought about RUT, the Return to the Uterus organization, which called for legalization of natural pregnancy the very instant a cure for SF was found. RUT was known to have close ties to the Network. It was obvious both organizations were made up of Utero women lacking the courage to free themselves from centuries of conditioning. But a Bio's membership was beyond imagining. Unless Kane had made a mistake, which was entirely possible.

The console buzzed.

"Crick? Is that you? So?"

"We found your Bio. She was spotted yesterday evening with her suitcase. This morning, a uniform at the East Side Terminal saw her get off the shuttle and into a cab. She must have spent the night in the airport somewhere."

"Which would prove that she really is the courier." Annabelle was thrilled. "Why else spend all night at Kennedy?"

"I agree," said Crick. "Especially in this kind of cold. The airport's practically unheated. We lucked out — we also found the taxi driver who picked her up in Manhattan.

"Where did he drop her off?"

"In front of the Plaza. I'm afraid that's where the trail ends. The driver said that he saw her go into the hotel, but that's it. We went over the guest list this morning, but nothing turned up. She might have met a contact there. I've got to say that having no file on her doesn't help matters. Maybe her accomplice in L.A. can help us out. We need to check with Kane."

"No time for that," Annabelle snapped. "There must be another way. The girl can't have gone very far. I don't know why she had to wait all night at Kennedy. I would have thought someone would come to pick her up. It seems so messy and complicated."

"Maybe she was waiting for instructions."

"Maybe. But that doesn't explain the stop at the Plaza. I know how these people in the Network think. The fewer points of contact the less chance of being spotted. Listen to me, Crick. Assume that she had a rendezvous somewhere in the area and that she was just passing time until then. That's our only chance. Otherwise we lose her. Take a look at the files on suspected Network contacts in Midtown. Or the East Side. You never know what might turn up."

"Let me put you on hold and check the computer."

Annabelle heard the clicks of a computer code being entered. At least she now knew what had happened to Milner's letter. That would greatly facilitate the surveillance of Verne.

"Annabelle?"

She jumped. It was Claudia Lombard's voice. Not only did she listen in on all the phone conversations, but now she interrupted them. Damn it to hell, she thought, is this old hag ever going to leave me alone?

"Yes, Claudia?" Annabelle replied in her smoothest voice.

"Forget about this New York search. It won't lead anywhere. You can pick the girl up when she meets up with Verne, and — "

"Weaver? Are you talking to someone?" Crick was back on the line. "Just the cat."

"Listen, I can't see much. Except, well, it's kind of a long shot."

"Fire away."

"You remember Myra Cornfeld? The old-timer?"

"I do. You brought her up when you came to the office a year ago. Something about a painting."

"That's her. She was involved with art auctions to aid the Network. We never did prove anything."

"What are you driving at?"

"I saw her name just now. She lives pretty far from the Plaza — Eighty-fifth and Park — but she was an old friend of Milner's."

"Of Milner's? You're positive?"

"Positive. She bragged about it when I went to pay her a little visit."

"What are you waiting for? Check it out!"

"The doorman is one of ours. I'll get him on the line. Hold on a second."

"What do you think, boss?" Annabelle asked into the microphone.

There was no answer, but she knew that Lombard hadn't missed a thing.

Crick's voice came back on the line. "Weaver? The doorman said the young Cornfeld girl came into the building this morning and was accompanied by a woman carrying a suitcase."

Annabelle made a great effort to control her voice.

"Crick. Have the whole building watched beginning right now. Use as many people as you need. I don't want her out of anyone's sight for a split second. If there's any question, just pick her up. Have you got that?"

"Yeah, I've got it. I'll start it up. What should we do if — "

"No ifs, Crick. I'm coming up. I'll be there in an hour, maybe an hour and a half. Send a chopper to LaGuardia. Leave instructions with the pilot so that I know where to find you. Understood?"

"Understood."

Annabelle had barely signed off when Claudia Lombard swept into the room. She made no attempt to hide her displeasure.

"Annabelle, what is this? They don't need you in New York. Crick can handle it all by himself. I don't want you to go." She uttered the last sentence in as firm a voice as she could.

Annabelle gave her a freezing look. "Of course I have to go, Claudia."

Lombard blinked. Annabelle was jubilant at the look of disbelief that passed over her face.

"But I just told you — "

"You know as well as I do how important this is," Annabelle continued, not about to let up. "You're the one who told me that. You explained to me that Howard Black was interested, perhaps the President herself. Imagine my report if we screw this up. I would have to say that — No, I love you too much to do that. I have a job to do and I'm going to do it."

"Do you mean — do you mean what you say when you say you love me, Annabelle?" Lombard's voice had lost all pretense of authority.

"Of course I do," Annabelle replied.

"Then show me," she murmured. "Hold me."

Annabelle put her hands around Claudia's head and kissed her on the mouth. Her feeling of triumph was so strong that Lombard took it for genuine passion. But Annabelle pulled back the second she felt Lombard opening her mouth to the kiss.

"I have to go," she said.

"Yes — go," whispered Lombard. She gave Annabelle a long look and then opened the door.

"Billy," she called, "would you bring down Ms. Weaver's bag, please?"

When she turned around, Annabelle was talking with headquarters, arranging for a helicopter to pick her up at Rock Creek.

2

Clara was sure it would hurt, but Myra Cornfeld was right: it was the best solution. She couldn't just walk around with Milner's letter in her handbag.

When Cornfeld had given her the tube — gold alloy, two centimeters in diameter and eight centimeters long, she had informed Clara with great precision — Clara had hesitated. The ironic gleam that appeared in the eyes of the venerable old lady indicated noncompliance wasn't an issue.

She took Milner's letter out of the envelope, and, without looking at it, rolled it as tightly as she could. After several attempts, she managed to make it fit into the tube.

Now comes the hard part, Clara told herself as she closed the bathroom door. She was remembering the first time she'd tried to put something inside her.

When she was a teenager, Clara had spent part of a summer on a farm in Utah. The excursion had been organized by Mormons. Not ones to take the laws of the Almighty lightly, Mormons held to the belief that procreation by natural means was a sacred duty, much like not working on the Sabbath or prayer before food. Their obstinacy was put to the test when the Fuchs Amendment's constitutionality was established. That SFV could automatically be transmitted to children by an infected father did not shake their faith in the slightest. The Lord worked in mysterious ways, and true Christians had no choice but to accept whatever was allotted to them in this vale of tears.

Nonviolent opposition to Federal decree was widespread in Utah; the federal government practically had to run the state. The National Guard was called in several times to break up the unending series of strikes instigated by the Mormon hierarchy, which was determined that no Center for Applied Eugenics would open its doors in Utah, not on their watch. Officially, the number of births fell to zero. Everyone knew that Mormon children were being brought into the world secretly, in country retreats. As for the ASP implants — they met with ferocious resistance. The crackdown organized by the FBBS had been swift and brutal.

During Clara's stay in Utah, things had quieted down. Seven out of the eight children in the Smith family were already married and were living in the area. Only Jonathan, the teenage son, stayed on the family farm. Jonathan was sullen, diffident, and moody. He seemed to ignore Clara, who spent her days reading and riding her bicycle.

One morning she was surprised when Jonathan asked her if she wanted to go and see something with him.

"I'll bet you've never seen this anywhere before," he said with cryptic sarcasm.

Whatever this mysterious thing was, it was taking place on a nearby horse farm. Clara agreed to go.

They took off on their bikes. When they got there, the first thing that struck Clara was that even though the weather was beautiful, all the doors to the stalls were shut. She could hear muffled whinnying. She followed Jonathan down a passageway between stables leading to a paddock around which several people were standing. Mostly men. No one paid them any attention.

Jonathan gestured to her to park her bike and not to make any noise. A heady odor floated in the clear air.

Then Clara heard a long whinny, the sound of which made her skin crawl. She wanted to go back, but Jonathan, seeing her hesitate, took her firmly by the hand and led her toward the group of men — farmhands by the looks of them, leaning against or sitting on the wooden fence surrounding the paddock. The newcomers found a shady spot next to a tree.

Two horses were in the paddock, which was covered with fine sand.

One of the horses, an Appaloosa, its dappled coat twitching in nervous spasms, was being held down by two men. The other, a magnificent bay thoroughbred, circled freely around the Appaloosa, its ears pricked forward, its neck so extended that the head was nearly horizontal. The snorting sounds it made seemed to come from its very bowels.

"A stallion acts like that when he smells a female in heat," Jonathan explained. "Look at his muzzle. See, he raises his upper lip to show his teeth and locks his jaw. And his eyes. Look how big they get. Geez, it's like he's gone crazy."

Clara understood only then what Jonathan had invited her to watch. She felt her anxiety mounting.

"Let's leave. Come on, Jonathan."

"What's the matter?" he sneered. "Scared?"

He held her by the arm.

"You're gonna see something amazing. See, the two men are holding down the female. The guy in the red sweater is using a twitch. The string attached to the end is hooked around her lip. They use it to keep her from running off when the stud makes his move. The other guy is holding down her back leg with a rope. See," he went on excitedly, "they've also lifted the tail with tape . . . There! See? Western Dancer looks like he's ready!"

The stallion neighed wildly and reared. The mare neighed in terrified reply and planted her ears straight back.

Fascinated, Clara couldn't take her eyes off the swollen, red, foot-and-a-half-long member that had become erect under the animal's abdomen. With one swift and amazingly powerful movement, the stallion slammed itself on the back of the mare, his front hooves on either flank, and pushed himself into her.

A cheer went up from among the spectators.

"He got her on the first shot, did you see? What a stud! What a stud!" Jonathan was ecstatic. All his timidity was gone.

The stallion neighed at full volume, his nostrils buried in the mare's mane. The muscles in his haunches knotted and rippled. After a relatively brief time — at most thirty seconds, maybe a second or two longer — the nostrils opened, the eyes dilated, and his tail moved spasmodically.

"Shootin' his wad!" cried Jonathan, applauding right along with the other spectators. "Look, Clara, the horny old guy is shootin' his wad!"

There was no need to shout. Clara was giving all this her full attention. The stallion now seemed to be resting on the mare's back. He even licked her neck. After several minutes, his still-swollen member slid out. One of the two men grabbed his organ and plunged it in a bucket.

"That's to disinfect it," Jonathan was explaining. "You never know. Clara? Hey, Clara, what d'ya think?"

While all the spectators were laughing and slapping each other on the back, Clara had stood transfixed.

"We're going," she said with finality.

Jonathan followed her, sullen.

Clara didn't say a word on the way back to the farm and went straight into her room. Jonathan sulked.

But Clara wasn't thinking about Jonathan. She had other thoughts to occupy her. The image of the animal's penis obsessed her. The whole idea of it disturbed her — it had been so violent.

From a very young age, caressing her clitoris had always brought Clara extreme pleasure. The relatively recent discovery of orgasm had only accentuated the pleasure of this new activity, and it was becoming a large part of her life. There were no male figures involved in her fantasies, no image of male penetration. Girls, yes. She sometimes wondered if it was abnormal not to feel the frustrations other girls apparently felt, which they sometimes tried to talk about openly since the ASP had become a fact of life.

Everything she had heard about the sexual act was unlike what she had seen. The idea of being penetrated was incongruous. Like all the other Bios she knew, she thought that the revolution in sexual customs brought about by SF was definitive, whatever science came up with.

But on that particular summer night, the images of what she had seen fresh in her mind, she had been awakened by a strange ache in her loins. She tried caressing herself, but it didn't help — it hurt. Seized by a sudden resolution, she turned on a light, took a mirror off the wall. She leaned it against the foot of her bed, brought the light closer, and then spread her legs and, watching in the mirror, delicately drew back the lips of her vagina.

The skin was almost too sensitive to touch, but she was determined to peer inside herself. Yet all the contortions she put herself through came to naught. Finally, exhausted by the effort, she lay back down on the bed.

For the first time in her life, she looked at her anatomy. She was aware what the diagrams she'd seen at school meant. The words that she'd whispered to herself in the dark sounded strange but she re-peated them, as if convinced that they carried some answer.

The ache became more acute. Images of rutting horses were replaced by images of monsters, half-men and half-horses, to whom she was being forced to submit. The feeling of being penetrated was beginning to possess every thought. She wondered if she were going crazy.

114 /

She tossed and turned, until finally, unable to lie still, she sat up, her face covered with tears and her body bathed in sweat.

She had to do something.

Almost before she was conscious of what she was doing, she reached out and, trembling, took a candle sitting on a night table. As soon as she felt it in her hand, the feeling of what she desired overpowered her.

The sharp pain that she felt wasn't enough to stop her. She knew what female virginity was. What she wanted that night was to push the candle as deep inside her as she could.

Eventually the ache subsided.

She never did it again. But from that day onward, she knew something had changed, without being able to put into words what it was. But the desire to be penetrated had disappeared almost as quickly as it had appeared.

So there in Myra Cornfeld's bathroom, Clara was surprised to find she could insert the tube inside her body without discomfort. She withdrew and reinserted it several times, to make sure it hadn't simply disappeared.

Pleased with herself, she came out of the bathroom. Her hostess was talking to a man whom she introduced as Hermes.

3

A high-speed helicopter was waiting for Annabelle at LaGuardia. Ten minutes later, she was deposited on the Great Lawn in Central Park, near Cleopatra's Needle.

Paul Crick, standing with an agent, waved to her. The enormous coat he was wearing made him looked inflated. During the helicopter ride he had confirmed by radio that Clara Hastings was still inside Myra Cornfeld's apartment, and that the building was netted, as he put it.

Annabelle was ecstatic. The Network's courier wouldn't get away. When she went out, they would be able to follow her to the next contact. It ought to be quite a catch. Or they could simply go up and arrest everybody right now. Either way it would soon be over.

Annabelle swore lustily when she found herself standing in snow up to her shins. The spike-heeled ankle boots she had put on to go to Claudia Lombard's were useless in the snow. She trudged toward Crick, who was waiting a few yards away.

"The weather's no better here than in Washington," she said when she reached him.

"Gee, that's too bad," replied Crick.

Annabelle seemed to take no notice of Crick's sarcasm.

They headed off in the direction of 85th Street.

"I will never forget the time I've spent here," Clara said.

The old woman smiled. Her face seemed a dozen years younger.

"Nor I, Antigone. I hope I'll get to see you again before I die. Tell Verne that — " she paused in thought " — tell Verne that despite everything that happened, Joseph never stopped believing in him," she said finally. "I suspect he already knows that. Come, give me a kiss, my dear."

She took Clara in her arms, and the younger woman felt tears welling.

Clara followed Hermes out of the apartment. The door slammed behind them.

"Time to move out," Hermes said to her brusquely. Clara had barely exchanged three words with the man before they left.

Carrying Clara's suitcase, he walked past the elevator to the emergency stair door, pushed it open, and began climbing the steps.

"Would you mind telling me — " began Clara.

"Later."

Clara wanted to demand an explanation, but she knew that her mission now depended on him. He seemed aware of that as well.

So she followed him, seething. She hated men like him; their passive aggression was infuriating, and the way he had of looking at her made her feel transparent. Myra had introduced him to her as a valued member of the Network, but Clara wasn't impressed. She hoped they wouldn't have to be in each other's company for long.

They came to the top floor. Before them stretched a dark corridor. Several yards down a ladder was attached to the wall. It led to a trapdoor.

"I'll go first," Hermes told Clara. "You follow as soon as I get to the roof."

He climbed up and pushed open the trapdoor. A stream of gray light came into the corridor. Hermes pushed the suitcase through and then disappeared after it.

As soon as he did, Clara followed. She refused to take the hand he offered her and stepped out onto a terrace covered with snow and buffeted by wind.

Hermes went to the edge of the building. She tried to follow but slipped and fell to her knees. Hermes went back to help her up.

"If you want to have even the smallest chance of getting out of here, you will need to follow orders. Do I make myself clear?"

"Yes. But that doesn't mean you can treat me like a child."

Hermes said nothing, but held on to her arm. A parapet bordered the terrace. Numbed by the wind, Clara felt no desire to stand around and admire the skyline that spread out before them against the rose-colored sky of the winter afternoon.

"That's the way down." He pointed to a fire escape. "Put these on. Otherwise you'll never make it. The stairs are covered with ice."

He gave her a pair of lightweight climbing boots he had hidden inside his parka.

At least he seems to know what he's doing, Clara thought, bending down in the snow to put them on.

"Castor to Major," came the voice over the videoless.

Annabelle had just sat down in the back seat of the unmarked vehicle. Crick was sitting next to her.

The agent in the front seat took the call. "Major to Castor. Go."

"The subject just appeared in the back of the building. Someone is with her. I repeat. She is not alone. A male. They probably came down the fire escape. Give me your instructions."

Crick put on a headset. "This is Major. Follow them. Use Plan Four. Clear? Plan Four. Don't let them spot you. Got it? Reply."

"Got it. Plan Four. Out."

"Just what is Plan Four?" Annabelle asked.

"We dog them using relay teams. There was a contingency plan in case she wasn't alone. We might have to pick them up in the street. Her companion is probably arsenaled. We'll see."

"No screwups, right?" said Annabelle. "Any doubt and we just pick them up."

"There's only two of them," Crick said in reply. "I've got fourteen operatives out there. No way we're going to lose them."

"We're not walking all the way to the airport I hope," said Clara.

"Ask questions later," replied Hermes. "Follow five yards behind me. I'll warn you if there is any change in menu." With that, he headed down 85th Street and without turning around, crossed Park Avenue, going east.

Clara had trouble keeping up. Her winged messenger was apparently unhindered by the icy pavement. He had twice saved her life during the climb down the fire escape.

He's a professional, she thought, as she trotted toward Lexington

Avenue. That was clear. The speed and agility of his movement indicated long practice. She wondered if he was a police agent, like Lobell. His bearing was ramrod stiff.

Hermes turned left on Lexington. She saw him disappear into the 86th Street subway station. But the light had changed, and she couldn't follow.

When she finally got to the station, Hermes was nowhere to be seen. Looking around wildly for him, Clara bought a card and went through the portal.

There were a few people around. Huddled forms in corners and on benches trying to stay warm. Hermes was sitting calmly on a bench a little ways off. Furious, she hurried toward him. He turned his back to her. She stopped immediately. What was she supposed to do?

A train hissed into the station. Clara watched Hermes. The train stopped and the doors opened, letting several passengers out, several passengers on. Hermes didn't move. Then, just when the doors were about to close, he made a small gesture with his hand, rose quickly, and stepped on board. Clara barely had enough time to jump into the car before the doors shut behind her.

She had the bench all to herself. Across from her sat two teenagers, too engrossed in their headset videos to pay any attention. Clara saw Hermes get up. He sat down next to her.

"You could have warned me when you went into the subway, you know." Her voice was controlled, but she was livid.

"You did just fine," Hermes replied with light irony. "Sometimes you have to improvise."

"You were the one who said we had to act like strangers," she went on in the same tone. "So why are you sitting next to me?"

"Change in menu. We can stop play-acting. We've been spotted."

"What?"

"We're being followed. There are two FBBS agents in the car behind us and one in the car ahead of us. Actually, I'm not positive about that one."

"Are you sure?"

"One I know from sight. She was one of the best shots on the force. I crossed paths with the other during some alcohol trafficking, when he was working for the FBI."

"How did they know where to find us?"

"I'm afraid it doesn't look good for Myra Cornfeld," replied Hermes.

Clara was alarmed. "You mean that her apartment is being watched? Shouldn't we warn her? Call her?"

"Too late. I don't think they'll do her any great harm. She's an institution, that woman."

They were silent, almost out of respect.

The subway came to the 77th Street stop. Hermes glanced sidelong at the people getting off and on the car. They started moving again.

"There still may be a way out of this," said Hermes, leaning toward her.

"How?"

"I know how they operate. They're hoping to identify our next contact. That's why they haven't just picked us up. What we're going to do is take advantage of their greed."

"So, captain, what are your orders? You *are* in the military, aren't you?"

A look first of surprise and then pleasure crossed Hermes' face.

"The way you walk gives you away," Clara added.

"You may be right." He was smiling. "I'm not saying. The less you know . . . OK. Listen carefully. We get off at Forty-second Street, just like we'd planned."

The car went south on Lexington. Traffic was heavy, despite the snow.

"*They just passed Fifty-ninth Street.*"

"Where do they think they're going?" sneered Annabelle. She was feeling vaguely insecure.

"The courier is supposed to deliver a message to Paul Verne," she said, thinking out loud, "and he meanwhile is in Chicago about to get on a train for San Francisco. It's almost as if the Network doesn't know that Verne isn't in New York. You've got to admit that this whole situation is a little strange."

"Stupid, if you want my opinion," replied Crick. "Why send someone from California when that's where Verne lives? Why not wait for him to get home? Is the Network taking us for a ride, or what?"

"I doubt it," Annabelle snapped. "If there was a plan this whole mess-up would be more logical. Milner's courier would be the key."

"*Subjects have just gotten off the subway at Grand Central. They're out in the open. Teams Two and Five are tailing. Team Four is waiting above ground. I'll be back in touch.*"

"Forty-second Street. Fast!"

The driver hit a switch; a siren poked up through the roof and began to howl.

"If the hood isn't keeping up the game, it means he knows he's been spotted," said Annabelle. "They're probably heading for a train."

"I agree," replied Crick. "But how did they know they were being tailed?"

"That," said Annabelle, "is a damn good question."

The couple crossed 42nd Street at a leisurely pace. Hermes guided Clara between the cars, which were bumper to bumper. The sidewalks were packed.

They crossed Lexington first, then Third Avenue, and finally stopped in front of a luxury apartment building. After checking the address, they went in.

The second they disappeared, several people converged on the building.

"They've gone into a building on Forty-second. 235 East, between Second and Third. Almost in front of the old Daily News *building."*

"We'll be there in two minutes," Crick responded. "Do nothing until we get there. Find out what floor and apartment they've gone to. Tell the truck to park in front of the building."

"OK, Major."

"Crank it," Crick ordered the driver. "We were right to take our time," he said, turning to Annabelle. "They must not have picked up on us after all, and thought further precautions unnecessary."

"Maybe. But I hope you appreciate the comedy of it all. In the space of five minutes, you have interpreted the exact same behavior in two completely different ways. Each time your deduction has been perfectly logical."

Crick burst out laughing.

Hermes and Clara got out of the elevator on the sixteenth floor. He led her through a fire exit and down several steps, until they came to a narrow metal door. He took out a set of keys, found the right one, and opened the door.

"This way," he said.

They went single file into a tight, dimly lit space, barely large enough to hold them. Hermes closed the door behind him and locked it.

"We're not staying here, are we?" said Clara, feeling slightly claustrophobic, not used to such close company with a man.

Hermes put a finger to his lips. He touched a hidden switch, and another door opened.

Clara stepped in and found herself in the bedroom of a comfortably furnished apartment.

"Home," said Hermes, closing the door to the closet. "We've

changed buildings. We're in the building adjacent to the one we entered."

"This is how you come home?" Clara asked, a little bewildered.

"Yes, it's a little more discreet. If you need to use the bathroom, now is the time. We'll be leaving immediately. My vehicle is parked in the basement garage. The FBBS won't be watching the exit on 237. They're more interested in the building next door."

"We've searched the building. The elevator voice-command record indicates they got out on the sixteenth floor."

"We'll be right there," replied Crick. He hit another button in the console in front of him and was in touch with the FBBS New York office.

"Get all that? Call when you have something."

He turned toward Annabelle.

"This ought to be a nice little roundup."

"I want an hour alone with Clara Hastings."

"Sure. Whatever you say, Weaver," Crick said with a smile.

Annabelle sent a warning look his way, but he had turned his attention out the window.

There was nowhere to park. The FBBS truck had arrived ahead of them and was parked in front of 235, the only other free spot.

"Pull up in front of the garage next door," said Crick.

"Ready?" asked Hermes.

Clara nodded.

"OK, here we go. Let me add only that I think you look very becoming in that hat."

Clara tried to smile. Before leaving the apartment, Hermes had had the ridiculous idea of suggesting she put on a wide-brimmed hat that had been hanging in his closet. "All you see is hat," he said, laughing.

The car moved slowly up the ramp exit of the garage. Clara was stiff with fear. She had seen Hermes take out a high-powered revolver and place it in his lap.

She had been wrong about him. Network men didn't behave the same way with women that other men did. She thought of Lieutenant Lobell, and the pilot and Wes Marshall, even though he'd been acting strangely lately. They all had ASPs, just as Hermes did, so the difference must be psychological. The old-fashioned gallantry was a form of resistance.

Hermes stopped the car and gave a voice command. The heavy steel door began to rise.

"Someone's parked right in front," said Hermes, gritting his teeth.

Clara could see a vehicle directly in their path. A woman and two men who had obviously just gotten out of the car were standing on the sidewalk.

"Hang on!" yelled Hermes.

Hermes slammed the steering wheel sharply to the right.

Only Annabelle saw the car coming. Then the sight of a giant hat inside the cab made her realize something odd was happening. She cried out to Crick at the moment the vehicle swerved onto the sidewalk.

"It's them!"

Crick and the other agent immediately pulled out their weapons and aimed them at the car.

"Not the woman! Don't shoot the woman!" screamed Annabelle.

They lowered their sights to the tires and fired.

Hermes swung the steering wheel to avoid a hydrant.

He had just seen an open space. In seconds the car could be back on the street. It was already a miracle they hadn't run anyone over. Pedestrians scattered as if by magic. Clara saw someone jump between two parked cars.

The car jolted and skidded toward a window in which, as Clara saw with utter clarity, was a display of perfumes. They slammed into it in a shower of glass. The car came to a stop. An alarm sounded.

It took Clara a few seconds to realize she was unhurt. The car's safety devices had all worked perfectly. Hermes hadn't even stopped talking.

"Those *bastards*. They hit the tires. OK. Don't move," he told Clara. "Pretend like you've been knocked out."

She watched him open the door halfway and slide out onto the floor of the store. The powerful odor of perfumes mixing filled the car.

"You got them, boss."

"Go get the agents," Crick ordered his subordinate. Then, to Annabelle, "You should wait here."

"No way. I'm coming with you."

Holding his gun, Crick ran in the direction of the accident, Annabelle following. A small crowd had formed around the store. The back of the car was hanging out of the front of what had been a perfume shop.

"Away from the car! Get away from the car!" cried an agent, waving his gun in the direction of several gawking pedestrians, who staggered backward, wide-eyed.

"They must have been knocked out," Crick said, squeezing between a fender and the wall. "Sweet Jesus, what a stench."

In the sideview mirror of the car, miraculously unbroken, Annabelle saw the young woman, head slumped. She moved toward the door on her side.

"Weaver, damn it, you aren't armed," Crick yelled, moving, crouched over, around the other side of the car.

Annabelle was about to open the passenger door when she felt someone poke a hard metal object into her back.

"Move and it's over," said a voice behind her.

Annabelle realized she had just done one of the stupidest things in her life.

"Hey! Over there! Throw me your gun!" Hermes yelled.

Crick stood up.

"There's no way you're getting out of here," he spat, dropping his revolver on the floor, kicking it under the car, and raising his arms.

"Antigone, get out of the car and pick it up," said Hermes.

Dazed, Clara got out of the car from the driver's side. She picked up Crick's gun and pointed it at him.

"You and I are going to walk out to the sidewalk," Hermes said to Annabelle, "and we are going to get into your car. If one of your people makes any kind of move, I will kill you. Antigone, wait here until I come back for you. If that man budges an inch, shoot."

"I understand." Clara was trembling with fear but was determined to follow orders.

Crick gave Annabelle a meaningful look. He hoped she knew that Hastings's bodyguard had absolutely no chance. For the moment, the best thing to do was whatever he said.

"Let's go," said Hermes. "I'm right behind you."

Annabelle emerged on the street, her arms raised. A crowd of spectators were standing a few hundred feet away, held in place by police.

"This is how we walk — you facing the street, me with my back to the buildings. Understand?"

"Yes," Annabelle snarled.

"OK, let's keep moving. Slowly."

Annabelle walked sideways, Hermes's arm around her waist. From the corner of her eye she saw FBBS agents crossing the street. She recognized Maud Lister, the best shot in the Bureau, holding a Mauser.

"All of you listen!" shouted Hermes in the direction of the agents. "Anyone opens fire and I will cancel Weaver."

"How did you know who I am?" asked Annabelle, who was perfectly cool.

"I have my ways," replied Hermes.

Annabelle was genuinely stunned. Her photo had never been circulated; few, even those inside, knew her position.

"How — "

"Let's chat about it some other time," said Hermes. "We're nearly there. Tell one of your drones to bring the keys to the car."

"And then what?"

"And then we'll see. Someone bring the keys to the car!" he yelled suddenly.

An amplified voice replied.

"OK, we're bringing over the keys. But you have no chance. Throw down your weapon and — "

"The keys!" Hermes shouted again.

With the barrel of the gun he poked Annabelle lightly in the back, enough to make her jump and cry out in surprise. Several seconds later, an agent crossed the street, which was now closed to traffic.

"Switch on the ignition and leave the door open," ordered Hermes.

The agent did what was asked, then moved away.

"Now's the tricky part," Hermes hissed into Annabelle's ear. "Because this is when your people are going to take their shot. You're going to drive."

He suddenly grabbed Annabelle, encircling her with his arm, and ran to the car. Seconds later, he was leaning against the side of the car, behind Annabelle, his shield.

"There. Wasn't so hard. I'm going to slide in first, then climb over to the backseat. I don't need to remind you that I still am pointing this gun at you. Get ready."

Annabelle heard him open the door.

"Now!" he cried.

They got into the front seat.

As soon as she closed the door, there was the sound of a gunshot. The back window disintegrated. Hermes gasped. Annabelle wanted to turn around, but the gun hadn't moved.

"Get the car moving," he said.

She pulled out.

"Stop in front of the perfume store."

"Have you been hit?" Annabelle asked, after some hesitation.

"Your people don't seem to think much of you, Weaver. I could do what I threatened and kill you."

"They did exactly the right thing," snapped Annabelle vehemently. "You know as well as I do that I'm your only chance."

"Not quite," said Hermes. "There's your estimable colleague Paul Crick."

Annabelle said nothing. The thought of sending the car through a storefront crossed her mind. But the right moment for action would come. She was sure of it.

Meanwhile, Clara stood motionless in the perfume store, her gun frozen on Crick. He had tried to get her to talk, but she had obstinately refused. When she heard the gunshot, she felt as if it had gone through her.

"I think your escort just bought the farm," Crick said. "It was inevitable. Look, young lady, why don't you give yourself up? There's no way out of this now."

"Shut up."

Should she just kill him? What about the letter? If Hermes was hurt, there would be nothing she could do. Surrender? Kill herself? Then the car pulled up in front. She felt a spasm of relief.

"All right, Antigone. Up to you!" shouted Hermes.

She gestured to Crick to move. He glared at her and looked in the direction of the car. The rear door was open.

"Time to go," said Hermes to Clara. His voice sounded muffled. "Leave your friend there. We're finished with him."

In a flash Crick spun around and with the palm of his hand struck Clara's forearm. The gun flew out of her hand. Crick grabbed her and, pivoting, tried to put her between him and the car. Clara fought back with desperate energy. Then a gun flashed. Crick's face turned pale, and he melted to the ground.

"Damn it, run!" said Hermes, smoke curling from his revolver.

Clara jumped into the car.

Chapter 6

1

Robert Kane was in a foul mood. He'd awakened that morning to find a vicious sty developing under the lash of his right eye. As per orders from Annabelle Weaver, he had hung around the Kenmore Hotel across from Lafayette Park, waiting for Calvin Marshall, for more than an hour.

Finally he left a message telling Marshall he'd be waiting for him at the Palms, an L.A. drink-tank across the street.

A mysterious character, this Marshall. Kane knew he'd been involved in several state and federal operations. Kane had already seen him in action once, during a firefight in the Mojave Desert. Some militant celebrities had built a camp there and were planning to use it as a base for organizing operations against the FBBS. The control and competence Marshall had shown during the operation were incontestable. He was a loner, but he knew how to mobilize people.

Kane had always wondered to whom Marshall actually answered. FBI director Howard Black, went one rumor. Whatever the case, his power was no rumor. Weaver had left no doubt about his being in charge. The order came directly from Claudia Lombard. Still, while he acknowledged Marshall's tactical prowess, Kane didn't understand why they needed a mercenary. The L.A. police already had plenty of competent officers. They could handle the operation.

Kane sighed in exasperation and watched the locals nursing their low-energy druggie drinks at the bar. The place was dimly lit and the atmosphere stank of mental paralysis. Men only, latter-day barflies, their skin the color of a lampshade, a few grizzled hairs on their chins in spots they had missed shaving, sweat-soiled printed shirts.

Kane sneered at the whole pathetic lot of them. Why hadn't SF just killed them all off? It would be a mercy slaughter. Alcohol may have been banned, but drug replacements had produced the same human flotsam and jetsam. Had SF never been, these same losers would be snuffing out their lights with scotch instead of the diluted Cocaid, of which they drank four or five glasses a day.

Alcohol was becoming a national preoccupation again. The FBBS had its hands full with a growing number of people who advocated provoking ASP discharges through alcohol, so that men could actually learn to enjoy the side effects. A Bureau psychiatrist had confirmed that under certain circumstances it was possible to "eroticize the ASP discharge." Kane still thought it was all lunacy. When had America had more crazies than now? He was mopping the sweat off his forehead when the door to the bar opened. A blade of light hit the floor.

Kane recognized Marshall's profile. He was tall, black, well built, and wearing the same paramilitary vest he always wore, the one that gave him quick access to his designer weapons. Without giving Kane a glance, he went straight to the bar to order a Zapp®, one of the high-energy Cocaids. The bartender seemed to know him and hopped right into filling the order. A decrepit old man on a stool stared googly-eyed.

Marshall drank slowly, without showing the slightest interest in the attention he was attracting. After he had emptied the glass, he took a crumpled bill out of his pocket and threw it on the counter. Then he got up and brushed against the man staring at him — the impact, though slight, almost knocked the old barfly off his stool. Marshall was out the door in two or three long strides.

Kane went after him. The sunlight was nearly blinding. Kane adjusted his sun visor and saw Marshall go into Lafayette Park on the other side of Wilshire Boulevard. He followed a hundred yards behind. Marshall settled his bulk on a park bench.

Kane approached the bench, looked around to make sure they weren't being observed, then sat on the opposite end.

"You're needed," he said to Marshall without turning his head.

"So I understand."

"Direct order," Kane went on.

"You can cram your direct order up your ass."

"Easy, Marshall. This is a big operation. We're after the leader of the L.A. Network; somehow he was picked up by a Latino gang. We need your skills. We want to go after their stronghold."

Marshall turned his head toward Kane.

"You mean Kess Sherman?" There was almost interest in his tone.

Kane said nothing. He hadn't expected anyone outside of the FBBS to know the name.

"Can I ask you how you know?"

Marshall laughed.

"My kid brother," he replied to the surprised Kane. "You may meet him one of these days. A reader. He still thinks that books are better than the real thing. Also a Network sympathizer, the damn fool. He tried to convert me once. He talked about Kess Sherman. A writer of some kind. He went apocalyptic when he learned who I sometimes worked for. He hangs around with a Bio Network groupie."

"Clara Hastings?" Kane chanced, his eyes narrowing.

"Could be, I don't know. I saw them at Le Dome not too long ago and he pretended not to see me. My brother is a pointy-headed screwup. When do you want me?"

"Now," said Kane.

Marshall thought for a moment.

"I need an hour. Tell me where I can find you."

"At the corner of Brooklyn and Eastern avenues in East L.A. There's an old gas station there. Our HQ is inside an oversize van parked next to it. Ten minutes from here."

"I know where it is. An hour."

Marshall rose and strode off toward Wilshire Boulevard.

2

The noise level began to grow as the room filled. Sherman realized that his moment had come.

When Loca walked down the central aisle to the front, accompanied by one of her sisters, a hush fell. The leader of the Virginas sat in the first row, like the president at a gala event.

Sherman had no illusions about what was in store. He had already seen what kind of brutality the Virginas were capable of. Curiously, however, he found himself feeling more detached than ever, and this kept him from wallowing in despair. His body was nearly anesthetized by the combined effects of exhaustion and that drink they'd given him a little earlier. If anything, he felt a numbed anticipation about how things would proceed.

From the moment of Loca's entrance, he couldn't take his eyes off her. For the leader of the most blood-curdling of all the gang cults, she was surprisingly petite. She was the only one to wear jewelry — a necklace of precious stones that dangled between her breasts. When he looked at her somber, immense eyes, he understood the fascination she held for her followers.

She was a woman of exceptional beauty — no, handsomeness was the word. The purity of her traits suggested an Aztec mask. The whiteness of her half-closed eyelids accentuated the power of her dark gaze.

A high priestess, thought Sherman, then almost laughed out loud at his own fatuousness. So these were the last moments of life. The sacrifice — however the Virginas translated that word — would put an end to the whole silly business.

Despite his bravado, he was a little pained to see the young woman in whose company he had spent the afternoon join the others. Three woman had taken a place on the stage. Each wore a long dress, buckled tightly, and shirts with small white clerical collars. They looked like demonized deacons. Except that one of them had a laser rifle, latest model, resting on her hip — and was pointing it at him. Only Special Forces were supposed to have a weapon like that.

One approached him, took his penis, and began to caress it, singing the same inane lullaby he'd heard earlier.

The "sacrifice," Sherman suspected, would probably consist of these aging virgins first arousing him, then burning off his penis with the laser rifle right at the moment of ASP discharge.

He was simply unable to feel the dangerous urgency of the situation. It was as if he had already died and was watching his final minutes in a virtual reality playback.

Even the idea that a new ASP discharge was about to surge through him didn't dispel his strangely euphoric mood; it seemed to have the opposite effect. The stroking was relaxing him. It felt good. His eyes were slowly closing.

A daydream. One night, a fire had broken out in a neighbor's house when he and Jane were living in West Hollywood. The flames had reached the wooden roof. Waiting for the firefighters to arrive, Jane and he had done everything they could to help the frantic owner. Suddenly an ember fell on Sherman and set his shirt on fire. Jane's cry of alarm was unforgettable. Later, she had made a salve from fresh herbs — she was a gifted nurse — and covered his burned shoulders with it. The pain went away. Afterward, they had made love all night long. The longing wouldn't exhaust itself . . .

When he heard shouting in the room, Sherman realized what was happening.

The woman who had been stroking his erect penis stopped.

There was no ASP discharge. Only an erection.

Sherman realized that he had somehow succeeded in mastering the effects of the ASP. Delirium lifted his soul. Most of the Virginas had never seen a man in this state. They were too young. A feeling of triumph began to swell inside him, until, into the silence of the room, his voice erupted and his body and his soul cried a name:

"Jane!"

Then he blacked out.

Sherman awoke lying on a bed in a small room. His whole body throbbed — except his thigh, which he couldn't feel. His hands were swollen and red, and showed the strap marks. He'd been washed and clothed in a genuine silk long-shirt. He moved his hand down to his penis, and felt through the fabric that what he had feared had not happened. The mutilation had been postponed. For the moment.

Someone entered the room. It hurt to turn his head, but he did, slowly, and recognized his young guard. She was carrying a tray.

"You're awake!" she exclaimed with unconcealed enthusiasm, putting the tray on a table next to the bed. "Feel OK?"

Sherman rolled his eyes.

"You've lost a lot of blood. I had big-time problems bandaging your arm. I had to put sutures on the wound," she added with some pride. "Now I'm going to give you some blue milk."

"Blue milk?" Sherman managed to croak.

"That's what you drank earlier. The sister who invented it calls it that. I wonder why, you know, because it's really red."

She poured the dark liquid into a glass and made Sherman drink it. He almost immediately began to feel the effects.

"You're talking to me again," he said. His mouth was pasty, and words came out in clumps.

"What happened earlier has changed everything." She became thoughtful. Finally she said, "We all wondered how you did it. With the ASP and everything. How'd you beat it?"

"I'm not wearing one."

"Yes, you are. The first time, you had an attack. I was there."

"What's your name?"

"Ascension. I go by Asu. You know, we knew that one day men would learn how to control the discharges. Just by themselves. Yeah, and with the help of — "

"And with the help of what?"

"Nothing. But you're the first one we've seen. When I first saw you, I knew that — "

"Asu. Leave us." A voice from behind.

"OK, Loca," said the young woman, and left quickly.

Face to face with Loca, Sherman found once again he was captivated

130 /

by her. The rose tattoo on her left cheek made her look more mysterious.

She sat on the foot of the bed and watched him in silence.

Here was someone, Sherman thought, who knew how to play her strengths. She was someone who could break down anyone's resistance.

"I guess you want to ask me something," said Sherman.

Loca burst out laughing. Something about the sound of it surprised him. He realized it was because the laughter was so girlish. It was the laughter of a very young woman.

This amazon was barely out of her teens.

"I do want to ask you some questions," she said. Her accent lent her words even greater authority.

"To start with, tell me who you are. And please — no lying. I can check whatever you tell me."

Answering Loca's questions about his identity and personal history, Sherman weighed the pros and cons of discussing the Network. Saying the wrong thing to the wrong person could be dangerous. On the other hand, the risk would be even greater for hundreds of Network regional groups if he didn't succeed in contacting Wesley Marshall and telling him how closely they were being watched by the FBBS. The Network moles in Washington would tell them the extent of the FBBS's operations, and how to take new measures. Above all, they needed to regain contact with Engelhardt, and fast. The NOX would change the rules of the game.

Sherman knew he had to convert Loca, to bring her gang into the fold. The problem was, that beyond tabloid generalities, Sherman knew very little about the Virginas. The mystery of that strange ceremony in which he would have been the main event was still unexplained. Something Asu had said before Loca entered came back made him decide to take the risk.

"Now my turn."

Loca's eyes narrowed.

"You've got nothing to ask," she replied.

"Please, Loca, just one question. It would help me know better what you want to learn from about me."

"OK, *Sherman*. Let's hear your question. Fair warning, though. It's your neck. Ask."

"Tell me about the sacrifice? I mean, to what deity do you do it?"

Loca froze. The whole room seemed to drop in temperature. He had the impression that she was lasering through his thoughts with her eyes.

"Who told you anything?" she said with contained fury. "Talk to me, little man, or I will have you on your knees."

"No one told me anything, Loca. Believe me. What happened told me. You stopped the sacrifice as soon as you saw that I'd conquered the ASP. That is right, isn't it?"

A look of surprise altered Loca's features.

"You have conquered the ASP?" Her voice was almost timid.

"Yes, I have conquered the ASP." The thought and the pride of the idea emboldened him. "Any man can do it."

"Whose name did you cry out?" asked Loca.

"A woman I once knew. We were in love."

Both were silent, taken aback by this sudden emotional honesty. For the first time, Loca smiled.

"You are different, Kess Sherman, but I'm only starting to believe you."

"You can believe me. I did it. It can be done," Sherman repeated.

"The Virginas want the men to return," declared Loca. A flash of rage darkened her expression. "The useless ones we burn. We make them disappear."

"The useless ones? Do you mean — "

"Men infected by the black snake, the ASP that lives in them and keeps them from being truly alive. That keeps them from the Plumed Snake, Quetzalcoatl."

"The Aztec god?" Sherman suddenly found things were taking an unreal turn.

"The Plumed Snake. The god of our ancestors. The one who left us helpless before the proclamations of the black snake. Sacred Fire is only the latest sign of the black snake."

Sherman was so fascinated he almost forgot his pain. The Virginas were banded together to fight the Fuchs Amendment. Regular sacrifices must provide a way of keeping to the path, holding on to their hate for the ASP, symbol of the new order. The inhuman cruelty of the ritual thus became symbolic sacrifice of male impotence — in all the senses of the word — to get at the anger that gnawed at them.

"Loca, tell me, what would have happened if I'd had an ASP discharge during the ceremony?"

"Your infected member would have been burned away," she replied in a voice devoid of feeling. "Each time that we do away with a representative of the black snake, the time of Quetzalcoatl, the creator of men and arts, the serpent with the feathers of the quetzal bird on his head, will grow nearer. On that day, men will be freed of Sacred Fire, the last and final evil that Tezcatlipoca, the Black Serpent, the God who limps, has breathed into our bodies since the departure of his brother."

"Brother?"

"Centuries ago, in the cities of the gods, long before the Europeans, Tezcatlipoca was jealous of his brother's beauty. One day, to get rid of his brother, he set a trap. He told him to come over and showed him his image in a smoked glass."

"Why was that a trap?"

"A god must never see his own image, or he goes loco," Loca replied, a little impatient with this gringo's ignorance.

Sherman noticed how Loca's beauty had become even more impressive while she was recounting the story.

"And that is what happened," she continued. "Quetzalcoatl began to drink *pulque*, and got so drunk that he lay with his sister Quezaltepatl, who his brother had also invited to the feast. When he came out of his drunkenness, he knew what he had done and left the country, first putting a curse on all men who, like him, fell in love with their own image. Ever since, the Black Serpent has ruled. We are waiting for Quetzalcoatl's return, for it will mean the return of our power."

Loca was silent for a moment, then added: "The day will come when men will overcome the Black Serpent."

"What must men do to overcome the Black Serpent?"

"Drive away the black pain when it comes. Learn to control the fire of their desire, not to give in to it. When that day comes, Quetzalcoatl will be back among us, and once again we will live as our ancestors lived."

Loca's eyes were nearly closed.

Sherman thought about what Loca was telling him. The Aztec god Quetzalcoatl was supposed to have been driven mad the day he confused his godly power — his immateriality — with his reflection, which he had seen for the first time in the mirror his brother held out to him. The temptation to measure his power, his potency, overcame him and led him to transgress the only law that he shared with other men in the Aztec cosmogony — he had sex with his sister. When he understood the full significance of his act, it was too late. So he took leave of the world, and the Black Serpent filled the vacuum. The evil in the world stems from man's misuse of his potency and virility. The argument had surrounded sexually transmitted diseases since syphilis. Once taboos fall, chaos follows. Many had viewed the arrival of AIDS as no coincidence, and Sacred Fire had confirmed their fears. The Virginas turned the ASP back into an asp and looked to legends for an answer.

"Loca, listen to me." Sherman knew now what he had to do. "The uniforms and the Eastern Government are looking for me. I was hiding from them when you found me. I am one of the leaders of the Network. Have you heard of the Network?"

"Yes."

"In a way, Loca, you and I are fighting for the same cause."

3

"Are you hurt?" Clara asked anxiously.

"My chest," Hermes replied, grimacing. "Trouble breathing, but OK. Grazed my ribs."

Clara began to move toward the wounded man.

"Damn it! Keep your gun on Weaver!" cried Hermes.

"Turn right on Second Avenue. And stay in the left lane."

The car hit a bump and he cried out in agony. "Shit! We were almost out of there and I get hit. It was probably fucking Maud Lister. Or maybe Betty Shrine."

Annabelle made a clucking sound with her tongue. "You really do know all the names, don't you. I'll have to remember that when I get back to Washington."

"*If* you get back. Turn right on Thirty-seventh Street."

Clara said nothing.

"This is all a waste of time," continued Annabelle. "You know as well as I do that you're being followed. You've got no chance of getting away."

"I'm banking that your morons come to the same conclusion," said Hermes.

Clara turned and looked behind her. With all the cars, she couldn't tell which ones might be following them. She wondered what Hermes could possibly do to get them out of this.

"Clara Hastings?" This from Annabelle.

Clara couldn't hide her surprise. The FBBS knew her name!

"Are you talking to me?" she replied, deciding to cling to her anonymity.

How many times had Wes explained that that's how it always went: you mistakenly divulge a name or an address thinking the uniforms already know it.

"I saw your photo about an hour ago," Annabelle went on. "Do you know who I am? I'm the boss of the man that your charming friend here just killed a few minutes ago."

Hermes started to laugh. "Paul Crick? He asked for it. You should thank me for getting rid of him for you," he sneered. "Well, now we've all been introduced. That's nice."

Hermes began a hacking cough. He put his hand over his mouth, and when he took it away he was cupping blood in it.

"Turn down Park, then left again on Thirty-fourth," he said, in a weaker voice.

"You're — " Clara had begun, distraught.

"Don't — move — your — gun."

He swore, then wiped some blood off his coat.

"Hastings. Listen to me. Your friend here is not thinking straight," said Annabelle. "He's wounded more seriously than he wants to admit. The bullet has hit a lung. We've been driving in circles for ten minutes. I'm telling you, we're getting nowhere. If you give up, I will personally take charge of your case. You still haven't done anything."

"Enough, Weaver," said Hermes, in a voice that had recovered some of its authority. "You're far better off keeping your mouth shut. Go straight across Second Avenue and stay on Thirty-fourth."

Annabelle followed his instructions.

From the moment she'd realized they were driving in circles, she hadn't stopped trying to dope out Hermes' plan. It wasn't haphazard. He was a professional. She glanced in the rearview mirror and caught Clara Hastings's eye. Her long hair made her look even prettier. How could a Bio wind up like this? The idea of finding herself alone with Hastings was an increasingly delectable one. It might just be a conversion experience.

"Now turn left on First Avenue," said Hermes.

"We're going in circles!" Annabelle couldn't control her exasperation. "Good Christ, what are you doing?"

None of this made any sense. Soon they would be back on the corner of Forty-second Street, a few hundred yards from the perfume store. Right in front of —

That was it. Hermes was heading toward the U.N. All the running in circles was to keep the FBBS from setting up a roadblock.

Annabelle watched the two of them in the mirror. Hermes looked as if he were at death's door. He was slumped on the seat. But his eyes were watching everything on the street. No one had thought about the U.N. — the one place in New York where the FBBS had no jurisdiction.

Annabelle calculated rapidly. If they made it into the main building, they had a chance. The Network probably had plenty of sympathizers within the international organizations. In the time that it took to alert the agents responsible for interior policing, who themselves had to defer to the authority of other forces, which in turn were controlled by the Secretariat — maybe even the Secretary General — they could disappear into the woodwork. She had to try to stop them.

The United Nations building rose up before them just a hundred yards ahead on the right, between First Avenue and the East River. Annabelle spotted the plates of two cars belonging to the Bureau ahead of them. There were probably some behind her. To save her, the FBBS were going to have to shoot the two fugitives.

Hermes was sitting up straight, tensing himself for something. Annabelle was sure of her suspicions.

"Keep to the right," he said when the car passed in front of the U.N. bookstore, on the corner of 42nd Street. "Hey! What are you — I told you — "

Annabelle had suddenly accelerated, taking advantage of a break in traffic, and turned the controls sharply to the left, pointing the car in the direction of the U.N. Plaza Hotel on the other side of the avenue. Then she flung herself on the floor of the car and curled up in a ball. Clara had no time to react. The car was zigzagging wildly.

With a superhuman effort, Hermes pushed Clara off him and threw himself over the front seat. He grabbed the wheel and spun it to the right. There was a series of shocks and collisions; the vehicle went up on the sidewalk and smashed straight into the U.N. main gate, several yards from the entry.

Two guards who had been following the whole scene ran toward them. They opened the door and pulled Clara out of the confusion of air bags and internal alarms.

"No, wait — him — " she sputtered, pointing to Hermes, who from the shock of collision had been thrown back, passed out.

"Take him, too. Please."

"There's no time."

Clara let herself be hustled off.

She was inside the U.N. building by the time the FBBS had surrounded the car.

4

"The old cineplex the Virginas use as a HQ is located here, on the corner of New York Street and Dangler Avenue." Sergeant Elipas jabbed the spot on the enlarged aerial map with his finger.

He had an audience of three men inside the police van. Two, Captain Paul Williams, L.A. police chief, and Robert Kane, were listening intently. Calvin Marshall straddled a chair a few yards away from the others, smoking a cigarillo that fouled the air in the van. This irritated the captain, who sent him dagger looks that Marshall ignored entirely. Kane — though the smoke irritated his sty — was enjoying the drama. The captain was clearly not used to insubordination.

Sergeant Elipas went on: "The neighborhood around New York forms a rectangle between the intersection of the freeways from Long Beach and Pomona on the west, and the intersection of Brooklyn and Mednik avenues on the east. Farther along on the right is Belvedere Park. That's their border with the Compadres. If you want to know what I think, taking them by surprise is completely unrealistic."

He looked significantly at the chief and then sat down.

"As I have just explained," began the captain, after coughing a few times to let the barbarian Marshall understand he wouldn't put up with the smoke for long, "it would be much less risky if we came to some kind of agreement with Loca. I know her. If we can get her attention she'll hand Sherman over to us."

"What would you offer her?" asked Kane, an ironic glint in his eye.

"I think I know what would interest her," Williams replied suavely. "Right now she's trafficking in furs. Yesterday evening she received a shipment of them. We could — "

"How would you know that?" Kane interrupted.

"We have our sources," the captain said evasively.

"Yeah? So when are you going to pick her up for illegal trafficking, violation of commercial codes, theft, and concealment of stolen property?"

A weighty silence fell. Captain Williams looked nervously over at Sergeant Elipas, who was busying himself with some papers.

"Agent Kane, maybe I should explain how things work in our city. The Virginas — "

"Here's what I think." Calvin Marshall brought both feet down hard on the floor of the van, interrupting the captain's stammering explanations.

Williams's face reddened. Kane wondered if he was going to have a coronary.

"We approach fast, so that the Virginas have no time to react. Otherwise they roast Sherman. Just to punish him. You said the doors are made of steel. Right, Sergeant?" Marshall turned to Elipas, who looked confused.

"Yes, Chief. I mean, yes — sir."

Kane nearly burst out laughing.

"Fine," Marshall went on. "We'll need to use Plastechite. How many hands can I count on?" He turned toward Captain Williams.

"Fifty," replied the captain gruffly. "If you need more — "

Marshall cut him off. "Fifty will do."

He studied the map in silence. "We'll attack tonight."

"Tonight?" The captain nearly fell off his chair. "It's way too dangerous! We need daylight, so that the attack choppers can — "

"You can hear those things coming for half a mile. They're useless. We'll use the infrared equipment."

"Of course. We've got all the latest — "

"That's swell. We'll need four or five headsets, and night lasers. Arm your agents with riot guns and pellets, and dispersion equipment — tear gas, toxic grenades, that sort of stuff. Oh, right. And two or three armored shields. Have you got those?"

"Yes, we have those." Williams's voice was barely audible.

Marshall sat down again, stretched out his endlessly long legs, and lit another cigarillo.

5

Sherman was finding it impossible to keep his eyes closed. The heavy throbbing in his thigh seemed to be returning, but from a distance, across some faraway threshold. He wanted to be held in maternal arms. Was he delirious?

Delirious or not, he knew one thing. The manic food binging from which he suffered beginning the day the ASP was implanted had mysteriously disappeared. He had eaten nothing for twenty-four hours and felt none of the side effects he'd grown used to over the last ten years. In fact, despite the pain in his leg, he had never felt better.

"Homer! What in hell happened to you?" thundered a voice.

Sherman turned his head to find Wesley Marshall hovering over him anxiously. His friend took his hand. Sherman did his best to hide his grimace of pain.

"Polynices. About damn time. Wasn't sure I'd see you again."

Sherman saw Loca come into the room behind Wesley.

"Thanks for keeping your word," he said to her.

"You know our agreement, *Homer*," Loca replied. "I'll leave you alone together for a few minutes. Then you will let me know how you will pay me back."

"An agreement is an agreement," said Sherman with solemnity.

The young woman gave them both a long look, then closed the door behind her.

"Who are these people?" asked Wesley, sitting on the bed.

"Allies. I'll explain later. First, my message. Did you go to my place?"

"I got your message. A girl named Asu brought it to me. I am smitten. And I went to your place. The birds have flown. By now the Network has been warned."

Sherman breathed out a long sigh. For the first time since his meeting with Engelhardt, he felt he could relax.

"Now things can follow their course," he said.

Sherman had met Wesley two years earlier in Westwood, near UCLA, during an anti-Fuchs demonstration that ended in the death of one student. The police had been helped by a contingent of counter-demonstrating pro-Fuchs groups, and together they had attacked the crowd just when Sherman was preparing to speak. In the chaos that followed, he was chased by two agents. They had run him down, pinned him against the wall, and were about to go to work on him when Wesley came like a bolt out of nowhere. With uncanny speed, he sent them sprawling with a powerfully calculated shoulder shove. Sherman later learned that the National Committee had charged Wesley with watching out for him.

Wesley was from Oakland. An expert in martial arts, he had studied comparative literature and was a gifted linguist. His erudition was impressive — he could pick up any discussion about literature and philosophy and hold his own with anyone. Several weeks later, when Sherman was named chief of the Southern California Network, he chose Wesley as his second-in-command.

Sherman now told Wes about everything that had happened that day. He said nothing about the sacrifice, however — no reason to jeopardize the new friendship between the Virginas and the Network. Then he talked about the extraordinary proposal Engelhardt had made.

"Do you understand what this means?" asked Sherman.

"I think I do. This is big. The NOX could be sent around the world. How do you know he wasn't just blowing smoke?"

"Why would he? The man is guided by one principle, and one

principle alone. Money. He'd lose business if the thing turned out to be pseudo. Engelhardt is no fool."

Sherman was realizing how tired he was. Maybe, finally, he might be able to sleep.

"Time for you to leave," he said to Wesley. "Get in touch with Herakles, so that he can prepare a communiqué for the National Council."

"No way I'm leaving you here."

"Loca won't let me go," said Sherman. "That was part of the agreement. She promised to get a doctor."

"What agreement are you talking about?"

"I told her about the NOX. She's interested. I told her I could get them. I just hope the NC goes along with me. Explain the situation to Herakles. The Virginas are going to be invaluable."

"You don't seriously believe you're going to stay here until the deal with Engelhardt is struck, do you? That could take weeks, Kess. It's not worth it. What do these women have to do with the NOX, anyway?"

"A question of faith, my friend," Sherman replied with a cryptic smile.

For several minutes shouting had been coming from the corridor. The door opened wide and Loca appeared. Wesley stood up.

"Something is up with the uniforms," she said, her voice hard with tension. "A sister was walking in front of the post office. It's a war if they've found out we've got you."

Sherman wanted to sit up, but the pain kept him from moving. All he could do was lift his head.

"What are you going to do?" he asked. "For our agreement to hold, Polynices must get out of here."

Loca said nothing. She was studying Sherman carefully.

"If you think it's me they're after, Loca, hand me over. All I ask is that you protect Polynices. He'll live up to our agreement. But he must go."

"No! No way." Wesley was livid. "There is no way of keeping to any agreement if you're handed over."

"You will do what I tell you because there is no choice. Because it's an order."

"This is a very touching scene, both of you, but your boss here" — Loca looked at Wesley — "he has made us an interesting offer."

There was a knock at the door. Loca opened it. A Virginas whispered something in her ear.

"¡El fin del mundo!" Loca exclaimed. "The Compadres are proposing an alliance! They just learned that the police are moving into the neighborhood tomorrow. I think I'm going to take them up on it. Maybe the attack will lead to something."

She turned to Wesley.

"You, Poly-whatever. Say good-bye to your friend and follow me." She walked out without closing the door.

"Good luck, Wes. Give everyone my best," Sherman said.

"Isn't there another way? I don't know — how can I just — "

"Go," said Sherman.

They shook hands. Wesley Marshall gave his friend one last look, was about to say something, stopped himself, and left the room.

6

Clara sat in the guards' office. As soon as night fell, she would be put on a boat for Flushing, across the East River, where a plane was waiting. The guards who had come to her rescue were Networkers who had been informed of the sudden change in Hermes' plans and were waiting at the U.N. main gate. They were also marked men and would have to disappear.

The FBBS had lost no time in getting in touch with the U.N. secretariat. They were duly informed that, as the affair involved the security of the United Nations itself, no decision could be made in the absence of the Secretary General.

Clara was becoming impressed by the extent of the Network's reach. It had managed to find a way around every obstacle. The National Council thought her mission that important.

Flattering as it might be, Clara felt other emotions overpowering her. For the first time since Wes had given her Milner's letter, she wondered whether her mission could be worth endangering the lives of so many people: Lieutenant Lobell, Myra Cornfeld, her niece, and now Hermes. The idea that he was badly wounded and being interrogated by the FBBS haunted her.

Alone, in the windowless nondescript office, Clara felt her courage flagging. She knew she had incurred the wrath of the most powerful federal agency. She would not soon forget Annabelle Weaver's face. Meeting her had made the FBBS that much more real — up till then the organization was faceless, an anonymous machine of oppression. She thought about her suitcase, now lost for the second time, before she fell asleep.

At nightfall she was awakened and taken through the U.N. garden to the East River dock, where a small boat was waiting. Heavy fog would prevent them from being spotted, the captain told her. It would take about thirty minutes to get there, but despite the bitter wind she sat in the stern of the boat.

The towers of Manhattan stretched as far as the eye could see; it was as if they had been launched right out of the brackish water of the river, forming a titanic curtain pierced by the glitter of innumerable lights. Much farther away on the right, the lights of Queens provided the sketchy outline of some docks and a street.

She could make out the outline of the captain in the cabin, a ghostly silhouette lit by the glow of his controls.

Clara shivered. Manhattan had abruptly disappeared behind the buildings on Roosevelt Island. In the shadows behind her she could no longer make out the boat's milky wake. She did notice that the engine was working harder — then heard the sound of ice breaking. The captain had said that navigation on the river would have to stop for several days if the cold didn't let up.

Clara felt as if she were embarked on a voyage that would never end. She thought about the man toward whom she had been running for two days now, Paul Verne. She wondered if he looked like the man she'd seen on television: composed, aloof, a man who gave thoughtful but logical speeches.

What would influence such a man to take a train to California? It didn't seem to fit with what she knew about Verne. He was overwhelmed with work. Maybe that was it. Maybe he just needed a little time to think through some medical problem.

Or maybe it was something more personal. Was he married? Had he adopted children? She couldn't guess. But she could understand his trying to get away from all the people who cluttered his life. A strange way of doing it, though: instead of running away from them at full speed, he was moving toward them at a snail's pace.

She found that idea intriguing, even a little exciting. Paul Verne was taking on human proportions. It pleased her to imagine that the world-famous scientist was searching for something he wasn't able to find under a microscope or in the circles of power in which he spent most of his life.

Clara soon convinced herself that this ludicrous train trip was nothing less than a personal quest — a quest in which she had no choice but to join in. She was running after a man who was himself running after a shadow.

"Aren't you freezing?" came the voice of the captain. He was leaning out of the cabin.

"No, thanks, I'm fine," Clara called back.

Just at that moment the boat passed Roosevelt Island and the luminous splendor of Manhattan returned off the starboard side.

"We head east and go by Hell's Gate," the captain continued. "So we're leaving Manhattan. Sure you don't want to head back?" he added, smiling.

"No, thank you."

He stuck his head back in the cabin.

The boat had reached the eastern shore and was heading down a canal that ran beneath a highway. The headlights from the cars made arabesques in the foggy air.

Clara was remembering the day she found out she was a Bio. The news had created a void. A feeling of loss had left its mark on everything she did afterward.

Being born a Bio meant being born to an existence deprived of family history. She had no stories, no family myths or legends, the links between genealogy and history. Those spawned and gestated in laboratory equipment, as she was, had been denied that singular connection between two biological constitutions.

Once, as a young child, she had been struck by something one of the characters on a TV sitcom said to another. A mother had looked at the daughter and said, "When I was carrying you, I hoped you'd turn out like Grandma, my father's mother, the one I have a picture of."

Clara had thought about those words before going to sleep — she mumbled them, as if in prayer, with the secret hope that they might make her dream of that grandma. She never dared to talk about it with her adoptive parents. Sweet though they were, they were unable to offer the words and stories that might answer the silent appeal issuing from her whole being. She grew up believing no one could.

She remembered a fight she'd once had with Wes Marshall. "What it comes down to is that you're like me," he'd told her. "I know. I was adopted, too." But he didn't know. There was a world of difference between being an adopted Utero child and a Bio. At least with an adopted Utero somewhere there was human history. Someone had conceived him, carried him, delivered him, then chosen — for whatever reason — to let him go. A Bio was born in and to a sterilized laboratory setting. There was no one.

Clara believed her whole presence had been shaped by the absence of corporeal history. The night from which she emerged was the darkest of all — like a cataclysm, something from nothing, a big bang.

Is that why she was on this boat? Was her search for Paul Verne a quest for her own identity, a rite of initiation? Carrying the letter inside her had given her that extraordinary thought.

Up till then she had been almost indifferent as to the contents of the letter. Now she was terribly curious what it was that Joseph Milner had to tell Paul Verne. Was it so important that people had to die over it? She focused on the letter, sharpening her senses to the point that she was sure she could feel the slender gold tube inside her.

"We're past Hell's Gate," yelled the captain. "Last chance to come inside to get warm."

This time Clara took him up on the offer.

7

Wesley glanced at his watch. Ten to nine. He had been with Sherman for an hour.

"Two blocks from here you'll find the the bridge that goes over the freeway," Asu told him, pointing her finger west. "From here on you're on your own."

They had just come out onto Brooklyn Avenue.

When he arrived, Wesley had come to the bridge over the Long Beach Highway, parked his motorcycle, and then crossed over on foot. Asu was waiting for him there to guide him to the Virginas head-quarters. The building's other exits, the ones on the corner of Dangler Avenue and New York Street, were barricaded.

It was unnaturally, suffocatingly hot. He had heard that the East Coast was caught up in a blizzard. But here, in the starless night of L.A., dusty swirls of wind announced a rainstorm. The streetlights gave everything an eerie and foreboding yellow glow.

As Asu left him, she offered him her hand.

Outside of his mother, Wesley had known no real intimacy with a woman, at least before Clara Hastings.

But since his ASP had been removed, something had changed. The idea of any physical contact, even with Clara, the smallest touch, terrified him. He started avoiding being alone with her and arranged meetings in public places.

Clara said nothing, but he knew she suspected something was different now. He had planned to tell her he no longer had an implant when he gave her the letter, but he couldn't bring himself to do it.

He'd been amazingly lucky that the AS patrol hadn't tracked him down yet. So far, Network connections were working. But they wouldn't work forever. That was what Wesley Marshall was thinking as he went across the overpass.

Something was wrong. He glanced around. Nothing seemed different. He looked down at the freeway. That was what was wrong. Not one single car was in the lane going north, whereas the lane going south was backed up. When he'd arrived, both lanes were busy. Every nerve in his body was tingling.

He was about to move on when he saw a procession of vehicles approaching from the north lane. They were using both lanes. He reflexively dropped to a crouch and then, carefully, peered over the side of the bridge.

The vehicles stopped and lined up along the side of the road. Armed uniforms were getting out. Attack gear.

He knew immediately this was in preparation for the storming of the Virginas stronghold. Loca had mentioned it, but she had said it wouldn't happen until tomorrow. It was happening now.

Wesley broke into a run, still crouching. His HD White Lightning was leaning against a concrete pillar, a glory of chrome and muscle.

He pulled his keys out of his leather jacket and opened the storage container on the back. Tools, oil, and then, beneath it in a separate container, the communicator. He unfolded the antenna and punched in some numbers.

"Agamemnon? Polynices. I found Homer. No way he can be moved. He's being held prisoner in East L.A. by the Virginas. He says that they're allies now. Yeah, punch it through. Their headquarters is going to be stormed tonight. They must know he's in there. I'm going back in. I know, but I'm going anyway. Mine is not to reason why on this one. Some orders were made to be broken. Fine, think what you want, but first get this message through. It's important. It's from Homer — what Plato showed him during the meeting is no shadow. It's real, all right. They can guarantee a code number. Homer thinks no question that it's the best way to go. OK. Someone's got to get back to him, whether Homer gets through this or not. I'll keep you posted. Gotta go. That's right. To the end of things, my friend."

He folded the phone, then pulled out his priceless antique Glock from the bottom of the storage container. He put it in a holster inside his jacket. Then he closed the container and reset the antitheft explosive device.

He looked back over the bridge. More vehicles had arrived. They were massing for an attack. Whoever was running the show wasn't fooling around. They were moving fast. Wesley started to sprint back across the bridge toward the Virginas headquarters.

A guard was posted a few yards along Dangler.

"Who's there?"

"It's Wesley Marshall. I left with Asu a few minutes ago. I've got to see Loca right away."

He got laughter as a response.

"We were warned you might come back. I've been told to keep you out. Now beat it, little man!"

"Look, I'm not kidding here, I've got — "

"Beat it."

"Listen to me, damn you! Just listen. The uniforms are going to attack any second now. They're lining up along the freeway." He was almost screaming.

Wesley heard people talking in low voices.

"If you're lying . . ."

"Go and see for yourself. Just do it fast."

Wesley sat on the curb and began to scratch furiously at his tonsure.

Loca acted fast. Patrols were sent outside the barricades into the adjacent streets, and two more followed as backup. The others — a few dozen women in all — took up positions inside the old cineplex. It was too late to take the Compadres up on their offer of an alliance. Asu explained to Wesley that Sherman had taken a sleeping pill and was worlds away.

Wesley was impressed by the Virginas' weaponry. Marguerita — probably the oldest gang member — was handing out revolvers and automatic pistols, pump-action shotguns, gas grenades. He himself was given a Beretta Scorpio and ten clips. He followed Asu and two others up to the roof, a vast terrace covering the whole surface area of the building and surrounded by a low wall. The wind had stopped blowing. Off to the west, along the coast, flashes of lightning lit up the sky, followed by deep rumblings. The gathering clouds. Wesley believed in portents.

He leaned back and with some tape began to arrange, two by two, head to tail, the cartridge clips he had been given. A trick his brother had taught him to win time. To reload, all he had to do was rotate the block formed by the taped cartridges when one clip was empty. "The fraction of a second could save your sorry ass." His brother must have been all of twenty-two and in the Marines, a fact their mother deeply mourned. She had so wanted him to study medicine. Wesley was fourteen at the time. Older brother could do no wrong in the eyes of the admiring younger brother. Things had changed since then.

When he heard the first shots, he was thinking about ignorant armies

146 /

clashing by night. The portents told him he wouldn't get out of this one alive.

Wesley came to. His left shoulder was seized up in a spasm of pain. He was lucky — the bullet had simply gone straight through the muscle. He'd been hit when he went to help Asu, who had crumpled several yards away from him. She hadn't made a cry. The bullet struck him as he was passing in front of the top of the main staircase. Now he was lying at the bottom, with his red badge of courage.

The noise of the battle coming from the main theater was infernal. Shouts and cries mingled with fire bursts and explosions. He had only a few steps to climb to get back in the thick of it.

But he hesitated. Despite a nagging feeling that he was taking advantage of the excuse, he decided to go and see if there was anything he could do for Sherman.

He opened a small side door and closed it behind him.

The noise of the battle immediately faded. Panting, sweating profusely, he climbed the steps that led straight to a narrow door and went through it.

He was in the old projection room. It was as if the projectionist had just left the room for a moment. Amazingly, everything was intact: the two projectors, one of which was in working condition by the looks of it, the cooling covers for the projection lamps, the rewinding table, light board. Only the glass to the projection openings was broken. Wesley had the feeling that all he would have to do is lower a switch and the projectors would start up.

But of course he had to keep moving. He headed for the back of the room, opened yet another door, and found himself in the same corridor he had been in two hours earlier when he visited Sherman. He gently opened the first door.

There was enough light from the hallway for him to see that Sherman was asleep, oblivious to the battle raging all around him.

Wesley closed the door and went back to the projection room, where his energy seemed to evaporate. He collapsed in an armchair. The projection openings gave him a bird's-eye view down to the main theater below.

As he looked around the room he was in, his attention was attracted by something leaning against the wall. He picked it up and looked at it in disbelief. It was the laser rifle. Fully charged. How could something like this have found its way to the Virginas? He lay it across his lap, then passed out.

Minutes went by. Wesley woke to the sound of gunfire in the main theater below. He opened his eyes to see two Virginas running toward the stage, closely followed by uniforms in full protective armor.

"Freeze! Drop your weapons!"

The two women dropped their guns. Others appeared on the stage, arms raised, and climbed down the steps. Wesley thought about using the laser rifle. What good would that do? His perch in the projection room offered a clear target.

The gunfire stopped. Shouts echoed everywhere. They must be looking for Sherman. In a second or two, they'd break into the projection room. He would have to give himself up. What a miserable waste. He'd never get to use the rifle.

Now what he saw on the stage below — who he saw — made his heart stop. It was Calvin, his brother, wearing the same vest he always did, carrying a portable rocket launcher.

Wesley thought it might be a hallucination. He hadn't seen him in months. But it was no vision.

His heart was beating wildly, and he had trouble drawing breath. He suddenly had the impression that all his life he had been waiting for this moment: the two of them, face to face, armed, confronting each other like opposing armies.

One by one, he flicked the old-fashioned switches along the board. The stage lights came up and the curtain opened. All attention turned to the projection room.

"Hey! Up there! What's going on?" he heard someone shout.

One of the projectors lit up and an incandescent glow illuminated Calvin Marshall, leaning on one knee, his weapon trained on the projection room.

"Calvin!" Wesley yelled.

He wanted to yell something out. But what?

"Hey, Calvin! Recognize my voice?"

Calvin Marshall froze.

"Wes?" he said finally. "That you?"

There was a silence.

"I should have known, Wes. Right, buddy? That this would have to happen to us. Know what I mean? Give up, little brother. I'll see you get treated right."

"Hey, Cal, guess what I'm holding? A laser rifle. Fully juiced, too. You wouldn't have time to pull the trigger. You hear me? A real damn LR."

"You're bluffing," Calvin replied. "No one outside of the army has one of those. No way."

"Whatever you say. Tell you what — make a bet with me. Just like we used to."

Calvin laughed.

"Those days are blown. Now — "

"You're not so sure you'll win that bet. That's it, right?"

"Sure, that's it," Calvin replied. "It would have been better if we hadn't met up."

"Too late, my brother."

"Like you say. Too late."

Neither spoke for a few seconds. The Virginas and the police agents guarding them watched, mesmerized by this confrontation between brothers.

"But anyway, Calvin? I wanted to ask you something," said Wesley.

Some uniforms out of Wesley's line of sight began moving toward the exit. One signaled to Calvin to keep his brother talking.

"No one move!" Calvin yelled suddenly. "This is my business. All of you — back off." He looked up at the projection room. "Go ahead, Wes. Ask away."

"Thanks, Calvin. It was a stupid idea. I would have lasered you before anyone got close. Anyway, what I wanted to ask you was about how you thought my friend and I could get out of here."

In spite of his fatigue, Wesley never took his eyes from his brother's finger, poised on the trigger of the launcher. He distinctly saw the rocket that in a fraction of a split second could streak out of the tube and obliterate the projection room. It was as if his eyes were suddenly able to telescope objects.

"I would like to depart from the premises with my friend," said Wesley.

"You mean Kess Sherman?"

"I do."

"And what do I get?"

"My undying gratitude."

Calvin burst out laughing. Wesley noticed that his brother had moved his weapon slightly off target. His nerves went on full alert. His brother had taught him well: you lulled the enemy into a false sense of security, then you blew them away.

He had just enough time to realize that this time they were both going to lose the bet.

A line of incandescent light spurted from the rifle several fractions of a second before the rocket exploded in the room.

Part II

Part II

Chapter 7

1

As he was being driven down Pennsylvania Avenue, Howard Black looked at the huge Willard Building, where representatives from twenty of the twenty-four states in the Union had met in secrecy one last time in 1861 in a final effort to avert civil war.

This was the hour of glory of Attorney General Harris Taylor, for in that same building an international conference had been taking place, bringing together the home secretaries, secretaries of state, interior ministers, and attorneys general of all the developed countries, plus a few others. To get it off the ground, Black was well aware, Taylor had needed to assuage every nation's police system. Security had been stranglehold tight since Sacred Fire.

Black smiled. His opinion of the attorney general remained unchanged. Taylor was incompetent. He had been convinced of that when he was still Taylor's deputy, right before his nomination to run the FBI.

Black was feeling pleased with himself. He had just learned from Claudia Lombard that Kess Sherman had been at long last picked up. As for the Verne business, everything seemed to be going according to plan, even though the situation would need constant monitoring.

He was looking forward to reading the Milner letter. None of the messages they had decoded gave any indication what goals Socrates hoped to accomplish, nor provided any clear picture of who even belonged to it. Indeed, these messages were characterized by a pedantic banality focusing on some scientific or philosophical issue. The best decoders in the Bureau discovered no ulterior message or hidden urgency in these communications. If there was a key to them, it remained beyond the grasp of the FBBS.

Black was also persuaded that Paul Verne had nothing to do with Socrates — yet. He probably knew it by name and little more. Few seemed to know very much about this organization. During the opening ceremonies at the international conference at the Willard, he had learned directly from Hugo Hölbling, the Austrian secretary of the interior, that Milner had killed himself. Hölbling promised to send Black everything he could from the Milner security file kept by the Austrian police — though he disagreed with Black that Milner's suicide had any connection whatsoever with Socrates and its activities.

Was that old fox Hölbling hiding something? Black was convinced he was. The thought troubled him, and he began scratching his tonsure. What would be valuable would be knowing Verne's reaction when he found out about the letter. Milner was doubtless trying to enlist his protégé for some mission. That would be something the old man would do. Black had carefully studied the eminent scientist's psychological profile.

But any letter written by someone about to commit suicide is going to bring up more than the weather.

"Tony," Black called to the driver. "I've changed my mind. Would you take me to the Safeway on Wisconsin please?"

"OK, Mr. Black. But if you want one of the bigger stores we're near New York Avenue, and I could — "

"No, Tony. I want the Safeway."

Black hadn't been to this Safeway for ages. In the old days, the wide stretches of Wisconsin Avenue above Georgetown had been the favored heterosexual pickup places for government workers. Grocery stores in particular were popular locales. Today the mating game was played only by women. Still, men — ASPs notwithstanding — continued to play an important, if passive, role. They watched. Walking behind their shopping carts, they were observers on whom not one single detail of the chase was lost. Their looks of envy, even lust, constituted, paradoxically enough, reward enough for women in search of adventure. Taunting men was a popular pastime.

Black most enjoyed watching men watch women. He would sometimes wait for hours to witness the delicious poignancy and pain of sexual nostalgia — men who continued to look for some kind of fulfillment. Spotting them threw Black into deep meditative onanism.

They reached the Safeway. Tony pulled up in front, and Black went into the store by himself. He spotted a handsome blond young man who walking up and down the aisle for several minutes, clearly attracted by the sight of a young woman in a particularly striking outfit: her buttocks were covered in transparent material, and with each step she offered an unobstructed view of their roundness and the delicate shading of the cleft.

154 /

His hands on the cart, into which he had thrown several canned goods, Black stopped at a location affording a strategic view of the whole scene. The young woman could tell the man was watching her and continued nonchalantly to fill her cart.

She disappeared around a corner, then reappeared a few seconds later in the company of a middle-aged woman. They were smiling and talking. Black saw the older woman brush her hand across the younger woman's ass. Very interesting. Far more interesting was the young man's reaction: he stood motionless, his eyes eloquent with indescribable agony.

It was one of the most beautifully expressive scenes Black had ever witnessed. It had it all: the cruelty of ostentation and the helplessness of impotence. The women gave the young man a look of disdain and strutted toward the checkout.

The young man sensed he had been watched and seemed to sag.

Afterward, on the way back downtown, Black relived the Safeway scene and the intense pleasure it had given him. His excitement was such that he felt his body expand — as if some part of his being emerged from the shadows and, for a few seconds at least, came to life.

There were other images, spattered with blood and gore, that came and went like short electric impulses flashing upon the inward eye. He had had these half-visions since he was a boy and had never been fully aware of their existence. They lived and thrived in his unconscious mind alone. Black would have been the first to be surprised were he ever to become conscious of them.

A severed head — that of the beautiful young man he had just seen in the Safeway. The eyes had the expression they'd had when Black saw him watching the two women walk out together.

The image evaporated. Black's conscious mind never stopped thinking about his earlier chat with the president.

When Elizabeth Hughes had called him this morning, her excuse for inviting him to the White House was to ask his opinion of her speech for the closing ceremonies of the Harris conference.

What — or who — was really on her mind was Paul Verne. She had met the biologist many times when she had been chairman of the Biosociology Commission. The idea that a secret society was trying to get in touch with him, even to recruit him into their ranks, both fascinated and worried her.

Lounging comfortably in the Gold Room, she had adopted a look of concern when she asked Black if he thought it necessary to bring the matter to the attention of the CIA. Black hedged to buy some time. Involving two agencies brought considerable risk. The FBI would do better on its own, he replied. Acting alone might in fact be necessary.

He was surprised when the president seemed satisfied with his replies. The fact was she'd made her point: he could do what he thought best in the Verne business, but he had to consider the consequences fully. Failure was simply unacceptable.

"I'm glad we understand one another, Howard," she said warmly, bringing the chat to a close. "I'm giving you a free hand in this because I've never had any cause to regret my faith in you. For the time being, let's just leave the Senate out of this, too, shall we? When we have to, we can explain that time was a critical factor in your successful handling of the situation."

Black was in complete agreement with this. He thought congressional oversight a complete waste of time and a needless distraction. He would assume all the responsibility in the matter, just as he had for the last nine years.

For the moment, therefore, there was absolutely no point in telling the President about the role that Colonel Eastwood was playing in the Verne Affair. Eastwood had been put at Black's disposal by his old friend General Tom Kutler, head of MID, the Military Intelligence Department, at the Pentagon.

"Do what you want with him, Howard," Tom had told him. "He's superbly trained. I just don't want to know anything about it. As far as I'm concerned, the man is on extended leave."

Black had taken a risk on Colonel Eastwood — a big risk. After two years, he had succeeded in infiltrating the Network, without having to hide his Pentagon connection. Just the opposite. He used the connection to help the Network and finally succeeded in convincing everyone of his sincerity. Particularly when he saved an important member of the National Council from falling into FBBS hands.

The instructions Black had given the colonel were clear: were he picked up by the FBBS, who had declared him their sworn enemy, under no conditions was he authorized to reveal his connection to MID, nor to mention his direct contact with the FBI director.

For the last two days, the capable Colonel Eastwood had been in up to his tonsure in the Verne business. Yesterday, in New York, he'd personally taken charge of the case of Clara Hastings, the courier of Milner's letter.

For the young woman to meet Verne without raising any suspicions, Black had had to come up with a plan, and had asked for help from Kutler. Taken aback at first by what the FBI director was asking of him, Kutler had ended up agreeing, particularly once Black had given him his assurances that the president herself had been informed and that the plan had her blessing.

Yesterday, in New York, Eastwood — Hermes was his Network name — had been badly wounded and picked up by the FBBS.

2

The worst part of the whole long, strange trip from New York was the Nebraska border crossing at Council Bluffs. Just as they had earlier, the passengers shuffled off the train at two in the morning to hand over their passcards and submit to still another ASP Supervision. From either inefficiency or sadism, they'd had to spend an entire hour standing on the train platform before the border police had finally decided to process them.

As soon as they found out who Verne was, the uniforms had fallen all over themselves trying to make it up. They immediately offered to escort him back to his compartment. Verne told them that he intended to wait with the others.

Not that he expected his fellow passengers to appreciate, let alone admire, his democratic impulse. They felt the same hostility toward him that they felt toward any public official. Every time someone in authority exercised power, an involuntary, sullen irritation rose within him. Lately it had gotten worse.

It's like some teenage crisis, he thought.

Yet he couldn't help it. Naturally inclined to resent authority, he wondered if his feelings weren't from a sort of allergic reaction rather than from moral repugnance. He was used to taking in stride the advantages afforded by his position. The farther west he went, however, the more he despised the deference shown him.

Among the passengers waiting their turn to go through the checkpoints, Verne noticed a little girl clutching a reproduction of an antique doll. His mother used to have a porcelain doll. It was one of the only surviving relics of her Polish childhood — she kept it on the top shelf of the bookcase in the sitting room. Verne remembered vividly the unwavering look of those blue glass eyes. The doll had bright cheeks and curly blond hair, and wore a wide-brimmed hat with a red ribbon. Her dress was made of some printed fabric tied in the back, and she wore real shoes with straps. That's why she was called Mary Jane Pumps.

One day when his mother was out, Paul climbed on a chair to reach this little porcelain object of desire. He almost had her when he lost his balance. The doll fell from the shelf to the floor, where it shattered. Horrified, Paul had tried to glue the pieces of her face back together, without success. He had carefully placed the doll's remains on the kitchen table, then taken out a sheet of paper from his notebook, and, using his brand-new pen, wrote a letter to his mother telling her that as punishment he should be sent away to boarding school.

When his mother saw the doll, she paled and put her hand over her mouth but said nothing. Her silence was even more terrible than her anger. Later, she framed the letter and put it on the shelf where the doll had once sat.

Since then, the image of a broken doll lying on the floor was embedded deeper than thought in Verne's mind, anchored by the pain he had brought to the person he had loved most in the world.

During the course of the night, as the train crossed the plains, Verne wondered if the image of the doll lived at the deepest level of his existence. He was seized by a desire to vanish forever, as if this offered the only hope he had of ridding himself of the feeling of despair that had weighted him since learning Milner was dead. He would never have imagined grief would do this to him.

The train seemed to be hurtling down, straight down. Under the roomette light, the air in the compartment closed in around him, tightening and constricting him with each vibration. It was becoming intolerable. He would get off at the next town and take a plane. But to where? San Francisco? The last place he wanted to go. It was the middle of the night. A hotel room wouldn't do him any good.

Milner had once told him about his bunkmate at the Buna Monowitz concentration camp. He had spent three months living cheek by jowl with this man, yet he had only really observed him after the man had been "selected" for the gas chambers and had given Milner his only treasure: a spoon.

He had a sweet face, Joe Milner. It had never hardened, even when he had walked out of the conference. Perhaps that was what made his unwavering opposition to the Fuchs Amendment so haunting to Paul — his face. He understood Milner's position only too well. But twenty million people were stricken with SF in the United States alone — that was the official number issued by the Center for Disease Control; the actual number was probably much higher.

A pale sliver of white was growing on the horizon, just above the snow blanketing the flat expanse of Nebraska, rendering it slightly iridescent. For a moment the train followed the banks of the Platte

River, whose current carried chunks of ice fashioned into grotesque formations. Then it moved away, rejoining the whiteness, where earth and sky melted into one.

Everything floated in an opaque silence. The pale winter sunlight hardly penetrated the icy mist.

Suddenly, there was a tremendous jolt.

The train's brakes began to squeal. Verne barely had time to grab hold of the edge of the table before the brakes locked completely, emitting a high-pitched shriek almost beyond endurance. Everything on the tray pitched onto the floor.

Verne braced himself for an impact that he was sure would come.

The squealing stopped, and with one final, groaning spasm, the train ground to a halt.

Somehow Verne had managed to remain standing during all this. It took him a few seconds to recognize the presence of a shuddering, concussive beating. He looked out the window but could see nothing.

There was shouting in the corridor. Verne opened the door. A young conductor was trying to herd passengers back into their compartments.

"Listen, folks, just return to your compartments. We'll be starting up again soon. Please, now."

"What's making that noise?" Verne yelled.

"Couldn't say, sir. The chief conductor will be passing through in just a minute. Please, if you wouldn't mind closing the door to your compartment. I appreciate your cooperation."

Verne shrugged and did as he was told.

From the window he saw a squad of men in parkas and snow camouflage, carrying machine guns. A paramilitary group, from the look of it. Why would they stop a train in the middle of nowhere?

The voices in the hallway had stopped, but not the beating sound.

A fist hammered on his door.

"Open up!" thundered a voice. "Public Security Corps."

Public Security Corps? Verne had never heard of it.

He opened the door and found himself nose to nose with a soldier. Others guarded either end of the corridor. He was about to close the door, almost out of reflex, when the man stuck his arm inside.

"Dr. Verne." A statement, not a question.

Stunned, Verne nodded.

"Do what I tell you, and you won't get hurt. Gather your belongings, put on your coat, and follow me."

"But, I don't understand — "

"You have two minutes, Dr. Verne."

Verne glanced at the men. Their parkas bore no insignias. Fuming with rage, he threw his things into his suitcase and put on his coat. He was escorted toward the exit.

Outside, men were lined up along the tracks.

Raising his eyes, he saw an enormous, two-propeller helicopter hovering above the train. The source of the beating noise.

Verne felt slightly reassured when he saw the helicopter had army decals on the side. Someone gave him a slight push from behind. Carrying his suitcase, Verne moved toward the front of the train.

Passengers stared at him from inside the train. Passing one window, Verne saw the little girl with the doll and waved. The child smiled and started to wave back, but her hand was slapped down by a woman behind her. She looked at Verne as if at someone being led to the gallows. He wouldn't have been all that surprised to pass in front of the engine and see a firing squad. Instead he found himself looking at a high-speed armored truck parked across the rails, its gun turret pointed straight at the train.

A little farther off, another helicopter was sitting on the snow. Paul was herded into the armored truck, which moved off toward it.

3

Clara was so exhausted she was near despair.

Two men had been waiting for her at the dock. They'd said nothing during the drive to the airport, where a private jet was waiting. The pilot informed her it would be a four-hour flight, and then, without another word, closed the door to the cockpit.

The flight was a nightmare. The jet flew at low altitudes and seemed to jump from one air pocket into another. Clara kept imagining the worst — that she had been kidnapped and was being taken to Haiti, where there were rumors the population was being subjected to grisly biological experiments by giant pharmaceutical companies.

She didn't begin to relax until after they had landed in the middle of the night at what looked like a military base — Quonset huts covered in snow, bright lights stuck on tall poles, electrified fence, guards.

A soldier took her in a jeep to a group of two-story buildings, each one identical to the next. Clara was too tired to ask questions, and the soldier probably wouldn't have answered anyway. He took her into an overheated room in which there was a bunk bed, a table, and a chair. Nothing more. The soldier turned to leave.

"Wait, can't you tell me where — "

"No. Orders. Breakfast at 0700 hours."

He closed the door and locked it.

That the Network had accomplices in the military didn't surprise Clara in the least. They would probably take her to some town, so that she could board Verne's train. Her mission would soon be over.

She couldn't sleep. Looking at the sky through the bars on the window, she sat up for hours. Every now and then she heard a distant, shrill whistle that seemed to come from the sky.

As it got lighter she could see that beyond the electric fence was nothing but white expanse, stretching as far as the eye could see.

Just before six A.M. the air shuddered with what must have been a squadron of helicopters taking off from the base.

At seven, she was brought coffee, toast, and a small container of orange juice on a tray.

"You're going to meet someone named Verne around 0900 hours," he told her.

"Here . . . at the base?"

"Affirmative."

Clara left her breakfast untouched. She stood motionless for a long time, then went into the bathroom. She took off her jeans and underwear, then, crouching, inserted two fingers into her vagina.

The precious vial wasn't there.

Her nerves froze. She didn't even feel the cramps settling into her legs.

She rolled over on her back and, lying flat on the tiles, performed a more thorough search. Finally she succeeded in locating the tube. She closed her eyes in relief.

When she was dressed, she carefully pulled the letter from the tube and slipped it into her bra. She threw the tube into the toilet and flushed. Then she lay down and went to sleep.

Just after nine, helicopter blades woke her.

Several minutes later, someone knocked on the door.

"Follow me, please," a soldier told her.

Outside, the temperature had dropped several degrees, yet the sun was blinding. Two helicopters had landed on the snow; their blades were still turning. Soldiers were moving in her direction.

It was so bright she shielded her eyes, so she didn't see the man in civilian clothes carrying the suitcase until he was only a few feet away. In the full sunlight she couldn't really see him — he was a dark shadow.

And then he was standing in front of her.

"It's you, isn't it?" she asked, as soon as she could make out his features.

Her legs gave out under her, and she collapsed in the snow.

Verne didn't immediately grasp what had happened. He had only noticed someone wearing a dark coat in the company of a soldier on the edge of the landing zone. He had approached her with the simple supposition that someone in civilian clothes was probably in charge.

He was impatient to confront whomever was responsible for this whole ridiculous adventure. He had enough friends in high places not to panic, but he was still furious.

Maybe that was why he had not caught what this person had said to him before fainting.

His medical reflexes shifted into gear. He took off his coat and kneeled. The soldiers shuffled uneasily and made a circle around them.

"I'll get a medic," said the soldier who had accompanied her.

"I *am* a medic!" Verne snapped. It was when he lifted Clara's head off the snow to prop it up with his coat that he realized the person was a woman. He was so startled he let her drop.

A soft laugh came from behind him.

"Dr. Verne, maybe you should let my men handle this. You can reintroduce yourself to her a little later."

Verne stood up and looked at the newcomer. Nothing distinguished the man who had spoken from the other soldiers, except the fact that he wasn't carrying a weapon.

"Are you in charge here?" he asked the man. "I think I deserve some kind of explanation."

The man smiled and gave the soldiers a signal.

"I'll join you in a few minutes. Meanwhile, would you be so good as to follow Private Hays? He'll show you to my office."

The man strode off toward one of the buildings.

Verne followed Private Hays for a few steps, then turned back to look once more at the young woman lying in the snow.

"Coffee?" said the officer, lighting a Tabatz cigar.

"Thank you," said Verne.

Even when he spoke about the blandest subjects, the man's voice carried a slightly menacing note. Verne studied him. The graying temples, the bristling mustache, the regulation tie impeccably knotted. He gave the impression of being a man whose entire military career had been spent doing desk work. Or intelligence work.

He was silent, waiting for Verne to open up. An old strategy, thought

Verne, who was beginning to enjoy himself. At the very least it would break the morose mood that had hounded him since he'd left New York.

Verne had no intention of launching too quickly into dialogue. He was at something of a disadvantage, after all — sitting at a military base in the middle of Nebraska where not one of the soldiers bore any indication as to which outfit they belonged to. He decided to take the offensive.

"I don't recall you telling me your name," Verne said, swallowing some coffee, which, he was a little surprised to discover, was not at all bad.

"Colonel James Bradbury," replied the officer with a thin smile, making it clear enough he had made the name up. "But I would guess you're even more anxious to know what the hell's going on. Well, Dr. Verne, you are in an MID camp. MID stands for Military Intelligence Division. Perhaps you've heard of it?"

"Perhaps," replied Verne. He was beginning to understand.

He was being held by the secret agency headed by Tom Kutler. The MID had been created by the Army to pursue the interests of the CIA, whose wings had been clipped after one too many scandals. The MID didn't have to deal with legislative oversight and could conduct covert operations with greater ease. Verne had heard a U.S. representative complain that it had become more and more difficult to figure out what the MID was up to. It was another outgrowth of Fuchs, plain and simple.

"You do know that I'm a member of the Biosociology Commission. I can't believe MID would go to all this trouble without some firm objective in mind — and one that, I assume, involves me. I also assume that at some point you'll let me in on the secret. What you've done is completely illegal."

Colonel Bradbury stubbed out his cigar.

"Whether or not your invitation to join us was legal is of secondary importance, Doctor."

Verne thought back to the young woman lying in the snow.

"That may be for others to decide."

"Whatever you say. Still, I'm willing to bet that within the hour you'll dislike us a little less."

The phone purred. Bradbury picked it up and listened.

"Got it," he said, hanging up.

He rose, towering over Verne.

"I have been instructed to put you in contact with the young woman you saw earlier. I know you find our methods a little crude, but it was good practice for my men. As soon as you've finished with the young woman — she goes by the code name Antigone — "

"Antigone?"

"Affirmative. As soon as you have finished with Antigone, I will assist you in completing your trip. If you want, I can take you directly to San Francisco."

Verne said nothing.

"Crazy, if you ask me. All this for a simple meeting," Bradbury added dismissively. "Anyway, I've just been informed that Antigone has regained consciousness and is feeling better. She's ready to meet with you."

"What about her?" Verne asked. "What will you do with her after I've talked to her?"

The colonel's face became a mask.

"My orders are she stays here."

It was Verne's turn to get up.

"Colonel," he said, "this whole business is obviously more complicated than you're letting on. If you'd lead me to this young woman now, I'd be happy to talk with her. But my discussion with you is not at an end."

"Whatever you say, Doctor."

The medical facility was located near the perimeter of the base.

An intern told Verne that the young woman had just gone out for a walk and pointed in the direction she'd taken.

Verne followed a path between two snow-covered fields. It was a windless, crystalline day. The skeletal trees stood out against the stunning blueness of the sky. Verne found tracks in the snow and followed them. It felt good, the light crunch of the snow beneath his shoes — wonderful to move his muscles after so many hours cooped up in a train compartment.

Antigone. The Greek names Network members were given were another indication of the total lack of maturity on the part of a few thousand troublemakers who somehow believed they had the right to oppose measures the SF epidemic had rendered so obviously necessary. But a woman, a Network member, organizing a meeting at an ultra-secret military base with the complicity of the MID — this surpassed all understanding. Verne was convinced Colonel Bradbury was toying with him — insulting him, even — which had the advantage of proving that they thought him harmless. But why would the MID kidnap a public official? Verne knew he had few friends in the administration, but still it was an enormous risk. Covert operations sanctioned by the White House were an old story, and too often they had disastrous consequences.

At a turn in the path Verne saw Clara. She had her back to him and had on the same dark coat she had been wearing an hour earlier. She wheeled around quickly when she heard him approach. For a fraction of a second, Verne thought he recognized her. He decided he didn't.

It had been a long time since he'd seen a woman with long hair. It distressed him less to think of her charm than of the disarming fact that for a brief moment, when he'd first seen her, he had mistaken her for a man. He stared at her, unblinking. She raised her eyebrows.

"Well, Doctor. Your diagnosis?" she said with light sarcasm.

Verne laughed.

"I apologize for staring. I'm assuming you are glad to see me even though the last time we met you fainted."

They both laughed and began to walk side by side. For a while they said nothing.

The path ran along the edge of the compound. Concrete fence posts and iron crossbars formed parallel universes of white.

Clara had the same feeling she had had after regaining consciousness: behind the feverishness was something else, something that left her feeling vulnerable and exposed. Walking next to the man she had been chasing for what seemed more like an eternity — two days — she resisted the desire simply to hand him the letter and then run straight out into the obliterating whiteness of the field.

She stumbled. Verne dexterously caught her elbow, surprised at how fragile she was.

Clara balled her fists hard in the pockets of her coat and pushed them against her stomach. She glanced at his profile. A dark line, almost like mascara, stretched from the folds of his eyelids nearly to his temples. He'll just have to wait a little longer, she thought. I am not ready yet.

He was wondering if the space between them and the double fencing was mined.

"I feel like I've been chasing you forever," Clara said, her voice tremulous.

"I can't be that hard to track down."

She was instantly furious.

"One man is dead — maybe two — I'm not even sure. The FBBS is breathing down my neck. And *you* aren't hard to track down?"

"The FBBS? What are you talking about?"

"I probably shouldn't be telling you this. My name is Clara Hastings. The Network has sent me. I have a letter to give you."

So Bradbury was right, thought Verne. The Network was moving heaven and earth to get a message through to a member of the Commission. They had commandeered a train with the help of the army. Verne was at a loss. All they had to do was come find him at Inverness! And now here he was, a guest — if that was the right word — at a MID military base, in the company of a young Network worker, nearly young enough to be a Bio — telling him sweetly that she had a letter to give him. It was completely absurd.

"All this for a letter?"

"Yes. From Vienna."

Verne was dumbfounded. A letter from Joe Milner? After so many years? Was it possible? Is that what the old man would do before silencing his own voice?

Verne stopped walking. His pallor now matched Clara's.

"Dr. Verne? Are you all right?" asked Clara. She touched his arm lightly.

Verne looked straight at her. "Excuse me. This letter. Are you carrying it with you?"

Clara felt the contact of the paper against her breast. She wanted to say no, she wasn't, that she had lost it somewhere in the confusion. It's not that she wanted to read it, not at all. Just keep it with her. Her legs trembled. She felt as if she were hemorrhaging, breathing her last breath.

"Yes," she managed to say. "I have it."

She pointed a finger at her breast.

"Wait. I need to think a moment," said Verne. "Something is not right. The Network, Milner — that connection I understand. But the MID? What does the MID have to do with any of this?" he asked her. "Why is it helping you?"

"I don't know," said Clara, in a weak voice. "I don't even know what MID stands for."

"Let's keep walking."

Verne's mind was spinning. The idea that Joe had sent him a letter elated him. This innocent young woman was carrying the last word and testament of his friend and mentor.

The path curved away from the compound and followed a white wooden fence that ran along the boundary of the medical facility. The drone of a plane landing some distance off interrupted their thoughts. Then there was silence again. They could see buildings through the trees.

"I don't understand why the MID is involved in all this," said Verne again. "I'm sorry, but would you mind telling me how you got here?"

Clara told Verne that the letter had made its way to the Network via an Austrian scientist during a twenty-four-hour stopover in San Francisco, and it was urgent that it be delivered to Verne while he was at the U.N. in New York. She explained what had happened from then on: the airport business, the FBBS chase, Cornfeld's intervention, Hermes, and finally her arrival here at the base.

When she was finished, Clara felt drained.

Verne had listened intently. "I would guess your organization has some operatives in the MID. That's one plausible explanation. Another is that the MID has set this up to find out what I would do the minute I was given the letter. My being at the U.N. probably has something to do with the contents. That's why it was critical for you to give it to me there."

"Is it too late, then?"

"I don't know. Maybe not."

They were silent, both preoccupied with thoughts about the whole intrigue.

"I am sure we are being watched," said Verne. "I've met with the officer who runs the base. He said nothing to me about any letter. He may not know the reason for our encounter, surprising as that sounds. Everything in this whole affair is surprising. Perhaps you should give it to me now."

They were passing a grove of pines that obstructed the view of the medical facility. Clara turned. She slid her hand under her coat and sweater and down into the neckline of her blouse. She withdrew the letter and handed it to Verne. He took it quickly and plunged his hand deep into his coat pocket. The letter had been warmed by her body.

Verne looked at her and was troubled. For the first time he realized how attracted he was to her.

He gripped the letter hard in his hand.

Chapter 8

1

Locking the door behind him, Verne sat down at a table pushed up against the cinder block wall. He looked around the room. A cockroach scurried along the floor with an energy and purpose he found almost comforting. He resisted an impulse to catch the creature, put it on the table, and watch it navigate the unevenness of the tabletop — into which were carved the names of previous occupants.

Shivering despite the heat pumping through the radiator, Verne finally took the letter out of his pocket and very carefully unfolded the onionskin pages, pushing them flat against the tabletop.

The handwriting was tiny and precise — as if done with a feather quill. The mere sight of it absorbed Verne. He immediately lost track of time and place.

My dear friend,

My room is freezing this morning and I cannot seem to get out of bed. I have lived in this little apartment for over a year now and I have to admit — for all its other charms — that it is not well heated. It is located on the top floor of an old apartment building, right on the edge of what the Viennese call the *Innere Stadt,* where the old ramparts used to be. Living here has aged me. Lately, I don't go out at all. I stay inside and move between my bed and the easy chair by the window. I pass the time looking at the sky above the clocktower of the Irish Church.

My street has a terrible-sounding name — Bird's Cry Street, the *Schreyvogelgasse.* My mother's name was Lea Vogel. That name, among all the other millions, still echoes in my ear.

Vienna. All you need to do is walk the Ring, the circular avenue around the city, which boasts all those hideous palaces Franz-Joseph built toward the end of the nineteenth century to replace the old fortifications, to sense the grandiose illusions of old Austria. Here the imperial circle was closed — the Ring was supposed to hold the Habsburg dynasty together for a thousand years. It failed.

Twice in this decrepit old city, fattened by a lost empire, the world came to an end. History was turned inside out like a glove: in 1914, when Ferdinand was assassinated, and in 1938, when Austria was swallowed up by the Third Reich. Since then, Viennese intellectuals and artists have shouldered the full burden of history. A peculiar sort of wisdom sometimes comes from disillusionment.

The last time I crossed the Ring it was to fulfill an old desire of mine: to visit the house where Beethoven died almost two hundred years ago. It is located on the Street of the Black Spaniards, in the Heiligenstadt district, not far from Bergasse, where Sigmund Freud worked for most of his life. I also discovered that this was the house where Otto Weininger committed suicide in 1903.

Vienna overwhelms the senses. Viewed from here, the world is like a theatrical backdrop on a stage, after the curtain has dropped.

Out of the darkest nights comes the light. *Mehr Licht,* as Goethe said. My dear Paul. It has been twelve years since we saw and spoke to each other. I have missed you more than you can imagine.

When I first came back to Vienna from the United States, I lived with an old childhood friend, a physician named Albert Kloster. We had been block mates once. His son, Hermann, is a painter. It was at Hermann's house that I met Hanna Mazel, piano teacher to Hermann's daughter.

A week later, I moved in with her. Hanna had a beautiful apartment that overlooked the Prater. I started to work on a book, and she would play Berg or Webern on the piano. My retirement annuity and the money she earned from lessons was more than enough. We slept in the same bed — something that had not happened to me in years. We went to Switzerland for vacations, near Lenzerheide, to an alpine chalet some centuries old — near a glacier, whose strange formations I used to be able to see through the birch trees.

I used to meet up with a group of artists and intellectuals, mostly friends of Hermann. At first I went as a favor to him. Then, despite my skepticism about those kinds of pretentious gatherings, I went for my own reasons. I had got very attached to them. Mostly we talked about the Sacred Fire epidemic. These people were distinguished in their fields and had contacts all over the world.

That was how I first learned about Socrates, of which they were all members. Initially I assumed Socrates was really just an intellectual parlor society. Once we became known to the public authorities, however, we were looked upon as conspirators. Their paranoid reactions to our existence opened my eyes to things. Free and open discussion of the disease troubled them. For the simple reason that they could not control it. I was followed. All my communications were monitored. I had nothing to hide. I would have happily been willing to answer anyone's questions, if only they had bothered to pose them. But direct interrogation was far too simple an approach.

All this bothered me little — I still enjoyed a certain notoriety, except when I was permitted to understand the authorities were openly watching me. One day, when I went to one of our meetings, two inspectors searched Hanna's apartment. Another time I was asked to go to police headquarters on some flimsy pretext. Then, some local members of Socrates began to disappear. They would reappear after a few days looking haggard and incapable of saying what had happened to them. Apartments were broken into, our friends were harassed openly on the street — and always without explanation. We began to live in fear.

Meanwhile, the newspapers were filled with endless debate about what Austria should do, faced with the choice between the American ASP and the Russian Laïka. As you doubtless know, the Parliament opted for the Laïka. The age limit for the implantations was arbitrarily set at seventy, so there was no need for me to emigrate to Switzerland.

Little by little I learned how to become what they thought I was. I knew how to look behind me without seeming to; I was aware of even the smallest noise. Hanna used to make fun of me. She believed that the police wouldn't dare to touch a hair on my head. I was too well known, she said. In this unsettled atmosphere, the state continued to broadcast reassuring programs about the measures being taken against the epidemic, the statistics, the hopes for a cure.

One evening, I took a taxi home from a meeting. When I got out, a red light illuminated the sky. Smoke floated heavily in the air. Flashing lights pulsed over a crowd, held behind a barricade by the police.

Nothing was left of the building where Hanna Mazel and I had lived for nine years together. Her remains were never discovered, and nothing of any value was salvaged from the fire. My two manuscripts were reduced to ashes. No one knows what happened, exactly. The inquiry got nowhere. My last memory of Hanna is of her profile, at her piano — a Bösendorfer that had belonged to her father — at the moment when I was closing the door to leave.

I must close that door again. The year that I have just spent on Bird's Cry Road has at least permitted me to become certain. I have no more bitterness left. Meeting Hanna at all was a miracle. Through her I discovered life has very little to do with what we expect of it. Everything happened in a most unexpected way, like a true gift. If I had hoped for anything, nothing would have happened. I am sure it is the same with our having met, you and me.

I remember our first conversation. You must, too. Vienna brought us together even then. I had mentioned the connection between the Rhine and the Danube. You had said the two rivers didn't flow in the same direction. A common language resonates in both of our spirits — even if my German carries an inaudible Yiddish accent (a gift of my Galacian ancestors!). Someone has pointed out that Yiddish resembles Alsatian.

The two rivers have continued to run, each in its own direction, but the tongue that should unite them has not. Did you know that nearly all the six million Jews who lost their life in the camps spoke the same language, in some form or other? It seems unfathomable. Nothing really happened in Europe after the Holocaust — what I mean is, nothing that has so determined human history. Some process has been halted, and it is as if everything that made universal understanding possible has now and forever become suspect, and this is because every individual has become a stranger to himself. The rupture comes from within.

One would have liked to believe this terrible isolation would exhaust itself because we are, all of us, living with Sacred Fire. The opposite has happened, however, and here in Vienna, of all places, that fact takes on a greater weight of truth than elsewhere. The retrovirus has struck at our natural capacity to perpetuate the species. What we most feared.

More disturbing is the lack of surprise. For all its devastating cruelty the disease was even nearly welcomed here. In their vanity, scientists contributed to this deadly embrace. They said, now we have something really serious to deal with. This has nothing to do with literature or philosophy, they said. This grounds us, firmly and purely, in the material. Those who discovered the smallest genetic particles known — and I am among them — believed they were breathing in the essence of the universe.

Think of the power. Think of all those ethical commissions that took dominion everywhere — socio/ethical; bio/ethical; politico/ethical; scientifico/ethical. I even heard of the creation of a etho/ethical commission. In our scientific wisdom we devoted ourselves to formulating our views about everything and nothing. The universe of science had expanded. Any candidate for public office who might dare run a campaign without the support of a group of scientific experts faces certain defeat. The United States may be constitutionally more sensible about religious separation, but no less than Europe has it become the private reserve for the science lobbies. Why? Where is the lesson in it? Where is it taking us? And you, Paul, are you going to continue to go along with this charade? Do you believe in that Big Lie — that a simple scientific discovery will solve the problem facing humanity? You know as well as I do — God help me —

that I would be the last to underestimate the importance of research and scientific inquiry. The question is, what kind of research?

I have begun to believe that what has been most affected by Sacred Fire is our relationship to death. We hear nothing about the future now. There are no more promises. Our time is immersed in fatalism, and the only hope we imagine is regressive in nature — going back to a time before the epidemic, before pollution, before ethnic cleansing. All that life brings is death — even from the decomposition of life, animal-vegetal life, from the soil and the earth. Life has lost all of its connections with the mineral and solar splendors that playwrights have celebrated since the Sophoclean Age. Death no longer comes on rocks warmed by the midday sun — the Greeks thought midday to be the hour of death. Death is a descent into the noxious and fetid jungle of denial. Even faith in the redemptive destruction of bombs, in the fire of neutrons and protons, has evaporated. Now we are consumed in, and by, germs — mutating, retroactivating, and most of all anonymous viruses. Anonymous most of all. Life devours itself, aborts itself. The miasmas of endless life, without breaks or cycles or seasons. Nameless death reigns supreme. A lightless destruction in the darkness of pure biology. A tragedy without protagonist. Oedipus no longer has a place among us and Moses no longer makes any sense. No one will take us to the promised land. We have even forgotten that anyone ever could.

I know that I am indulging myself. Living in Vienna has that effect on people. This is a city that has always dwelled on memory. More than Paris or London or New York. Vienna is a reminder that there is no reconciliation between civilization — what remains of it — and the triumphant technical achievements it nurtured with such love in its bosom. Viewed from the crumbling heights of these decaying ramparts, the crisis of medical research looks like history turning in upon itself.

Paul, you may think me senile. But I tell you living here forces one into a kind of excess of lucidity — its only advantage, perhaps. I am convinced our inability to defeat the epidemic is the logical outgrowth of history. The same advances medicine made years ago in the fight against AIDS are themselves responsible for our losing this larger battle. We lack the concepts with which to *imagine* Sacred Fire. Technology seems to have become a substitute for the founding myths of our society, and we are watching an invisible yet profound crisis change our way of understanding that technology.

It has been some time now since biology could no longer hide its failure: in concrete terms, it could not find a cure for SF. The failure of all prophylactic and therapeutic attempts to deal with SF signals nothing less than the end of the Pasteurian Age in which we were all raised — the irony being, of course, that the AIDS virus was first isolated at the Pasteur

Institute. What should have been the crowning achievement carried the seeds of its demise.

The time has come for a profound reevaluation of the concepts we are using to guide our work on the SF retrovirus. Of course, that doesn't mean that we should throw out what we have already learned a thousand times over about the molecular, chemical, biological, and genetic systems at work. We need not so much to question our field of knowledge as to modify radically how we look at it. This will involve a methodological return to our past, or that of our science, so that we can sift what we know through the screen of Western history itself.

I have come to the conclusion that if, as is likely, some fundamental aspect of SF escapes our understanding, that will be because over time some concept has been permitted to remain in the shadows. Its absence in our thinking explains why science has arrived at the present impasse. If my hypothesis contains even a grain of truth, that should be enough to force us to search for what had been eliminated from our conception of the universe, and the way we have constructed it to fit our understanding of reality.

I propose that we consider the appearance of SF, as well as its endemic spread, as the result of amnesia.

Is it proper to look for the connections between SF's microbiology and historical events? For most people, such proposals represent a regression into the most backward sort of metaphysical speculation. Still, we cannot escape the possibility that human history has influenced the retrovirus.

Anthropomorphizing the disease haunts our thinking. We speak of SF's "intentions," of its Machiavellian behavior. In article after article we discuss the ruses the virus uses to disguise itself, the "markers" the organism uses once it has penetrated our system to elude the body's defenses. I do not believe this is mere rhetoric, just a way of talking about the disease. I *do* believe this kind of language affects how we understand the virus, and even influences the virus itself.

Every discovery alters reality. Antibiotics have had more of an impact on the evolution of microorganisms than centuries of natural selection. More and more frequently, phenomena occur without our knowing to what degree they have been predetermined by our existence and our influence. We are still unable to explain why AIDS appeared in the 1980s. Hypotheses abound, many of them persuasive and probing, but you know as well as I that behind these scientific constructions we find some like your compatriot Ambroise Paré, who in the sixteenth century proclaimed syphilis "the wrath of God, Who has permitted this disease to ravage humanity as punishment for its lasciviousness and unbounded concupiscence?"

Our own thoughts unnerve us. The idea of a "cellular intelligence" seems insanity, and yet we cannot let it go. We cannot make our belief that an intelligence is at work disappear. All we can do is put it into a blind spot where it escapes our scrutiny. In other words, just when we think we have finally kicked the age-old quarrel about predetermination out the front door, in it comes through the window. The retrovirus throws our thinking off track. We might say that it is doubly "retro" in that sense, because it has invalidated that precious creed that has existed almost since the discovery of DNA: "Every molecule of DNA codes for a molecule of RNA, but never the reverse." It is also "retro" because it has reintroduced into history, and into the history of science in particular, conceptions we assumed we had rid ourselves of forever, having banned them to the world of the irrational and supernatural.

My dear Paul, I believe that what we need, now more than ever, is another Copernican revolution, a reversal of perspective, so that we can finally conceive of multiple causality, contradictory and dangerous though it might be. Even if it forces us to place our materialist faith in science into doubt.

My work on the Maggie gene leads me to the hypothesis that there can be an active exchange between the genome of a species and the world around it. The retrovirus is the first example — though there are surely thousands of others — of a human gene being actively penetrated by a "foreign" gene with an ability to disguise itself. Such a hypothesis opens up horizons of possibility. I envy you the time you have to explore them.

The revolution in thought that lies ahead of us will be comparable to what happened at the beginning of the twentieth century, when the dimension of time — relativity — was integrated into wave theory. It became necessary to integrate time into physical phenomena. So too, now, it is time to integrate time into biological phenomena. Not time as in a life, or lives, but the time of a species. By its very mode of behavior, the retrovirus forces us to go back into time. Until the discovery of Sacred Fire time "descended," if I can put it that way. This meant, paradoxically enough, that we didn't have to deal with it. The theoretical system in which we have lived ever since Darwin permitted us to posit and prove that life evolved toward ever greater complexity, from protozoans to mammals.

The "spatial" corollary to this idea allowed us to establish beyond question that the genetic code always unfolded in a centrifugal sense — from DNA to RNA, from RNA to a protein, from the gene to its product. "Reverse transcription" proved that the retrovirus moved backward, from RNA to DNA. Even if we are not, strictly speaking, dealing with a refutation of the rules established by Darwinian deontology, it forces us at least to question it. The coded message carrying SFV is centripetal in its relation to the host it infects. From the point of view of the cell, the outside world, as represented by the virus, acts directly upon its internal structure, and it has a mutating "intention" — if you'll excuse the anthropomorphism. The retrovirus is therefore capable of altering the memory of a species. That is what is so truly staggering. What we have to determine is what laws these modifications obey, and whether they indicate something about the relationship between the genetic product — the protein — and the genome itself: what I have in mind of course are the "binding proteins" and the direct action of these hormones on certain DNA sequences.

That is what we face, my friend. You of all people are qualified to investigate this. You have the training and you have the ability. But that is exactly what your colleagues on the Biosociology Commission do not want you to do. You are a witness to their hypocrisy, and to what they are doing with the power given them by the people they have been able to deceive. Do you still think you can somehow prevent them from taking even more power? You're their hostage! Do you not understand what price you pay by perverting democratic justice? I am convinced your participation is destroying you. Your official responsibilities and social position keep you from seizing the moment. You are also one of the very few who can overcome them.

Resign from the Commission. You must, if you hope to have a chance to achieve your goal, the one which we worked for together side by side for so many years. You will need as much freedom as you can find. Liberty is as necessary as breathing. It will give you the courage to take risks.

Paul, my dear friend, I am sorry that I did not get to see you and Melissa again. The reasons for our distance now seem to me unpardonable vanity. I was wrapped up in my self-righteousness, the sort that comes when we feel that what we do influences the course of things. Is that vanity the price of science? I do not think it has to be. Yet we are pushed into believing our own importance by our training and colleagues and admirers. Silly as school prizes.

Leaving love is the hardest of all. Everything else — But I am starting to take myself seriously again. I am still trying to convince you. Perhaps you are already convinced.

Joe M.

P.S. I need to add something about Socrates. Started in Vienna ten years ago, it has now spread worldwide. Socrates is open to intellectuals, scientists, artists — all who want to involve themselves with the means and ends of science in the face of the SF epidemic. It was founded to combat the paranoia gripping governments as soon as the words "science" and "biology" were uttered. Socrates chose to be unofficial — underground, I suppose you might say — and this contributed to its ludicrous reputation as a seditious organization with tentacles in every resistance movement that has sprung up around the world in the last few years.

This unfortunate development was all the more foreseeable because certain members of the association disagree, to put it mildly, about what should be done, and how active Socrates should be in dealing with the world SF has created, particularly in the way governments now dictate research goals to scientists.

Socrates has no political goal beyond that of promoting democracy wherever and whenever possible. That is a philosophical goal, a matter of ethics, and it means membership is non-exclusive. To join, one needs to be sponsored by two active members, so that everyone can see what interest your participation might bring to the aims and activities of Socrates. Each new member agrees to follow the rules of the association.

I should hope, my dear Paul, that what I have said might convince you to help Socrates. In fact, you might even need Socrates' help, sooner or later. It sometimes takes years for the right moment to come along. It is my ardent hope that the moment has come for you.

A small favor. I learned that Ban Zhao, a colleague, will be at the U.N. as part of a Chinese delegation between January 15 and 29. Would you pass along a formula to her? It's part of an RNA messenger. I have reason to believe she will find it of the greatest use in her research on metabolic change in nerve cells during hyperthermia. The formula is no secret, though my asking you to do this for me does violate that irritating international regulation about the open circulation of scientific knowledge.

I trust I'm not putting you in too difficult a position. I simply have no other way of getting in touch with her. Put the formula into her hands and greet her warmly for me. You will not regret it. Thank you, my friend. I count on you.

```
A G U A A U G U A T G C A U U T G A C C C U C C
G U A G A U A A G G G C G A G G G G G A G A U U
A A G G U A G A U U C A G A G G U A G A U G U A
T G C C U C U C G G U A G U A G A U A A G A G C
G C G C C C U C C T G A G G C A C C A A G U G C
G U A A A U C C A A C G U U A U G U U G A G U A
A A U G C A T T T G U A A A U A C A A A G U A G
G A G G U A T G A G A G G U A A A U C U C G A G
G U A G U A A A U G C A A A G G U A A A U G U A
T G C A G C U A U C C A T G C G C C C C C G U A
```

Chapter 9

1

What struck you first was the silence.

If you listened carefully, you could hear, just barely, the sound of blood circulating through plastic tubes. More than likely, however, this was simply an illusion. There was no reason you should be able to.

The hydraulic pumps were located on the floor above, and all the piping went into them. So did all the other "nutrient providers," as Carol Gardner, director of the first Center for Applied Eugenics, used to call the life-sustaining equipment, the machinery that provided oxygen and food and maintained the necessary electrolyte and hormonal balances. Everything was controlled by a central computer that monitored the levels in each unit every twenty seconds and reacted instantly when there was an imbalance.

Melissa had always resisted visiting the "hold," as it was called. The sight of fifty APUs — Artificial Placentation Units — in groups of little pentagons in each one of the gestation rooms, was itself extraordinary enough, and she had no desire to listen to Carol Gardner go on and on about all the latest technical developments. Still, the whole setup was perhaps the most impressive achievement in the course of humanity's inexorable advance.

Lately Melissa had been visiting the Center for what might be called spiritual reasons, the way some people occasionally felt the need to go to church or to temple. Golden Gate Island — Alcatraz in former days — was something of a holy place.

Melissa had been sleeping badly, and last night had been the worst. She had finally fallen into an exhausted sleep just before dawn. That was when she'd had a dream.

It was of a young woman, strangely familiar, standing next to a window. She wore a flower-print dress that concealed her figure, and her head was inclined forward slightly. Her fair hair was done up in a bun. The shadows made it hard to see her expression, but she seemed to be listening to something. Just as Melissa was waking she smiled, and though it was a sweet smile it cut through Melissa's breast like a sharp knife.

She sat bolt upright in bed.

What had the woman been listening to? She had been standing absolutely still — like an ancient daguerreotype, sepia-colored and poignant. During the drive over to the Center today, Melissa tried to locate the source for the dream but couldn't.

She fell into a silence when she entered the hold. In the nursery's pale light, the APUs gave the impression of being suspended. Faced with this eerie spectacle, Melissa again felt the strange sensation of an acoustic void: first dizziness, and then the desire to stop and breathe in — ingest — the indescribable taste of silence. There was a primordial density to life here.

In the Six-Month Room, the one Melissa preferred, everything felt as though it were bathed in opalescent seawater, pale glowing green. Fifty little domes of glass on tables, each about a foot and a half high, two feet long, a foot wide, and a yard apart.

As they approached the time of delivery, all light was removed — everything was black, day and night, at least so far as normal vision went. This was because the air was being filled with all the luminous energy needed for the growing awareness of these future infants.

Melissa walked up to the first unit, the one closest to the door. Inside, she could see the colloidal water that permitted the sustenance of the embryonic system. Through the milkiness, the transparent amniotic pouch was clearly visible, and inside it was the fetus: the disproportionately sized head, the legs crouched like an Oriental wise man.

She found the spectacle mesmerizing: the delicate nostrils, the diaphanous eyelids, the tiny fingers and perfectly formed fingernails. She nearly gasped when she saw that the fetus seemed to be sucking its thumb. The only perceptible movement was the umbilical cord, which, vibrating to the rhythm of the beating heart, connected the abdomen to the placenta, whose cotyledons were firmly anchored in the uterine endometer covering the back of the unit, where the exchange of "maternal" blood took place. An artificial vein carried the blood out of the APU and transported it directly into a room below, where it was recycled and then pumped back up into the unit.

The fetuses appeared in blissful sleep.

Produced by technological artifice, ignorant of the experience of a maternal bond, who were these creatures? Everything possible was done to give them a chance to develop under conditions approximating those of the mother's body — the beat of the heart and other visceral sounds were piped into the APU at regular intervals, and latex sacs were put around the amniotic pouch during the final months of development, so that when it moved the fetus would come up against something resembling the muscled wall of the mother's uterus.

But there was no way these devices could replace what would not be measured in biochemical, physiological, or mechanical terms — something whose importance was becoming increasingly apparent to Melissa, despite the fact that her upbringing and medical training conformed to the canons of scientific materialism. Something was missing.

Did maternal love have only an emotional dimension to it — or was there more to it?

Melissa thought again of the young woman in her dream, standing in the soft light of the window. Then she remembered a photograph of her grandmother, taken when she was pregnant with Melissa's mother.

That was the trigger. Melissa had thought she had no memory of her grandmother, who died when she was very young. Yet it was clearly her grandmother who had come to her in a dream, smiling.

She sobbed and backed away from the APUs. The room had turned nightmarish: fifty mushroom clouds in boxes, little atomic explosions — each with diabolical powers only temporarily contained in a fragile state of precariousness, each waiting for its moment of liberation. The room was a closing trap. Threads of some unnameable malevolence were being woven together into the fabric of the future, a fabric that threatened at every second to rip open and explode in apocalyptic fury. Melissa took a step forward. She wanted to destroy these creatures and smash their bubbles.

She stopped, horrified with herself, and she ran from the room. Never had she known such rage.

She was outside, panting.

It was pouring, but the rainwater refreshed her. She walked down to the sea.

San Francisco Bay spread out before her. Through the light mist that had settled over its roiling waters, she saw the city's towers.

"Dr. Verne?" called a voice behind her.

She raised her head and turned. It was the CAE receptionist, calling from a window.

"There's a message for you. I think it's from Dr. Verne."

Melissa hurried back inside.

2

Annabelle emerged from the bathroom, a towel turban around her head, and paused before the full-length mirror in the bedroom.

She performed a critical evaluation of her muscle tone, then did a one-quarter turn to look at the line of her back, of which she was particularly proud. Annabelle judged her body to be nearly flawless. She could spend hours looking at it, scrutinizing each square inch. Sometimes she made faces, sometimes she made extravagant poses — show stoppers — until she laughed at herself in girlish delight.

Today, however, she was in no mood for such silliness. The idea that she had to check in with Claudia Lombard hung over her like Damocles' sword. Lombard had tried several times to reach her in New York, but Annabelle had managed to elude her.

"I'm fed up with that bitch," Annabelle told her reflection, "and I'm not going to let her get me."

There was no way she would ever again put herself at the mercy of Claudia Lombard. The few hours she had spent in Georgetown were more than enough. Yet the New York debacle meant she would have no choice. Now more than ever she had to keep seeking the good will — and stoking the desire — of her boss.

The New York business had compromised Annabelle terribly.

Not that she felt personally responsible for Paul Crick's death. The moron had acted like a rookie. Fooling around with a gun aimed at his chest. The Network man Hermes was right when he'd said he had rid the FBBS of an embarrassment. Too bad he'd gone into a coma right after his arrest. She would have enjoyed applying the thumbscrews.

The Mount Sinai doctors were being cautious about his chances for recovery. The bullet had lodged a fraction of an inch from his heart, and he'd lost plenty of blood. Even if he didn't die of a massive hemorrhage, it would be weeks before Annabelle would be able to have at him.

After the accident, Annabelle had been forced to leave the FBBS barricade at the U.N. to help with the interrogation of Myra Cornfeld and her niece, even though she was positive she would learn little from either woman. The old lady was well connected. She was of far greater use to them free than in custody. Annabelle must find a moment to suggest that to her boss. But what was the point? Soon none of this would matter anyway.

A wave of rage crashed over her. Why hadn't she pulled out all the stops to get her hands on Clara Hastings? After hours of discussion, the spokesman for the Secretary General of the U.N. had finally authorized an FBBS agent to speed-search the building, accompanied by a U.N. representative. All the agent could do was confirm that Hastings was not on the premises. Neither were the two U.N. guards who had helped her after the accident. When they were found, they would simply say that all they'd done was help a young lady in distress. She'd left in the middle of the night without leaving her address.

Annabelle had not informed the FBBS she was back in Washington. She was angry. She needed some time to think. She could still smell Mary Peale's body. Mary had made the bed and left. No message, as usual. Who had that slut gone off with for the weekend?

Annabelle sighed. She cupped her breasts with her hands and started to caress them. They were still a little sore from the accident.

Annabelle told herself, again, she should break things off with Mary Peale. She also knew her resolve would weaken and that in a couple of hours she would try to reach her, just like she did every day, to ask when she could see her again.

She couldn't have cared less about Kess Sherman's capture, which Kane had announced with such triumph just a few hours earlier. Still, maybe the head of the Southern California Network would tell her something new. She would call Dr. Cline and ask him to come up with some imaginative new serum. Sherman would pour out his heart.

What most obsessed Annabelle at the moment was the disappearance of Clara Hastings. The singular combination of the Bio's timidity and determination had impressed her. Was there a way of bringing her back into the fold? The thought of using her as a double agent, having Hastings completely at her mercy, was too delicious for words.

Lombard would remind her to concentrate on the message, not the messenger, but Annabelle hadn't given much thought to this mysterious letter that supposedly threatened national security. On the other hand, whoever had the letter had the girl. Paul Verne was on his train and closely watched; he was a sure pickup. Actually, the fact that Verne had taken a train was a blessing. It would all be over in twenty-four hours. The letter would be in FBBS hands, and Clara Hastings would be in Washington — where Annabelle would be able to get her hands on her. If Annabelle still had a job, that is.

What if she waited until the Bio was picked up before checking in? No. Impossible. She knew Claudia too well: if she didn't go in tomorrow morning, the whole world would be after her.

She continued to rub her breasts while she thought. The towel had fallen off her head. She looked at herself in the mirror, erect, a little stiff, tense even, hands cupping her breasts, legs apart, the shaved pubis clearly showing the ridge of the vulva.

Her nipples hardened. She slipped her hands between her thighs and began to caress herself, slowly, delicately, speeding the motion of the fingers little by little.

She watched her face, anxious to view her own excitement mount. Her hips began swaying, and she bent over slightly. A sound came from deep in her throat.

"Put me through to Morgan," Annabelle asked phone reception.

She had dressed and was impeccably made up.

"Bill? Annabelle."

"How are you, Weaver?" a man's voice asked. "This is a surprise. Still falling all over the boss?"

"Cut the shit, Bill. Keep it in the little boy's room."

"Hey, I was only kidding!"

"Listen, Bill, I need a favor. It's urgent and a little delicate. You said that you were ready any time to pay me back when I needed it."

"I meant it. You pulled me from the abyss when Lombard was ready to cast me in."

"OK, then can you still get into the main banks?"

"What do you mean, 'can I still get in?' That's my job!"

"And into the coded files?"

"Sure. But — "

"Can you screen into everything?"

"Almost. Except if it's about FBBS personnel, and what the FBI steals from me."

"How often does that happen?"

"It happens."

"How can someone get hold of a FBBS personnel file?"

Bill's end was silent for a moment.

"You need two to do that. I only know half the code key."

"Who knows the other?"

"Haldane. Who are you after, Weaver?"

"Don't worry. It isn't you."

"Who is it?"

"You're sure your line is protected?"

"I changed the code yesterday."

"I'm after the boss."

An impressed silence.

"Well, well. I've got to hand it to you. You're really going for broke this time. What exactly do you want?"

182 /

"The eligibility report the FBI gave the Senate confirmation commission."

Bill was silent for a second or two.

"I'm going to have to conjure with this. Someone's sure to find out. All they have to do is consult the list of operations over the course of the last few days. You can't erase that."

"Bill, don't give me the routine. You tell them you made a mistake. You say anything you want. Can you do it or not?"

"I'll have to bring Haldane in on it."

Another silence. Then he added: "Maybe there's another way. You need this when?"

"Today."

"What? Are you nuts? I don't even know where Haldane is!"

"It's today or never."

"That serious?"

"That serious."

"OK. Sit tight. I'll call you back in five minutes. Either I get Haldane and convince him or it's a no-go and at least you'll know."

"Bill, my man, you're a honey. I'll wait for your call."

"You just want me because of my access, you big bully!"

"You got it, pal."

Annabelle went into the kitchen and got a carbonated Cocaid out of the refrigerator. She took it to the living room and sat down.

Well, this was it. She had played all her cards. Either she dug up dirt on Papa Lombard, or she was bounced.

She hadn't even finished draining her glass when her console purred. Annabelle waited until she heard Bill's voice before picking up.

"You're on," he said. "Meet me at Hoover in an hour. My recent poker luck has helped you. Haldane owes me some money. Bring twenty-five bills with you."

"Twenty-five hundred? What happened to friendship and favors?"

"Haldane says take it or leave it."

"OK. Twenty-five bills."

"In cash. In an hour."

"In cash. In an hour."

Annabelle switched off. "God, you'd think they actually had balls," she said out loud.

3

There was nothing in the world Howard Black loved more than a restorative Sunday evening at home. His mother sat comfortably in her favorite chair in front of the fireplace — the green leather recliner with the crocheted doilies.

Doris Black loved to talk. Now that most of her friends were resting peacefully in the First Presbyterian church cemetery, she regaled her son with endless prattle. Howard would read the *Chronicle* and grunt in acknowledgment every so often at something his mother said. When her son wasn't there, Jackie, the cleaning lady, a large Latino woman nearly her age who had been with them for eighteen years, did the listening. Howard thought Jackie had a distinct advantage in being almost completely deaf.

This Sunday was like the others. After the service at First Presbyterian, which the Black household attended regularly, Jackie had gone to Bethesda to visit her daughter. Howard had spent his afternoon upstairs in his study. His mother watched one of her favorite shows. They'd eaten a frugal meal together in the kitchen and settled themselves in the living room. Howard turned on the gas in the fireplace, then sat across from her to read a few pages out of the Bible. Mrs. Black, her eyes closed, her legs covered in a blanket, rested her head against the lace antimacassar on the back of the chair.

As usual, at about this point, his mother was no longer listening and letting her thoughts drift, from the combined effect of her son's caressing voice and the soothing warmth of the room.

She was remembering the Bible lessons Howard gave as a teenager to the Sunday school children. Everyone in the congregation predicted a brilliant future in the ministry for the young man. Providence, however, had other plans.

Mrs. Black had now nearly forgotten that her family started as Lutherans, before Howard decided that they should switch their allegiance to First Presbyterian. A judicious choice. This new community enjoyed considerable prestige among the conservative white middle class.

Her son had succeeded at everything he tried. First as an Eagle Scout, then at his first job at the Library of Congress. After law school, as an attorney general for the District of Columbia, and then professor at George Washington University. Finally, as director of the FBI.

Her one source of worry was that Howard seemed inclined to do nothing to continue the family name. That had been a closed issue for some time, and when the epidemic struck it seemed to prove to her the absolute rightness of his innate good judgment. She had been proud to tell her friends that Howard was among the first to agree to an implant, at a time when it had not yet become obligatory.

"I'm going to bed, Howard. I'm very tired."

She raised herself with difficulty. Her son helped her to her room, which, to avoid stairs, had been moved into the old dining room on the first floor.

Afterward, Black sat back down in his chair. He was feeling content. He had always lived with his mother. She was a part of the order of the world. Ever since the death of his father (Howard was twelve when his father died suddenly from a coronary while presiding in his courtroom), he had known he would never leave her.

Black sank into his thoughts. He recalled his conversation with Tom Kutler. Everything had gone according to plan: Paul Verne and the Network messenger had met at the MID base at Maywood, Nebraska. Military secret service had had no difficulty finding Joseph Milner's letter. A copy was now in the hands of FBI cryptologists. Black had asked to be notified when Verne returned to New York.

Kutler also talked about Hermes. The general was worried about his man. He had asked Black to get him out of Mount Sinai and transfer him to Bethesda. Black had told him it was impossible until he'd had surgery.

Hermes would never come out of the coma. That would simplify things with the FBBS. Claudia Lombard was a danger. If she learned about the role the MID agent was playing in the Network, she might stir things up. Black imagined himself trying to explain to the director of the FBBS that he had been controlling the Milner affair from the beginning. That afternoon she'd called Larry Walton, his secretary, to grill him about the raid and Verne's abduction.

At some point things would boil over. Maybe the time had come to replace Lombard. Keeping one's colleagues in the same position for too long was always dangerous.

Black leaned into the chair. The image of the man he'd seen at the Safeway that morning came back. For a split second, he relived the ecstasy of it, then dozed off.

The phone buzzed. Black glanced at his watch. Five past ten. He'd been asleep for nearly an hour.

"Yes? Ah, Haldane. Whose dossier did she want to see? Well, I'll be . . . No, no. Do nothing for the moment. Wait for me to call you back. You're at the office? . . . Don't move. Five minutes?"

Fascinating. One of Lombard's own inner circle was snooping

around in her file. Naturally, Black had ways of stopping insurrection. But if an agent had decided it was worth taking such a risk — for she must have known that sooner or later Lombard would find out about it — she must have had a good reason.

A dim memory crossed his mind. He punched in some numbers.

"Powell? Black. Strictly confidential. Monitor Annabelle Weaver's movements. And trace them over the last two days. She was in charge of the Network messenger. She went to New York . . . Ah yes, she was the one in the car . . . Can she be reached? No one knows . . . Very well, thank you, Powell."

It was as he had suspected. The young woman had met Hermes. Things were perhaps more complicated than they seemed. Annabelle Weaver was sending him a message. She was saying, "Let me rifle through the past of Claudia Lombard and I won't make any trouble." Good. They would just have to wait and see what she'd do. He would give her until tomorrow morning. An interesting question: what would she do when she discovered Lombard once had Mafia connections? Soon he would have to meet this audacious young woman.

Black punched in a new set of numbers.

3

Claudia Lombard woke with her heart pounding. She was sure she'd heard a noise. Titus was asleep in a chair, illuminated by a ray of light that filtered between the curtains. Caesar was lying on the puff. Lombard got out of bed, went to the window, and gently pulled back the curtain.

Everything seemed normal. The snow glistened under the spotlights around the fence. The guard was shuffling in front of the gate, his hands in his pockets. It looked bitterly cold. Lombard couldn't see the two FBBS agents who watched the house night and day from their unmarked vehicle. At least they were warm.

Feeling some relief, she turned on a light, put on her peignoir and fuzzy slippers, and went downstairs to the kitchen to put some water on to boil — she had long been in the habit of drinking a cup of tea in the middle of the night. She sat down at the kitchen table.

Lombard was preoccupied with what had happened in New York over the weekend: the death of Paul Crick and the disappearance of Clara Hastings. All Saturday night she had been expecting to learn that the special agents aboard the California Zephyr had picked up Hastings the moment she met Paul Verne.

Then, in the small hours of Sunday morning, came the extraordinary news that the train had been attacked by a small armed band using sophisticated weaponry and that they had spirited Verne away. Right from under the nose of the FBBS agents.

First the messenger and now the leading Commission biologist — whisked away as if by magic. There was little hope now of retrieving Milner's letter.

On Sunday Lombard had called Black's secretary, Larry Walton, to ask him to set up a meeting with Black. She thought it curious Larry had not sounded particularly upset, even though he must have known what had happened. He told her he wasn't sure she would get to see Black before Monday afternoon.

Lombard found the underreaction very strange. On American soil, an armed group had made a full-scale assault in broad daylight. This was not some small incident. In fact, the whole operation raised a host of questions: what connection did the attackers have to the Network? Had the Network grown so powerful that it could pull off such a sophisticated and sustained maneuver? Did it have confederates in the U.S. military? It would seem it did. The FBBS would have to move fast. Up to this point the Network had been less organized, capable only of isolated incidents: surprise attacks on FBBS offices or AS checkpoints, subversive literature, destruction of FBBS property and files. What had happened out there on the plains was on a whole different level.

Did someone decide to hand the Verne affair over to another service, such as the CIA, which would have a better bead on its international implications? Lombard wondered if that might explain Walton's diffidence. He was under orders. There was no mention of the attack on TV. Who would have the power to impose a media blackout?

Larry Walton called back at the end of the afternoon to tell her she had an appointment with Black the next day at four. Having fulfilled her obligation, Lombard had stopped worrying. But she hadn't stopped thinking.

The New York mess affected her directly. There was nothing to indicate that Annabelle Weaver was personally responsible, but what infuriated Lombard was that Annabelle had found a means of getting away — probably to seek the charms of one Mary Peale. She had already decided on a punishment: Weaver would be assigned to some obscure FBBS office in Oregon.

Suddenly the lights went out.

Lombard tried to control her nerves, glancing out the window to see if the blackout affected the whole neighborhood, or simply her house.

She heard a swishing sound in the hall — someone walking.

She wanted to call Billy, but nothing came out of her throat.

The lights came back on.

Two men were standing in the kitchen on either side of the doorway.

"What do you want?"

"You are Claudia Lombard?"

"Yes, but — "

She was about to cry out for the guards. A razor appeared in the hands of one of the men.

"No sound. Please do not disobey. Do what we tell you."

They were Asian, dressed in dark suits with immaculate white shirts and black ties. On their foreheads, bandannas emblazoned with Japanese characters. Yakuza! The heavy hand of the famous Japanese Mafia had terrorized large chunks of American territory. Lombard had read a recent report on exchanges of information and personnel between the Japanese and American cartels.

The men stood immobile, their eyes fixed on her. She knew they would slice people up with a smile. Where was Billy? And where the hell were the guards? At least now she knew who she was dealing with — the Yakuza were ferociously disciplined, and they never committed violence indiscriminately.

"I understand," she said, regaining her composure. "Now what do you want?"

"We are fulfilling our mission."

She knew this was a nearly sacred responsibility.

"And what is your mission?"

"To bring you with us."

"I will not leave this house."

The eyebrows on the man who had spoken knit very slightly. The other man moved with uncanny speed and seized Lombard's arm in one hand. He then stood stock still — waiting for instructions.

His touch was not light. Lombard felt as if her arm were in a metal vice. She noticed the missing portion of the pinkie, a distinctive mark of the Yakuza.

"Ms. Lombard," said the leader, "if I ask him to, my friend is capable of inflicting pain. Please do as I told you."

"I . . . will . . . do whatever you want."

"Then we must go."

The speaker signaled to his friend, who then dropped Lombard's arm.

188 /

They were in the hallway. The leader went ahead and took down two coats that were hanging from a hook; he handed one to his partner, after saying a few words in Japanese.

"I have just told my partner to strike you if you offer any resistance. I will tell you again. Please do what I ask. Now please put this on."

He handed her a cape that she put on over her peignoir. Then he opened the door and walked out without in the least trying to shield himself from the bright lights.

He was making no attempt to hide. Lombard knew this was not a good sign. What was going to happen to her? Maybe it was an FBBS matter, and they would take her home afterward and explain. Then she thought of Billy, and her heart sank.

They went down the walk. The gate creaked open. Lombard thought briefly of all the sophisticated alarm systems that the FBBS had placed around the house. These men must have thought of absolutely everything.

They came out onto the street.

Two cars waited by the curb. The uniform Lombard had seen only a quarter of an hour earlier was gone. The security vehicle wasn't in its normal place. She tried not to think of what had been done to them.

The door opened.

Seconds later, she was seated between the two Yakuza. At the controls was a third, dressed identically. The vehicle moved off. Lombard could tell from the lights in the rearview mirror that they were being followed.

"You will be so kind as to please put on this blindfold," said the man on the right.

Exasperated by the excessive formality, Lombard took the blindfold and did as she was asked.

She had just enough time to notice that they were heading down Wisconsin Avenue, before her vision was lost.

Her eyes were still blindfolded when she was helped out of the car.

A pungent odor filled the air. It was even colder than before. Lombard shivered. At least she was sure that they hadn't gone beyond D.C. limits. They had been driving for only ten minutes, maybe less.

She tried to concentrate on what was going on around her. Someone had her arm and was guiding her. She couldn't hear anyone else.

Then, suddenly, it was overpoweringly hot. They had gone inside. She was led step by step up a staircase.

A door closed behind them.

Several steps forward, then her guide let go.

"Please, sit down."

It was the voice of the Yakuza leader. Someone behind her pulled her gently back. Lombard let herself go. She felt relief to be sitting in a chair.

Someone took her cape. Despite the silence, she was sure that others were in the room. She felt watched.

"OK, Claudia. You can take off the blindfold now."

Only one voice had that nasal tonality, that singular mix of childishness and cruelty.

"Engelhardt!" she cried, unable to contain her surprise.

The capo let out a laugh that sounded like a squealing mouse. Lombard tried to unknot the blindfold.

"You could at least help me, instead of laughing!"

"I'm having too much fun watching the celebrated director of the FBBS in her bathrobe wrestling with a blindfold. Believe me, Claudia, I wouldn't change places with you for a million bucks."

"Stop boasting, Michael. You'd sell your own mother for a good deal less."

Engelhardt said nothing.

Lombard finally succeeded in sliding off the blindfold, but the sudden brightness made her shut her eyes. She fluttered her eyelashes while they adjusted to the light.

She was sitting in a small room. The walls were peeling, and there was no shade on the floor lamp. Before her, at a simple table on which sat a bottle and some glasses, sat Engelhardt himself. Next to Engelhardt sat another man: powerful looking, steel-gray hair, face like a boxer's.

In the corner of the room, his eyes leveled at her, was the Yakuza — he was standing as he had in her kitchen, a coiled spring.

Lombard looked back at Engelhardt. His eyes still unnerved her. He had changed little since the last time she'd seen him in Miami, but his method of setting up a meeting certainly had. In Miami, he used to reserve the room that adjoined hers, and they had spent an afternoon in discreet conversation.

"Well? Satisfied?" he asked. "This is George Mattei. We're on his turf and he set up this meeting for me. Thanks, George."

The man grunted. He seemed bored by the whole situation. He looked more like a bodyguard than a don. But Lombard knew from experience appearances could be deceiving.

"Michael, since when have you started to kidnap people in order to talk with them? I can't believe you would do something like this. I will never forgive you for — "

Engelhardt leaped off his chair, came at her in a fury, and using his full arm, backhanded her across the face. The sound of the blow resonated in the room.

"Don't give me any of your shit!" he shouted, his face distorted with rage.

"I — I — don't understand, Michael." Lombard held her cheek. Tears were streaming down her face as much from humiliation as pain. "What is wrong with you?"

"What is wrong with me? Hear that, George? The director of the FBBS wants to know. And I'm supposed to tell her! *I'm* supposed to goddamn tell *her!*" He was roaring. Then he panted for a second. "The FBBS screws me over and I have to tell its boss what *her own* organization did to *me*. Hilarious! A laugh riot. That's what this fucking is."

"Maybe you should needle her," said George Mattei, speaking for the first time.

Lombard cowered. Engelhardt was terrifying her. She had never seen him like this, and she had known him for some time.

Years earlier, Claudia's father, Peter Lombardi, had abandoned his brilliant legal career to devote his services to Vincent Sullivan, who was running for the Senate. He told people that the senator had what it takes to be president. After Sullivan's victory, her father became edgy and unhappy. Six months after that, he want on a mysterious trip to Canada. Sullivan's suicide had taken place during his absence, and Lombardi was questioned by the police. There were rumors about foul play and influence peddling. Michael Engelhardt was often seen in Lombardi's office. The Sullivan affair was closed in a couple of weeks and ruled a suicide. Just before his own death in a car accident, Lombardi had confided to his daughter that Engelhardt had helped him.

Many years later, after her nomination to head the FBBS, Lombard got a call from Engelhardt. Despite his reputation, she hadn't hesitated to meet with him.

Lombard had done some small services for him — closing her eyes on the alcohol trafficking, one of his main businesses, for example. Like many women, Lombard viewed this second Prohibition as a denial of a woman's fundamental rights. It seemed unfair that women should be deprived of a luxury simply because men were forbidden from indulging in it. As a result, because it was legal, women consumed Cocaid products — and its effects, she felt, were far more deleterious than a little alcohol.

Yet despite their working relationship, Engelhardt never told her what exactly he had done for her father. And Lombard didn't want to know.

"Claudia, did you hear what my friend here suggests?" he said with gleeful malevolence. "That maybe I should have you poked with something to refresh your memory. What do you think?"

"Michael, I swear to God I have no idea what you're talking about."

Engelhardt squinted at Lombard. He was pleased to see she looked haggard.

"You know who Kess Sherman is?" he asked dryly.

"The guy from the L.A. Network?"

"That's the one." He turned to Mattei. "The distinguished lady knows who he is."

"Yes," said Lombard. "I also know we brought him in two days ago."

"Good! And this morning's newspapers are all about the storming of the Virginas H.Q. in L.A.!"

Lombard was becoming exasperated. "Was something going on between Sherman and you?"

"You didn't know that I had a meeting with him a couple of days ago? No? You didn't know that it was after that meeting that the police began pursuit? That the FBBS was staked out near my offices? That I lost two of my best men in that fucking mess?" He was yelling now.

"No!" Lombard shouted back, her voice raw. "I mean . . . yes, I knew there was a chase, and that the L.A. police helped. But no one informed me that you were involved, nor that you'd been watched. This is crazy! I don't understand."

Engelhardt walked to the other side of the table and sat down. He leveled his eyes on Lombard, his eyelids half closed.

"Annabelle Weaver works for you," he said calmly.

"Yes. Why?"

"She knew what was going on. One of your agents reports to her — Robert Kane. I have my sources. And they seem to be better than your sources."

"You have contacts inside the Network?" Lombard asked.

"So you're asking the questions now? Yes. And I had a meeting with Sherman. We've discovered something we thought might interest the Network. Something that might help them elude AS checkpoints."

"They've been looking for that for ages. It can't exist. No one believes in it anymore."

Engelhardt laughed.

"Neither do I. But I found something that might give them the *illusion* that it exists. You add it to the ASP and it neutralizes it for a little while. My friend here and I are wearing one now. It works for a while. We sell you the means to detect the modification. Either way we get paid. The Networkers get cocky and start coming out of the woodwork, and the FBBS has a surefire way of picking them up trying to get past AS checkpoints — and before you know it you have a whole bunch of them under lock and key. Right when I was putting this thing of beauty into operation, the FBBS decides to blunder in. Fucking idiots!"

"Let me go," Lombard said huskily.

"You still have a few things to tell me."

"Let me go and I'll give you Weaver."

Engelhardt looked at her with interest.

"Why shouldn't I just approach her myself and make a deal?"

"She's out of the loop."

"Is that so? How did that happen?"

Lombard saw no reason why she shouldn't tell Engelhardt about the weekend's events. In the final analysis, by telling her about his Network meeting, he had done her a big favor. By not informing her of the Sherman-Engelhardt meeting, Annabelle had obviously hoped to jeopardize her control. This would be Lombard's chance to prove who had power over whom.

Lombard reminded herself to see if Black had met with Annabelle lately. You couldn't be too careful.

Then she talked about the Paul Verne affair. She talked about Clara Hastings, the Milner letter, and, after only the briefest hesitation, about the train assault. It would all be in the newspapers anyway.

Engelhardt listened to her without blinking.

"Well, well," said Engelhardt when she'd finished. "Now what interest would you have in that letter?"

"Socrates."

"That pointy-head organization? They must be more powerful than I'd thought for you to be interested. It's true they have the advantage of being international — an advantage I'm familiar with," he added, looking at the Yakuza. Then he glanced over at Mattei, who was looking more awake.

"Okay. I'm going to think all this over. For now, though, you stay with us."

"Michael, be reasonable. The FBI is already looking for me. Let me go. It's in your best interests. I'll give you Weaver."

"Weaver doesn't interest me, Claudia. What do you want us to do with her? You're going to need some patience. We're not talking a few hours. It takes time to get everyone together. You'll stay with our friend over there." He pointed at her captor and nodded.

The Yakuza took her arm.

In silence, Lombard allowed the man to lead her away. The two men watched them leave the room, their faces impassive.

5

Clara's body ached everywhere. There were thousands of insects under her skin, scampering to save themselves from a fire. Absorbed by unfamiliar sensations, she had lain in bed, sprawled out for hours, her eyes open — she was the white sands of a desert waiting for a few drops to fall from heaven.

Her immobility was the result of a dizziness that would not go away. Sensations were taking on a different dimension. She felt as if her very being hummed in response to the objects around it, and that each atom of the universe was in the same trance she was. Whatever lay behind all of her free-floating thoughts resisted the puniness of doubt. The word *god* could have even come to her mind, but it would have been alien to her, and evaporated from her thoughts like a bubble the moment it was pronounced.

She wasn't wondering what it was all about. Or she had not yet started. The response came before the question. Her soul was filled with a joy she would have thought unattainable. She didn't dare let herself follow the images beckoning from the horizons of her consciousness. She willed them away the second they appeared. Seeing them was already unbearable enough. She knew what they were bringing; they would come back soon enough. For the moment she wanted to savor this new dimension of feeling that had her in thrall. Suffering mattered little. What mattered was that the pain brought intimacy, subverting everything else, making everything else insignificant, or welcome, depending.

She thought she would begin by giving her name. They call me Clara Hastings. I know what I feel. By what miracle is that possible, that I know that — me, born from a void, a vacuum?

She knew that what held her would never let her go. This first time was also the last. Time focused upon a single point, a point without a point, the shape of the immaterial coming before materiality. Words hurtled through her universe like meteorites. She understood them. They came from before things were. Clara felt as if she were remembering a language she had never spoken.

I am sick, she told herself. I can't move. And it was true she was sick and couldn't move. But what joy. She loved, she burned. I have to call out to it. Tears began flowing. Another name was there. Paul. Paul Verne. She knew. She had always known.

Dr. Arnold Strumwasser was a large man of about sixty with a potbelly and thick glasses. He looked as if he watched the world through the glass walls of an aquarium.

Strumwasser was actually an excellent clinician, with considerable medical expertise. He lacked one thing — ambition. He had been delighted with his assignment to the MID base. Becoming chief of staff at a hospital, two years before retirement, was an unexpected boon.

He loved his work and was liked by the soldiers on the base. Without having really sought the role, he had become their most trusted confidant. The camp pastor felt jealous and had even said a word about it to Colonel Bradbury.

Besides his patients, Strumwasser had one ruling passion: biology. As soon as his duties were completed, he would return to his living quarters on the top floor of the hospital and spend his evenings reading the scientific journals he subscribed to or the latest government-issue research manuals. He knew the names and faces of most of the leading scientists.

When Paul Verne entered his office at seven in the morning — Strumwasser was in the habit of doing a rapid tour of the patients before the hospital staff arrived — he knew right away who he was. A visit from Paul Verne was more thrilling than a visit from the president.

"You're Paul Verne, all right," he blustered, having risen and come out from behind his desk to greet his visitor. "I don't know what to say. I'm very honored. Kind of surprised, too. What are you doing in this godforsaken place? Please, sit down. My name's Strumwasser."

"An unusual name. German?"

"Yes, that's right. My ancestors came from the Black Forest region. I'm fourth generation."

"Not far from where I'm from — just on the other side of the Rhine. I'm from Alsace originally."

"I know. In fact, you might be surprised at how much I know about you. Alsace, Paris, Berkeley, discovery of SF, the Reiss Institute — I can't tell you how happy I am to meet you. But, I'm sorry, you probably came here to ask me something, not have me jabber at you. If I can be of service, I would consider it an honor."

Verne smiled despite himself. He was touched by the kindness of the man. It wasn't something he would have expected to find in this remote military base.

"Doctor, thank you. I appreciate your warmth. I may have need of your help, though I don't know yet. I'm here to inquire after the health of a young woman whom you hospitalized this morning, Clara Hastings. Do you know her?"

"Of course."

"I was supposed to meet her this morning. A soldier told me she was here. I'm a little worried. She fainted once yesterday. Have you had a look at her? May I see her?"

"Of course, of course. I had a feeling that your visit might have something to do with her. I examined her this morning at six, Dr. Verne. She's running a temperature of 103. She's disoriented and delirious. Oh, and she also kept repeating your name."

"My name?"

"Yes, your name. Paul. Sometimes she would also say your last name. Verne. Paul Verne. Sometimes a whole sequence of gibberish, of which I understood not a single word. Then, a single sentence, in absolute clarity, 'The name on the letter I'm carrying is Paul Verne.' Sort of a way of showing affection for you, I guess."

"Affection?"

"Well, yes. Affection. None of my business. Of course, affection like that has become something like an obscenity these days — affection between a man and a woman or the other way around. My God, you know, it wasn't always like that. It's only because of — well, you of all people know what I mean. Not that people don't still have feelings. I mean, I wonder why I'm blathering on like this. You asked me how she was doing. Dr. Verne, your friend is having one hell of a sharp attack of rheumatic fever. I put her on antibiotics. I'm waiting to see the results of a throat sample and some blood tests."

He turned and went back to sit down behind his desk. Verne got up.

"Can I see her?"

"Yes, sure. God, I'm sorry. I was just so eager to make your acquaintance. You see, I have so many questions to ask you. I've read all your articles. I was wondering if I could ask you a question or two."

"Perhaps another time."

"Of course. Follow me."

They left the office and began walking down the corridor that led to the rooms.

"Her fever should break in twenty-four hours. At least I hope so. Just to be extra sure, we'll do an electrocardiogram. But I really don't think there will be complications. As soon as I get the lab results — they told me we were probably dealing with a pretty severe streptococcal infection — I will start the appropriate antibiotics."

Strumwasser opened a door and went in. Verne followed.

Clara lay quietly in her bed. The starched sheet covered her up to the chin. Only her face was exposed.

He stepped toward the bed.

While Dr. Strumwasser continued to inform him in a low voice of the results of his thorough examination, Verne could not help noticing how lovely she was. He was suddenly overwhelmed by emotion and had to catch hold of the bar on the bed.

Each breath she took pulled him forward. He was terrified by the idea that he would fall on top of her and cause injury. But he couldn't help it. It was the price to be paid to life, the cost of the shadow in which he'd lived.

Clara opened her eyes.

He saw that she was smiling at him. He wondered if he would forget all this, if it were not already a memory.

"Well, now, look here! She's come back to life," said Strumwasser from behind in a booming voice. "How are you feeling, Ms. Hastings? We were pretty worried about you, you know."

"A little better," said Clara weakly. "I've . . . put . . . you to a lot of trouble. I'm sorry."

An orderly entered the room to say that Colonel Bradbury was expecting Dr. Verne in the hospital waiting room. Verne smiled at Clara and then turned to Strumwasser.

"I will come to see you in your office after my talk with the colonel. You offered your services. I may take you up on that offer."

Chapter 10

1

"She's suffering from an acute attack of rheumatic fever," Verne said to the colonel, his hands thrust deep into the pocket of his overcoat.

They had just come out of the hospital. The sun was circled by a dark halo.

"Looks bad," said Colonel Bradbury, looking up.

"Actually, it's easy to treat. She should be back on her feet in twenty-four hours. Unless a cardiac condition develops, and while we're on the subject — "

"I was talking about the weather," interrupted Bradbury, laughing. "Doctor, please, I wasn't trying to challenge your diagnosis of Clara Hastings's condition."

Verne said nothing in reply. The man irritated him.

"I have no doubt Hastings will pull through. What worries me is the weather. Snow storm on the way. You would be well advised to get out of here fast. Unless you *want* to be stranded. All the planes will be grounded in a few hours. By the way, you still haven't told me where you're heading from here. If you want to go back to San Francisco, we can have you there in an hour."

Why not San Francisco? thought Verne. Melissa was there, the Institute, friends. Yet he had absolutely no desire to go back.

"What about Clara Hastings?" he asked.

Bradbury took a deep breath.

"I've told you, Dr. Verne, I'm waiting for instructions. In any case — "

"In any case, what?"

"She has completed her mission. Why the concern?"

"Her mission? What are you talking about?"

"Listen to me, Verne. You don't mobilize MID just to provide a setting for a rendezvous. Right?"

Verne was silent.

"Let me do you a favor," the colonel continued, his voice taking on sarcasm. "Hiding the truth isn't going to do me any good. How about if we talk over by that blue spruce over there."

Verne nodded, and they walked for a moment without speaking, their breath making clouds of vapor in the frigid air.

"Down in Wisconsin, there's a blue spruce just like this one," the colonel said. "We used to decorate it at Christmas. Most trees now are made out of that collagenic junk. Whatever happened to non-extrudents?"

Verne thought of Clara. Only yesterday they had taken this same path. He was suddenly remembering the way she walked in snow. She put her toe down first. Her head tilted forward slightly, her attention fixed, as if the simple act of walking was cause enough for deep meditation. He also remembered how serious she looked when she handed him Milner's letter — her expression bespoke participation in some kind of sacrament. There was something childlike about it. Children are often obsessed by ritual, whether playing or eating, and capable of the highest seriousness, higher than any adult.

"Do you have the letter with you?"

"What?"

"Do you have Milner's letter with you?"

"Milner's letter? What do you mean?"

"Come on, Verne. It was the first thing we looked for when Hastings checked into the hospital yesterday morning, after she fainted. We made a photocopy of it before putting it back where we found it. In her bra, I believe. Why so surprised?"

Verne wasn't surprised. As soon as Clara mentioned the letter, he knew Washington would want to know if it contained a secret message. That was why a member of the Network had been given all that help. He also knew it had something to do with Socrates and its connections with resistance organizations. The full resources of the FBI were now being brought to bear on the letter. Maybe they hoped they could use it to crack a code.

They were going to break their backs over that biochemical formula Milner had asked him to give the Chinese scientist. Verne was convinced they would find nothing.

Surely Milner was correct when he wrote that Socrates was a non-political organization. Still, the Hughes Administration had its own reasons. Knowing what was going on in research laboratories had become a matter of the utmost important to the government. It feared independence in the laboratory far more than terrorism in airports and traffic tunnels.

Bradbury could not repress a smile as he watched Verne. He was enjoying this, particularly after what had happened yesterday evening.

"I don't know what to say about your regrettable lack of discretion in reading a private letter from one of my old friends," said Verne finally.

"I understand how you feel. But my job carries obligations. Just like yours. Besides all that philosophical blather, your friend asks you to meet with this Chinese scientist at the U.N. to pass along a formula. He says himself she's in Socrates. We have good reason to suspect that Socrates is a lot more than a group of intellectuals sitting around thinking deep thoughts. For one thing, they share their results with one another before they share them with the authorities. You know as well as I do that any scientific discovery has to be submitted to the government of the country in which it has taken place before it can be sent outside. It's a U.N. resolution."

"Yes, Colonel. And you also know as well as I do that most scientists ignore that resolution. No country has ever indicted anyone for the kind of exchange you're referring to. Freedom of communication is the basis of science. If you enforce that resolution, you condemn us all."

"I'm not so sure. Whatever happens, we're all at the same point as far as SF goes. Things are going to change, Doctor. High time someone looked into what really goes on in those high-powered commissions and labs. Socrates poses a real danger to the State, and the State is our last and best defense against annihilation."

"You've got to be joking, Colonel."

"Listen, Verne, I don't have that much time. You may think I'm joking. I don't really give a shit. I think that our agency, or the FBBS, will figure out what's really going on. We'll decode Socrates' messages — the ones we've already picked up. We will know how Socrates is organized, we will know where it meets, and we will know what its goals are. Only a matter of time, now. Milner's letter is one of our most important catches. That formula."

"It's perfectly ordinary."

"Is it? We'll see about that. I have instructions to let you leave, but the girl from the Network stays. She'll be turned over to the FBBS. I have no idea what they want her for. MID couldn't care less about what happens. Unless — "

"Unless what?"

"I let her go with you."

"And?"

"You tell me what's really in that letter. Milner was doing more than singing his swan song — even if he did live on Bird Cry Street, or whatever it's called. The mission he asked you to perform proves that.

The rest is camouflage. Washington will back me on this. You get her for what you know."

"The problem, Colonel Bradbury, is that that formula is an ordinary RNA sequence and of no interest to you. I'm sorry."

Colonel Bradbury scratched his tonsure. "No, I'm the one who's sorry. I'll be in my office all afternoon if you change your mind."

Verne turned and strode in the direction of the hospital.

2

". . . authorities are still speculating about who might have been responsible for the attack yesterday morning. A well-placed source said the attack was planned and carried out by an elite group from the Network, the self-styled organization of resistance to public health directives. The attackers succeeded in stopping a train bound for San Francisco near Maywood, Nebraska, two hundred miles east of Denver. The reasons behind the act of piracy are still unknown. No damage was done to the train and nothing was taken from it or its passengers. Eyewitnesses are being held in Lincoln while the affair is under investigation. Our reporter has been dispatched to City Hall in Lincoln, and we'll know more after she has contacted the district attorney in charge of the investigation. More details then."

"Yeah, right," Annabelle sneered.

As she did every morning, she had programmed the wall screen for the eight o'clock news. The morning anchor was using her best new-speak to cover the fact that her information came directly from the police. Authorities were trying to figure out how to vaccinate the truth.

The anchor made no reference to Paul Verne, but Annabelle was certain he was the reason for the attack. The whole thing was staged by someone to make it look as if he'd been kidnapped, so that they could put him in touch with Milner's envoy. Were that the case, the Network had definitely scored a point.

She went into the kitchen and voice-commanded another screen, then sat down at the counter to eat her cereal. The anchor now had Remington paintings in the background and was comparing the events in Nebraska to the old Wild West. Annabelle rolled her eyes. News for public consumption.

After the ads came the next item: the storming of the Virginas headquarters in Los Angeles late Saturday night. This time, no detail was lacking. Captain Paul Williams, the L.A. chief of police, was interviewed on the scene, narrating the whole thing with nauseating smugness, Annabelle thought.

Hearing him go on about the strategy employed in the siege, without making any reference to FBBS assistance, Annabelle almost regretted the way the Virginas had been taken. The reporter noted that Loca had so far escaped capture, as had several of her immediate cohorts, and then related the extraordinary double death of the Marshall brothers.

"Calvin Marshall, former Marine, was given his fourth Purple Heart, posthumously, and was buried with full honors in the military cemetery of his native Oakland."

Williams went on to say that his deceased brother, Wesley Marshall, member of the Network, brother to and killer of the deceased hero, was to undergo the Punishment of Ashes. His remains would be scattered in an unknown location.

There were more ads, followed by the SF body count, state by state, as reported by the Center for Disease Control in Atlanta. California and New York were still leading the way. This tolling of the bell was followed by a report from a lab at the National Institutes of Health, where the director was listing all the promising results from the latest medical research on SF.

Annabelle had had enough and called off the screen.

She again tried to reach Mary Peale. No response.

At the Union Station intersection, Annabelle almost rear-ended a truck. She made an obscene gesture at the driver, who looked at her, moonfaced, as she veered down E Street heading west.

Normally she enjoyed walking the mile and a half from her apartment to the FBI building, but this morning she decided to drive her little convertible — which she adored — to work.

She was not in a good mood. Her visit last night to the FBI basement had been a disappointment.

Everything had gone according to plan. She gave the money to Bill Morgan. He and his friend were waiting for her at precisely ten P.M. at Hoover. The guard put their cards through the control and let them pass without so much as a look.

Annabelle knew that if the direction didn't already know about her little nighttime raid they soon would. Her excuses for investigating Lombard's past would be worthless. As the assistant to the director of FBBS, Annabelle had, at least in theory, the right to demand the cooperation of Morgan and Haldane. They would get off with a reprimand. In her case, things would be different. She was playing her trump card. Either she would succeed in toppling Claudia Lombard, or she would be a good candidate for an assignment in the Alaskan back-and-beyond.

The trio had begun by stopping at Morgan's office. They'd split up. Annabelle waited by herself while her accomplices keyed first into the main bank, and then into the top-secret personnel files. Morgan came to get her and ushered her into an office with a terminal where the name "Claudia Lombard" glowed on the screen.

"You're all set. You press here to open the file, this one to scroll, this one to exit. All we could get you was a half-hour. After that the system goes into automatic alert, and security will ask to see your warrant. Best not to complicate things. Half an hour ought to do it, right? Another thing — no copies. It's against regulations. Call me if you finish early. I'm right next door."

Annabelle spent the full half-hour in the Lombard file. She went through everything: testimony to Congress, photos, personal statements. By the end she knew a good number of things about Lombard that she had not known before — her tastes, favorite places, the trajectory of her career.

The file contained very little about the Sullivan business, which had affected Lombard only indirectly.

Claudia's father, Peter Lombardi, had been the personal counselor and right-hand man to the senator from Indiana for three years. Lombardi was in Canada the day his boss was found dead.

The coroner's report showed that Vincent Sullivan had died from an overdose of sleeping pills. He left a letter in which he made it clear what he was going to do, though without explanation why.

Still, there were troubling details. The preceding afternoon, the senator had played a round of golf with one of his closest friends, Senator Calwell of Mississippi. According to Calwell's testimony, Sullivan had seemed in good spirits. Moreover, Calwell had affirmed that during play Sullivan had mentioned a memorandum he had been preparing that he hoped to deliver before the full Senate in the next few days. Frances Mason, the Senate majority leader, was stunned to learn about the memorandum when questioned about it. It was the first she had heard of it.

Nothing was discovered among the deceased's papers. His wife confirmed that her husband had been working on something that had occupied nearly all of his time, but said he wouldn't talk about it. No, she had not been aware of any depressive tendencies on his part.

The final — though by no means the least significant — bit of curiosity was that Sullivan was alone the night of his suicide. His two housekeepers were gone: one was on vacation, and the other had been picked up on the street that day and mistakenly arrested in connection with a robbery. That same day, the senator's wife was hospitalized for a minor operation. Peter Lombardi's alibi was absolutely solid — he was in Ottawa. A year later he was dead.

Annabelle did find one thing that made her heart skip a beat. For a second she thought it might be what she was looking for: the file mentioned that Peter Lombardi had established his reputation as a lawyer of considerable ability through his brilliant defense of Michael Engelhardt, in a tax-evasion case brought by the federal government. Engelhardt was acquitted. But on reflection it seemed less important to Annabelle — plenty of lawyers defended the Mafia. That was just part of being a lawyer.

For the second time in twelve hours, Annabelle drove into the Hoover parking garage and pulled into her space.

She all but snarled at a secretary who greeted her in the elevator. The idea of finding herself on the receiving end of hysterical reproaches from the FBBS director completely depressed her. She could only cherish the hope that Lombard would be too preoccupied with the incredible news about the train attack to bother with her. But that, she knew, was wishful thinking.

Annabelle decided that if her boss was in Black's office, she would compose a terse letter of resignation, get her things together, and walk out the door. If she could only get away so easily.

The secretary raised his nose from his screen when Annabelle came into the office anteroom.

"Oh, Ms. Weaver! Director Black has been asking for you. He wants you to join him in his office."

Director Black? Lombard was supposed to be with the director, thought Annabelle. Unless . . .

"Where's the boss?" she snapped.

"No one has seen her this morning and she's not at home."

"You mean she hasn't come into the office?"

That was a first. Normally she should have come to her office before joining Black. Annabelle could not imagine her going directly to a meeting with the director. Something was wrong.

"Call his office and tell them I'm on my way."

Annabelle took the elevator to the sixth floor. A guard stood outside the door. She went through the weapons detector and into Black's secretary's office. There she found Larry Walton, a slender man with precise manners and a dark suit.

"Weaver," he said in an affected tone, "could you wait for a moment? The director will see you shortly."

He rose and disappeared through a door.

Annabelle was impressed. She had encountered the FBI director only rarely. She was not even sure he knew who she was.

Walton reappeared and signaled her to follow.

The office she found herself in was straight out of the last century — the 1930s, to be precise, Annabelle thought — and was huge. A broad terrace ran the length of it, and from the windows there was a stunning view of Pennsylvania Avenue with the Capitol dome gleaming in the morning sun.

"Please sit down, Weaver."

Black's legs were crossed, and reading glasses were perched on his nose. He was busy flipping through a folder. He waved at a chair without looking up.

"Be with you in a second."

Annabelle looked at him. She was instantly conscious of how imposing a man he was. She had never before felt intimidated by a man.

Black put the folder down on a low table, ran his fingers through his thinning, carefully combed hair, and began to observe Annabelle with unwavering blue eyes.

Son of a bitch is trying to rattle me, she thought, determined she wouldn't let him know he'd succeeded. She wished she had worn pants.

Annabelle crossed her legs and turned away from his look. Hanging from the wall was a painting depicting a cheerful countryside viewed from above, with a human form falling from the sky.

"The Fall of Icarus," said Black. "You know the story, of course."

Annabelle knew the story as well as anyone. She hesitated for a fraction of a second before shaking her head.

"No? You surprise me. A man builds wings for himself and his son Icarus so that they can escape captivity. He attaches the feathers with wax. Icarus flies too close to the sun, which melts the wax, and he plummets to his death. An object lesson for us all. Do you know Michael Engelhardt?"

The question that came without missing a beat startled Annabelle. Her mind raced. Pure coincidence? In two days, the capo's name had come up twice. First the secret meeting between Sherman and Engelhardt, which she had decided to keep from her boss, and then Lombard's file.

She cleared her throat. "You mean the Mafia capo?"

"That is precisely who I mean."

"I have heard of him, yes."

Black folded his fingers, his elbows resting on the arms of the chair.

"An extraordinary man. I will tell you something about him that perhaps you don't know."

The tone of Black's voice turned professorial. Annabelle had heard that about him.

"Would you care for a carbonated Cocaid?"

He'd surprised her again. "Uh, thank you, no."

Black's eyes sharpened. "Don't say no on my account. I am aware of Lombard's stance on the beverage, but I personally see no reason why it shouldn't be consumed. Are you sure you wouldn't care — "

"If you insist."

"Quite happily."

He leaned over and spoke gently into a microphone built into the armrest.

Annabelle knew that everything was being monitored and recorded.

She began to relax. What she had most feared had not happened — and the subject of her trip to New York had not come up at all.

She noted that the FBI director wore a gold signet ring with a yellow diamond on the pinkie of his left hand.

The thought that Black might be gay came to her, and she had to suppress a smile. At that moment he fixed her with a look of such coldness that she felt paralyzed.

Larry Walton came in carrying a tray. He put a bottle in front of Annabelle, together with a glass with a mint leaf and some ice cubes. Wordless, he glided out.

"You won't have something?"

"Thank you, no."

For the first time, she noticed a glimmer of a smile. He was using his whole arsenal. Watching someone cave in under an icy stare was an old trick.

She took a big gulp of the drink.

"Michael Engelhardt was born outside of Chicago, the son of immigrant parents. His father became a foreman at a local factory. Michael took to the streets young and gained a reputation. At age fifteen he bludgeoned a rival to death with a steel pipe. Three years in juvenile detention, that was all, and when he got out he joined the army and volunteered for a branch carrying out CIA directives in Central America. Do you follow me?"

"Closely." Her favorite drink was already both sharpening and lightening her reflexes amazingly.

"That was where he made the acquaintance of Juan Meyer, the cocaine dealer who worked the U.S.-Colombia route. You may remember that Meyer died a number of years ago trying to break out of prison. He trained Engelhardt, taught his protégé everything about cocaine — from harvest to refining to transportation, and then how to launder the money, use connections, bribe public officials, and so forth. He did a first-rate job.

"At the time Meyer was picked up in Rio Negro, many were convinced Engelhardt had betrayed him — that was very much his style — but there was no proof. Anyway, Meyer was extradited to the U.S. from South America and was killed during his transfer from Florida to Illinois, where he was wanted in connection with some robbery that took place years earlier. That was before the courts in Colombia stopped extraditing narcotraffickers — mostly because the local Mafia was pressuring them. Michael Engelhardt went on to become one of the biggest *padroni* in the business."

Black rose out of his chair and walked over to the window.

Annabelle knew that now he would get to the nub. Her worries were over. She wouldn't be here if he didn't have some use for her.

"Since the discovery of Sacred Fire leaders worldwide have met frequently to discuss the conditions necessary to gain back control of their countries. An enormous amount of work was done in a short time. The basic elements of what became the Fuchs Amendment came together. Nathan Gray was able to put them into execution almost immediately.

"For political leaders, the necessity for widespread implantation of the ASP was slowed by the accompanying necessity to outlaw alcohol. You may be familiar with the secondary effects of alcohol on the cerebral metabolism of ASP wearers. Prohibition posed the most difficult problems — the way it was ingrained in our national consciousness as a needless exercise in morality. Do you follow me?"

"Of course."

"To avoid drama, something was needed to replace alcohol, something that had the same psychological and physiological effects, but that didn't cause . . . problems. Tests demonstrated cocaine was the best alternative. Not only does it not cause those unpleasant sensations, but in the long run, it has the capacity to reinforce the inhibiting effect the implant has upon sexual functions."

"A very positive side effect."

"As you say. We had expected cocaine substitution would involve a massive effort of imagination and organizational will — at every level. Producing it in liquid form was decided upon very early for the simple reason that it is easier to monitor the dosage levels. Measures needed to be taken to oversee production. The powers of the FDA increased exponentially because of the responsibility."

Why was this lesson in contemporary history necessary? Annabelle wondered.

"The organization of cocaine production in the early years of legality," continued Black, "was not without major problems, particularly in the form of competition from former suppliers. But those problems were greatly relieved by the widespread implantation of the ASP. Holland is a good example. After the government refused to legalize cocaine, the riots were widespread. Six thousand were killed, give or take. That number is highly confidential, by the way."

Annabelle knew the director was touching on the problems the government had had with the Mafia after the families lost control of the cocaine market. The fall in the price of the drug had forced them to look for more lucrative commodities. The Waikiki Agreement, which involved the Japanese and the American organizations, was part of a new attempt to internationalize the syndicates, just when disharmony among the sisterhood of nations could not have been greater.

"The paradox of all this, today," Black continued, "is that the Mafia finds itself once again in the position of fighting Prohibition. By trafficking in alcohol, they put all sociopolitical organizations that were in a position to fight SF in danger. Another paradox is that the new Prohibition's strongest opposition comes from women, who feel their fundamental rights are compromised. While we're on the subject," said Black, looking straight at Annabelle, "what is your position?"

"I prefer coke," she replied, "as you might have guessed."

She didn't want to be drawn into a debate, although she was thinking about the Worshipers of the Sacred Fire, mostly men, who advocated the systematic release of an ASP discharge using alcohol to put themselves closer to the godhead. A ticket to paradise. The latest statistics collected by the FBBS suggested that four million men were worshiping. Four million!

"The suppression of the alcohol market became an absolute necessity," said Black. "Legislative action is being studied by the Senate that proposes, among other things, that publicity for Cocaid products be underwritten by public health departments. Anyway, the situation today is that we are basically at war against the Mafia and the Waikiki Cartel, as the Americans and the Japanese named their organization after their agreement. Are you with me?"

"Yes, Director Black. But I was thinking..."

She stopped herself.

"No," he said with a half-smile. "Please go on."

"I was thinking of Joseph Milner's letter."

"In what relation?"

"If I've grasped the significance of what happened over this last weekend, the letter got away from us. Lombard confirmed to me that Socrates is directly involved. Socrates is an organization with international connections, like the Cartel, which you haven't mentioned. I began wondering if they aren't connected in some manner."

"The Cartel and Socrates?"

"Yes, sir."

Black took a handkerchief from his pocket and began wiping his fingers with it, one after the other. Annabelle watched in fascination.

"An interesting suggestion," he said finally. "It had not crossed my mind, but I think it has real merit. I'll put someone on that."

Black continued not to mention Lombard.

"Perhaps it would be a good idea to pass the word along to Director Lombard," said Annabelle, deciding to go for it. She had finished her bottle of Cocaid.

Black raised his eyebrows.

"Ah. You may not see her anytime soon," he said, finally.

"Has something happened?"

The question had an urgency that seemed to annoy Black.

"According to information that arrived this morning, Engelhardt is in Washington."

"But what — "

"Engelhardt never leaves his territory unless he has a very good reason," continued Black, ignoring the interruption. "I understand that he dislikes the climate here."

Annabelle was about to pull out the stops. If Lombard had talked to Black over the weekend, she was screwed. She breathed in slowly.

"And to think that Engelhardt had a meeting with Kess Sherman just two days ago," she said with emphasis.

This time, Black's surprise was indisputably genuine.

"What are you telling me?"

Annabelle gave a quick recap of what she'd heard from Robert Kane about their meeting.

"Sherman ended up taking refuge at the headquarters of the Virginas, which is where he was eventually arrested."

"Now *this* is fascinating ."

The director was clearly shaken. He had not talked to Lombard.

"And you believe that Engelhardt wanted to talk to the head of the Network?" asked Black.

"So it seems to me, sir."

"No one has mentioned this to me. What could Engelhardt want with those misguided idealists? It makes no sense. You spoke to Lombard about this?"

Annabelle knew the moment had come.

"Yes, over the weekend. I had intended to see her this morning to — "

"Impossible," interrupted Black. "She has disappeared."

"Disappeared? I don't follow."

"She was kidnapped. The uniform guarding the front of the house was found in the bushes. As were the two FBBS agents. All eliminated in the same fashion."

"And . . . Director Lombard?"

"No trace. The murders all carried the same trademark, that of the Yakuza, the Japanese Mafia."

"The Cartel kidnapped Lombard?"

"That is what I think."

"So Engelhardt — "

"I believe he is responsible."

"But why? I don't get it. Is he planning to blackmail us?"

"Perhaps. One thing is certain, and that is that Engelhardt wants something. We're doing everything we can to find out what it is. The problem is that strategically we are not in the best of positions. Engelhardt has all the means to create a scandal." He hesitated before he continued. "Director Lombard has been maintaining contacts with him for a number of years."

Annabelle averted her eyes. What she had been looking for in Lombard's file last night was true, and since confirmation came directly from Black, the news had obvious implications. It suggested he wanted to form an alliance against Lombard. Her disappearance had started all this. Could Black be worried about something? Did the Mafia have something on him? That seemed impossible.

"Having said that," Black added, "I also think that you know more than you let on. Am I wrong?"

Annabelle knew there was no point in holding back.

"I take it you are referring to my nocturnal visit to the files."

"Precisely. What was it you hoped to find, if I may ask?"

"First, let me say that I knew you would be told of my action."

"Go on."

"I learned that Lombard's father had been Engelhardt's lawyer in a tax case in which he was very nearly indicted."

"That is correct," Black said. "Your conclusions?"

"I wondered if this story had been brought to the attention of the Senate Confirmation Committee, or if it had been removed from the record. If the latter, Lombard would have been a possible subject to pressure, even blackmail perhaps."

"And — "

"It wasn't the case. The case was there in black and white. Since the Committee decided not to pursue the matter further, I thought I'd seen enough."

Black laced his fingers and cracked the knuckles.

"Well, you were wrong."

"Sir?"

"The Committee had to write the story off because of lack of evidence. The Committee was also presided over by a friend of Lombard's. So you see — "

Annabelle couldn't help interrupting. "You mean the Mafia played a role in nominating Claudia Lombard to run the FBBS?"

Black laughed.

"Slow down, Weaver. I'm the one who nominated Claudia Lombard. If you knew your boss better, you would know that she is not the kind of person who would compromise herself to any great extent with anyone."

That, Annabelle thought, has yet to be established. She resolved to push ahead with her own investigation.

"As soon as Engelhardt contacts us," Black continued, "I want you to meet with him, or whoever speaks for him. Above all, we have to get Lombard back. You are going to serve as my liaison. You are not to talk about this to anyone else," he said in conclusion, "and most definitely not to your young friend in the State Department. I forget her name."

"Mary Peale," said Annabelle in as neutral a voice as she could muster.

"Mary Peale, yes. And always carry some communication device with you. I want to be in touch with you at any hour of the night or day." He sighed deeply. "That will be all, Weaver."

He spoke to the armrest. Larry Walton entered.

Annabelle knew Black's factotum hadn't missed a syllable of the whole conversation. She rose and followed Walton out of the office.

Annabelle could barely contain her elation. The tables had turned. Lombard was no longer a danger. If and when the boss was freed — well, then she would see. She had time to prepare.

She was going to have Kess Sherman sent to Washington. She wanted to know what he had been doing in Engelhardt's stronghold to begin with. Perhaps that would give her something she could use.

Then, like a ripple on a pond, a memory drifted by. Several weeks earlier, she had noticed in the paper that the late Senator Sullivan's widow, Susan, had appeared on a list of dignitaries offering their support to a philanthropic project to help children afflicted with SF.

She needed to find her.

Chapter 11

1

Sacred Fire had decimated communities in the western parts of Marin County — refuge to every counterculture for more than half a century. Yet in the backwaters of the county still lived the artisans, writers, musicians, gurus, jewelry makers, and leather workers; with them lived all the earliest incarnations of the established cults — the New Agers, Returners, environmentalist radicals, and, of course, Worshipers and Apocalyptics.

West Marin had long been on the frontlines of the epidemic. The "sustainable communities" north of San Francisco, which carried on the sturdiest of all American traditions — the mentality of the frontier — huddled together for protection. Scores had died, whole families were wiped out. Survivors carried only the shadowy remains of utopian dreams lovingly created at the dawn of each new age. Most stayed, to wait out the siege and wait for hope to return.

Despite what one might have expected from communities where anarchic traditions were so firmly anchored, few men had resisted ASP implantation. In fact, Marin men had been among the first to sacrifice their sexuality, acutely conscious of their responsibility to check the progress of SFV. Progressively communal educational traditions permitted them to absorb children from the CAEs with comparative ease.

Religious allusions became more pronounced than they ever had been, and Apocalyptic Millenarianism continued in full force. Zen also enjoyed a healthy revival, as did the Hindu cults popular in the old days. Some found Tibetan Buddhism better suited to an age in which suffering and physical pain were the major preoccupations. In sweet synchronicity, the exercises of transcendental meditation coexisted with the most pronounced expressions of Judeo-Christian traditions so dear to American mythology.

In this way the microsocieties of west Marin would doubtless have adjusted to the New Resignation, if, when the Fuchs Amendment had begun to be vigorously enforced, the true designs of the Eastern Government had not become clear. It wasn't a question of health; it was a matter of power. "Read your Orwell," people said grimly to each other.

The first signs of revolt took some time to manifest themselves. But when they did, police reprisal was swift and sure. The libertarian reputation these communities maintained meant the authorities had already been observing them warily. Nerves frayed on both sides and tension mounted.

It was a simple drug deal that hardened opposition. One day, perhaps as an excuse to assert their authority, the FBBS, FBI, FDA, and DEA began a systematic hunt for marijuana producers in the region. By so doing they went right at one of the oldest traditions in west Marin. Planes equipped with infrared cameras photographed the entire region, enabling agents to use spectroscopic analysis to locate the exact places it was being grown. House searches, raids of public places, and arrests followed in rapid succession. No longer outraged, people were enraged.

Not that marijuana enjoyed anything like the popularity it had during the golden age of California. In fact, most residents of west Marin had long since given up using mild drugs. It was a question, rather, of what it represented, the freedoms it stood for.

Cocaine and its derivatives had come to represent the technocracy, a pure product of the power of money. Growing dope, on the other hand, was viewed nostalgically as a craft; marijuana itself was regarded the way dandelion wine used to be — a home remedy. Anybody could grow it on their balcony and in their garden.

Moreover, people learned that marijuana consumption had no more deleterious effect on the ASP wearer than did cocaine. If smoking it was a crime, it was said, that was only because the government couldn't control production. Folk songs on the subject came back into fashion.

When cocaine beverages were legalized to replace alcohol there was a general outcry. Inhabitants began questioning the truth of government proclamations. For some men of west Marin, the desire to rediscover the freedoms of their bodies had become the most potent instigator for revolt. For others, it was their opinion about the effects of cocaine versus marijuana.

Soon enough, Marin gave rise to one of the most radical wings of the Network. Within several months, the majority of the county inhabitants were involved. At first they put up posters and flyers (FUCK FUCHS! FUCHS FUCKS!) or offered safe haven to someone being sought by the FBBS. Soon the resistance methods became more violent: shootings, destruction of government property, and so on.

Their eyes were opened. Fuchs was nothing but mind control.

Following their marriage, Paul and Melissa Verne settled in Inverness, in Marin County. They fit into the community with surprising ease. No one seemed to resent Paul for having discovered SF or, even more surprisingly, for being a member of the Commission. The tolerance of the region, combined with Verne's own reputation for honesty and integrity, permitted the couple to be accepted into the community. Not into all its secrets, however. A tacit agreement existed between them and their neighbors — that they would never discuss their work, neither at the Rosemary (at Point Reyes, where the Vernes went on Sundays to have brunch) nor at the parties, get-togethers, or barbecues to which they were invited. It was something of a miracle that trust had never been lost and that the bonds of friendship had grown so strong.

Which was why Melissa was not surprised on Monday morning when she saw Tim Lamar coming up the front walk. Lamar lived in a house on stilts he had built himself on the edge of Tomales Bay.

Toby began barking with joyous enthusiasm. Melissa went outside to greet Tim. The fog had lifted and was moving south toward Stinson Beach.

"Hey, Mel, good to see you," Tim said, squeezing her arm.

"Come in, Tim," she said, turning her back to hide her confusion at the physical contact. "Nice of you to come over."

Tim was about thirty-eight. Tall and well built, he had curly red hair, blue eyes, and an open face. He always wore jeans and a plaid shirt, sleeves rolled up above the elbows revealing muscular arms.

"You're lucky to catch me here," she said behind him, crossing the living room. "Normally I'd be down at the Institute."

"I was passing through the valley. Actually, um, Mel, I came to see Paul. Is he around?"

"No, he's not. How about some tea?"

"I'd love some."

From the terrace it was a straight drop down to Tomales Bay, which ran for fifteen miles along a northwest-southeast axis.

From the other side of the bay, toward the east, herds of cows nibbled the grass on the rolling hillsides, which formed a sharp contrast to the thick conifer forests of Point Reyes National Park, in the middle of which the Vernes had built their house.

The ocean was about a mile west, across the edge of the park. There was a forest and an immense plain covered with tall grass that sloped gently down to the Pacific. From afar, under the line of the horizon, the ocean seemed little more than an extension of the sky — the same grays mixed with barely distinguishable colors — bordered by the irregular festoons of Limantour Beach. Toward the north was Kings Point — Point Reyes — and Drake Bay.

Melissa played with a fossil she and Paul had picked up at the foot of the cliffs at Sculptured Beach — the rust-colored skeleton of a fish only a few inches long but millions of years old.

Wearing T-shirt and jeans, she was lying on a mattress in a corner of the terrace. Tim sat in a cane chair with his legs apart, picking his teeth with a wooden match. On the ground, on a tray, were the remains of breakfast. The silence between them was occasionally broken by the cry of sparrows whipping by.

"Mel, I really need to see Paul. It's important. Where is he?"

Melissa tried to respond, but all she could produce were sobs.

"Melissa, good God, what's the matter? Can't you tell me?"

"Yes, I can tell you. I'm not feeling well. That's what's wrong."

Tim got up.

"I've got a joint in my car."

"Tim, no. All it does is depress me."

"This time it will do you some good."

Melissa stubbed out the joint. For the first time in two days she felt herself relax and yield to the warming caresses of the sun.

Tim had been right, but it was so pitiful — smoking a joint at her age. And this sudden ludicrous lucidity — she wanted to melt into the luminous immensity of the scenery around her.

"Why do you need to see Paul? Can't you talk to me?"

"I can talk to you. But I would have preferred to talk to him."

He paused. "It's about the ASP. A friend of mine told me they had discovered a way of replacing it with a fake one."

"Fake?"

"Yes. The AS checkpoints couldn't tell it from a real ASP. Can you imagine what that would mean?"

Melissa was fond of Tim. He was a gifted sculptor who worked on pieces of sequoia he found on the beach. Most of his pieces were of men in hats. All sorts of men — he let the shape and the grain of the wood guide him — wearing cloche hats that came down to the eyebrows. The sculptures were all sizes, some without legs or torsos, sometimes wearing ties. Their totemic rigidity made her think a little of the sculptures on Easter Island. His work gave the same impression of indestructibility. Yet the material had once been living cells.

Although Melissa was a great admirer of Tim and his work, she also knew that he had trouble expressing himself — his language was simple, and his facial expressions and gestures a little exaggerated. He had once kissed her.

"How's your work going?" she ventured, to break the silence.

Tim smiled.

"I just finished my *Man with Hat #83*. Mel, you haven't said anything. Is a thing like that possible or not?"

"The fake ASP. That's what you want to ask Paul?"

"Yes. Don't you see? The FBBS couldn't control our lives. We would be free. Free to make love."

"Free to die of SF," she said dryly.

Tim didn't reply.

"When you say 'we,' are you referring to the Network?" she asked.

The expression on Tim's face hardened a little.

"Melissa, all I want to know is, can a fake ASP exist?"

"Why not? It's always possible to undo what technology has done. It wouldn't be easy, and it would require skill, time, and money. Why can't you tell me what this is all about?"

Tim glanced around him, as if he were afraid someone was listening.

"One of our people was arrested in L.A."

"You mean Kess Sherman? The news about that attack on the Virginas headquarters is everywhere, Tim."

"He was supposed to meet someone about a fake ASP. That was when he was picked up by the Virginas. Whoever he met claimed he could make fake ASPs, and he called it a NOX, N-O-X — non-operating-ASP — and he wanted to offer it to us. Now we don't know how to proceed. All we can do is wait."

"Who was the person he met with?" asked Melissa.

"I don't know. Seriously." He laughed, then added, "OK, I know. But I can't tell you."

"Aha!"

"Look, it's not my business. I was just wondering if Paul had ever heard of the NOX — you know, since he's on the Commission and everything."

"I doubt it, Tim. He would have mentioned it to me. Anyway — " She stopped.

"Mel, tell me what's wrong."

"Paul isn't coming back," she blurted out.

"Where is he?"

"What does it matter where he is? I don't know. When he found out Joe Milner was dead he decided to take a train back to San Francisco instead of flying. He told me he needed time to think things over. This morning he called again. His voice was completely different; he was jumpy and evasive. He told me he wasn't going to come back. He had something he had to do. It doesn't make sense, any of it. He's abandoning me and the Institute right when we need him the most."

She started to cry. "Why? Why is he doing this?" she managed through her tears.

"He has to have his reasons," Tim said. "Get a hold of yourself. I'm sure he'll be back."

"No, he's not coming back. I can *feel* it."

"What makes you think so? He didn't say that, did he?"

"He did! He said, 'You know that I love you' — "

"And because he said 'You know that I love you,' you think — "

"That is exactly what I think. Don't you get it? He means he doesn't love me!"

The phone hummed. She picked it up without thinking and wiped her eyes. It was Margaret Brittain.

"Melissa? Have you got a cold or something?"

"Yes . . . a cold."

"Listen, Melissa, I just left Chamberlain's office, and I'm afraid the news is not good. Chamberlain is furious with Paul, and his not being at the Institute when I visited didn't help. In fact, he's decided to remove him as director."

"But — "

"He's thinking of putting Doris Hathaway in charge."

Melissa's eyes cleared immediately.

"You can't be serious! That would mean the end of the Institute."

"You're being overdramatic. Doris has her good points. On the other hand, I am aware that her rapport with the research staff isn't great — I know how attached they are to Verne. That's where you come in."

"Me?'

"Yes, you. Chamberlain happens to think highly of you."

"What are you talking about?"

"Well . . . I was wondering why you couldn't be a candidate for director."

"Me?"

"Yes. You."

"But that's not possible."

"Of course it's possible. Think, Melissa. You are perfectly capable of doing the job. Chamberlain would save face — because he would have his way with Verne. Yet the Institute wouldn't be stuck with Hathaway.

He's not an idiot, you know. He realized the danger of appointing Hathaway. And besides — "

"Besides?"

"The idea amuses him — um, *appeals* to him."

"Amuses him?"

"Shit, I let the cat out. OK, maybe it's for the best. He will agree if you accept it. He's convening the board immediately."

"This is sheer lunacy! Whose idea was it?"

"Mine."

Melissa didn't know how to respond. She knew that no one on the staff would stomach Hathaway as director.

"I have to talk to Paul first," she said firmly.

"I understand."

"But I'll think about it. Call me tomorrow."

"Melissa?" Brittain paused for effect. "Take it!"

"I told you I would think about it. Good-bye."

Melissa switched off and got up. She went to the edge of the terrace.

"They just offered me the directorship of the Institute," she said to Tim without looking at him.

"Paul's job?"

"Yes, Paul's job."

Tim said nothing. Melissa stared out at the sky, then, as if she were talking to herself, she continued, "You know, as I've gotten older I've had the same feeling the rest of the world has that nothing is eternal. But it's been an intuition, not a certainty. When you wake up in the morning you're sure that the person next to you loves you, that the road to work still goes there, that dogs still bark, that birds still fly, that trees are still green. And then everything changes. The person lying next to you is a stranger. The trees are blue, the dogs sing requiems, the birds crawl on the ground, and the road to work suddenly doesn't go there anymore. You can't even breathe air like before. You can take nothing for granted. You realize that you have always known that one day it would all change. Well, that day is here. Nothing is the same. Everything is different."

2

Strumwasser looked in the rearview mirror. The gleaming grill of the truck had disappeared from his field of vision.

At that instant a horn blasted from the left side with a force that nearly pushed him off the road. Like some enormous howling beast, the truck roared past the ambulance at top speed and, in a final vent of fury, flooded the windshield with a glutinous mixture of salt and mud.

Strumwasser considered pulling over, he was shaking so much. It was always the same. The minute he got behind the controls, all the vehicles he came upon were so many prehistoric monsters animated with but one single desire: to crush him like a bug. Maybe it was his enormous glasses that were at fault.

Maybe everything would be much better if he only agreed to have an operation for his myopia. But Strumwasser had long been convinced that he would die under anaesthesia. He would much rather see death coming head-on.

"That one really had it in for you," said Verne from the backseat.

"Did you see that? Incredible! It wasn't just me, was it? I'm driving at forty miles an hour and — "

"That may be why he was so furious. You're going too fast for him to pass, but too slow for him to stay behind you."

Cautiously, Strumwasser turned the ambulance at the exit marked North Platte.

"I wasn't going to drive any faster with the roads slippery like this. We only had to go ten miles on the Interstate. Just my luck to come across that monster."

He stopped at the intersection with Route 83, which went straight across the flatlands.

Not a tree in sight. The snow-covered expanse was empty except for a few immense grain silos on the horizon. A sign read NORTH PLATTE - 5 MILES. The afternoon light had turned milky, enveloping everything in a layer of fluorescent gauze.

"The snow'll be starting any minute."

"We'd better stop in town," Strumwasser said. "I could ask — "

"No," replied Verne. "Too risky. The colonel would have no trouble tracking us. Let's go on to Thedford, just as we'd planned, even if it takes four hours to do the fifty miles. Do you need to refuel?"

"We'll need to in North Platte. How's our patient?"

"She's fine," a small voice replied from the back.

In his rearview mirror, Strumwasser could see only a mass of brown hair spread out on the white sheets of the stretcher. On the other hand, he could see Paul Verne — who was sitting next to the young woman — quite well.

Strumwasser wasn't worried for himself. Sure, he risked early retirement. When the colonel interrogated him, he would simply say that

Clara Hastings's condition necessitated taking her to General Hospital in Lincoln. Or Denver. Denver would be even simpler. He knew the chief of medical services there.

But what would he say to the colonel when he asked him why he personally had had to go along?

"You look like you're enjoying this," said Verne.

"You know, I am. I just hope that the colonel doesn't come back before 1500 hours."

"The snowstorm will keep us beyond their reach for a while. Without it, we would already have been spotted by their chopper."

The colonel's departure on a routine mission had been a stroke of pure luck. The officer who replaced him during his absence was below Strumwasser in rank, which facilitated things considerably.

When Verne had come to ask his help to get Clara Hastings out, Strumwasser's first reflex had been to refuse. Not from fear, but because at first glance the plan didn't seem workable. Still, he found the energy with which Verne tried to convince him fascinating, and slowly he changed his mind.

The more he listened to Verne, the more sure he became that he was listening to the voice of pure conviction. Behind Verne's genius — his discoveries — was passion, his unrelenting and uncompromising desire to leave his mark on human events. Strumwasser decided to break out of the comfortable little space of his life, to join the ranks of the revolutionary. Verne offered him the unique opportunity of a great adventure.

Strumwasser quickly sketched a plan: as a patient, Clara Hastings was technically under his command, and, should he so choose, he could have her sent to General Hospital in Lincoln. Strumwasser would tell the guards that he wanted to accompany the patient. Because of the storm, they could seek shelter with a minister friend of Strumwasser's who lived in Thedford, a small town about seventy-five miles from the base. There, Clara could take a day or two to get back on her feet.

The officer temporarily in charge in Colonel Bradbury's absence tried vainly to argue with Strumwasser but ultimately had little choice except to countersign the order allowing the prisoner to be transferred. He didn't care about Verne, who was free to do as he wished.

The ambulance passed more enormous grain silos, then crossed the frozen South Platte River. The first houses of North Platte began to appear.

Several minutes later, they were in the middle of a town that looked as if time had left it virtually untouched. There was still a town square with a snow-covered gazebo — First Bank, stores, white-steepled churches. A few cars were parked on the street, and one or two muffled inhabitants struggled by.

"Pull up in front of that convenience store," Verne said. "We're going to need some food. I haven't eaten since last night."

Strumwasser stopped the ambulance and Verne got out.

"You two seem to know each other better than you're letting on," Strumwasser said to Clara.

"I met Dr. Verne for the first time yesterday at the base," Clara said warily. "What makes you think we met before?"

"I don't know. It just seems like — well, that there's some kind of intimacy."

"No," Clara said, a little heatedly. She let her head fall on the pillow.

"Don't be upset, Ms. Hastings. I'm doing all I can to help."

"Yes, I know," Clara replied, without raising her head. "But I don't see what you're driving at."

"Well, something here intrigues me. If what you say is true — not that I don't I believe you — then I'm wondering why you seem to be so — so intimate with this man."

"Why do you keep using that old-fashioned term, 'intimate'?"

"Maybe it is the wrong word. But seems to me Verne has a way of making people see things they normally don't. He . . . shakes things up. There's something appealing about it. I imagine his friends are very attached to him. And probably his enemies, too. Here he comes."

Verne got into the ambulance and slammed the door.

"We have to move," he said to Strumwasser. "Fast."

"What?"

"You heard me. I think we've been spotted."

Strumwasser pulled out.

"Look," said Verne.

A uniform emerged from the grocery store. When he saw the ambulance pull off, he spoke into a portable.

"We should have known that someone might alert the police," said Verne. "Now he'll know that we're not heading toward Lincoln, but taking 83 north. Step on it, Strumwasser. I'll take over when we're at the edge of town."

The major accelerated. No one seemed to be following.

"At Stapleton we'll take a detour through Tryon," he said. "That's about twenty-five miles off. We can take a back road that heads west. It's a little longer, but maybe — "

"Good idea," said Verne. "Take it."

"Maybe that uniform was just verifying something. Could be it had nothing to do with us."

"Maybe. But we should play it safe."

The last houses of North Platte were slipping behind them. They crossed the North Platte River, which joined its twin a few miles to the east. Strumwasser was worried. If they had been seen, taking Verne and Hastings to the minister was a bad idea. If they took the Tryon route they had another fifty or sixty miles to go.

"Shit," he suddenly exclaimed. "We're in trouble."

"What?"

"We forgot to refuel. We don't have enough gas to get us to Thedford."

"What about Stapleton?"

"I don't know. I'm not even sure we'll get that far. I can't locate it on the computer."

"Pull over," Verne ordered. "I'll drive."

Strumwasser pulled over and got out of the ambulance. The air was frigid. To the north, the horizon had disappeared altogether. He shivered. For the first time he wondered if he would survive his adventure.

"The storm's just about on top of us," he said.

Somehow Verne was managing to keep the ambulance on the road, but he was driving mainly on intuition. He felt as if a chemical reaction was taking place inside his head, fusing his optical nerves. The gray luminescence seemed to come from the bottom of the universe — light that was darker than dark.

Verne tried squinting. Out of the corner of his eye he could catch the line of electric poles that whipped past at regular intervals, like the vibrations of a cello string being plucked.

He was dimly aware of music playing in his head — the music of mental strain and, in the eerie light, the regular cadence of the poles.

"Do you know Beethoven's sixteenth quartet?" he suddenly asked, without taking his eyes off the shadow theater playing out before him.

"Yes," came a weak voice. Clara's. Strumwasser was sound asleep.

"How are you feeling?" Verne asked, trying to sound clinical.

"My joints feel better, and my throat's OK now. I think I'm still running a fever. Strumwasser's treatment seems to be working." She paused. "Will we get through all this?"

"I can't say. We're nearly out of fuel. The worst of the storm is still ahead of us."

"Talk to me about the Sixteenth Quartet."

"It was Beethoven's last quartet. He died only a few months after he finished it. The last part of his life was not easy. He was depressed over the suicide of his nephew Karl, whom he adored and thought of as his adopted son. He was penniless and lived on the whim of his brother. He never heard the quartet because of his deafness — we know it wasn't even played until long after his death.

"Beethoven was the first creator who I really knew in my life. I must have been eight when I heard the Ninth Symphony. My parents took me to a concert in the cathedral at Strasbourg. I wondered how one person could have created all that sound. Sound he never even heard.

"Einstein wrote out his equations on the backs of envelopes. When he had conceived of the theory of relativity, the universe — the billions of light years of infinite space — was entirely inside his head. Decades were necessary before the proof was available for what he had already found inside his own head. With Beethoven, it's the same thing. His work is as real as the theory of relativity. Millions of people are witnesses to that." Verne paused. "I think I am getting a little carried away."

"That's all right."

"You see, when I asked you earlier if you knew the Sixteenth, one of its last themes was running through my head. Did you know that on the manuscript Beethoven wrote an epigraph, right at the end? Do you speak German?"

"A little."

"He wrote: '*Muss es sein? Es muss sein!*' 'Must it be? It must be!' No one has ever really understood what he meant. We always talk about Beethoven's need to use the grand myths as his points of reference — destiny, despair, death. I think the answer is in his music. The question is posed by his violins, like a streak across the sky: 'Must it be?' The cello responds in counterpoint by strokes that take the breath away. Like an earthquake. It answers, 'Yes, it must be. You must yield.' Do you remember that tension? You think it's over, and then — suddenly — there is lightness, dance music, something from some popular song. It comes out of nowhere and ends in a *pizzicati* of chords. It really lasts a minute and then — poof. Gone. Beethoven has revoked grand seriousness. Life may be tragic, it seems to say, but that's all the more reason to laugh at it."

When Verne finished Clara said nothing, and for a second he wondered what had made him go on like that. He was catching Milner's disease for grand rhetoric.

It had begun to snow. The rhythm of the poles, like cello bows, were playing notes from Beethoven's sixteenth quartet.

* * *

The wind sent clouds of crystals swirling around the ambulance. Driving was becoming treacherous. Controls indicated they were going barely twenty-five miles per hour. They would never get to Thedford at that rate.

Verne looked in the mirror. Clara was asleep. His back was hurting; grimacing, he adjusted the seat. He was thinking that they would probably have to stop at a motel in Stapleton, twenty miles off, and that the police would be waiting for them.

Visibility was diminishing. The wind was blowing harder. The snow began to strafe horizontally. The wipers has a hard time keeping up.

Verne pulled over. He had no idea how far he was from Stapleton. Strumwasser was right. The town wasn't in the computer.

He'd heard of snowstorms that lasted for days, of travelers found frozen to death in their cars. Their reserves probably didn't amount to more than — Verne played with the controls — three hours at most. The temperature outside had fallen to 15 below zero.

Nothing to do except to call for help. Verne decided to wait for daybreak.

Chapter 12

1

"Look, I don't care if you're from the FBBS or not," replied the voice at the *Washington Post,* as if it had been giving the same refrain for some minutes. "I can't give you Susan Sullivan's address. I'm very sorry — "

Furious, Annabelle switched off. Only one thing to do: ask for the address of Vincent Sullivan's widow from *Post* columnist Liz Claret, the head of the pro-gestation group RUT. The idea of asking for anything from Liz, who she'd known in college, revolted Annabelle.

But the call went better than expected. Liz gave her Sullivan's address "for the sake of our old friendship."

The address was in northern Virginia in Nova Park, a luxury retirement community on the Potomac. Despite the formal instructions that Black had given her that same morning, Annabelle jumped into her car and headed for Nova Park.

Annabelle drove into the parking lot near the luxury condos. She looked around at the hundred-year-old elms and parked in front of a four-story structure, an antebellum revival with graceful colonnades and a long front porch.

The reception area was as large as a baseball infield, decorated with little clusters of chairs and tables separated by exotic plants. Annabelle headed toward a uniformed hostess and asked her whether she could see Mrs. Susan Sullivan. This seemed to surprise her, but she picked up a phone and asked Annabelle to wait.

A few minutes later, a woman of around fifty, whose front bangs formed a nearly perfect triangle, came up to Annabelle looking stiff and formal. She was, she said, the director of the home. In a cold voice she asked Annabelle what business she had with Mrs. Sullivan. Realizing that a simple explanation probably wouldn't suffice, Annabelle pulled out her FBBS badge and informed her she was on official business.

"In that case, I will ask you to be brief. A nurse will direct you to her room." She walked off briskly, her heels clicking on the marble floor.

In the elevator, the nurse — a sort of caricature of the director — made no sign of acknowledging Annabelle. He led her into a huge room that was shrouded in darkness. It took a few seconds to see anything, but gradually Annabelle could detect the figure lying on an immense brass bed.

"Susie?" said the nurse in a singsong voice, "You have a visitor!"

Annabelle immediately felt ill at ease. The heat of the room made breathing difficult. An acrid smell floated in the air. The nurse raised the blind slightly and a ray of light came in, illuminating the foot of the bed.

"You can sit here," said the nurse, addressing Annabelle for the first time and pointing to a chair near the bed. "I'll be back in ten minutes. If you need me before then, use that." He indicated the buzzer on the wall, then left the room, carefully closing the door behind him.

Susan Sullivan hadn't moved a muscle during all this. She was propped up on cushions, and her tiny head was nearly lost in the vast softness of the bed. Her cheekbones were pronounced, her skin wrinkled, her hair thin, and she wore a pink nightgown with a lace border, which revealed her fleshless shoulders. Her arms were in repose in front of her on a sheet. Enormous blue veins ran along the back of her hands, looking as if they were about to break free of her transparent skin. She wore a huge diamond ring on her right hand. Her expression was vacant.

Annabelle was unsure what to do. She wouldn't be able to get anything out of this creature, who looked as if she had already departed from the world. Who, she wondered, could be distributing her fortune for philanthropic causes, and signing her name to charity appeals in the *Washington Post?*

"Who are you?" The voice was remarkably clear.

"My name is Annabelle Weaver, Mrs. Sullivan."

Beneath plucked eyebrows clumsily redrawn with a pencil, Susan Sullivan's dark eyes were extraordinarily penetrating. Annabelle thought her first impression must have been wrong and was feeling relief.

"I'm from the FBBS. Um, the Federal Bureau of Biological Supervision. We enforce the Fuchs Law. You've probably heard of it?"

The old woman had turned her head toward the window, and now showed only her profile. Annabelle had no idea if Sullivan was getting a word she said. She decided to go to the heart of the matter.

"So you see I came to ask you if you had the smallest clue about the death of your husband that you haven't already given to the police. Mrs. Sullivan, I personally don't buy the suicide verdict. Like lots of people, I think Senator Sullivan's death had something to do with the announcement he planned to make to the Senate. Do you know anything about that? I know that you were asked these questions years ago, but have you thought of anything since that time? Something you didn't know at the time? A man as distinguished and successful as your late husband wouldn't simply decide to do himself in. It doesn't make sense. On the other hand, to discover what he wanted to announce to the Senate would be of the very greatest importance to our country. Because I think your husband was" — Annabelle paused — "assassinated."

Susan Sullivan didn't move. The silence grew heavy. Annabelle got up and leaned over the bed. The old woman's expression was blank, but tears were streaming down her cheeks.

"You think so, too, don't you, Mrs. Sullivan?" she said at last. No response.

Annabelle punched the intercom button in frustration. She wasn't going to get anything out of this bag of bones.

The nurse came in.

"She didn't tell you anything, did she?" he asked, going over to the bed. Then he added in a raised voice, "All right, Susie. Now it's time to rest."

He helped the old woman stretch out, then went over to the window and lowered the blind.

"The director would like a word with you," he told Annabelle.

With a brusque gesture, the director motioned Annabelle to sit down. All Annabelle wanted to do was get out of there as quickly as possible and head back to town.

"I assume you learned little from Mrs. Sullivan."

Annabelle said nothing.

"Before you leave," continued the director, "I just wanted to inform you of one thing. Management of Mrs. Sullivan's money is our responsibility. This is entirely legal. When Mrs. Sullivan signed the papers directing that we take over responsibility, she was very much in control of her faculties. Since then, keeping the excellent reputation of our house has been in part due to this poor woman's fortune, and — "

She didn't finish her sentence. Annabelle turned, and saw the nurse heading toward them, carrying in his hand a packet the size of a small book. He handed it to Annabelle. The director looked as if she was going to intercept it, but Annabelle was faster.

"Mrs. Sullivan asked me to give this to you," said the nurse. He was visibly shaken.

"Mrs. Sullivan?" cut in the director, whose eyes never left the packet. "What on earth are you talking about, Mr. Hast?"

"I don't understand it. She — she turned to me and started to talk. For the first time in three years! She gave me a key. I can't imagine where it came from. She told me to look in the suitcase, the one she never opens, do you remember? Inside I found odds and ends — letters, photos, and this packet. She told me to give it to the woman who was just visiting. So I, I, uh, did as she asked. Perhaps I should have . . ."

He gave the director a questioning look and got a glacial glare as reply.

"Well, if you'll both excuse me," said Annabelle, getting up. "Thank you for your assistance."

She hurried across the marble floor and out the door.

2

The unmarked official vehicle bumped down the snow-covered dirt road. Howard Black asked his driver to turn off the heat. His mohair coat was warm enough.

He was very annoyed. Taking risks did not appeal to him. The meeting with Gabriel had been prepared down to the last detail, but an unforeseeable circumstance could always arise, and the unforeseeable was precisely what Black could not permit to happen. The meeting place had been fixed for Anacostia Park, the same place he had met Gabriel the first time, years earlier. Two special agents watched all the roads leading to the intersection at Maple.

No one was allowed within five hundred feet of the meeting place. Black was relying on the expertise of Betty Shrine, in whose hands he had put surveillance and supervision. He had no doubts whatsoever about her ability; he had used her before, for operations even more delicate than this.

Black was edgy, though he would have been unable to say why. Perhaps just the idea of seeing Gabriel again was the reason. Their first meeting was before Fuchs.

Black watched the Anacostia River. A figure lost in a dark coat was striding toward the Bureau vehicle parked a few feet from Black's sedan.

Betty Shrine got out and exchanged a few words with the man, then pointed a finger toward the top of the hill. The man headed off into the trees; Shrine approached Black's car.

He lowered the window.

"Two cars have arrived at Charlie point, Director Black," Shrine told him. "Brook met someone named Sal, who was with three others. He came here to warn me, because I've said no radio contact."

"Good."

"This Sal wants you to go by foot to the maple," she went on. "Gabriel will only join you if sees you're alone. I can't say I'd recommend that you — "

"Thank you, Shrine. I'll go."

"But, Director — "

"That will be all." Black looked at his driver. "Tony."

Tony got out and opened the rear door of the sedan. Black got out a little stiffly and buttoned his mohair coat. Then he started walking up the side of the hill, where a large maple tree a century old stood.

Black had not been to this place since his last meeting with Gabriel. That day, the heat had been so intense Gabriel had arrived in a short-sleeved shirt, his jacket draped over his arm. The maple was in full leaf. Today, the bare branches chiseled the frigid blueness of the sky.

That last time, he was not yet even a member of the National Political Action Committee for Public Health — the former NPACPH — which had played such an important role in electing Nathan Gray president. How far he had come since then.

"Sir?" Shrine was following several feet behind him.

"What is it now?"

"I just wanted to inform you, sir, that this Sal what's-his-name's men, well, sir — "

"What, Shrine?"

"They're wearing full-cover headwear!"

"So what?"

"Well, nothing. I just wanted you to know."

"Yes, I see, Shrine. Excellent job. You can leave me now. I will come back in about fifteen minutes. You can let them go. I don't want any sudden interventions from your end. Is that clear?"

"Yes, sir."

The snow crunched under Black's boots. Hats! That was all he needed. Another one of Gabriel's provocations. His tendency recently to show off was not a good sign. The man thought he was above the law.

It would soon be necessary to get rid of him, but for that Black knew he would have to wait for a signal from Hughes. He could settle a few scores then. For the moment, what was most important was keeping things running smoothly. This behavior must have some justification. Only some new development would make him that cocky.

Black had taken two precautions. The first was to bring Annabelle Weaver into his orbit. Security had informed him that this afternoon the young woman had visited a retirement home in Nova Park. Ms. Weaver certainly didn't lack initiative. But that was all right: he was used to that. He had been tempted to confront her, but decided it would be wiser, in the long run, not to let her know he knew what she was up to.

The second precaution involved Hermes. That same morning, he had been informed that by accident someone at New York Hospital had disconnected the artificial respirator that had been keeping him alive; one difficulty resolved. The double agent had done what he was supposed to do and had now been put out of his misery.

Black reached the top of the hill.

Washington was spread out at his feet. The white marble of the Capitol dome had taken on a bronze tint. The Washington Monument towered above the snow-covered trees on the mall.

Black turned to watch for Gabriel's arrival. He thought about Milner's letter, with which he had familiarized himself. There seemed to be little more in it than ornate phrasing and philosophical woolgathering, but he knew the formula contained some kind of message. The Bureau's cryptography unit had gotten through the first level, but were still stumped by what they found. In time, they'd figure it all out. Black was convinced of it.

Gabriel appeared, moving at a brisk pace. He looked even smaller than usual, but his face hadn't changed. The man was ageless.

"Well, old friend," Black said, spreading out his arms. "It's been a long time."

Engelhardt's face creased into a smile.

3

Once outside the gates of Nova Park, Annabelle pulled over.

The packet was wrapped in old Christmas paper decorated with holly leaves. Under thick cotton gauze, she found a plastic box held together with tape. The box hadn't been opened for some time.

Annabelle cut through the tape with her pocket knife and opened it. She found two digital micro-cassettes inside.

Her heart pounding, she made out the inscriptions on the two labels marked I and II: there were initials — "V" and "S" — an abbreviation — "senat.com." — then some dates. These were the tapes Sullivan had been using to prepare the famous speech. The dates indicated they had been made just seventeen days before his death.

As soon as she got home, Annabelle called Larry Walton, who, to her great relief, told her there had still been no word from or about Claudia Lombard. Then she tried once again to reach Mary Peale. She wasn't at home either. A message told her that the young woman had left the office for the day.

Annabelle made a Cocaid cocktail and switched on the sound system. Not being able to reach Mary exasperated her. She drank quickly. Mary liked to shroud her life in mystery, but she had never disappeared for more than twenty-four hours at a time.

Annabelle concentrated on the tapes. Nervously she inserted one into the machine.

What fascinated her first was the sound of the voice of a man who had been dead so many years. She was probably the first person ever to hear the tape. Sullivan sounded self-assured. Like someone with something to say.

He read off a list of names that sounded as if they came straight out of comic books. Some had addresses and telephone numbers: "Robert Daytripper, Canal Street, 5345–6869" or "Mike the Magnificent, Dead Heroes Square, 5342–9898," and so on. A code, of course. At the very least it proved that Sullivan was attempting to conceal things, even from his personal staff, which would explain why nothing of any interest was found among his effects.

Annabelle forgot all about Mary Peale.

Gradually, the pieces began to fit, and she realized she would be able to decipher the names without the Bureau's experts. No one else need listen to these tapes, at least not yet. The idea of marching into Black's office with conclusive proof intoxicated her.

The name "Eagleman" kept coming back. He seemed to play a major role in what Sullivan referred to over and over as "the business." Other names also came back — Gabriel, Little Eagle — and, less often, Jackal.

"The business" obviously involved a number of levels, and the senator seemed intimate with them all. Annabelle's attention was caught by one of the names.

"The Wop is a real problem. Saw his daughter the other night. She doesn't seem to know what's going on. Amazing. I mean, Jesus Christ, she was one of Cauldron's first senior appointments — "

Annabelle's nerves tingled. That had to be a reference to Claudia Lombard. She listened to the passage again.

". . . April 14. Just left the Wop. He confirmed what he told me last month. There will be an agreement between the Committee and the Organization, but that things were at a critical stage. The Jackal represented the Committee, Gabriel the Organization. They've gotten stuck on the Organization's demand for a five-year pasta monopoly. No way. Eagleman won't go for it. The Jackal proposed two years, to be followed with controlling interest in other products and merchandising: drinks, gum, that sort of thing. The product will continue to arrive by plane or by boat from the south, and be delivered via Florida to a group controlled by Eagleman. In exchange, the Organization will put everything it's got behind Eagleman. Again asked the Wop why he was handing over his real boss. He could have gone on two-timing without my knowing about it. From friendship, he said. As if he thought I would swallow that bullshit. Also talked about his daughter. She has a career now. That was maybe closer to the truth. You could tell by the way he smiled when he talked about her. A bastard with a big paternal heart. Classic case. Have to steer free of him when this is over. I can't stand seeing him every day. For three years he's been telling Gabriel every time I pick my nose. He's betrayed once, and he'll do it again. No question about that."

The tape stopped, but it had told enough. Lombardi worked for Gabriel, who had to be Engelhardt, even though he'd also been Sullivan's chief of staff for three years. Then he decided to turn on his Mafia boss. Maybe for love of his daughter and her promising career. Maybe he thought coming clean would help her out? Maybe for other reasons. The lawyer had decided to hand Engelhardt to the senator on a platter. As a sign of his good faith, he had disclosed the agreement being hammered out between a committee powerful enough to go head-to-head with the Mafia — probably a political lobby with some influence — and Engelhardt's organization. The product was cocaine, of course. At the time, the powder was being shipped by the planeload between Latin American countries under the exclusive control of the American Mafia and its local syndicates.

Why would a Washington lobby deal directly with organized crime over the coke market? For money? It didn't seem likely. Not on that scale. There must be some tangible political reason. The Committee must have known the serious risks involved in joining up with the

Mafia. Only politics could give that kind of power, so long as it was pushed along by the right number of people in the right places. That was why the Mafia had given Peter Lombardi the job of spying on Sullivan. It wanted to know what was going on in the corridors of power.

And why would the Mafia want to spy on a Democrat who was so resolutely opposed to Fuchs?

This all happened the same year the SF virus was isolated. That was why powerful groups were looking for ways to pressure the federal government into taking drastic measures to stop the epidemic, even if it meant suspending all civil rights. The battle for what would become the Fuchs Amendment had begun, led by the conservative wings of the parties and by the National Political Action Committee for Public Health, a coalition of groups, principally fundamentalist. Evangelism enjoyed a resurgence that made the earlier movements and their hell-fire rhetoric seem tame. Jeremiads streamed from every pulpit. Even the Catholic groups relented on the issue of artificial gestation, despite their earlier vehemence. Now it was the only immaculate conception. Nathan Gray's candidacy was in the works.

Annabelle understood that many of the original cast of characters were still major players in Washington. Through his act of betrayal — if betrayal it was — the Wop had given Sullivan the proof that negotiations with the Mafia had taken place at the very highest levels. The massive production of coke had been undertaken to prepare for one of the major provisions of the Fuchs Amendment.

Were it revealed, the whole business would have caused a firestorm. Fuchs supporters would not have succeeded in getting a conservative on the ticket. The Gray election had been decided by one of the smallest percentages in American electoral history. Everything could have turned out very differently.

Annabelle's self-confidence began to flag as soon as outlines began to become clear. She was fully conscious of the fact that "the business" was way over her head. What happened to Senator Sullivan could more than easily happen to her. She could just imagine the director of Susan Sullivan's nursing home telling some FBI agent that she had been given a package. Now what she needed were allies, powerful allies. Telling the whole story to Black and giving him the tapes would serve a dual purpose: protect herself and prove her loyalty.

That evening she went to the Red Moon, a woman's nightclub she had frequented for some time. Wearing balloon pants, a black silk jacket, and onyx earrings in the shape of conch shells, Annabelle had trouble making it through the crowd of regulars. The place was packed. She breathed in the sweet smell of perspiration and perfume. Periodically the flash of a strobe blinded her, and the wild arabesques of hyperdance floated above the crowd of Washington's most stylish women.

Couples moved hip to hip to the eerie, pulsating music. Everyone danced while looking at their feet — below them, through the transparent floor, floated their images reproduced by cameras and mirrors. A neat effect. Naked breasts with nipples painted or tattooed bobbled through transparent blouses.

It was warm. Annabelle started to relax. She adored the Red Moon and came often, usually just before she hooked up with Mary. The thought of Mary caused a familiar pang.

Annabelle sat down with a group of friends. A woman of about fifty, bluish hair in a buzz-cut, lower lid elaborately made up, was engaging her in conversation. This was a woman who wanted to make her evening something to remember.

Annabelle wasn't interested. She responded in monosyllables and sipped her drink, sometimes checking to make sure her phone was activated. All she wanted to do was dance herself to exhaustion and then go home.

An old torch song replaced the frenetic music. The lights went low. Couples moved into tighter embrace, dipping their hands into the foldings of clothes. Aroused, Annabelle was about to say yes to Blue Hair when she suddenly saw Mary Peale.

She was wearing an outfit Annabelle had given her for her birthday and dancing with a redhead whose ring-spangled hands encircled her waist. She was leaning her head back, her eyes closed in what seemed total ecstasy.

Annabelle knocked over some glasses when she got up.

Conversations around her stopped mid-sentence.

She leapt onto the dance floor, grabbed the redhead by the shoulders, and shoved her away, sending her sprawling on the floor. The images below were of a sea of legs.

Mary hadn't moved. A trace of a smile played on her lips. The sound of Annabelle's hand striking her cheek was like a pistol shot.

Couples stared for a few seconds, then went back to their dancing. One hand on her burning cheek, Mary continued to stare at Annabelle. Now she wasn't smiling.

Flushed with confusion and rage, the redhead got up and was about to tear into Annabelle when a barmaid whispered a few words in her ear. She moved off without a word.

"I'll meet you out front in precisely five minutes," said Annabelle in a tight voice.

The crowd melted before her all the way to the exit.

Annabelle drove erratically. Blood was pounding in her head. The memory of the couple in locked embrace obsessed her. Mary must have spent the weekend with the redhead.

"I hope you had fun," she said without turning her head. "That girl must have given what you wanted, to judge from your absence from the office today."

Mary turned to look at Annabelle.

"Yes, she did," she said with heavy sarcasm. "More than I ever — "

"Ever what?"

"Forget it. You wouldn't understand."

"Wouldn't I, Mary?" said Annabelle after a pause. "We'll see about that as soon as we get home."

The front door slammed shut behind them.

"Get into my goddamn bed," snapped Annabelle.

Mary had taken off her seal coat, which glimmered under the soft lighting of the living room. Holding it negligently in one hand, she was dragging it along the floor.

Without a word, she turned and revealed her bare back. She nonchalantly strolled into Annabelle's bedroom. Annabelle could not help admiring her beauty despite the rage that was tearing through her. She hurt everywhere. She poured herself a drink — the tenth she'd had that day. Three was dangerous dosage. Maybe she should have followed the lead of the RUTters and taken alcohol. But the idea of a drunken loss of control disgusted her.

She took another swallow and felt a sudden heaviness. Her heart was beating madly. She told herself to calm down, but her fury was so blinding she didn't know what to do with it.

She jumped up and strode into the bedroom.

Mary hadn't turned on the light. A dim light from outside provided the only illumination. The bed was undone. Annabelle stopped in the doorway long enough for her eyes to adjust. Slowly she could make out Mary's body. She was lying on her back, her arms folded across her chest.

Annabelle went to the bureau and opened a drawer. It took her a few seconds to find what she was looking for — a snakeskin belt that had belonged to her father. She seized the buckle in her left hand — her strong hand — and turned toward Mary.

"Do you know what I'm going to do?"

"Yes," said the young woman from the shadows.

"You've got nothing to say?"

"No." Then Mary paused, and added, "Afterward, everything will be over between us. Right?"

Mary's words bit deeply into Annabelle. She raised her arm. The air whistled. The dry snap of the whip was sharp.

Annabelle let herself go. She roared, drunk with her own strength, with each stroke climbing steadily to the peak of ecstasy. It was a revelation to her, this release — a joy.

She barely heard Mary's cries.

When she stopped, the phone was buzzing loudly. She was seated on the bed next to Mary, who lay still.

From its own weight, the belt slipped out of Annabelle's hand and dropped on the floor.

4

Wrapped in her mantle of blue-black velvet edged with red, the Young Virgin is seated in the cool, shimmering light that streams through the vaulted Gothic windows. Her head is tilted back, her face turned away just slightly, her hands are clasped. She pleads with the archangel who hovers over her in a cloud of red and gold, his surprisingly masculine features informed by the solemnity of his mission. A banner of red cloth trails from his gesture of benediction.

At the Virgin's feet an enormous Bible rests upon a chest of precious wood. It is open, for the archangel has surprised Mary while she was reading. On the verso page (farthest away from the observer), printed in Gothic letters, the prophecy of Isaiah is visible. It was upon that which Mary had apparently been meditating at the moment of the angel's appearance:

Ecce Virgo concipiet et pariet filium et vocabitur nomen eius Emmanuel. And a virgin will become with child and give birth to a son, and He shall be called Emmanuel (VII, Verse 14).

On the opposite page was the exact same verse. The painter had decided not to inscribe the next verse of the prophecy, the fifteenth, which would have read: *Butyrum et mel comedet ut sciat reprobare malum et eligere bonum.* He shall eat curds and honey when he knows how to refuse the evil and choose the good (VII, Verse 15).

Each time the Annunciation came to him in a dream, Verne struggled all over again with the question of why Grunewald had reproduced the same passage twice. An inventory of possibilities greeted him in his deepest sleep. In the morning, however, he would wake with the bitter feeling of having somehow lost the key.

This time was different. The answer was becoming clear. His dreaming mind had found a new possibility and was turning it over and over, testing it, questioning it. A feeling of triumph began to spread. He had finally succeeded in solving the greatest puzzle of all.

His luminous thought was that, originally, one of the two pages of the Bible in the painting was to have been blank. But a scribe had committed an unpardonable mistake. By accident — or by design — he had closed the Holy Book when the ink was still wet, so that the page was copied onto the next page.

In his sleep, Verne wanted to turn but couldn't.

"I'm dreaming," he murmured in half-sleep.

For a second, he was afraid he would forget the answer when he woke. No, it was still there.

He fell back into the dream and began the same reasoning process.

Something was wrong. The hypothesis wasn't holding up. How obvious the error was! Had it been correct, the text on one of the pages would have appeared backward, as in a mirror.

Verne's disillusionment was as great as the joy he had experienced only minutes earlier. He had always known both scriptural texts in the painting were readable. His desire to solve the puzzle had allowed him to triumph over memory.

Grunewald's intentions were once again incomprehensible. Sleep would not be restful now.

He opened his eyes.

It was totally black, deathly quiet and frigid.

He sat bolt upright. He struggled to remember where he was, looked at his watch: five minutes before ten. He was lying on the stretcher with Clara Hastings.

Several hours earlier, the two men had had to face reality. Despite all the economizing, they were going to lose all heat. Outside, it was bitterly cold. The computer read minus 15 and the temperature felt as though it might go lower. Clara woke up only long enough to swallow a few gulps of water.

Verne feared broncho-pulminary complications. The two blankets wouldn't protect her from this cold.

Calling for help now would do no good. Even if they succeeded in reaching someone, who would risk going out after them in a raging snowstorm in the middle of the night? They had to wait for daylight and hope that the storm would spend itself. And stay warm any way they could.

Verne had the only overcoat with a heating unit. Clara's had been left at the base. Strumwasser had only a parka.

"You know what you must do," Strumwasser told him. "You must get under the covers with Ms. Hastings."

"That's out of the question!"

"If you cover yourselves with your overcoat, you will save her life and yours. As for me, I am going to sleep on the front seat. Good night. Wake me when the coffee's ready."

He laughed and lay down.

Immobile, Verne had waited for Strumwasser to fall asleep. Then, holding his breath, he had leaned over Clara and tried clumsily to wake her.

"Dr. Verne, stop playing around and get into the stretcher. All you're doing is your duty as a doctor, period."

Shivering, Verne took off his overcoat, activated the heating mechanism, and covered Clara's sleeping form with it. Then he slid in next to her; he could just manage not to touch her by staying on the extreme edge of the stretcher.

As soon as Clara sensed his presence, she had moved over to let him in. Verne thought she had awakened. He lay still, until he realized from her breathing that she was still in a deep sleep. He stayed awake for hours, dozing fitfully, until at last he'd fallen asleep. That was when he dreamed about the Annunciation scene in the *Retable*, just as he had done so often since his childhood. Repeating verse fourteen from *Isaiah* made sense for a painting showing the Annunciation, of course. But Verne had always been struck by the absence of verse fifteen. The child Mary was carrying would undo original sin and restore to us the power of hope and the salvation of choice.

Lying in the dark, the wind howling, snow covering the windows, Verne thought about that brief moment of joy he had found. It was what he felt when he discovered a missing piece to a puzzle in molecular biology. Those rare moments were what sustained him.

But now, as always, the solution to the *Retable* was beyond his grip.

He had been taught a lesson he would remember. How could he be sure the same thing wouldn't happen in his research? All scientists were susceptible to being deluded by their own cleverness. Why was it so difficult to imagine they could blind themselves to something fundamental?

Verne unconsciously moved closer to Clara. Feeling that his body was beginning to stiffen from the cold, he tried to turn. He had barely moved when she put her arm around him.

He was petrified with fear. Was she asleep? What should he do?

He felt something. For half a second, he feared it might be the first signs of an ASP discharge. But it was something else.

A strange feeling of resignation began to grow in him, as if the very matter of that which he was made were undergoing transmutation. Distant as he might be from contact with Clara's skin, because of covers and clothes, there was intimacy between them, and it was opening a new horizon.

He turned and enfolded her in his arms. Fear had disappeared.

They stayed locked in each other's arms all night long.

They heard the wind slowly dying down, but they did not see the sun rising over the immense plain of white beneath which they were entombed.

Chapter 13

1

Sitt Hokkee was grateful to the storm for letting up.

From the top of his tractor, he looked out over Gray Knoll, where he came every day to check on the fox traps. Yesterday evening, before the storm and after returning from a meeting with the tribal healer, he'd found a beautiful male, its spine snapped cleanly by the steel jaws. Sitt Hokkee was also grateful death had been so merciful to the animal.

He had decided to head off early toward Arnold, a small farming community, and not wait for the county snowplow to go through first. They might take days. He was going to ask Peter McCormack for $2,000 for this pelt, even though he knew that the old black marketeer would try hard to bargain down. That was part of the game. The process could take hours. This time, however, Hokkee was determined to hold firm. The superb blue-silver fur of the animal was longer than a yard. Worth plenty more than $2,000.

Once he had the money he'd put some of it in an old strongbox, where Turtle Neck, the deputy sheriff, had kept his fishing gear. And he'd give some of it to Joe Chilsom, the tribe's silversmith. The rest would go for the new barn he wanted to build this summer, if the Spirits of the Prairie gave him one or two more furs of that caliber.

The plainsman drove slowly, careful not to drift off the path hidden under the snow. He could see the line of poles along the side of the highway to his left. They went off at a sixty-degree angle before heading back in the direction of Douglas Well. The odd twists and turns of the road in this region were the result of a dispute from years earlier. Two ranch owners had come to blows over water rights.

Hokkee's thoughts, however, were of his two-year-old son. For three days, Ben had been in bed with a sore throat. The evening before Hokkee had gone to the tribal healer to get a concoction of herbs he had made especially for the boy.

He was about to pass over the second sharp turn of Douglas Well, when several yards ahead he saw a mound blocking the path. He stopped the tractor, then reached for his rifle.

It must be the vehicle he'd heard about on his police radio this morning. There was a manhunt in progress for three persons, a woman and two men, driving an ambulance.

Hokkee leaned down and got the snow shovel from under his seat, put on his snow shoes, jumped off the tractor, and headed in the direction of the mound.

The pale sun was breaking through the fog the snowstorm had left in its wake. Hokkee began to bore into the glittering mass until he struck something hard — a windshield.

He went back to his tractor and took a phone out of his trunk.

2

Kess Sherman was thoroughly enjoying himself. He had just downed his second Zapp, brought to him by a sullen female flight attendant. This was the first time he had traveled in the prisoner dock of a plane, and he was going to make the most of it. His gaze was deliberately focused on the attendant's legs, which were sheathed in transparent material. What the hell — a few months more or less of prison wouldn't make much of a difference. Simply being charged with "salacious solicitation" was enough to merit a jail sentence, but he was feeling pretty cocky. And sexual.

The attendant could very easily have reported Sherman's look to the U.S. marshall in the seat next to him, Cleeve O'Casey. The agent's attention seemed entirely absorbed by his true-crime magazine.

"You should stop drinking, Mr. Sherman," O'Casey said without lifting his nose from the magazine. "I want no trouble out of you until I hand you over to the people at D.C. jail. Right?"

"Not to worry, Marshall O'Casey," Sherman replied. "Cocaine never kept anyone from going to jail."

Sherman was lying on a stretcher that took up three seats. O'Casey occupied the fourth. He was a large man of about thirty, whose tonsure was shaved to exaggeration — at least eight inches in diameter — as was the fashion among federal agents.

A mark, just like any other, thought Sherman, watching him out of the corner of his eye.

The other seats in the section were empty, except for the one occupied by the medic, who was fast asleep, his head against the window.

The plane hit an air pocket, and Sherman groaned. The pain in his wounded thigh was still a nearly constant companion. The doctor at the L.A. jail had said it was twisted ligaments, and had put him in a cast until the damage could be operated on. The spasm disappeared — the cocaine helped. Sherman closed his eyes and thought about the last few days.

He had refused legal counsel. A young lawyer from the Public Defender's office had advised him to refuse extradition. The lawyer believed in opposing federal jurisdiction for the sake of state's rights.

But Sherman hadn't resisted. As a member of the Network, he much preferred having his case brought closer to federal corridors.

"Are you listening to me?" said a voice emanating from somewhere near his feet.

Sherman snapped out of his reverie.

"Sorry, O'Casey, I was daydreaming."

"Well, is that how it happened or not?" asked the agent.

"Is that how what happened?" replied Sherman

"Did the Marshall brothers really know they were apocalypting each other when they did it? You know, did they, like, recognize each other?"

Sherman sighed. The whole business appealed to people whose minds fed on junk-food virtual realities. He knew that it would become a film video within the week. *O.K. Corral: The Sequel.* Poor Wesley. The agents who'd found Sherman had regaled him with the story of his friend's fiery demise. It was all anyone had talked about for the last two days.

On the other hand, he had heard nothing about what happened to Loca. The young lawyer he'd talked to said she'd gotten away, together with a few members of her gang. There was some kind of tunnel.

"Sherman, I asked you — "

"Damnit, O'Casey, it isn't any of your fucking business, now is it?" Sherman cried, losing his cool.

The flight attendant appeared.

"I suppose you want to know, too, right?" said Sherman to her with savage sarcasm.

"Please lower your voice a little," she said in a tone both threatening and neutral. "You're disturbing the other passengers."

"So sorry. It's just that this gumshoe here — "

O'Casey's face went deep red.

"You smartass — "

"My apologies, O'Casey," Sherman interrupted him. "No hard feelings? I just harrowed hell, so cut me some slack. You were asking about the Marshall brothers? I'll tell you something. The Marshall brothers died the way people have died since the dawn of time — with the hope that it would serve some higher purpose. Once and for all, someone should announce that nobody's death serves anything. Follow me?"

"Not where you're going," growled the agent, turning back to his magazine.

"Forget it, then."

Sherman decided to get some sleep.

3

Margaret Brittain called Melissa two days after she'd offered her Paul's job to ask her what she had decided. Rather than answer, Melissa proposed that Margaret come with her to visit one of her oldest friends, Clayton Powys, who had been squatting for years in a log cabin on Laird's Landing, a rocky inlet in Point Reyes National Park.

"We'll have time to talk there. The walk along the national seashore is wonderful."

To Melissa's surprise, Margaret accepted.

On the drive over to Laird's Landing, Melissa explained that Clayton was a painter who lived hand to mouth. He had a commission to paint a canvas that would go into Paul's collection. In the meantime, Melissa regularly went out to see him to give him money or supplies.

When the two women arrived, the old man — white-haired, bushy-bearded, laugh-lined, potbellied — was just leaving. "For an appointment," he announced with comic exaggeration.

Melissa guessed it was a Network meeting. He begged them to come back later in the afternoon, and they agreed. To pass the time, Margaret and Melissa decided to walk in the fields above Tomales Bay.

Melissa was in a somber mood. She didn't want to talk about the directorship but knew she had to.

"The staff doesn't understand what's happening. They can't believe that Paul would desert them, and they can't accept the idea that Hathaway might take his place. They agree to my candidacy on condition that they can talk to Paul about it first."

"What did you tell them about Paul?

"Very little," replied Melissa. "I said that he was busy with the Commission, and that it involved the security of the country."

"Mel, I'm so glad that you're going to take it. The next time you talk to Paul you can ask him — "

"No, it has to come from you," Melissa replied.

"What happens if we can't reach him?"

"Then Hathaway gets the job."

Margaret could tell that Melissa wouldn't budge on this.

The two women walked in silence along the crest of the cliff. Below them, the sun reflected off the waters of Tomales Bay.

"I love this part of the world," said Melissa. "Do you see that little hamlet over there? It's called Marshall. Once a week Clayton rows over to it."

"What for?"

"To play poker. He won Laird's Landing in a poker game."

"You're kidding."

"I'm not. One night, at the Saint Vitus Dance, a bar in Marshall, he played a hand when he was completely drunk, and it was a winning hand."

Melissa enjoyed recounting the legends surrounding their old friend.

"The loser was a squatter by the name of Cahunga Smith. He took Clayton out back where his boat was moored. Clayton says the boat didn't have a rudder and that it was a miracle Cahunga managed to get back and forth across Tomales Bay.

"Anyway, after that famous poker game, they lived together for a year. Cahunga taught Clayton all he knew. Then one day Cahunga just vanished. Clayton maintains he went off looking for a secret place, so that before he died he could commune with the spirits of the forest. He also insists that after Cahunga Smith's disappearance, he slowly transformed into Cahunga, just as Cahunga had been transformed into the man who had squatted there before him.

"So he goes across the bay several times a month in that same rudderless boat, mostly to moan and groan about the injustice of this second Prohibition to the bartender at the Saint Vitus. He keeps at it until the guy produces a bottle of whiskey."

The sun was beginning to set when they returned to Clayton Powys's cabin.

They went inside and sat down at a table made of white wood, so massive it took up nearly one side of the main room, which, because the windows were open on three sides, felt and looked like the hold of a beached ship.

Melissa saw that the pine tree that used to shade the room had disappeared. All that was left was a stump, charred by lightning.

"There's almost nothing worse than losing somebody you love," she murmured. "When you realize that you've been betrayed, the rage is poisonous."

"Can't you forgive Paul?"

"Forgive him for what? A mid-life crisis? Paul only deceived me. I've been lying to myself for years."

"Maybe he just needed to be alone. You said that Milner's death affected him deeply."

"Milner was as much my friend as his. That's not it. The problem is his need for solitude — a term he seems to define as not being with me. This has been going on for years. I just refused to see that he was pulling back from me."

Melissa's tone surprised Margaret.

"He hasn't loved you for some time?"

"The question never even came up. He took things for granted, which is typically masculine. We were married, we made love, then stopped because of SF. But SF covered a multitude of sins. Things would have gone that way even without the epidemic. I belonged to him, and so it wasn't ever discussed. My mistake was in having accepted his way of seeing."

"You couldn't know that."

"I do know that, Margaret. We always know."

Melissa stared out into the dusk. A squadron of pelicans glided over the surf in formation.

"There was always the research. We shared a passion for biology, and that meant we were able to avoid confronting all the rest. Maybe I'm being hard, I don't know. I don't even care that much about the directorship, and if I took it, it would be because I'd never see him again. He will never come back."

"Why do you say that?"

"Paul would never agree to work any place I was the director. Ancient masculine prejudices still endure. It's as simple as that."

The door behind them slammed. Clayton Powys was striding across the room, his face lit up in a generous grin.

"I'm glad you two are still here. How about dinner?"

"Actually, Clayton — "

"No excuses, Melissa. I caught two mullets, and they are beauties. Now introduce me to your charming companion."

*   *   *

246 /

Over dinner, Clayton asked Melissa if she would agree to come talk sometime soon to a few of his friends about the ASP. Melissa knew he was talking about the Network.

"On one condition. That you finish the painting."

4

Claudia Lombard balanced herself on one leg on a chair perched on top of the table. Her other leg was attached to a radiator by a metal chain, stretched to the limit.

In this acrobatic position, the director of the FBBS pressed her forehead against the pane of glass and strained to see something besides the patch of daylight she had been staring at for three days. She felt as if she had been suspended in midair. A building, a plane, a tree, anything — but she saw nothing. Suddenly dizzy, she lost her balance and only managed to avoid falling by pushing against the wall with her hand. A sob of rage rose in her throat. Every effort to escape visually from this room had come to naught.

Gingerly, she climbed down from the improvised perch, put the chair back in its place, and collapsed in a heap on the mattress that lay on the floor.

She had been waiting for days to look out that window. Two hours earlier, at the moment when the Silent One, as she called him, was locking one of the two chains that were attached to the radiator — just as he did every morning after she finished washing herself — she pretended to faint. The Silent One never lost his composure: he applied his fingers to a pressure point behind her ears. She was alert immediately. Then he left, and as she hoped, forgot to check whether the steel ring was attached snugly enough to her ankle.

As soon as he was gone she worked the manacle off with the help of some soap. This took an hour, and for a nervous moment or two, she'd wondered if it wasn't a lost cause: the ring was so wedged against the bone that it seemed as if it were embedded in her flesh. Crying from the pain, Lombard finally succeeded.

She bandaged the wound with a piece of her nightgown. Then, with soaring hopes, began her fruitless ascent.

Sitting on the mattress, Lombard gently removed the improvised bandage. She knew the Silent One wouldn't be back for a few hours, but when he did he would immediately see what she had done, because she couldn't put the chain back around her swollen ankle.

Lombard tore off another piece of her nightgown, dipped it in the water pail, carefully washed the wound with soap, then fashioned a new bandage. When she finished she lay back and looked at the light.

In addition to providing no reference point, looking out the window had also told her nothing about those noises — the ones she heard at regular intervals coming from the other side of the wall. They were deafening. An amplified human sound mixed with the rhythmic stamping of feet. Sometimes, extraordinarily loud wheezing and rasping followed, as if someone were slaughtering a animal. Occasionally would come a cry of such feral savagery that it froze the blood in her veins. This whole disturbing symphony would last for an hour, then stop abruptly — leaving her exhausted.

Lombard managed to get up and positioned herself over the bucket next to the mattress. In the unbroken silence of the room, the trill of urine sounded obscenely loud. Having to use the bucket was the worst of her humiliations.

The first night in the cramped and clammy cell, she had banged her fists on the metallic door, until the Yakuza had rushed in and, ignoring her screams, chained her roughly to the radiator.

Since then, the Silent One came three times a day to bring her a bowl of clumpy rice and unidentifiable vegetables. She had tried to speak to him, but he was absolutely indifferent. Nothing would move him to respond — screaming, howling, crying, cajoling.

In the morning, she was also given a bucket of water with which to wash herself and some drinking water. The Silent One undid her manacles and then, without the least conception of modesty, positioned himself near the door, where he would sit, eyes half closed, and wait. She had given up asking him to look elsewhere, and turned her back. When she was finished, he reattached the chains to her ankles. He would then walk out carrying the bucket at arm's length. He'd bring it back to her a few minutes later, clean. Lombard dared do nothing but meekly obey him. He terrified her.

At first, she was persuaded that she would be released the following morning. Engelhardt wanted to teach her a lesson for having had him tailed in L.A. — that was all. At the right moment she would tell him that it was nothing but a misunderstanding. An unfortunate series of circumstances. The FBBS had wanted Kess Sherman, not him.

As for this business about the NOX, she would tell him she found the idea amusing. She would tell him he was absolutely right, it would indeed provide an excellent way to spot Networkers the moment they went through the checkpoints. He would know that it was in his interests to work with her instead of keeping her locked up in this shithole.

But Lombard had had three days for her rage to ripen, and her point of view had changed. The simple fact that it had been possible for someone of her stature to disappear in the middle of Washington, D.C., was proof enough that others were involved — and they had to come from the top. The best-case scenario was that Black had begun negotiating with the Mafia and things had gotten complicated.

The worst-case? Black wanted to be rid of her.

The idea seemed too monstrous to be true, and at first she had dismissed it. But the suspicion remained, and it grew into certainty. This whole wretched business had something to do with Annabelle Weaver. Her assistant had betrayed her on at least two counts: one, by saying nothing about this meeting between Engelhardt and Sherman; two, by avoiding her after the New York disaster. Lombard knew her beautiful protégée well enough to suspect she would engage in such unacceptable behavior only if convinced she had something on her boss.

Annabelle had gotten the support of someone highly placed in the administration. The director of the FBI himself. Lombard was convinced of it. The same man who had named her to her position and stood behind her during the confirmation hearings had suddenly decided to let her rot in a cell. Engelhardt became secondary to Lombard. Now she had but one reason to live: to get out of that cell and settle a score with that bitch who, just a few days earlier, she had felt so powerfully drawn to.

The cell door swung open. The Silent One was accompanied by his superior.

"Good morning," the Yakuza said with humiliating formality. "I hope your stay here hasn't been too painful. Mr. Engelhardt wishes to meet with you this afternoon. I have brought some of your clothes. You can now get dressed."

"This afternoon? What time is it? I need a shower. These are my clothes! When did you go back to my house?" In her weakened state, the thought nearly unhinged Lombard.

"Several hours after we picked you up."

"The same night? But how did you — "

"Please. Mr. Engelhardt will answer all your questions."

He turned to his assistant and said a few words in Japanese. The Silent One knelt at Lombard's feet. She recoiled. They had seen she had gotten one of the metal rings off.

"You shouldn't have put yourself through so much," said the Yakuza. "We will come for you in two hours."

* * *

Lombard sat on the chair, waiting. Her rolled-up nightgown and peignoir were under her arm.

At least they had shown some taste in clothes. They had brought her best black mohair suit, stockings, and leather boots of matching color, as well as her dark gray coat with pink trim.

Being dressed almost made Lombard feel her old self. The idea that she would soon see the outside world again filled her with hope. She thought about Caesar and Titus, and wondered how they'd survived her absence. Poor babies. And how had the media handled the kidnapping? How would her colleagues on Pennsylvania Avenue treat her when she went back to the office?

The noises started again from the other side of the wall. It sounded like a gored animal gasping for breath on a blistering day.

She went to the door and turned the handle. To her surprise, the door opened. Before her was a hallway lit only by a bare light bulb. She hesitated, then went back, picked her coat off the chair, and, carrying her little bundle, limped out the door.

Moving as stealthily as she could, she hugged the wall until she came to a T. Both corridors ended in a door. She turned to the door on the right. Locked.

She went to the other door. The stamping of feet she had been hearing grew louder. She was seized by the impulse to cross herself, an impulse she hadn't had in years. She squared her shoulders, made the sign of the cross, and turned the handle.

A flood of light streamed into the hallway.

Lombard took a step forward and found herself on the roof terrace of an apartment building. Washington was all around her. The sky was crystalline.

The light forced her to close her eyes, but the feel of it on her face was exhilarating.

The deafening noise had stopped.

She squinted. A dozen or so Yakuza in black combat pajamas and leather halters were standing like statues around her. They wore helmets, and had swords in their hands.

With a movement as rapid as it was precise, the one nearest her sheathed his sword. In a flash of the eye — and in one fluid, simultaneous motion — the others did the same.

Lombard realized she had stumbled on a training session between a sensei and his Yakuza. It was their exercises that had produced the noises she'd been hearing for the last three days.

The leader glided toward her and removed his helmet with ceremony.

"You have done as you were to have done," he said with respect. "I congratulate you."

He inclined his head very slightly. Lombard saw his tonsure. In perfect unison, the others removed their helmets and performed the same gesture of respect. Flabbergasted, and without fully realizing what she was doing, she returned the gesture.

At that moment they let out a terrifying cry. Out of the corner of Lombard's eye, her head still bowed, she saw a movement. A blinding flash of light sliced through her at nearly the very second her severed head struck the cement of the terrace.

Chapter 14

1

Paul Verne lay his head back in the straw and thought about the miracle of the man from the Pawnee reservation digging them out. He was jolted by a noise that made the floor of the barn shake.

He got up and shinnied down the ladder from the loft. Bracing his feet on the twig-covered floor, he eased open the sliding door a few inches to look out.

In a swirl of snow, he saw a helicopter hovering a few feet above the ground, throwing off multicolored flashes of light.

Sitt Hokkee was moving across the broad front porch of his rough stone house. He stopped at the top of the steps, his legs apart, a rifle cradled in his arms. His anorak had a fur collar, and his long black hair was held by a leather headband. The whole effect was to give him the appearance of a noble savage from one of the early Westerns.

Verne knew that if Hokkee felt his family was in the slightest danger, he would not hesitate to use that rifle.

The first time Paul had seen Ben Hokkee being held by his mother, he had been struck by the child's resemblance to his parents: he had the dark look of his mother and his father's features. Verne had not come upon a newborn Utero in ten years, and the feelings it aroused were unnerving. Hokkee wasn't tonsured.

With amazing delicacy, the helicopter — boldly marked SHERIFF — set down on the snow. The whine of the turbos quieted, and the huge blade slowed until it was slicing listlessly through the icy clear air. A door slid open and a uniform jumped out. Verne could clearly see the pilot through the bulbous windscreen, sitting motionless. Hokkee watched impassively as the uniform ran toward him.

Verne was not especially worried, though this meant the Nebraska police were after them, too, on top of the FBBS, the MID, and whatever other federal agencies had joined the chase. But the fact that the first official visit to the farm was from a sheriff was actually reassuring. The Pawnee had probably come to an agreement with the local police regarding internal affairs on the Reservation.

The uniform was making sweeping gestures. Suddenly, he turned and pointed at the barn.

Verne's heart stopped. Instinctively, he drew back into the shadows. If the sheriff decided to check out the barn they were finished. There was no way of hiding an ambulance. Hokkee had felt there was no point in even trying — covering it with hay was the only possibility, and that wouldn't stand up to a serious search.

Had the sheriff spotted some tire tracks? Hokkee had been so careful to cover them up.

Verne saw Hokkee break into a broad grin and make a gesture in the direction of his house. After a moment's hesitation, the sheriff shook his head, saluted Hokkee, and retraced his steps to the chopper.

With a deafening roar, the machine took off and flew over the farm.

"Kind of a close call," murmured Clara from behind, startling Verne. He turned toward the young woman, who was wearing the clothes Mow Hokkee had given her — jeans, leather boots, brown wool turtleneck, and a brightly embroidered shawl. Preoccupied as he had been with the visitors, Verne hadn't heard her climb down from the loft where they had spent the night. The dark circles under her eyes contrasted with her pale skin.

She smiled.

He could still feel the impression her body had made against his. His center of gravity had somehow been displaced, outside his body, somewhere — nearby and familiar, but also strange.

They had not talked about what had passed between them. In the barn, they had slept apart, separated by a wall of hay.

Paul knew that what he had felt in the ambulance would not be understood in any scientific fashion. Nor would science explain why he had been spared an ASP discharge. At first, he thought it might have something to do with the frigid temperature, but the more he thought the more he doubted it. He was in thrall of something larger than himself.

Clara respected his silence. She wanted to show him that she knew how to wait.

"Mr. Hokkee is coming to pay us a visit," she said.

The beating of the helicopter blades faded, then disappeared, as their rescuer made his way toward the barn. He'd left his rifle on the front porch. Verne slid the barn door open.

"Greetings," Sitt said. "Warm enough last night?"

/ 253

The question was directed at Verne. He seemed to ignore Clara's presence.

"Yes, thank you," Verne replied, then indicated the young woman. "And I know that Clara is also very grateful. For everything you've done."

Sitt Hokkee turned toward her, as if discovering her for the first time.

"I am very glad for that," he said with great formality.

"Kind of a rude awakening, that little visit by the police," Verne ventured.

Sitt looked at him sharply, then brightened. "Please, come join me and my family in my house. After breakfast, we can talk things over while the women take care of the child."

Clara caught Verne's glance and rolled her eyes.

"I think I'll go and help Mow with a woman's work," she said, hardly bothering to conceal her irritation.

She left the barn.

Sitt watched her walk toward the house, then turned to Paul and smiled.

"She is still young. She will learn that it is necessary to leave to men what should be left to men."

"You may be right," replied Verne, surprised.

"I am curious whether you really believe that I am right."

"Yes, well, I'm not sure."

"White people have a strange way of showing politeness. But I respect your honesty. What I said is of the greatest importance for the order of the world. Shall we go?"

"I'd like to be by myself for a few minutes."

"Take as much time as you need."

He left and followed Clara's tracks in the snow.

The two fugitives had quickly understood that so long as they were grateful guests, they should respect Pawnee ways and keep their opinions to themselves. The quaint phallocentric customs here amused Verne, even pleased him. Clara was neither amused nor pleased.

What Sitt had said made an impression on Verne. He would never have imagined that for a Pawnee the relationship between a man and a woman would have any effect on the order of the universe. An eye-opening idea. In most societies — the ones he had known — male-female relations had little more than sociological or political interest, and the love that was supposed to bind them together, even love of the platonic sort that SF had given rise to, was pure sentimentality.

Paradoxically, the SF epidemic had had some positive side effects for certain minorities. For the Pawnees, like other Native American tribes, it had restored their belief in the legends and myths that for decades had slept in memory. The old ways returned with unexpected vigor, for the epidemic symbolized nothing less than the failure of modern civilization and reinforced their faith in the culture and tradition that existed before the white man's arrival.

Verne walked over to the ambulance, opened the door, and sat in the front seat. He looked at the stretcher he had slept on with Clara. He was struck by how narrow it was. If Strumwasser had not suggested he share it with the young woman, Verne might have been the only one to survive. He increasingly had the impression that people were put in his path simply to help him along this voyage of discovery.

Like poor Strumwasser, who had not made it. The good doctor had frozen to death sometime during that long night.

After Sitt had found them, he had moved into action. He signaled friends, and when they arrived they took things in hand with remarkable skill — like every clandestine organization, they were accustomed to working fast. A second tractor arrived to help Sitt tow the ambulance to the farm. Another followed behind to cover their tracks.

Verne had learned that the Pawnee were part of an association called Vine Deloria, named after an activist for Native American rights.

The breakfast was regal: corn, coffee, eggs, fresh bread, jams and jellies. Clara ate hungrily. She really was feeling better; Strumwasser's cure had worked. Everybody's attention was held by little Ben in his high chair; he was clearly used to being the main attrraction.

After breakfast, the two young women cleared the table and left the room, taking Ben with them. Sitt motioned to Verne to sit near the fireplace, in a simple but comfortable handmade wooden chair. Sitt lit a pipe, and the acrid smell of tobacco filled the room. Verne waited patiently for the man to speak.

"I have heard that you are an important man. A scientist. My great uncle was a man of science. He lived in South Dakota and is still very well known among the tribes."

"What was his field?"

"There is only one true science among our tribes. The science of the spirits. The spirits that live in things. Everything else . . ."

He tapped his pipe on the hearth.

"Everything else has little value. Science has only brought sickness. Now there is Sacred Fire. White people are getting better at naming their diseases, worse at finding cures. Was fire ever sacred where you are from?"

Verne smiled. "A very good question. Yes. But long ago, I think."

"If fire had remained truly sacred, and water, and the mountains, and the animals, perhaps this disease would not have come among you."

"You may be right."

"How can you stand wearing your Pikkiemak?"

"My what?"

"Your head device. Pikkiemak is the name of a snake in one of our legends. He rolled himself up at the feet of two lovers one night when there was a full moon, and no one could pull them apart. They died like that. The force alone separates things. Brings things together and separates them. Union without separation is weak, and so is the other way around. The two are necessary. How can you stand wearing your Pikkiemak?"

"I, ah, I manage all right. You don't wear one, do you?"

"No."

Verne decided he should keep his thoughts to himself.

"The thing is, you sort of forget you have one on."

"But it doesn't forget it has you. It is terrible to have to wear a device that remembers for you."

"What do you mean?"

"Everything that acts as our memory — computers, videos, and the Pikkiemaks. The more they remember for you, the more you forget."

"That's not exactly right."

Verne tried to explain to Sitt what a computer could do: the unlimited number of connections it could make with all the other computers in the world.

Sitt Hokkee listened for a while in silence, then retorted, "But with all your memory, you cannot cure Sacred Fire. The disease spreads and you cannot stop it. Disease becomes increasingly more complicated, more and more difficult to cure, and machines also become more and more complicated, containers of more connections. They are linked. The disease will always win, because you have forgotten what is essential."

"What is that?"

"You have forgotten the effect of the full moon on the two lovers I told you about."

Unexpectedly, Sitt began to laugh, until tears came to his eyes. Verne watched him, irritated and perplexed.

Sitt finally stopped, and relit his pipe.

"Please excuse me. But I think that if you want to be a man of science, you must always keep in mind the influence of the full moon."

He reached into his pocket and brought out an antique watch, which he consulted with a look of high purpose.

"A gift from my great uncle . . . I have to go to the Council early this afternoon to discuss your case. I will bring back news. The uniform you saw this morning came by to warn me that you must leave before this evening. Tomorrow at the very latest."

"He came to warn us?" Verne was flabbergasted.

"He is one of us. We have to prepare for your departure. Until then, I have to ask you to stay in the barn with your wife."

"Sitt, I . . . Clara is not my wife. She is . . ."

Again, the rafters echoed with Sitt's laughter. Verne stared at him, nonplussed.

"Verne, my friend," he said when at long last he had recovered his breath, "Clara is your wife."

Then Sitt got up and put on his fur-lined anorak.

"White people always forget the essentials," he said with genial seriousness.

He waved to Verne, took his rifle from the rack near the door, and went out.

Verne stayed where he was. He was thinking about Milner's letter. Reaching under his sweater, he retrieved it from his shirt pocket. Strangely, it was the first time he'd looked at it in three days. There had been more important things to worry about.

He unfolded it and began to read. He was so absorbed he did not immediately notice that Clara was standing over him, a look of anguish on her face.

She stopped in front of him.

"Paul," she said, in a tight voice.

He raised his eyes.

"Paul, I'm going back to Los Angeles right away."

2

Howard Black gave his overcoat to the attendant in Dr. Bernard Beadle's lab. He kept his kid gloves.

As he headed down the long corridor, he glanced at Larry Walton, who was walking beside him. As always, the obsequiousness of his assistant irritated him. He knew his mannerisms by heart. As soon as Walton sensed his boss was looking at him, his nostrils pinched, the corners of his mouth tightened, and his long neck stretched a little farther forward, like a horse anticipating the whip. The man was turning more and more into Uriah Heep with each passing day.

"Walton, did you inform the family?"

"Yes, Director. I sent a message to Italy as soon as we got word."

"Italy? No family in America?"

"Apparently not, Director. Her great aunt, who is Italian, the sister of her paternal grandmother, has a large family in Naples."

"Walton, spare me arcane details."

"Yes . . . sir."

"What about Weaver? Where is she?"

"She's back at headquarters, Director. I believe that she went to the penitentiary hospital this morning."

"Yes, of course. To visit Sherman."

"I believe so, Director."

A man in a white lab coat opened a door and directed them inside. Black held back for a moment, but sensing that Walton was watching, he squared his shoulders, lifted his chin, and strode into the room. Another corridor presented itself to view.

"We're not there yet?" he said with forced humor to the attendant.

"Almost, Director. Just a little farther."

"Walton. That little — what is her name? — You know, Weaver's young female acquaintance."

"Mary Peale, Director."

"Yes, Mary Peale. Is she still at Weaver's apartment?"

"She's been there since Monday evening, Director. Over two days."

"I see. Has the State Department been notified?"

"Yes, sir. I've informed Campbell that Peale's absence is connected with business affecting national security."

Walton exasperated him — the man had no passion, no hook — but he was decidedly useful.

"And they bought it?"

"No, sir. But they're far too clever to push the issue."

Black smiled. It would cost him nothing to do Weaver a favor.

Another door appeared on their left. Black suddenly had the urge to ask Walton to get down on all fours. With amazing precision, he could see the long neck of his secretary being sliced by the door, his head rolling onto the floor.

"We're here, Director."

The orderly disappeared through a side door, leaving them room to pass. Black turned toward Walton, sighed deeply, and went in. His secretary followed at his heels.

The room was large, and its walls were covered in white tiles. There was a sweet, slightly nauseating smell in the air. Three marble tables were lined up, and above them hung blindingly bright lights.

The top of the table nearest them, which was empty, was striated with what looked a little like channels, all leading to a drain. The outline of a body was visible beneath a white sheet on the second table, with a protuberance the size of a balloon perched on its stomach.

Dr. Beadle was standing at the third table, his back to them. He turned his head when he heard Black enter.

Small, oily, completely bald, he sported an immense walrus mustache and was wearing a T-shirt and large rubber apron that came all the way down to his white boots. In his right hand he held pincers larger than any Black had ever seen.

"Ah yes, Director Black," he said, laying the pincers on the table. "I didn't think you'd be here so early. If I'd known I wouldn't have started on this one. Be with you in a second."

He turned toward his aide, a young man standing on the other side of the table.

"We'll finish this one later," he said.

He covered the cadaver with the sheet, but not before Black had got a look. He felt with panic that he might faint. Walton's presence steeled him — the idea of showing any weakness before his assistant was unacceptable. Hands behind his back, he leaned against the wall near the door and tried to look indifferent.

Walton — who was also leaning against the wall — was as white as the sheet covering the body, which gave Black a small measure of satisfaction. Dr. Beadle turned around. Black noticed with horror that he hadn't removed the rubber gloves he'd been wearing to rummage around in someone's intestines.

"This way, gentlemen," said Beadle, motioning them toward the form on the second table.

Black turned ashen. A bare foot was sticking out from under the sheet. There was a tag on the big toe.

Dr. Beadle took hold of the sheet covering the body.

"No wait, I . . ." Black stammered.

His eyes dilated in horror. He sensed Walton edging closer. Beadle was watching him, waiting for him to finish his sentence

"I — wanted you to tell me again where the body was found."

"I never told you the first time," said Beadle. "The police found it in Chinatown. In two separate garbage cans. But look closely. Something very strange indeed."

And with that he lifted the sheet. At that very instant, Black heard something falling — Walton had collapsed in a heap on the tiled floor. The orderly was going over to help. Black forced his attention back to the table.

Eyes wide open, Lombard's head was sitting on her stomach. Black's fear was overwhelmed by his fascination.

"Your secretary is a little weak-nerved," said Beadle. "A very pretty piece of work we have here, don't you think?"

Black settled back into the seat of his limo, his eyes fixed on Tony's tonsure. There was no doubt about it. The perfection of the decapitation was a signature. Dr. Beadle was right to admire it. He had never in his life seen something like that — a perfect cross section — no vertebra had been crushed, as often happens with saws. The sword had cut through the neck at the left side. Only the Yakuza had that kind of skill, that degree of artistry.

Engelhardt had warned Black the Cartel was going to take the offensive. That it would strike hard and fast at the highest levels.

Black still found this business about the NOX unclear. When Engelhardt first told him about it, he hadn't believed him. He was convinced that NOXes were really false ASPs, that they would not allow men to free themselves of the prostheses with impunity. What Engelhardt had said about its usefulness as a way of helping the government round up Networkers simply didn't wash. The Network leaders weren't idiots; they would know very quickly if the thing worked or not.

Now Black was more uncertain. If the NOX was for real it could create a nightmare for the FBBS. NOXes would become what drugs were in years past. There would be the same network of dealers, traffickers, all organized by the demand for an outlawed commodity: sex. The same stigmas would attach to the NOX that had once been attached to drugs. There would be the non-users, the vast majority of people, those who went along with regulations and obeyed laws, and the users.

Why not, after all? Black personally saw nothing wrong with this. For him the important thing was to make it look as if he was using the full resources of the FBI to go after the Mafia, while at the same time keeping the unofficial ties between them as strong as ever. The Mafia would always exist. The question was not — nor had it ever been — to eradicate it. The question was getting it to play by the rules. It was all a matter of territory.

The government turned a blind eye to the alcohol trade. But liberalization of cocaine production had created a void. That the Mafia would put out a contract on Claudia Lombard was ample proof it thought it had found something to fill the void: the NOX.

Let them believe they had rattled him by killing the FBBS director. Black was convinced that Lombard's assassination, paradoxically, would give him leverage.

Thank heavens for Annabelle Weaver. The Sullivan tapes she had given him were going to prove very useful. More leverage. All that was necessary now was for Annabelle to meet Engelhardt and pass along the good word. The secret agreements between everyone were very explicit on the tapes. Black congratulated himself for having had the sense to let Weaver follow her nose.

This new war with the Mafia might be long and bloody. Black needed an event that would get the administration behind him. Something like a scandal. Verne? Ever since the man had run off with the Bio, Black was nourishing the hope that the man who isolated SF would be the carrier of a useful controversy.

That would be a crowning achievement, Howard Black was thinking to himself at the moment his limo reached the Hoover building.

He was too preoccupied with the thought to notice Annabelle Weaver's sports coupe pulling out of the garage onto 9th Street.

3

Clara lay sprawled in the hayloft, hands cradling her head, watching dust particles drift languorously in the rays of sunshine.

She had just heard about the Virginas raid. She felt numb. The radio report had said a tribunal in L.A. had ruled that Wesley Marshall be given the Punishment of Ashes.

The Network fought ash dispersion because it sapped the spirit and imagination of people, deprived them of a way of focusing their grief. Municipal morgues were sometimes raided and ashes stolen. In a culture living constantly with death, burial rites — what dignity remained to them — were of the greatest importance. The ashes of criminals were given decent burials; the ashes of those who resisted ASP controls were not.

Clara herself cared little about burial rites, though she knew many of her compatriots did. Ever since cremation had become national law, ashes had replaced the body and taken on a substantiality they had not had before. She'd even joked about this with Wes.

The memory now pained her.

Wes had given the best part of himself. He had opened her eyes to the perversity of the administration, and shown her a way . . . without ever giving up on her when she fell back into despair. It was thanks to him that she had accepted who she was, however she came into the world. Her debt to him ran deeper than words.

When she'd told Verne about her decision to return to L.A., even though the news shook him, he hadn't tried to persuade her to change her mind. She was grateful to him for that. Then a messenger from the Tribal Council had arrived asking him to join their meeting. She was waiting for him to return.

The pains in her joints were gone, but Clara felt drained. She was letting herself feel exhausted. Before she'd heard the news about Wes, she had been letting herself enjoy the freedoms that came with being in love.

Her memory grew hazy whenever she tried to remember events after leaving the MID base. That first meeting at the airfield — had she seen Verne's face before passing out? She couldn't remember. She knew she'd said to him, "It's you, isn't it?" Or something like that. She also knew an image of Paul impressed itself upon her, immediately and irrevocably. Even if she never saw him again, Clara knew she was changed forever.

She heard the barn door opening.

"Clara?"

"I'm coming, Paul."

"No, wait. What were you doing?"

"I'm lying down. Thinking."

"Please stay there."

Clara smiled. Dust particles still danced in the shafts of sunlight.

She heard the creaking of the ladder. Her heart was beating so hard it felt as if it would break her open. She closed her eyes. The idea of being looked at by him without seeing him exhilarated her.

She heard him approaching. He was kneeling down next to her. And then there was silence.

She could hear him breathing.

"Kiss me," she said.

His lips were on hers. This first kiss lasted only a few seconds, a few beats of the heart. It was unbearably tender.

She began to cry. It was all impossible now.

"I met with the whole Council," Verne said.

He was sitting a few feet from Clara, leaning against a hand-carved beam. Their hands were joined.

"It was actually very moving. A dozen men sat in a circle in a communal hut. Sitt is obviously a man of some importance in the community. He sat on the right hand of an elderly man, who said nothing. You got the feeling the old man was only there to make speech possible. You might be interested to know that a chief is named by a woman, a grandmother. Being a chief is all he does. The one sitting across from him explained the role the community was playing in helping us. Not only are they fully aware of who we are, but they know what we are. They know why we're being chased. I'm wanted, too — for purposes of interrogation, the police are saying. When I asked them why they didn't just hand us over to the authorities, they replied I would be told later on. They agree to help you get back to Los Angeles. You'll travel through reservations — Navajo, Hopi, Papagos, moving by night. It should take two days. You leave tonight. A truck will arrive."

"What about you?" she asked quietly.

"I will head east. They want me to meet some people, and I agreed. They didn't say who or why. Afterward, I will be free to do as I please. Somehow I have to get back to New York. I'll take a plane tomorrow. Our paths divide."

They remained silent for a minute.

"Hey, up there!" Sitt's voice rang out from outside the barn. "The truck will be here in twenty minutes. I'll be waiting up at the house. Can you hear me?"

"Loud and clear!" Verne shouted back.

Clara was playing with a piece of hay. She turned to him.

"Paul," she said. "I want you to do something for me. I want you to talk to me about Milner's letter."

Verne remembered what she'd said earlier about the letter, and the way she'd concealed it.

"What drove you apart?" she went on.

"I — I don't know what to say. I should have proposed that you read it yourself. If you want to, you — "

"I don't want to. I simply want to know what drove you and Joseph Milner apart. Did it have to do with the work you were doing on SF?"

"He thought so. I don't. His letter begins with a long reflection on European culture and Vienna in particular. He believed there was a strong connection between history and our inability to cure — let alone understand — Sacred Fire. Let's go for a walk. I need to breathe."

Verne insisted on giving her the overcoat that had saved their lives. He wore a coat he had been given by Sitt Hokkee.

Chapter 15

1

The press conference Director Black called was to begin at one P.M. at FBI headquarters. Annabelle decided to make a quick visit to her apartment.

In the middle of Pennsylvania Avenue, the low-battery light flashed on the dashboard. She realized she had forgotten to recharge. Probably because she had been so upset. The news about Lombard's assassination had been terribly unnerving.

For the first time, a doubt that the FBBS would take care of its own had entered Annabelle's consciousness, and it was growing. Too many questions, not enough answers. Did Black know why it had happened? Why had he made Annabelle wait three days before letting her make arrangements to meet with Engelhardt and negotiate Lombard's release?

Annabelle was convinced at first that Black's silence meant there were unforeseen difficulties in the negotiations with the Mafia. He probably didn't want his intervention to further endanger Lombard's life.

But now? What should she think now? From Engelhardt's point of view murdering Lombard made no sense. The FBI was well aware he was responsible for the kidnapping. Moreover, Lombard's disappearance would cost the Mafia a valuable insider. The way she was killed had all the earmarks of an execution — a calculated act.

There was no doubt about it: Engelhardt was sending a message to the FBI. Why did he think he could get away with it?

Annabelle thought back to her last meeting with Black. He had asked her to listen to the Sullivan tapes with him, in his office, and she interpreted this as yet another sign of his confidence. Before that, Black had asked her about Susan Sullivan, and gently needled her about not keeping him informed of her actions.

While Sullivan's voice played through the speakers, Black paced around the office. After fifteen minutes, he abruptly turned the tape off.

"These aren't telling me anything new."

Annabelle was incredulous. "You already knew about the agreement between the Committee and the organization Sullivan is talking about?"

"Of course I knew about it. We were making preparations for a secret agreement between the Committee for Public Health and the Mafia."

"But I thought — I'm afraid I don't get it. The NPACPH supported Nathan Gray for president. And if I — you — "

"Yes, I was in on it. In fact, I'm the Coyote Sullivan refers to. I should think he could have chosen a better code name. But that was how he was. We called him the Seal. I can't quite remember why, perhaps because he was adept at swimming in the cold undercurrents. He insinuated himself into everything. Nathan Gray is Eagleman, Elizabeth Hughes is Little Eagle — she was already on the Gray ticket. And I met Gabriel a number of times during the intervening years."

"Who is Gabriel?"

"Engelhardt, obviously. He was negotiating for the Mafia. There are times, my dear Weaver, when national interests simply outweigh personal feelings. SF was threatening to wipe out the country. We needed people who were ready to face the hard facts. The Committee for Public Health did. If the Fuchs Amendment was going to work, we had to bring in the Mafia. To suddenly legalize cocaine without first negotiating with them would have been an overt act of war. And the only way to avoid war was dialogue. Otherwise, the whole thing would have collapsed."

"And Senator Sullivan's death?"

"Not clear. That's the least you can say about it. Police found no clues. There were plenty of people who hated him — Sullivan was a political hack — but supposedly he told no one what he knew about the negotiations with the Mafia. Except maybe Peter Lombardi, whose departure for Canada on business several days before the murder was a little too fortuitous. As you know, he was later found dead himself, on a deserted stretch of highway. A Mafia signature. Lombardi was in charge of keeping Sullivan under surveillance. He probably got wind that Sullivan was going to make the negotiations public."

Annabelle zipped between two trucks and headed off down M Street. From the Mafia point of view, Claudia Lombard's death could only mean one thing: a declaration of war against the Hughes administration. If the Cartel decided to take such a risk it was only because it had something new that had strengthened its hand.

Little by little, Annabelle was getting accustomed to the idea of Lombard's death. In a way she felt relieved. Her position at the FBBS was strengthened. The New York business was now dead and buried. And she would be forever free of the woman's irritating and pathetic advances.

But she was not yet on easy street. Black was going to have to be diabolically smooth with the press. The slightest mistake would be disastrous. He had to explain how it was possible that someone as important as the director of the FBBS could simply vanish for three days without anyone knowing where she was, and then turn up in garbage cans. Decapitated, no less.

Annabelle felt rage. She had no idea what was going on. Once again she found herself blindly obligated to someone in a position of power. No, that would not happen again.

She was sure of one thing at least: something in Black's well-laid plans had gone wrong. Otherwise Lombard would still be alive and making her life miserable.

Annabelle pushed open the door to her apartment. Both arms were filled with groceries.

"Mary!" she cried, kicking the door closed. "It's me."

No response. She put down the bags on the kitchen counter, threw her coat on the coach, and went into the bedroom.

The curtains were closed and the room was dark. Mary was sitting in the shadows wearing a bathrobe. Her body was rigid, her hands on her knees, her face impassive. Annabelle sat almost demurely at her feet. She took one of Mary's hands and lifted her eyes toward her young friend.

"Mary," she said, softly. "Mary, I know you can hear me. I wanted to tell you how glad I am you're staying here. That you're here every time I come home. Say something to me, baby. I wish you'd say something. I went to see Kess Sherman this morning at the prison hospital and interrogated him under serum. Strange man. They've reimplanted his ASP. He didn't tell us much. I asked him all about the meeting he had with Engelhardt in L.A. He rambled on about an ASP — a NOX, he called it — that the Mafia was planning to put on the market. Once it's in place, there's no way of detecting it. The guy was delirious. Pretty soon there would be no more ASPs, he said, the FBBS would be powerless. The whole thing is a crock. Engelhardt was toying with them. But I should talk to Black about it. Hey, I'm babbling, aren't I?"

Annabelle got up and pulled Mary to her feet. Like a sleepwalker, the young woman allowed herself to be led over to the bed, where Annabelle sat her down. On the night table was first-aid equipment: bandages, ointments, a basin.

Annabelle lifted off Mary's nightgown. The thorax was completely swathed in gauze, which Annabelle very carefully unrolled.

Then Annabelle removed the bandages that covered the rest of her body. Only the breasts were clean of wounds.

She carefully washed the wounds with compresses dipped in liquid soap. The wounds gave off a putrid odor, but she didn't notice. She even smiled, an expression no one outside that apartment had ever witnessed.

"You'll see, Mary. Pretty soon you'll start to talk again."

Mary's features shuddered at the pain, but her expression didn't change.

When she was finished, Annabelle kneeled before her. She waited for a long time for the young woman to show some sign of recognition. Then, very slowly, she leaned toward her. Barely had her lips brushed against Mary's breasts than the young woman, without seeming to break out of her trance, shoved her away with tremendous force.

Annabelle sprawled on the floor. She jumped up, her features disfigured, and hurled herself at Mary, ready to strike. But she stopped. Mary's face was blank once again. Annabelle melted to her knees and burst into sobs, her hands covering her face as if in prayer.

Mary didn't move.

2

Verne and Clara walked along the banks of a frozen creek. The deep snow had transformed bushes and trees into wondrous forms. The sun was about to disappear behind the hill, and in the dying light the snow crystals created an unending spread of white sparks.

Hands plunged deep into the pockets of his borrowed parka, Verne was speaking softly.

"Misha Oblomov's agonies lasted for weeks. Before his death, which I could not explain, I discovered that the HIV retrovirus had mutated, and that it had eluded standard treatment by invading the sperm cells. In those days, everyone was rushing to perfect an AIDS vaccine. I had been preoccupied with the fever, which is the universal symptom of the disease. The monocytes in the blood act very strangely in this fever — monocytes are a kind of leukocyte — and this had to do with the leukocytes. With SF, the activated monocytes produce a pyrogenic protein called interleukin–1, which creates the fever. I studied that protein."

"Can you explain it to me?"

"If the temperature of the blood rises to a temperature of 101 degrees — what normally happens in most SF cases — it produces 'heat-shock proteins,' or HSPs. These proteins don't exist when the blood is at normal temperatures. We discovered that the blood of Sacred Fire patients contained abnormally high quantities of HSPs. Four or five times as many as in the blood of a healthy person when it is heated to the same temperature. We also discovered the blood of some healthy people never produced HSPs, even after being heated. We called them 'HSP negative.' Fine. We have never found SF cells in people who are HSP negative."

"You mean they're immune?"

"That's our hypothesis. Until someone proves otherwise, I don't see what else it could be. *If* we find out that the subjects all have a particular biological configuration somehow involving their blood — so that it doesn't produce HSPs when heated — and *if* these subjects never get SF, we will have made an important first step toward a treatment."

"A natural immunity."

"Exactly. Then we would need to discover how that immunity works and why there are no HSPs. After that you figure out how to inoculate vulnerable people. But I'm afraid all this is a very long way off."

It was almost night. Clara slid her hand into the pocket of Verne's coat and took his hand in hers.

"What are your thoughts about the origins of these HS proteins?"

"Probably they're fossil proteins. Useful to us at a stage in our evolution when our thermic balance was higher — in other words, when we were still birds, a few million years ago. There we enter the privileged domain of Joseph Milner — genetic archaeology. The Maggie gene. Eight thousand years old, according to Milner's calculations. His duplication of the Maggie gene was a technical masterpiece. Many scientists think that it was clever and nothing more — there is nothing to prove Maggie existed in any of our ancestors. It could have been a particular species, they argue, cousins of an extinct line. If that were the case, then it would be nothing more than a scientific curiosity."

"But what do you think?"

"I think Milner's discovery is amazing, but I wouldn't have gone as far as he did in his conclusions. Milner's followers believe Maggie represents a revolution in science. Joe hoped to prove that our ancestors had a gene that suddenly disappeared, without our knowing why. We had lost a piece of our phylogenetic past. If that were so, the consequences would be enormous. Do you understand why?"

"Not really."

"I'll try to explain. In biology, we have a spatial perception of time. A million years of evolution produces a molecule of DNA, and all we can do is map that molecule out on paper. The history of this molecule appears only as a projection on the space of that piece of paper. That's how we see it. We cannot trace what is transmitted from generation to generation through time. In other words, we have no way of tracing the increasing complexity of a DNA molecule — from the moment, millions of years ago, when the first amino acid appeared at the bottom of a pond, to today. We see the vast difference between the most elementary of all living things, the virus, and the specialized cells of our bodies, but we know nothing, or virtually nothing, about the history that links them. The dimension of time is absent in our formulas. We work in a kind of time-zero, a vacuum, like children who say 'yesterday' to designate the space behind them, and 'tomorrow' for what is in front.

"The question Milner poses is this — how can the element of time be introduced into our research? Not time in some mythical, imaginary, or even metaphysical sense, but as an active element of biological evolution.

"Milner's questions plunge us into nearly pure theory. Here's an example — why did the AIDS virus appear when it did? The scientific response is that it was chance. Plus the conditions necessary for it to spread, such as the promiscuity, drug abuse, population growth, migration patterns, and so on. Without realizing it, we do away with the whole question of time by subdividing it into categories — chance, on the one hand; a series of statistical hypotheses on the other. You could add hygiene to the list. Why not? The number of baths in a given population, the amount of soap used, and so on. All this data really tells us nothing. The truth is we still don't know why AIDS appeared when it did."

"So Milner thought that it wasn't just by chance that AIDS appeared back in the 1980s."

"He also thought it wasn't just by chance that what was involved was a retrovirus. What we lacked, he felt, were concepts that might help us evaluate the influence time has on phenomena."

"In other words," said Clara, "saying it was chance was a way of avoiding the question of time."

"Precisely. Milner thought that the fact we were dealing with a retrovirus forced us to ask this very question. In neo-Darwinian terms, the retrovirus is an anomaly. It 'knows' too much, so to speak. It does things way out of proportion to the protocols of scientific thought. A fundamental principle of biology, as written before the discovery of the retrovirus, is that extranuclear RNA can't become DNA, moving from the periphery to the center. Retroviruses force us to rethink our conception of the organisms' defense system, the differentiation between the 'self' and 'non-self,' and also reproduction. Everything that constitutes us as multicellular animals. This, Milner believed, was the revenge of time on space.

"All this is pure speculation. We haven't the slightest idea how to make time as useful to our work as space. It is not at all clear that we can do in biology what Einstein did in physics. I know what Milner was looking for. I'm just not sure we can find it. Above all, we should stay on the plane of scientific rationality, which is our only foolproof approach. That's where we will find the concepts that are missing. *If* we find them.

"Milner, of course, didn't believe this," Verne continued. "He was even open to the occult. Very different from occultism."

"I don't understand the difference."

"Occultism tries to ascribe a supernatural agency to observed phenomena. That didn't interest Milner. For him, it was simply a question of finding a new way of thinking. He became convinced that our way of studying life was a screen. We were creating barriers. Science does more than rationalize the world. It creates new ills we could not fight because of the limitations of our approach. That's what Milner meant when he said we have to look for what we have forgotten. What we have forgotten will reappear, but masked behind wildly unscientific modes of thinking — legends, religions, myths. Maybe now you can understand why following him was so dizzying. He was looking for a whole new ethic."

"A new ethic?"

"Yes. The old ethic — supporting the Fuchs Amendment, suspending democracy to save the population, as a means of gaining time to come up with a cure — Milner believed would guarantee we'd never find that cure. There was no continuity between our research and our ethical, ideological, and political stances. He believed defending democracy should be an integral part of scientific research. The progress of thought and spirituality are inseparable from the progress of science. I didn't agree with him. If we abandoned Fuchs and the principles behind it we would be left with a democracy of the dead."

"Do you still feel that?"

"Yes, though I am not without my doubts."

"I get the feeling that you're closer to Milner than you want to admit," said Clara.

"Maybe. But I got tired. Joe would go from outrageous optimism to the darkest pits of despair."

Headlights appeared.

They stood still, barely visible in the falling darkness.

She wanted to add something, but changed her mind.

Then she was in Verne's arms, and this time their kiss seemed to last forever.

3

The auditorium of the Hoover building was packed, and the atmosphere was tense. Black's relations with the press had never been cordial — he told them virtually nothing, and almost never held press conferences.

Every Washington journalist and correspondent was there early, some an hour, waiting for Black to arrive at the podium.

Annabelle didn't have an easy time claiming her place in the section cordoned off for personnel at the side of the stage. It was chaos. A dozen technicians maneuvered television cameras. At least two hundred journalists were crammed into the seats. Others lined the walls and stood three deep at the back of the room. All the major news anchors had come in person.

Annabelle saw Betty Shrine sitting across from her on the platform. Whenever she caught Annabelle's eye, she jabbed her finger at her and smiled. What was Shrine trying to say?

Annabelle glanced at her watch. Black was ten minutes late. This was not his style. She felt nervous, especially when she noticed two other assistants who had been close to Lombard whispering to each other. Probably wondering who would replace Lombard.

Finally, Black appeared through a side door. Annabelle caught a glimpse of Larry Walton. He, also, was staring at Annabelle.

What was going on? Why all this high drama? Annabelle wondered.

Black stepped up to the microphones, one hand in his suit pocket. He waited for the room to become quiet.

The director of the FBI was one of the few men in Washington to dress the way the old gumshoes used to — pinstriped suit, conservative tie, sky-blue button-down shirt.

The hubbub slowly died down, but Black remained silent. He was taking his time, raising the factor of intimidation.

Then he turned his gaze to Annabelle and held it for so long that it was followed by everyone in attendance.

Annabelle fought an urge to get up and leave. Black began to speak.

"Ladies and gentlemen of the press, I have just finished talking to the President. That is why I am a little behind schedule. I should add that I also tried to contact Attorney General Taylor, but I have learned that he is unfortunately out of town. Doubtless he is preoccupied with the international colloquium he has so brilliantly organized in our capital."

A few snickers. Everyone knew there was no love lost between Black and Taylor.

"Despite the delay, I hope I have your full attention . . ."

Why all this soap opera? Annabelle thought.

". . . because I'm afraid that what I reveal to you today will raise a good number of questions we may not have time to answer. I am therefore going to speak for a few minutes, then Larry Walton, whom you all know, will make himself available to all of you for as long as you like."

There was grumbling. Unperturbed, Black waited for the room to quiet.

"You would be wrong not to take full advantage of Mr. Walton. He knows as much as I do."

"Not enough to avoid questions," mumbled a voice.

The laughter that followed was disorderly and loud. Black was unmoved. Annabelle had the feeling he was enjoying the scene immensely. He waited, even began looking at his watch.

Silence was finally restored. Black scratched his tonsure.

"Ladies and gentlemen, I'm afraid I am here to deliver some tragic news. Claudia Lombard, the director of the FBBS, has been found assassinated."

Everyone in the room gasped.

"Her body was found at six this morning in two garbage cans at the intersection of H and Sixth streets."

"Sir, did you say *two* garbage cans?"

"I did indeed. Two garbage cans. Director Lombard had been decapitated."

The room seemed to erupt.

Annabelle thought she could discern the trace of a smile on Black's face. Larry Walton was still partially hidden behind the side door. His hands were shielding his eyes, as if he didn't want to witness some horrific vision. He was deathly pale.

"Your attention, ladies and gentlemen, please," continued Black. "I will tell you as much as we know at this point. But you must allow me to speak."

It was quiet again.

"Claudia Lombard was discovered dismembered. She was fully dressed, and according to the medical examiner, Dr. Bernard Beadle, there were no other indications of violence or abuse except for some minor injuries to one of her ankles. I should add these are preliminary results. Dr. Beadle will be available tomorrow morning for your questions when he has completed a full autopsy."

Black paused. The room was eerily silent. The director was thoroughly enjoying the scene.

"You doubtless want to know what might have been the motive for the assassination. By murdering Claudia Lombard, this individual or group of individuals has declared war on the whole Bureau. You will also want to know what leads we have on the case, and I assure you we will keep you posted on all new developments over the course of the next few days. I give you my solemn word." Black sighed, as if trying to contain his feelings.

Christ, what a ham, Annabelle was thinking.

"I will need to be graphic for a moment. The head had been severed from the body with remarkable precision. Dr. Beadle will elaborate later, but indications are it was accomplished in a single stroke. I think you appreciate the significance of that feat. One blow — to cut through the neck at the level of the sixth vertebra, through the muscles, the carotids, the jugular veins, the tracheal artery, the nerves. The expertise would be admirable were it not so hideous."

The journalists were nearly as stunned by Black's fascination as by the details he was providing.

The guy is nuts, Annabelle was thinking.

"The murder, in other words, was as well planned as it was executed. And it has a signature, does it not?"

"Yakuza," came a voice.

"Absolutely correct, Ms. Sheller. Yakuza. Only the Japanese Mafia, with its long tradition in the martial arts, could accomplish such a feat. And only the Japanese Mafia might believe that it would be able to elude our grasp. What is their motive? Not gambling, nor drugs. I am convinced that we will discover that alcohol is involved."

He *cannot* be serious, thought Annabelle.

"We are working on the supposition that the Mafia has realized the profits to be made by selling alcohol to the Worshiping sects, which, as you know, have been growing. Alcohol that they use to unleash ASP discharges, which leads to 'orgiastic death,' as they term it. We have lately seized several boats loaded with alcohol. We are sure of their provenance. The money involved in operations such as these is enormous. That the traffic is being orchestrated by a criminal organization from outside the United States should not come as a surprise to anyone. This is the inevitable result of the weakening of the American Mafia, and its inability to resist foreign control."

Annabelle was having a hard time believing what Black was trying to pull off. Exonerating the American Mafia by criticizing their inability to "resist foreign control"! Annabelle could just imagine Engelhardt howling with delight at Black's fancy dialectic footwork.

"I need not remind you," continued Black solemnly, "that the entire affair involves our national security. We have contacted Japanese authorities, and Prime Minister Tokosato will be consulting with the President in" — Black looked at his watch — "about two hours. The National Security Council will convene immediately to discuss further measures. The White House will communicate its findings."

Then Black looked at Annabelle.

Now what? she wondered.

"The investigation into the Japanese connection began several weeks ago. I cannot provide details at this time, as that would jeopardize the lives of agents out in the field. Claudia Lombard had been leading this investigation. We believe that is why she was abducted from her home three days ago. We were informed that the Japanese wanted us to release two Yakuza currently in federal prison — Sato Kamakura and Teitaro Yoku. We refused to negotiate for their release, as always under such circumstances, and Director Lombard was murdered. We said nothing to you in the hope that we might save her life. We could not. Now we will concentrate all our efforts on bringing to justice those responsible.

"I have one more announcement. I am pleased to inform you that I am appointing Agent Annabelle Weaver to take charge of the investigation."

Every head turned toward Annabelle.

"Agent Weaver ably served Claudia Lombard as second-in-command, and her superior thought very highly of her. I will add that as soon as she has concluded the investigation, I will nominate her to assume the direction of the FBBS. The Bureau could not hope for a more dedicated and gifted leader. Thank you, ladies and gentlemen. Larry Walton will now take your questions."

Chapter 16

1

Verne peered through the porthole of his cabin. The sun was sinking below the horizon, and the water had turned green. In the distance he could see lights along the coast among what looked like clumps of trees.

He guessed the boat was anchored in a bay or estuary.

He lay back, exhausted. The plane ride he'd taken that same morning had not been smooth. At long last they had put down on a private airstrip. Verne climbed into the back of a truck and then, after a half-hour drive, was put aboard a small launch, and then onto a larger vessel. Two sailors had helped him aboard, then led him below. He was on a private yacht somewhere on the East Coast. The heady odor of iodine and the sound of sea gulls screaming above him filled the evening air.

He watched the watery reflections dancing on the ceiling, still too tense to sleep but soothed by the pitch and roll. He mused that if he should disappear now no one in the world would ever know what had happened to him.

A sailor wearing a T-shirt with SEAWOLF printed on it in white letters opened the door carrying some coffee. He handed it to Verne, then left, closing and locking the door behind him.

Verne sipped the coffee and thought of Clara. They would probably never see each other again. Too many obstacles stood in the way.

Soon he was lost in the contemplation of his cuneiform fingernail, staving off self-pity. The glass in the porthole began vibrating. They were raising the anchor.

When the sailor came back to get him the boat was moving.

It was night on the bridge. The yacht, a luxury liner of at least seventy-five feet, moved parallel to the shore. The air was cold, but Verne found it invigorating.

Verne entered the main cabin and found three men waiting for him.

One had a broken nose and cauliflower ears. He had obviously known the inside of a boxing ring. His gleaming white hair was plastered straight back. Next to him was a small, ageless-looking man, entirely bald, wearing a bathrobe of black-blue silk. The third was a Japanese in a dark suit, white shirt, deep-red tie. Verne happened to notice he was wearing a jade signet ring; part of a finger was missing.

Two men stood on either side of the door. One was wearing a hat. A fedora, by the look of it. It was hard not to stare at it.

"Ah, Dr. Verne. Come in and sit down," said the bald man, indicating a chair across from him.

"Have we been introduced?" Verne asked formally.

The bald man laughed. It sounded uncannily birdlike.

"Where the hell are my manners!" he exclaimed jauntily, getting to his feet.

"My name is Michael Engelhardt. This is my associate and friend George Mattei. And this is the honorable Kenzo Ozaki from Japan. Now, please, park yourself. I thought we'd have a friendly chat — kind of a discussion. When it's over you can go wherever you want. New York, am I right?"

Verne sat down, feeling sure he had heard the name Michael Engelhardt before.

"Where are we?" he asked, ignoring the question put to him.

"Chesapeake Bay," answered Engelhardt, obviously satisfied to find his guest so cooperative. "Only about thirty miles from Washington, as the crow flies. Had a good trip?"

"A little rocky."

He had just noticed Engelhardt's eyes were different colors.

"Perhaps you could tell me why you've invited me on your yacht," said Verne. "If that isn't asking too much."

The inevitable laugh. Verne expected it this time.

"Asking too much! I see you've got a sense of humor! You didn't ask to come here! But, please, let me say that I am very honored to have as guest on my boat Dr. Paul Verne, the guy who discovered SF, and an eminent member of the Biosociology Commission. I am *very* honored."

"I, too, am honored," said the man from Japan, inclining his head.

The boxer said nothing.

"Anyway, Dr. Verne, we've invited you here because of a specific problem we think maybe you can help us with. We would have also invited Ms. Hastings, if she hadn't needed to get back to L.A. in such a hurry. But I'll be honest and say that you're the one we really wanted to talk to. As you can tell, we have very good contacts with some of the tribes. You've been incredibly lucky. The night in the snowstorm—

that poor bastard who died in the ambulance. What a way to go. Anyway, you're here safe and sound and that's what counts. Right? And Ms. Hastings will get safe passage to L.A., thanks to our native brothers. Like us, they know that helping the Network is in their best interests. You probably understand the reasons we feel this way."

"I have no idea what you're talking about. Who is 'we'? Are you some kind of an organization?"

Engelhardt fixed his eyes hard on Verne.

"Yes, that's it," he said, in a tone diminished in enthusiasm. "We're an organization. We hope you'll work with us. The fact that you've been on the run for the last week gives me some encouragement. Am I right?"

Verne remembered. Someone named Engelhardt had been picked up by the FBI for running a bootlegging operation. He was released for lack of evidence. A Mafia capo. What would a capo want with a biologist? And what did he mean when he said he was helping the Network?

"No, you're wrong," Verne said finally. "The police are only looking for me to ask me about Clara Hastings. There are no charges pending, none that I am aware of. I was only doing my duty as a doctor. But I must say, I still don't understand — "

"That's why you're here, Doctor. So that you will understand."

It was Verne's turn to smile.

"Just tell me what your organization is."

"Dr. Verne. Why not just lay your cards on the table? We know everything about you. We know about your work at the Institute. We know about your wife Melissa, the Commission. You're a celebrity, Dr. Verne. That's the least we can say. And now you're on the lam. You don't go back to the Institute. You take the train. You've got every FBBS agent in the damn country looking for you. You help someone from the Network get away. I can't be telling you anything new if I say that the FBI is very interested in what you're up to. And you're pretending that you don't know a thing. How do you expect me to believe that, Dr. Verne?"

"But I'm telling you that — "

"What about that letter you're carrying?"

Verne was so surprised he nearly patted his pocket to make sure it was still there. Why on earth would the Mafia be interested in the letter?

"I'm not sure I understand."

"Sure you do. We both know Milner offed himself. Probably something to do with Socrates. He wanted you to pass along a formula to a Chinese scientist at the U.N. Let's get beyond this. What do you say?"

Verne was completely nonplussed.

"Why would you care about an organization like Socrates?"

Engelhardt stared silently at Verne. Then he laughed, and this time his Japanese colleague joined in.

"Dr. Verne. I'm having a hard time swallowing this. You are either one slippery bill of goods or naive beyond belief. Socrates is just a bunch of thinkers, right? Sure. Don't tell me you don't know that every police agency in the world is hunting them. Word is that even the Network is small-time next to Socrates. But I get the feeling you don't believe me."

"I don't."

"Then read Milner's letter again, Dr. Verne. Especially the message at the end."

"How on earth can you know about this?"

"The organization I work for has lots of friends. But I'll be honest and tell you we haven't learned how to break the Socrates code. These guys are pretty smart. Maybe you know something that can help us."

Verne was becoming aware of the fascination he was feeling for this man.

"Why are you so anxious to meet with a member of Socrates?" he asked abruptly.

"A good question. Maybe you know about the interests of our organization."

"Money."

"Right on the nose. Money. We want a business arrangement."

"From what you tell me about Socrates, I don't think money is what interests them."

"Correct once again, Doctor. And that means we're not competitors but partners. We have something to sell, and we get something in return. Sounds reasonable, doesn't it?"

Verne shrugged.

"Let me help you. Have you ever heard of Dr. Sozo Kawakami?"

"Yes, I have. Dr. Kawakami is a physiologist who specializes in neurology. I recall reading that he had succeeded in keeping a human brain functioning for a week using perfusion."

"One *month*." This from the Japanese man on the couch.

"Yes, possibly. What is the connection, Mr. Engelhardt?"

"Dr. Kawakami now lives in Nagasaki, where he works for our sister organization. My friend Kenzo here represents them." An exchange of nods. "The eminent doctor has succeeded in perfecting an ASP that is both harmless and undetectable."

"That's imposs — hard to believe. The implant's code. What about the code?"

"Thanks to a program developed by some Toshudo technicians, who have worked closely with Dr. Kawakami, this is not a problem. The NOX, as it is called, does exist. The three of us are living proof."

Verne looked at George Mattei, who without breaking his stony expression gave him a little wink.

"What we are trying to do now," continued Engelhardt, "is put together a network with international connections, one strong enough to deal with the governments and agencies. That's where Socrates comes in."

"What about Sacred Fire? Are you telling me that you plan to release male sexuality back into the world? You'd kill millions of people just to make a profit?"

"Kawakami and others think there are other ways of fighting the disease. It has to do with immunizing. I'm told that people without homosexual history in their family are protected. Homosexuality would be a sign proving that there's a defect in the family's heredity. Good riddance, you know? Natural selection."

"What you're saying is monstrous."

"All I want you to do is to translate the Socrates formula and put us in contact with the person you're supposed to meet at the U.N. In exchange we help you. Put you in contact with Clara Hastings again. And we give you a NOX."

"You want to fit me with a phony ASP?"

"Think it over. We'll take you to New York. In fact you'll be there by tomorrow morning. The boat will be anchored near New York for three days. All you have to do is come to the boat. We have everything needed right on board. Takes about half a day. You come out a different man."

"This is absolute lunacy! If you think — "

"Three days to make up your mind. If you don't agree, we have other means."

"What are you saying?"

"Something deadly serious, Dr. Verne. You'll do what we want, willingly or unwillingly. What I'm offering now is a chance to do it willingly. And it's a limited-time offer."

2

"Hyatt!" screamed Kess Sherman. "Hyatt, I need the bedpan!"

The fucking buzzer didn't seem to work.

He had just woken up, and his head was throbbing. For the first time in the week he had been in Washington, he was emerging from the torpor caused by all the injections he'd been administered — each one with a smile — by Dr. Cline.

There was no joy in his cell. The implant hadn't been smooth. No point hoping for patient-friendly post-operative care at a federal hospital. As for using a local anesthetic, normal procedure for the implantation of an ASP, Cline wouldn't hear of it. He was more interested in understanding how the Network had managed to disconnect it a year earlier without damaging anything. Cline had done a messy job, and Hyatt already had had to change Sherman's bandage a number of times.

For Sherman, the only source of satisfaction was the way he had resisted that hyena Annabelle Weaver, despite all the truth drugs they pumped into him. The same surgeon who removed the ASP had made him undergo hypnotic treatment for a few days after disconnection, as a way of protecting him from the FBBS. It had worked. The hypnotic suggestion would eventually collapse, however.

Sherman shifted his body. The pain in his left thigh was less acute. The deep sleep had at least refreshed him. Cline had assured him that the dislocation didn't need surgery.

"Mr. Hyatt! Damn it!" he howled. Where was the man?

The clock above the door indicated five to nine. This was the first time no one had come to wake him at seven-thirty with coffee and a bowl of cereal. His need to piss was overpowering. He didn't think he'd be able to make it across the room to fetch the bedpan, which was sitting on a table. The idea of being basted in his own urine was repulsive.

The cramps were getting worse. Had they left the bedpan across the room deliberately? Was he being watched? With the Virginas his private functions seemed to be of great interest to a general public. He couldn't help but laugh remembering — he knew he couldn't hold it much longer. What the hell. Who cared? He wasn't about to hold a press conference. He would end up in some prison counting each passing hour toward some hypothetical release date. Twenty years. At least twenty years.

There was the sound of a key turning in the lock, and the metal door swung open, revealing the form of Dennis Hyatt — thirty, thinning hair, affected gestures. Behind him was someone carrying a tray.

"Thank the lord, Mr. Hyatt, and pass the bedpan!" he cried.

"Are we hungry?" Hyatt asked, in a cheerful voice.

"No. Mr. Hyatt. The bedpan. Behind you — hurry!"

"Oh, my. Poor Mr. Sherman!"

Hyatt picked up the pan and hurried over to the bed with it. The color came back to Sherman's cheeks.

"How terrible! How could this have happened? I will make sure this gets reported!"

"Don't trouble yourself on my account, Mr. Hyatt. Things are better now. Water under the bridge. What happened this morning?"

"Oh, Mr. Sherman, it's this strike. Terrible, I'm telling you. The hospital staff has joined prison guards in asking for a salary increase. A picket line kept us from getting into the prison for two hours. Finally some kind of agreement was made. But even so, I wonder what could have happened to the night guard? You poor man!"

The door swung open again and in strode Annabelle Weaver, accompanied by a uniform.

"Good morning, Sherman," she said with enthusiastic sarcasm. "See? I just can't live without you." She looked at Hyatt. "Could you leave us alone for a bit? Thanks."

"Yes, we need to be alone," chimed in Sherman, doing a passable imitation of Annabelle's voice. "Oh, and don't worry. Ms. Weaver is in no danger from me, now that the spider is back in the ole web."

Hyatt harrumphed at Annabelle, then strode out under the watchful eye of the uniform, who followed him.

Annabelle pulled a chair up to the bed and sat down. Sherman chose this moment to bring out the filled bedpan from under the sheets.

"Ms. Weaver? Would you be so kind as to set this on the table behind you?"

Before she had time to think about it, Annabelle was holding the bedpan. She rose and, crinkling her nose, set it on the table. She sat back down with a murderous look in her eyes.

"Waiting is doing you no good, Sherman. Little fish like you — "

"Ms. Weaver, what have I ever done to you?"

"Little fish like you I pick up and swallow whole."

Calmed somewhat, she took a microphone out of her pocket and set it on her knees.

"Now, Sherman, I want to hear some more about those NOXes — those little phony implants you and the mafioso talked about. What did you say his name was? Engelhardt?"

"Weaver, what's the point?"

"I'm not through with you yet, Sherman. When I am, however, you will be sorry we ever crossed paths. So, tell me more about these NOXes."

3

The schoolbus stopped with a hiss of the air brakes.

"Bellevue. Last stop," yelled the driver, a Chicano whose long hair was knotted around his tonsure in concentric circles.

The passengers got up silently. The humidity that covered the windows made the air almost unbreathable. Verne let a man pass in front of him — a large, middle-aged black man with a feverish expression, a long beard with white streaks, a blanket over his shoulders — then buttoned his parka and got off.

The mammoth buildings of the ancient hospital disappeared into the mists that came in waves off the East River. Cold crept into the bones. Shivering, Verne followed the blanketed man, who was heading for the main building. They were a silent troop of homeless people, all over twenty-five — the cutoff age established by the Bureau of Human Resources.

Every evening at seven, a score of buses waited for passengers on Third Avenue to take them to either Bellevue or Fort Washington.

The younger ones had to make their own way. Every night, they gathered by the hundreds on the stairs of the subways, in Grand Central Station, under makeshift cardboard houses, in abandoned buildings, in all the public places where there were small sources or leakages of heat. They were almost entirely men. Most indigent women were cared for by WoMLiP, the Women's Movement for Liberation from Pregnancy.

Few escaped ending up in Special Hospitals in Harlem or the Bronx, or in centers run by the religious sects that had crowded into the cities. The FBBS method of surveillance was rigorous. Biomedical teams carefully monitored every movement of the indigent population and kept a close watch on their contact with the rest of the population.

Verne was aware of all this when he got on the Bellevue bus. Exhausted, he was relieved the line was moving fast. A clerk asked everyone to keep quiet and expose the electronic tag on their shoulder.

One by one they went through an ASP checkpoint under the scrutinizing eye of uniforms.

Verne was reminded of the Pennsylvania checkpoint. The two setups were depressingly alike.

"You're new," said a technician with the shaved head, glancing at Verne's bare shoulder.

"Yes, I mean I — "

"That way please," interrupted the man, pointing to a door and turning to the next in line.

In the adjacent room, the large man he had seen on the bus was sitting on a stool. The rolls of his bared stomach nearly covered his thighs. A nurse was applying a pad to his shoulder. The man grimaced.

"You can get dressed," the nurse said to the shoulder.

"Can I go to sleep?" said the man, rising slowly.

"No. Now you have to go into that room for some questions. Then you can sleep."

The man walked out with what Verne thought was remarkable dignity.

Verne wondered if he could do as well. At first, the idea of avoiding the Mafia and the FBBS by moving with a homeless troop seemed perfect. He'd left his bag at Grand Central, taking nothing but the clothes he was wearing. He had torn some holes in the sweater on the train and had rolled the parka in the mud. On the street he'd used every technique he could think of to throw anyone following him off his trail. A night in the subway made him wonder how long he was up to the challenge.

A hotel was out of the question. Hotels would be watched. Verne was convinced that Engelhardt was right — he probably was wanted for aiding and abetting Clara, a member of the Network, a felon. They would be watching his friends and colleagues, as well. Imposing on them would put them at too great a risk.

The most important thing was the mission Milner had given him. The rest he would have time to worry about later. Eventually he would go back to California, after he'd convinced the FBBS and the Mafia that he was of no use, and no danger to either. Maybe he'd see Clara if he went back. And then what?

He couldn't say. What had happened between Clara and him surpassed his understanding. Sometimes he thought about going back to the Institute and picking up where he had left off on his work. At other moments he was seized by an emotion of such intensity that it was hours before he felt himself again. His pulse rate even slowed.

He thought about what Engelhardt had proposed and how he'd

immediately refused the offer. The erotic dream he'd had the next night had strengthened his conviction. He had been awakened by an ASP discharge, just like during the early days after the implant.

"Did you hear me? You can go."

Verne glanced at his shoulder. He hadn't even felt the tag being applied.

"What? Oh."

Verne got up and buttoned his shirt. Then he went into another room, where he found himself facing a woman.

"Sit down." She repeated his number — TDB11955 — and told him under no circumstances could it be changed. Otherwise he would not be permitted into any New York City shelter. Did he understand? Did he have any ID?

"No," answered Verne.

"Nothing? A driver's license? Work certification?"

"No."

"Name?"

"Brown, William L."

She keyed it in.

"Okay, Mr. Brown. You've been assigned bed 1207. Twelfth floor. Take the E stairwell at the end of the corridor. The elevators do not work. Lights are extinguished at 8:45. If you have to use the bathroom, use the plastic bucket next to your bed. You must be out by seven tomorrow morning — bed made, bucket emptied and disinfected."

Verne rose and left the room.

The air was chilly and he put his parka back on. He was shivering as he walked toward the E stairwell, perhaps because he hadn't eaten. He had stopped at a soup kitchen but had been unable to finish what they gave him.

The stench in the corridor made Verne gag. The odor of urine and stale air was overpowering.

At stairwell E, at the end of the corridor, for the first time since he had been in New York, Verne was warm. Steam ducts emptied into the stairwell. The air smelled like rust.

Verne moved with difficulty through the clusters of men — handicapped, lung-hacking, arguing — on the landings.

On the fourth floor, a group of bystanders were urging on a fight.

Verne didn't think he'd make it to the twelfth floor. Each step was a kind of victory. Why was everyone staring at him? He looked and felt like one of them, but when he passed by conversations stopped midstream. He began to worry.

He caught a few words. It was his parka. His parka was creating the attention. He picked up the pace. Luckily, the population became sparser the higher he went. On the tenth floor landing he hurriedly removed his coat and folded it under his arm. He was sweating profusely.

On the eleventh floor, he caught up with the big black man from the bus. On the twelfth floor, there was no one. He picked up one of the buckets from the stack near the stairwell and went down the hallway.

The rooms had no doors. Cots had a number painted in bright red on the frame. There were no directions, and Verne wandered around until finally he found his number. The man from the bus was sitting on the adjacent bed.

There were no sheets, and the mattress was black with mold. Verne decided to lie on top of the blankets. He folded his parka into a pillow and lay down. Nausea from the stench of urine kept him awake. He glanced over at the man on the opposite bed.

The man had not taken his eyes off Verne.

"My name is Bill Brown," said Verne.

"Mine's Hannibal."

"Hannibal what?"

"Just Hannibal. My real name isn't important, Dr. Verne. And couldn't you have done better than *Brown?*"

Verne stared at him for a few seconds.

"How did you find me?"

"I was watching the front of the United Nations Plaza hotel. I saw you go by. The rest was simple."

"That means that others will have — "

"You were lucky. The FBBS and the Mafia didn't spot you. They were too busy watching each other. There was quite a crowd at the U.N. this afternoon."

"My problem is how to get into the U.N. If the FBBS or FBI stop me before I — "

Verne bit his lip. How did he know if this guy really was in the Network? It could be a trap.

"We'll get you into the U.N.," said Hannibal. "Maybe that will convince you that I am who I say I am."

Verne smiled at his perspicacity.

"And how will you do that, Hannibal?"

"We can do it. It was one of the first things Antigone asked us to work on when she got back to L.A."

"Antigone? You mean . . . ?" Verne cleared his throat. "How is she? Do you have any news?"

"Yes, I have news. Not good, I'm afraid."

"What do you mean not good?"

Verne's voice rose. Someone who happened to be shuffling past the doorway looked at him.

"You should be more careful, Mr. Brown," said Hannibal.

Hannibal got up and glanced in either direction down the corridor, then went and sat back down on the bed.

"It'll be all over the newspapers tomorrow. Antigone was arrested with two others during a raid on the Montebello Crematorium. It was a trap. Agents had suspected she would be part of an attempt to steal Polynices' ashes. They were right."

"Where is she now?"

"L.A. police headquarters. But I don't think they'll keep her long. She's broken a federal law, and the eastern feds want her."

Verne closed his eyes. If he needed proof of how he felt about Clara, he had it.

"You've got to get her out of there," he said.

Verne began to grasp that with these words he was crossing over definitively into illegality. The compromise he had managed to make with the public powers, a compromise in which his ideals and skepticism played equal parts, was finished.

4

Annabelle was having trouble sleeping. She was sitting in the living room in her pajamas, sipping some tea.

Mary Peale's mute presence was beginning to drag down her spirits. The young woman seemed completely normal: she ate, washed herself, slept. But she refused to let Annabelle near her. Since that night she had not uttered a single word and would sit in the bedroom chair for hours on end, waiting for Annabelle to come home.

Annabelle had thought that taking Mary outside might bring her to life, but she was like a sleepwalker. Once, she abruptly changed direction and started crossing a busy street. It was a miracle she hadn't been run over.

They didn't go out now.

Annabelle knew this could not go on.

She would have a talk with Mary's doctor and ask her to recommend a clinic. The government insurance agency had agreed to pay for treatment.

A slight noise coming from the bedroom distracted her attention. She listened. The door was open. Maybe Mary was awake.

Annabelle felt cold air on her face. She ran into the bedroom. The window was wide open. Mary was nowhere.

Annabelle went to the window and looked down.

On the sidewalk, four flights below, she could see Mary's nightgown fluttering on the sidewalk.

The next day, Annabelle went to the 12th Precinct police headquarters accompanied by Lieutenant Steve Holmes. Whatever his suspicions, Holmes had not detained the nominee for director of the FBBS, who needed to join Director Black on his way to the airport.

Black delivered his condolences in an emotionless voice. To Annabelle's great relief, he made no allusion to the fact that Mary had been staying with Annabelle. It was clear the suicide was of only marginal interest to him. What was interesting had happened before that.

Black had asked Annabelle to join him on his ride to the airport to discuss an appeal from the Boston Group, newly reconstituted and now going public, which had enjoined all American citizens to join them in a march protesting the Fuchs Amendment in Washington on April twenty-third.

"The President believes that a demonstration permit to march should be denied," Black explained to her. "I agree."

"I wonder if that isn't exactly what the anti-Fuchs forces hope will happen."

The limousine was leaving Federal Triangle and crossing the Mall.

It was warm for the twenty-fifth of January. A mild breeze came out of the southeast, an intimation that spring was less than two months away. Annabelle was feeling buoyant. The administration's concern over this demonstration did nothing to dampen her pleasure at being named acting director of the FBBS.

Mary's death had been an enormous relief.

"Come now. You're not going to suggest we should cede any power to the Network, are you?"

"No, Director. All I was saying was that — "

"Look at Harris Taylor, that spineless twit. He would be ready to put up with any kind of Network silliness rather than take any sort of political risk. Luckily, the President is in my corner. The march might actually be a publicity success, a bigger one than we can imagine. As many as a million might come. That's not to be sneezed at. Imagine the impact on the rest of the country. Maybe worldwide. No, the march cannot take place, and we should in any case begin to take precautionary measures — block access to the Capitol, tighten checkpoints, that sort of thing. It would be a good idea to open a temporary internment camp for disruptors who manage to get through our defenses."

"You're probably right."

"I know I'm right."

Annabelle sighed again.

"Will you be alone with the President?" she asked, changing the subject.

"I haven't the slightest idea. All that I know is that there is no way I can get out of spending a weekend at her ranch."

The limousine glided along the Tidal Basin, past the Jefferson Memorial.

"In high school," said Black after a pause, "one of my teachers forced us to memorize some lines from the Jefferson Memorial. 'I swear before almighty God to hate for all eternity any form of oppression to the human spirit.' I wonder what Mr. Jefferson would say today. He'd probably deliver sermons about how we have to fight tyranny. The human spirit? That's the easy part. The spirit defends itself without anyone's help. It's the body that's defenseless. It has appetites and needs and catches incurable diseases, and then you have to keep it from infecting other bodies. Any body poses a potential danger. I'm in far more danger from your biology than I am from your spirit. By the way, I want to chat with you about Clara Hastings."

"She's being held by the police in Los Angeles."

"I am aware of that. Take the local authorities out of the picture as quickly as possible and bring her here. Network lawyers are more than capable of finding some pretext to irritate us with."

They passed over Memorial Bridge.

"Would you like to meet with Clara Hastings personally?" Annabelle asked Black.

"I would indeed."

"Director, can you tell me why you are so interested in her?"

"Listen to me, Weaver. I hadn't intended to tell you this so early, but perhaps this is the right moment. The person I am really interested in is Paul Verne."

"Verne?"

"Yes. I believe he thinks he's very clever, but he is going to help us set things right."

"I don't follow."

"He is going to do us an immense favor, and help rid the country of a danger that threatens us all. Without knowing it, of course."

Black seemed to pause to admire his own mental processes.

"For that to come to pass, I need to meet Clara Hastings."

"But — "

"I'll tell you more next time. A delicate business. When the moment comes, Weaver, I'll need your help. For the time being, keep a tight rein on the FBBS, just as you have been. There has been more fallout from Lombard's assassination than I would have thought."

"I will, Director."

"Good. Well, I think we're there."

The limousine passed in front of the terminal and continued toward a guarded gate a few hundred yards farther along.

Annabelle was very much looking forward to meeting again with the young woman who had slipped through her fingers.

Chapter 17

1

The Gramercy Park Hotel, Hannibal explained to Verne, was owned by a South American company that contributed to the Network cause on a regular basis. The manager, a former Uruguayan soccer star named Ramon Saltillo, had set aside two furnished rooms in the basement for Network use, rooms that were off the regular police inspection route.

No one would have guessed that the unobtrusive metal door that opened onto the ground floor of an anonymous building on 22d Street was connected by an underground tunnel to the basement of the hotel.

Verne and Hannibal had left the Bellevue shelter at six in the morning and had gone straight to the Gramercy.

The first thing Verne did was take a long, hot shower. He was shaving when Hannibal came in to tell him that the Chinese Delegation had been invited to a Long Island villa belonging to the State Department. Hannibal's source had also told him that Ban Zhao, to whom Verne was supposed to pass along Milner's message, had postponed her return to China and could be reached at the U.N. at the beginning of the week.

Verne had the weekend to think things over.

The idea that he would be able to halt, if only for a few hours, the roller coaster his life had become these last few weeks was accompanied with relief. He hadn't stopped thinking about Clara. He knew what happened to anyone who resisted Fuchs, so he had no illusions about what would happen to her.

Why were anyone's ashes that important? What were they compared to freedom? Like many scientists, Verne felt that what happened to the body following death was of scientific importance alone. A corpse was a wax doll, nothing more. Only the living mattered.

Sitting on the bed studying his fingernail, he asked himself — again — why he hadn't stopped her. And again got the same answer. It would have done no good. He remembered Clara's expression. He recognized the look of pain and determination.

When Hannibal came back later with some food, Verne gave him a letter he had written to Melissa. The Network had offered to deliver it to her in person. In succinct terms, Paul had informed her of his decision to finish the mission Milner had entrusted him with, whatever the cost. Now that he was an outlaw, he would not communicate with her until the new order was established. Until then, he asked her to inform the Institute of his decision to request an extended leave of absence. He offered a few tender words.

Hannibal went out again and came back two hours later with the newspapers and Verne's suitcase, which he had picked up at Grand Central.

The account of Clara Hasting's arrest in Montebello, a suburb of Los Angeles, had made the front page of the *Times*. Two men were arrested with her. The article noted that this was the first time that a Bio was known to figure prominently in an organization whose primary objective was to combat the Fuchs Amendment. There followed some speculation about its being a young woman's attempt to look beyond her "artificial origins" by identifying herself with the uterean world. Verne asked Hannibal to find out as much as he could about Clara's arrest.

Alone again, Verne sat at a table. He knew that the time had come to focus his attention on Milner's letter. He took it out of his pocket and unfolded it on the tabletop, smoothing out its folds with the back of his hand.

The sight of the handwriting again moved him greatly, and he turned the pages slowly, then reread the passage about the virus being an entity from the depths of the ages, proof of the amnesia inevitably caused by human progress.

Verne was persuaded that Milner's rhetoric held scant scientific value, but his deep admiration for the tenacity of the argument Milner set forth had not diminished.

He turned finally to the last page and the biochemical formula.

Verne tried to imagine the old man in his garret, blocking out in capital letters the symbols that represented a strict sequence of purinic and pyramidic bases that form the basic composition of an RNA molecule.

The fact that Milner had used this particular way of communicating the formula was in itself rather curious. He obviously wanted to avoid the explanations that would have had to accompany a less symbolic formulation, in case it fell into the wrong hands. It would take time to decode it. Everyone who knew about the formula was utterly convinced that it contained a secret message. That was why they were unable to decipher it: they were looking for too much.

Verne was busy recopying the formula on a pad of paper when his attention was drawn to a small detail. He stared at it. There must be some mistake. There was absolutely no way it could be an RNA sequence. T stood for thymine, a nucleotide found in DNA but not in RNA, where they were transcribed as Us, for uracil. It was a mistake a schoolchild wouldn't make.

Verne looked at the formula more closely:

```
A G U A A U G U A T G C A U U T G A C C C U C C
G U A G A U A A G G G C G A G G G G G A G A U U
A A G G U A G A U U C A G A G G U A G A U G U A
T G C C U C U C G G U A G U A G A U A A G A G C
G C G C C C U C C T G A G G C A C C A A G U G C
G U A A A U C C A A C G U U A U G U U G A G U A
A A U G C A T T T G U A A A U A C A A A G U A G
G A G G U A T G A G A G G U A A A U C U C G A G
G U A G U A A A U G C A A A G G U A A A U G U A
T G C A G C U A U C C A T G C G C C C C C G U A
```

Once he'd recovered from his surprise, Verne proceeded to an operation that was mostly busywork. He copied out the formula, separating the RNA nucleotides — uracil, cytosine, adenine, and guanine — into groups of three, called codons. The original DNA messages are transferred to RNA by these codons and then carried from the nucleus to the cell's ribosomes, where they dictate the amino acid sequences that produce an infinite variety of proteins.

This is what he got:

AGU-AAU-GUA-TGC-AUU-TGA-CCC-UCC-GUA-GAU-
AAG-GGC-GAG-GGG-GAG-AUU-AAG-GUA-GAU-UCA-
GAG-GUA-GAU-GUA-TGC-CUC-UCG-GUA-GUA-GAU-
AAG-AGC-GCG-CCC-UCC-TGA-GGC-ACC-AAG-UGC-
GUA-AAU-CCA-ACG-UUA-UGU-UGA-GUA-AAU-GCA-
TTT-GUA-AAU-ACA-AAG-UAG-GAG-GUA-TGA-GAG-
GUA-AAU-CUC-GAG-GUA-GUA-AAU-GCA-AAG-GUA-
AAU-GUA-TGC-AGC-UAU-CCA-TGC-GCC-CCC-GUA

From a biochemical point of view, the formula couldn't exist. There is no thymine nucleotide in RNA, and no uracil nucleotide in DNA.

Verne knew that Milner would never have made such an error. The Ts had to have some special meaning. There was also the glaring problem of the formula having neither "start" nor "stop" codons, which are essential in "telling" the ribosomes where to begin and end the assemblage of each protein. Milner's formula should have begun with an AUG codon and ended with either a UAA, a UAG, or a UGA. And it didn't.

Suddenly the answer leapt out at Verne. Why not turn the whole formula around? If you reversed it, the necessary start and stop codons appeared. Verne hurriedly began writing the formula backward, noting that Milner had even doubled the codons to make it clear where a line ended. That meant the single stops within the formula represented proteins. Only someone accustomed to the rules of biochemical transcription could have thought of using a mirror permutation.

Verne was beginning to enjoy himself. He remembered the dream he'd had a few days earlier about the scriptural passages at the bottom of the *Retable*'s Annunciation panel. What would Joe Milner have said about that coincidence? He would have said that it wasn't a coincidence, but a premonition. It was all a part of prophetic time — what is behind us shall appear ahead.

It didn't take Verne long to break the text up into sequences beginning with an AUG start codon and ending with either UAA or UAG. The UGA indicated the termination point.

AUG-CCC-CCG-CGT-ACC-UAU-CGA-CGT-AUG-UAA-
AUG-GAA-ACG-UAA-
AUG-AUG-GAG-CUC-UAA-
AUG-GAG-AGT-AUG-GAG-GAU-GAA-ACA-UAA-
AUG-TTT-ACG-UAA-
AUG-AGU-UGU-AUU-GCA-ACC-UAA-
AUG-CGU-GAA-CCA-CGG-AGT-CCU-CCC-GCG-CGA-
GAA-UAG-
AUG-AUG-GCU-CUC-CGT-AUG-UAG-
AUG-GAG-ACU-UAG-
AUG-GAA-UUA-GAG-GGG-GAG-CGG-GAA-UAG-
AUG-CCU-CCC-AGT-UUA-CGT-AUG-UAA-UGA-

Beneath each normal RNA triplet Verne wrote the amino acid abbreviations for which it was code. He would figure out later what to do with the CGTs and AGTs. This produced an eleven-protein message:

AUG-CCC-CCG-CGT-ACC-UAU-CGA-CGT-AUG-UAA-
     pro pro ?   thr tyr arg ?   met

AUG-GAA-ACG-UAA-
    glu thr

AUG-AUG-GAG-CUC-UAA-
    met glu leu

AUG-GAG-AGT-AUG-GAG-GAU-GAA-ACA-UAA-
    cys ?   met glu asp glu thr

AUG-TTT-ACG-UAA-
    ?   thr

AUG-AGU-UGU-AUU-GCA-ACC-UAA-
    ser cys ile ala thr

AUG-CGU-GAA-CCA-CGG-AGT-CCU-CCC-GCG-CGA-GAA-
UAG-
    arg glu pro arg ?   pro pro ala arg glu

AUG-AUG-GCU-CUC-CGT-AUG-UAG-
    met ala leu ?   met

AUG-GAG-ACU-UAG-
    glu thr

AUG-GAA-UUA-GAG-GGG-GAG-CGG-GAA-UAG-
    glu leu glu gly glu arg glu

AUG-CCU-CCC-AGT-UUA-CGT-AUG-UAA-UGA
    pro pro ?   asp ?   met

What remained was to interpret the eleven polypeptides whose amino acid sequences he'd now parsed. He knew that the four RNA nucleotide triplets could be arranged in various combinations to produce sixty-four different codons. Since there were four "A" amino acids, as well as four beginning with "G," and only ten different first letters to the twenty amino acids found in nature, an initial letter code — taking the first letter from each amino acid name — wouldn't generate any meaning.

Then Verne remembered the international code that substitutes twenty Roman letters for sixty-one of the sixty-four amino acids (the remaining three being, of course, the start and stop codons). He jotted them below each codon. Then he had:

AUG-CCC-CCG-CGT-ACC-UAU-CGA-CGT-AUG-UAA-
    pro pro ?   thr tyr arg ?   met
    P   P   T   Y   R   M

AUG-GAA-ACG-UAA-
    glu thr
    E   T

AUG-AUG-GAG-CUC-UAA-
    met glu leu
    M   E   L

AUG-GAG-AGT-AUG-GAG-GAU-GAA-ACA-UAA-
    cys ?   met glu asp glu thr
    C   M   E   D   E   T

AUG-TTT-ACG-UAA-
    ?   thr
        T

AUG-AGU-UGU-AUU-GCA-ACC-UAA-
    ser cys ile ala thr
    S   C   I   A   T

AUG-CGU-GAA-CCA-CGG-AGT-CCU-CCC-GCG-CGA-GAA-
UAG-
    arg glu pro arg ?   pro pro ala arg glu
    R   E   P   R   P   P   A   R   E

AUG-AUG-GCU-CUC-CGT-AUG-UAG-
    met ala leu ?   met
    M   A   L   M

AUG-GAG-ACU-UAG-
    glu thr
    E   T

AUG-GAA-UUA-GAG-GGG-GAG-CGG-GAA-UAG-
    glu leu glu gly glu arg glu
    E   L   E   G   E   R   E

AUG-CCU-CCC-AGT-UUA-CGT-AUG-UAA-UGA-
    pro pro ?   asp ?   met
    P   P   N   M

Despite the gaps and transcription oddities, Verne recognized it immediately. *Isaiah*, chapter 7, verse 15. He'd just been thinking about it. *"Butyrum et mel comedet ut sciat reprobare malum et elegere bonum."* Milner had made his B by using two Ps. The mystery of the CGTs, TTTs, and AGTs was explained as well. Vowels.

Verne leaned back in the chair. He was exhilarated and more than a little pleased with himself. But the more he stared at the page, the more he felt as if a voice from the shadows had spoken to him. The still, small voice of the ages, invoking an authority almost as old as human history itself.

He shuddered. The message had been meant for him. Who else in the world would recognize that phrase from the Vulgate Bible? — "He shall eat curds and honey when he knows how to refuse the evil and choose the good."

Verne admired Milner's ingeniousness. Even if expert cryptographers managed to get to the Latin, or even discover that the passage was from *Isaiah*, how would they guess its connection to Grunewald's *Retable?* It wasn't even *in* the *Retable*. It would completely bewilder them, leave them convinced the code remained unbroken. Which was true. Milner had known all along that if Verne transcribed the formula he alone would understand the reference. Milner had also known that the *Retable* was a source of mystery and inspiration to Verne, that consciously and unconsciously he was drawn to it, as to a mirror that shows you what is ahead and what is behind. From the very beginning Milner and Verne had used it as a reference to Sacred Fire, the disease that eludes science's grasp because it seems to embody a different conception of time.

Milner's colleague in Socrates would be waiting to learn what Verne had decided. He wondered if, like Milner, Ban Zhao also believed it was as simple as refusing evil and choosing good.

2

Engelhardt went into a towering rage when he learned that Tony Calabretta had lost Paul Verne just two hours after the man had set foot in Manhattan.

"We followed Verne to Grand Central," George Mattei told Engelhardt.

"Yeah? And then what?"

"Tony said he just disappeared."

"Disappeared?" screamed Engelhardt. "How could he just disappear? They need a fucking helicopter to shadow someone?"

"Get a grip, boss," Mattei said. "It's not gonna help us get him. Don't worry. He can't have gone very far."

"Where's Tony?"

"I sent him to Bogota on the first plane out. Salazar will use him on one of the farms."

"You're soft, George. You know that? Tony screwed up. It's that simple. This stupid laboratory rat made an idiot of him, and you bought his excuses."

"OK, Michael. We'll put two teams on it, and we'll find the guy. Bogota will do Tony some good. Unless you want me to — ?"

"Nah. Let him twist in the wind awhile."

Nothing came of the search for Verne.

The yacht remained anchored in New York harbor for five days, just in case Verne changed his mind and resurfaced.

Mattei kept up tight surveillance on the U.N. building, but the only thing he saw were FBBS agents. At least that proved Verne had not been snatched by Betty Shriner and her crew.

Verne was the most wanted man in the city of New York. Engelhardt decided that he must have succeeded in getting into the U.N. on the first day. He was on the point of leaving New York for the West Coast when he got a message from Marcello Cavani. A summons to come to Gordon Heights.

Engelhardt's limousine left Interstate 84 and headed toward Brook-field. The capo was nervous. He hadn't been to Gordon Heights in ten years. The last time, Cavani had given him the news about Isabella and the boys. The older was studying law in Milan, and the younger went to the Chigiana in Siena, where he was learning the cello. Isabella still lived in Donnalucata, a little village on the southern coast of Sicily. She was much better now.

Engelhardt wished he had a drink. His eyes followed the line of bare elms on either side of the road. The bleakness of it all made him long for California.

He wondered again if he would ever be given permission to see Isabella. It had been twelve years. He had seen his kids when they came to the U.S. a couple of years ago. Peter, the oldest, had wanted to stay on, to study international law at Harvard. John's ambition was to become a soloist.

Engelhardt's limousine followed the shoreline of a frozen lake. On the other side appeared a strange-looking structure, a kind of giant mushroom emerging from among the trees. White smoke snaked from the chimney. Every time he saw it Engelhardt thought it looked like something straight out of Disney. He knew that monitors were observing their approach and had been ever since they crossed the intersection at Pinetree. This was Gordon Heights, home to Tomas Capecchi, the greatest of the American padroni.

The limousine pulled up before a white gate. Lucio honked. The gate opened. The limo pulled into the driveway that wound upward through several miles of woods, until it reached Gordon Heights, the hill on which Capecchi had built his home.

Engelhardt glanced at the huge bright-red metal Calder sculpture perched on the lawn like some mythical beast. Marcello once told him that Calder had lived in the area. When the sculptor died, his lawn was covered with these titanic creatures. They brought equally gargantuan prices.

They arrived at a snow-covered front lawn, spread before an immense white Victorian house. A semicircular front porch with columns framed the glass entryway.

Lucio signaled to Engelhardt to stay where he was. Engelhardt had no intention of moving. He remembered how things were done at Gordon Heights.

Two men in coal-black suits came out of the house. One opened the door for Engelhardt, the other stood behind the limo, watching.

"This way," said the man who held the door open.

Engelhardt was accompanied into the house through a side door equipped with a metal detector.

The floor of the huge hallway was Italian marble. Oversize mirrors hung from every wall. Engelhardt removed his coat and gave it to one of the bodyguards. The other opened double doors leading farther down the hall.

The living room was luxuriously furnished. Englehardt went to the window that overlooked the back garden. The view stretched all the way to a horizon of wooded hills. One-hundred-year-old oaks sloped gently down to a frozen pond. In summer, the slope was blanketed in flowers.

Engelhardt remembered the evenings he had spent here, twenty years earlier, with Isabella. They had met as lovers, secretly, at midnight in the park, while their friends swam in the pond. Not long after, Isabella told her father she was pregnant. The Padrone's men had come to get Englehardt. They had kept him locked up in the back room of a restaurant in Little Italy for two days. Then a black limousine picked him up and took him to Gordon Heights.

That first meeting with Capecchi had lasted only five minutes, but Engelhardt had known the moment he arrived he shouldn't panic. Being invited to Gordon Heights was a good sign. The Padrone asked only one question: when did he start having sex with Isabella?

Engelhardt told him it had happened here at Gordon Heights, at the graduation party. Capecchi did not reply. Engelhardt breathed a sigh of relief. Isabella hadn't told her father how things really happened, about Aspen.

Before letting Michael leave, Capecchi added two things. He said that for a true Sicilian, the fact that her daughter's lover was of German origin was reason enough to kill him. But he had learned that Michael's mother was Piedmontese. That was an extenuating circumstance.

He also told Michael the wedding would take place next month. The young couple would move to L.A., where he would work for Richie Washavsky — known as Warsaw — who managed their affairs out there.

Engelhardt remembered vividly how elated he felt when he left Gordon Heights that day.

Over the years Engelhardt had made himself indispensable. After Warsaw's death, he had taken over California operations. Isabella had given him two sons. They lived in Bel Air in a home that could modestly be described as a mansion.

One night, everything changed. He had come home late and, as usual, had gone in to kiss the boys while they were asleep. He was coming out of John's room when his attention was diverted by a commotion in his bedroom. He opened the door and came face to face with Bernardi, his lieutenant, his friend, desperately trying to put on his pants. Engelhardt took out his gun. He didn't even hear Isabella's screams.

The whole business was completely suppressed.

Two months later the Padrone personally came out to visit the family at their new home in Malibu. Isabella was sent to Sicily. Michael was told he would never see her again. As for the boys, Capecchi would decide later if their father could visit them.

Don Capecchi had told him on that visit that he was pleased with Engelhardt's work, in particular with his handling of the Sullivan affair. They wanted him to handle the Japanese Mafia, to create what would become the Cartel.

Just as he was about to leave, the Padrone turned.

"Aspen," he said. "Does that ring a bell? She said you forced her to have sex with you, even though she wanted to wait. You raped her and she covered for you. You're a son of a bitch, Michael. You lied to me and you have ruined my daughter's life. I should make you pay. But you are useful to us. We need you. When you are no longer useful — "

Engelhardt had not seen the Padrone since. He learned to live with the fear that some day he may be no longer useful to the organization. Had that day finally come?

"*Come stai*, Michael?"

He wheeled and saw Marcello Cavani, Capecchi's right hand. The man hadn't changed. A few more wrinkles, perhaps, but his hair was still jet black, and his bearing was stiff as ever.

"I'm okay, Marcello."

They embraced.

"You look the same, Michael. Really."

"So do you."

"Sit?"

Marcello pointed to a pair of easy chairs.

"Marcello, I've wanted to ask you, any news from Sicily?"

"Yeah, there's news. Good news. Everybody's doing fine. Isabella's doing great. Peter is going to come stateside next year."

"What?"

"Yeah, the Padrone found a job for him. I think he forgave him for being your kid, Michael. He also says you're doing a helluva job."

Engelhardt regarded him skeptically.

"No, I'm serious, Mike. He thinks you're doin' fine with the NOX business. Our Oriental friends swear by you. Maybe they like Germans better than Italians do."

Engelhardt relaxed a little. This wasn't going to be his final hour.

"On the other hand, there is the mess with this scientist."

"Paul Verne?"

"Yeah, Verne. His disappearance is a problem. You found him yet?"

"No. Not yet."

"Too bad. Verne's going to be important if we set up something with Socrates."

Cavanni was silent.

"Hey, Marcello."

"Yeah, Mike?"

"Do you know why the Padrone wanted me to come out here?"

Cavanni gave him a look of surprise. "Don't you know?"

A door opening interrupted them. A bodyguard walked in.

"Don Capecchi wants to see you."

Engelhardt rose, wondering what Marcello had been about about to tell him.

He followed the bodyguard to the first floor. The bodyguard knocked at the door leading to the antechamber to Capecchi's office. It opened immediately. Engelhardt found himself in the company of an old man, who eyed him silently for some time. Engelhardt smiled. Finally, wordlessly, the man got up and knocked twice. A voice answered. The Padrone's.

The room he went into was small. The light from the window was dimmed by a blind. Sitting at his desk, the Padrone was swathed in an old bathrobe. He was wearing socks.

He turned his head when he heard Engelhardt come in.

"Ah. Sit. I'll be with you in a moment."

He went back to his work.

Having never seen the Padrone except when he was wearing his gray flannels, tie, and pocket handkerchief, every hair in place, Engelhardt felt uncomfortable. He had never seen the great man looking so disheveled.

Il capo di tutti capi wearing socks!

Engelhardt looked around him. The walls of the room were completely lined with bookshelves. The old desk was a beautiful period piece, on top of which was an avalanche of papers and notes; postcards of famous paintings were pinned here and there. There were two books open, and a sheaf of paper with tiny scrawl covering its pages. The Padrone was writing a book.

Finally, he turned to Engelhardt.

"There, I'm finished. You look pale, Michael."

"Padrone, I'm sorry. This is all just a surprise. I didn't expect you to send for me." He mopped his forehead with a handkerchief.

"It is warm in this room," said the Padrone. "But I need to have it warm to write."

"You're writing something, Don Capecchi?"

"Yes, a piece on Spinoza's *Ethics*. Are you familiar with it?"

"Well, uh — "

"No, of course you're not. You would find it interesting. You will pardon my appearance, but I am close to finishing, and I want to waste as little time as possible."

"I understand."

"What are you doing about Paul Verne?"

"Padrone, it wasn't my fault. Tony Calabretta was supposed — "

"Yes. I know that. Have you found him?"

"No, Padrone. But I will."

"Stop looking. Concentrate on our friends in Washington instead. Go there and make contact with Black. I know he is cooking up something and I want to know what."

"Padrone, with respect. I saw him only a few days ago. He swore he would keep his hands off of the NOX business. He was going to draw public attention to our alcohol trafficking, so that we'd have an open field."

"I don't believe him. What did he say? Exactly."

"He told me that he was going to give us trouble about the alcohol, but he wouldn't touch the NOX business. So long as nothing leaked about Nathan Gray."

"Very shrewd. We are to be responsible for the smallest rumor. What about Claudia Lombard?"

"We helped him," replied Engelhardt. "He wanted to get rid of her."

"And he gave the FBBS to that girl. What is her name?"

"Weaver."

"Yes, Weaver. She is shrewd. We will need some kind of plan."

Don Capecchi was silent for several minutes.

"When are the next presidential elections?"

"In two years, Padrone."

"Yes. Elizabeth Hughes cannot run for a third term. Black wants to keep his spot at the FBI. He doesn't want to throw away the investment of all these years to some Democrat. He is negotiating with whoever might run on the Republican ticket. But who? Vice President Knight? Senator Dahl? Cleary? We don't know. I will guess that Black knows. Imagine that the rumor spreads that the Republican Party knew something about Gray's death."

"No Republican would have a chance."

"Precisely. So Black will have leverage over whoever is chosen to run on the Republican ticket. He is clever, this Black. His only problem is us. We could make it known in sufficient enough detail something about Gray and ruin everything for the Republicans. That is what he fears. That is also why he is going along with the NOX business. He needs our silence. For now at least. Because once the President is elected — Are you following me?"

"Yes, Padrone. We will lose our bargaining position."

"Correct. He could simply say that it was nothing but a pack of lies. We have to expect Black to counterattack after the next election. We have two years to make the NOX operation work. Two years during which they will not lift a finger against us. Unless . . ."

"Unless, Padrone?"

"Unless he finds a way of provoking a grass-roots movement against the NOX. Then he won't have to wait two years."

"How would he do that?"

"I cannot say, though I am sure he is considering it. That is why I want you to keep a close eye on him. Go back to Washington and stay there. I want weekly reports."

"That's all. Good-bye, Michael."

Don Capecchi returned to Spinoza.

Several minutes after Engelhardt left, someone knocked at the Padrone's door. It was Marcello Cavani, followed by the old bodyguard who had let Engelhardt in.

"Well, Don Facciotti," said the Padrone, addressing the older man. "Your thoughts?" Capecchi's voice was marked by a deep respect.

"I heard very clearly," said the old man in a feeble voice. "He is tired, Don Capecchi. He would betray us if he could find a way. He should go."

"I share your opinion," replied Capecchi. "We will need someone to replace him in our contacts with Black." He looked at Cavani.

"As you wish, Padrone."

"Is Verne still at the Gramercy Park Hotel?"

"Yes, Padrone."

"Tell Ramon Saltillo to send us anything he finds in the room. Paper in the wastebasket, for example. Verne is ready to negotiate with us to be rid of the ASP. That is what Simon reports, am I right?"

"Yes, Padrone."

"Good. Now things will move. A few more days, and we will have him. I would be very interested to know what he is going to say to the Chinese. Go and lie down for a while, Don Facciotti. I will see you a bit later."

The old man left the room.

Cavani was about to follow him.

"Marcello," Capecchi said, "what did you tell me Simon's Network name was?"

"Hannibal," he replied with a smile.

"Ah, yes, Hannibal. Not a bad name at all. Now leave me for a while."

Chapter 18

1

The driver for Marx Food, Inc., opened the rear door of the delivery van. Before Verne stretched an enormous subterranean depot piled high with an unbelievable quantity of merchandise waiting to be shipped to the various floors of the U.N. building. Two workers in blue coveralls started to unload the truck with a forklift; they showed no surprise whatsoever at the sight of Verne. He was evidently not the first person to use this mode of entering the U.N.

Verne jumped out, and a man dressed in a gray suit approached him.

"Dr. Verne, I presume? Steven Clark. How do you do. I've been instructed to accompany you to see Pierre Orsini. Excuse me, but I need to" — in a swift motion he pinned a badge on Verne's lapel — "now, if you'll follow me." He pointed toward the back of the depot.

The U.N. was buzzing like a beehive. Verne's guide led him skillfully through crowded hallways until he stopped in front of a door bearing a plaque: PIERRE ORSINI, SPOKESPERSON FOR THE SECRETARY GENERAL OF THE UNITED NATIONS.

The two men had just walked into an outer office when a glass door opened and a man came bursting out. He was about fifty, partly bald, in his shirt sleeves with a very loosened tie. He grimaced at the two men before him.

"What the hell do you want?" he asked Clark rudely. His English was heavily marked by French intonations.

"Mr. Orsini, this is — "

Orsini's expression changed abruptly.

"My God. Of course! Where is my head?" he exclaimed, extending his hand to Verne and smiling broadly. "You are Dr. Verne. Pierre Orsini." He gestured to Verne to go into his office.

"I'll be with you in a minute. The Security Council is meeting tomorrow, and as always, there is pandemonium."

The office itself was an indescribable mess. Bottles, glasses, papers strewn across a desk, behind which hung a poster depicting Ajaccio Bay in Corsica. The only window looked down on 43rd Street.

Verne sat down in one of the two visitor's chairs.

"I apologize for the chaos," Orsini said, entering and closing the door.

Despite his flamboyance and harried look, Orsini seemed to Verne like a kindred spirit.

"What's all this commotion about?" he asked Orsini. "Has there been bad news?"

"Things have been heating up since Russia began accusing Turkey of fomenting uprisings in central Asia."

"Yes, I've read about it."

"Well, the Five Powers, along with the non-permanent members of the Council — Albania, Brazil, and Thailand — all walked out of a meeting two days ago. Europe, with the English leading the charge — France following out of obligation, though it would have preferred not to, of course — has taken Russia's side in the matter, while the Americans are behind Turkey, an ally since the ancient days of NATO. That has been happening more and more frequently, I should add."

"What has?"

"The Europeans teaming up with Russians against the Americans."

"That's no reason why the Americans can't come to an agreement with the Russians."

"Should be an incentive, actually. Only the Europeans still believe they can play with the ex-superpowers. As for the Chinese, they stay out of it, at least for now. Lately they're even acting as mediators, and that might last until the Japanese get involved. At this point, everyone will be in favor of jumping on them. But I must be boring you."

"I'm enjoying it."

"I hope you know how happy I am to make your acquaintance, Dr. Verne. We almost met about two weeks ago, and I gather that much has happened since then. You sort of blasted out of here."

"An obligation."

"Well, happily, there are obligations that have brought you back to New York."

"Yes, there are." He was amused by Orsini's volubility. "Are you from Ajaccio?"

"Ah! My poster. You know Corsica? Yes — home of Napoleon, Tino Rossi, and *tutti quanti*. And you're from Alsace, as I remember."

306 /

"Yes, fairly nearby."

The phone buzzed. Orsini spoke quickly into it and switched off.

"That was Ann Van Bricken, from the World Health Organization. Do you know her?"

"By reputation. She is active on the issue of quarantining."

"Which is precisely the reason your Chinese colleague is coming to New York. As part of a delegation that will try to convince the General Assembly to put an end to the quarantining as a 'prime necessity' for refusing to abide by Resolution 1257 of the Security Council."

"Involving 'red countries.' "

"Yes, countries in which the growth rate of SF exceeds twenty percent per year, and that have refused so far to force their populations to have either ASPs or Laïkas implanted, as stipulated by WHO. That is the basis for denying entrance visas, freezing assets, and so forth. WHO is doing everything it can to change short-term policies. To soften the U.N. position, it has decided to subdivide the Reds into countries of primary and secondary importance, which takes into account the standard of living, GNP, and so forth. Generally, the Group One Reds, as they're called, consist of African countries with GNPs below the line. Group Two Reds consist of all the other countries refusing to abide by 1257 for religious or ideological reasons. Today, eighteen countries are involved — an enormous number. WHO has finally gotten the agreement of the Security Council and the Secretary General, so that the quarantining of Group One Reds can be suspended for humanitarian reasons. But the Council added a provision — that the General Assembly approve the suspension."

"You can understand WHO's refusal to go along with any U.N. resolution that makes things more difficult for countries already staggering under the burden of SF."

"Of course. However, WHO's crusade for the Group One countries has little chance of succeeding. As long as the mortality rate climbs, the vast majority of the countries will continue to support 1257. It becomes a vicious circle — WHO wants the Africans to handle their own problems as best they can on their own territory. The Africans have no objection in principle to the implants, but they want to control them. They say they have agencies as effective as the American FBBS to oversee things. But most countries in the General Assembly don't place great confidence in their ability to enforce implantation, particularly because ASPs are so unpopular in African cultures. So they continue to demand that WHO supervise everything. Ultimately, the Group One countries want to be treated like developed countries, but they don't have the means."

"Politics and Sacred Fire are not very good bedfellows, are they, Mr. Orsini?"

"No, Dr. Verne, they are not. The problem posed by the Group Two countries is also deeply political."

"You mean the theocracies?"

"Basically, yes. The Catholic countries that have gone back to Vatican I, like Poland; the Hindu cultures and their castes; the countries in which Buddhist thought is influential, where questions posed by an implant are philosophical. Everyone understands the scope of the problem, but they want to deal with it their way. For countries with large populations of Islamic extremists, SF has been the focus of a Holy War. Not against the disease — against the ASPs. Last month Indonesia, which has a majority Sunni Moslem population, declared a jihad. You should have seen the expression of the representative from Jakarta when he approached the podium to announce his country was resigning its membership on the U.N. Commission for Biological Control. Jakarta closed its WHO office a month ago. The Japanese are talking about armed intervention, under the pretext of endangerment to their population. No one wants to hear more talk of a war in the Pacific — except perhaps the Australians. Last reports are that they would quietly support the Japanese in exchange for help in annexing a few islands."

There was a silence as Orsini distractedly drew concentric circles on a piece of paper. He looked very tired.

"More than ever we need to act in concert," he said finally. "Yet every country is only looking out for itself."

"Fear. They are living in fear," replied Verne. "They are doing what they can."

"Or they don't give a damn," said Orsini. "*Après moi, le déluge.* That's why the initiative offered by Joseph Milner and his friends could be so important."

"You mean Milner's research?" asked Verne.

Orsini got up and put his hands on the desk. He looked straight at Verne.

"So they were right. You really don't know a thing. I have to tell you that I find that pretty stunning. But it's not my position to judge your ignorance. It's also time for your meeting. Ban Zhao will be here momentarily. You'll meet at the restaurant."

Verne found the choice surprising. "Are you sure that's the best place? I would have preferred a more discreet spot."

Orsini burst out laughing.

"We live in a glass house, Dr. Verne. Please believe me that as we speak, the main offices of the CIA, KGB, our own SGDE, and scores of other agencies are actively discussing what on earth the spokesperson for the U.N. Secretary General might be doing with a famous biologist and sometime member of the Biosociology Commission. Ban Zhao's choice is altogether a wise one. Public places are sometimes the most discreet of all."

The telephone buzzed again. Orsini spoke for a few seconds, hung up, then looked at Verne with a tragic expression.

"I have to contact Secretary General Kui. I'll have someone take you to the meeting place."

2

Howard Black's first two days at Pike's Canyon Ranch were interminable. The ranch was pleasant enough — a group of chalets nestled among pines, with a view of the bluish summit of Pikes Peak — but Black had not had a word from the president.

No one seemed able to tell him why Liz had decided to hole up in her residence for two days without attempting to contact either him or any of the other guests invited for the weekend.

Black killed time playing bridge with the undersecretary of the Treasury and the publisher of *USA Today*. They knew no more than he did.

Finally, on Sunday, just as Black was packing to leave, he got a call from President Hughes, asking him to stay on until Monday, so that he could join her on one of her trail rides, her favorite activity. Despite his fear and hatred of horses, Black had little choice but to accept.

Monday morning at seven A.M. sharp, Fred, one of the president's bodyguards, wearing spurred, silver-toed cowboy boots, a blue parka, and pearl-colored rancher's hat, came to get him. The president was waiting in the saddle on her chestnut quarter horse. Another bodyguard was on horseback next to her.

The morning was spent crossing the glorious snow-covered regions near Colorado Springs as Black jostled around atop Master, a six-year-old bay stallion with a will of his own and a marked tendency to stick close to the rump of Darling, the president's mare. The FBI director was having a miserable time of it.

The worst was when Hughes suddenly decided to leave the beaten path and head straight for the forest, which was down a very steep slope. Black's instinct was to pull back on the reins, but once Master realized that his rider was trying to keep him from joining his beloved Darling, he reared suddenly, whinnied, and broke into a gallop through the deep snow.

The president stopped to enjoy the spectacle of Black clinging with both arms to the neck of his horse. Only when he reached Darling did Master permit his rider some relief by flinging him off. He came to an undignified end in a snowdrift.

Fred the bodyguard leaped off his horse, helped Black to his feet, and brushed him off. The president's laughter rang loud and clear. Later, Black would remember with a pleasant shudder Fred's strong arms coming to his rescue.

Scraped and bruised but essentially unhurt, Black finished the ride on the back of Master, who, having regained his place at Darling's rump, was gentle as a lamb. Black's thoughts ran dark and deep. Had the president known what she was doing when she plunged ahead down the slope? Black believed the president had known exactly what Black's horse would do. Instead of enraging him, the idea that it was done intentionally made him thoughtful. He broke out of the mood only at the end of the ride when Hughes asked him to join her in her residence.

Seated before the fireplace, surrounded by hunting trophies, he waited for the president to change clothes. After a few minutes, she emerged in a satin jumpsuit knotted around the waist. Her buzz-cut accentuated the angularity of her features. Her reputation depended to a large extent on the vivacity of her gray eyes.

Mustering all her charm, Hughes asked Black if he really had recovered from the nasty fall, about which she was truly sorry. He assured her he had. She also apologized for having been reclusive for the last two days. The international situation, as perhaps he knew, was worsening. Finally she began to shed a little light on her recent strange behavior.

"How long have we known each other, Howard?" she asked abruptly.

"Nearly thirty years, Madame President."

"That's right. At the time you were — "

"An attorney for the Supreme Court for the District of Columbia."

"Ah, yes. And teaching at GW Law School, just when I arrived."

Black didn't feel this was an auspicious start to the conversation. This was the first time Liz had brought up their meeting in other than an allusive or nostalgic manner.

"Do you remember our interview in your office, when I was leaving GW?"

"Yes, of course. You were going to New York to get married."

"And I made you a promise, do you remember? I said, 'Someday, I am going to need your help.' "

"Actually, Madame President, those weren't your exact words."

"No?"

"What you said was that one day you'd call on me. Not, someday I'm going to need your help. They are not the same thing, if I may say so."

"Of course they are!" exclaimed President Hughes.

"As you wish — "

"Howard, it doesn't matter. What I was talking about was our first meeting, and our pact. It was a kind of pact, wasn't it?"

"Indeed, it was. And you have kept your part."

"How do you mean?"

"I mean, Madame President, that now you are calling on me."

"Stop being impertinent. I have appointed you to one of the most powerful and prestigious positions in government. And I am not in the least having second thoughts — you are still one of my closest allies. Someone on whom I can count. That is true, is it not, Howard?"

"Indeed, Madame President."

"I don't doubt it. That's the reason why, when Senator Dahl told me that — "

"I beg your pardon?"

"Senator Arthur Dahl. Of course you know him . . ."

"Naturally. I thought you said Senator *Moll*."

"That hick? No, I was talking about Senator Dahl. I met with him last Thursday at a reception. He asked if I could spare him a few minutes, during which he told me that if I didn't have any objections — you know how self-important he can sound — he would like to run in the presidential primaries. He added all sorts of niceties, then waited for me to respond. He was hoping to have my support before making the decision public. I have to see him next week at the White House with Clarissa Crowe, the new Republican Party chairperson. Howard, are you up on party politics?"

"I do my best."

"So then! Can you tell me why you haven't said a thing?"

"Because, Madame President, I don't want to waste your time by coming to talk to you every time I learn something about a politician. And Dahl also doesn't stand a chance."

"That's not the point, Howard. The point is that I learned you'd met with him a number of times to discuss his candidacy. Is that true?"

"Yes, I have, but who — "

"I suppose that was just coincidence?"

"No, it wasn't. I have also talked to the vice president and Governor Cleary. I will talk to anyone who looks as if he or she is going to take the risk and run for president."

"And you tell me nothing about it?"

"Madame President, it is my job to talk to them. I would have spoken to you about it when I had a clearer picture of what was going on."

"I must tell you that it is not my conception of your job. Beginning tomorrow, you will inform me, in very detailed fashion, what you have learned through your contact with all three men. Are there any others?"

"No, Madame President. Only those three. You want me to put it in writing?"

"Yes. In writing."

"You will have it by morning."

The president rose, making it clear the interview was over.

Controlling his fury, Black bowed his head to her. He was on the point of leaving, when he turned.

"Madame President, there is something I must tell you."

"Can't it wait?"

"I think not."

"So? What?"

"I have been the recipient of some faint echoes involving the Italians."

"The Italians?"

"They maintain they have some information about the plane crash in which President Gray was killed."

There was a pause.

"I had thought all that was cleared up," the president replied, warily, with an edge of nervousness.

"You know how these things work, Madame President. The Italians have become greedier. I think they intend to begin a new business in the next few months."

"What do you suggest doing?"

"That's exactly what I wanted to talk to you about this weekend. I believe that at any cost we must keep rumors from circulating. They would not be taken seriously by the press, but they might risk the success of some of the programs that you have implemented during your administration. It might give the Democrats the push they need."

"Howard, you're telling me nothing new. We've been over this a thousand times."

"Fortunately, I've maintained my contacts with the Italians, and this enables me to keep abreast of what's going on. It is all a question of strategy. What I wanted to tell you, Madame President, since you have asked, is that the meetings I've had with the future candidates of our party are connected with this."

"Meaning?"

"Meaning I want to make sure they will remain loyal to the administration. I think we will win the next election, but even if that is not the case, we need to help future Party candidates, whoever they are. I know how to do that. However, I wanted to say that if you are not pleased with the way in which I am performing my functions, I am ready to offer my — "

"I will not accept it."

"Fine. Until tomorrow, Madame President."

"Howard!"

"Madame President?"

"I want you to take Air Force One with me from Denver back to Washington. We need to go back over all this. We leave in an hour."

"As you wish."

He left, glowing with the satisfaction that he had managed to put a ray of fear into those celebrated eyes.

Deep in thought, he took the path that led to the main guest house a hundred yards away.

After a few yards he stopped, realizing that this was the first time he'd been alone at Pike's Canyon. Aside from the president, the resident servant, and the two bodyguards, he had seen no one since the beginning of the morning. Yet he knew that the ranch was under strict surveillance. Dozens of uniforms and their dogs stalked the perimeter of the ranch. There were even carefully concealed surface-to-air missiles, ready to knock out anything that approached by air.

But what struck him at this moment was the silence. Not a breath of wind among the pines and maples. He continued walking, finding the unreality of it all disagreeable. Off on one side, he saw a helipad and hangar through the trees. An all-terrain vehicle was parked in front of the hangar. He could hear music.

Walking up to it, he looked through the window.

In the middle of the hangar Fred, the young bodyguard who had been with him on horseback that morning, and Nigel, the other bodyguard, were face to face, a few feet apart, dancing. They were nude. The music was sultry jazz, and to its rhythms the two men moved their toned bodies, their arms raised above their heads, eyes half-closed.

Afraid they would see him, Black took a step back. But the dancers were completely absorbed in each other.

Fascinated, Black watched while Fred danced close to Nigel. Gradually, their movements slowed.

Only inches apart, they reached up to their ASPs and made circles with their fingers.

Suddenly, violently, they embraced each other.

Black gasped for breath. Never had he seen something that so excited him. He realized that he was witnessing for the first time a ritual of the Worshipers of the Sacred Fire.

He heard Nigel cry out and collapse to the ground. He was having a discharge.

Fred kneeled next to his partner and held his penis, bringing his mouth closer to it. Nigel was still shaking with spasms. Then at the moment when Fred put his lips around the tumescent member, he, too, collapsed.

Black sat down in the snow. Then, moving very slowly, as if regaining consciousness, he looked at his watch. The whole thing had lasted only three minutes.

His mouth tasted of bile. He looked inside. The two were resting, one lying on his back, the other on his stomach. Fred's arm lay across Nigel's chest.

Black staggered off in the direction of the guest house.

As he walked, his mind began to clear.

By the time he had reached his chalet, he had but one thought: to take Nigel's place in Fred's arms.

3

Verne could see the length of the East River from the windows of the restaurant, all the way to the Queensboro Bridge. A barge piled high with containers moved slowly upstream, parallel to the snow-covered U.N. garden. In the east, the sun was trying to break through the fog.

He looked around him. Only a few people were seated at the twenty or so tables in the room. The sounds of their conversation were barely audible. Breakfast was clearly not the big meal of the day. Perhaps everyone was at the Security Council meeting that Orsini had talked about.

Verne recognized Ban Zhao the minute she came into the restaurant. She was tall and supple, dressed in a long silk Chinese dress trimmed in green and blue, whose shimmer caught the morning sun. She was wearing black leather flats.

Verne rose awkwardly. Ban Zhao stood before him and smiled.

She was a little older than he had guessed from her walk. There were faint laugh lines around her eyes. Her hair was pulled back tightly in a chignon and diamond earrings hung from her long and pendulous earlobes. She reminded him of the face of a Buddha statue from the Kin Dynasty. He still had the poster from the exhibit somewhere.

"Dr. Verne?"

"Yes. Won't you sit down?"

Her every gesture informed him of the pleasure she took in being alive, as if each object she touched — tabletop, chair — had been created for her to discover.

Impressed as he was, he was convinced her movements were as precise and as fervent when she was by herself. She lifted her long arms with an almost unreal fluidity, her head slightly inclined as if she were listening for his thoughts. Verne felt a slight euphoria; Ban Zhao's beauty had an almost metaphysical grandeur.

They both ordered toast and coffee.

"Dr. Milner spoke often of you, Dr. Verne."

"Did you know him?"

"I did not have the chance to see him often, but I felt as if I knew him well. You were very close, were you not?"

"Several years ago we were. But we fell out of touch. He was very unhappy with the progress of events in the world."

"You believe that is why he committed suicide?"

"You don't think so, Dr. Zhao?"

"I am not sure. Perhaps he thought that he had finished his time."

"He gave up. He abandoned life."

"You are angry with him."

"Yes."

"There is a time when one has the right to give up. That may be the best proof that we have truly lived."

Verne had always found the idea of suicide as an alternative to aging revolting. He knew that what he was doing was accusing his old mentor of cowardice. Still, he was surprised by the calm that came over him talking with this woman. It reminded him of those precious moments he had known with his closest male friends. But he was also conscious of Ban Zhao's femininity, her restrained sensuality, without feeling the impatience, the urgency, he felt when he thought of Clara. In fact, he was discovering the singular pleasure of talking openly.

Watching her hold her coffee cup, he realized the work and discipline that must lie behind such grace: the forearm slightly bent, the effortless way she held an object, each finger in its rightful place. She gave the impression she guided things with her spirit as much as with her body.

"What part of China are you from?" he asked.

"I am from Beijing, where my grandchildren still live."

Verne blinked. Ban Zhao laughed.

"Dr. Verne, I am sixty-five years old. I have two children, and yes, I am a grandmother. My husband died last year. You have heard of him, perhaps. Ban Lushan. He was a physicist and studied cosmogony. He discovered that black holes emit rays. Are you familiar with this?"

"Everyone knows of his Ban Lushan rays," replied Verne reverently.

"I met him in Taiwan, where we moved after the Revolution. My father was a writer, and there was no room for him in the new China. But I have been to China since then, of course, since the Opening."

"What do you do?" asked Verne. "Milner wrote that you were a biologist."

"Not exactly a biologist, though I have worked in a biology lab. My work has more to do with researchers than with research."

"You are a science psychologist?"

Ban Zhao smiled. "Not in the least. I keep laboratory archives."

"Archives? You mean a register of experiments?"

"My objectives are much more ambitious. I keep laboratory history, and write accounts not only of the experiments but of what inspired them and brought them to their conclusion. The questions, discussions, the relations between the researchers. I am an observer whose job is to synthesize what happens in a laboratory into narrative. In a sense there are no true limits to what I do. Everybody is supposed to collaborate with me by offering their observations and thoughts. Yet the work has much more than simple literary interest. It has the great utility of measuring the progress of research."

"That is truly remarkable. Have you published your findings? When did you start?"

"You are reacting exactly the way Dr. Milner did when he came to Beijing."

"When was that?"

"Two years ago. That was the only time I met him, but he made a strong impression on me. He told me that what I did was one of the first concrete examples of what he had long thought necessary to reconsider the bases for scientific thought. I have published nothing. Most periodicals have turned down my submissions. They believe it is much too subjective, too artistic."

"What does your laboratory specialize in?"

"In Sacred Fire, like your Institute."

"Your notes — do they directly influence scientists in their work? I'm sorry to ask so many questions, but I find what you say fascinating."

"You flatter me, Dr. Verne. Yes, I believe my work has influenced certain researchers in their work, and their results. Please understand me, however, it is not for me to write the history of a laboratory, but to find and put together the sources of reflection and sensibility that are at play within it."

"Please explain. Are there other labs in China that do this?"

"Our ideas are beginning to spread. Until now, the government has left us alone. But several months ago an administrative inquiry was undertaken. I will admit to you that we are very worried."

"About what?"

"We can never be sure. Our methods put us in contact with many other laboratories and research institutions. The public powers do not always understand the value of this. To them, it seems suspicious. Our notes have already been the object of several nocturnal visits."

"I still don't understand why I have never heard of your work," replied Verne.

Ban Zhao smiled again.

"I do not find that surprising. Our work method involves radically changing the relationship between the researcher and the research objective, which does not yet deeply concern the government, so long as the theoretical goal of the research has not been altered — and with the government institutions. Their political logic leads states to block our path. We live in an age when the freedom to think has become a fiction. Incredible pressures affect all research. If a researcher believes that work such as mine might assist him or her, that it might explain, even demystify biological events, that is proof that a revolution is at work in the world of thought, and in its relationship with reality. This doubtless will draw a negative reaction from the public powers. It will be a battle. A battle we are seeking. Like Socrates."

"There we are."

"Yes, there we are."

Ban Zhao explained that her work was one example among many of the current revision of the origin of civilization made necessary by the onslaught of Sacred Fire. The collusion of established world powers was the most obvious result. They feared the very intellectual freedom that might have permitted researchers to find a cure. Organized religion had failed lamentably in its attempt to act as the guardian of human spirituality. That failure had resulted in a downward spiral of renunciations of the aesthetic, philosophical, and moral order in the face of scientific progress. It was as if that progress had released humanity from its responsibility to control its own destiny and encouraged it to cling to a single form of belief. Today they were the price of that renunciation.

Ban Zhao continued: "Reality is exacting its revenge. If we want to survive, we have to climb back up the slope. It is our scientific duty. My work persuades me that what is essential is to find where we have gone astray, within ourselves, in our mental habits and, even more so, in the theoretical bases for our experiments."

"It's your opinion that there should be no disjunction between the scientist and the object of study, whether a bicycle or a retrovirus?"

"That is so. But we are not suggesting a strict causality. It is not a question of describing the behavior of a retrovirus simply because the scientist looking at it has a headache."

"I did assume something like that," replied Verne, smiling. "I thought that was a part of Milner's thesis. I lacked a methodology, an experimental framework, such as yours. I felt that I was dealing with the mystical positions badly handled by Milner himself."

"It is not a simple problem, Dr. Verne."

"No indeed. But what can you tell me about your organization?"

"We call it Confucius. Like Socrates, it is made up of individuals from around the country who meet to deepen their understanding of the crisis in scientific research and to find practical solutions, such as those we use in our lab. That is all. We try every path that opens. At the moment we are looking at some of our country's founding myths and trying to evaluate how they have shaped our vision of the world. As you probably know, Chinese civilization owes a great deal to Confucius, Taoism, and Ch'an Buddhism. They are the principal sources of our millenarian culture. But we are not overlooking Marxism, whose role was dominant for so long. Today there are two aberrations triumphant in the world, against which we do battle with all of our strength. One consists of thinking that the progress of humanity is summarized in the progress of science. The other that scientific progress is summarized by the accumulation of material results. You might imagine our joy when we discovered the existence of Socrates in the West. Since then, we have been employing every means possible to maintain contact. Conditions at home and abroad require us to take certain precautions."

Verne wondered if Ban Zhao was aware how little he knew about Socrates.

"I need to ask you a personal question," Verne said abruptly. "I would like to know how you got to this point. I mean, what inspired you to do the kind of work you do?"

Ban Zhao appeared to hesitate, so Verne tried to explain. "I — you see — I feel as if everything is changing for me. And I don't really understand why."

"That is possible," replied Ban Zhao, smiling gently. "I am happy to answer your question. In the beginning I was trained to be a teacher of painting and art history. In Chinese culture, they are the same thing. I did a thesis on the classical painter Shitao. I consider him one of my masters. Have you heard of him?"

"The monk Bitter Pumpkin? I have indeed! I read his *Treatise on Painting* when I was a student." Verne was excited by the connection. "I remember one thing in particular. He wrote somewhere that the activity of the painter is not to imitate nature but to reproduce the very act by which nature creates. That touched me deeply."

"I, too, am moved, Dr. Verne," Ban Zhao replied. "I would not have thought you would know him. Few scientists in the West know Bitter Pumpkin. Now I begin to understand why Joseph Milner esteemed you so highly."

Verne could not conceal his feelings of pleasure.

"Shitao," Ban Zhao went on, "is among those who have best demonstrated the proximity that exists for Chinese people between painting and writing, especially poetry. This is not something many Westerners understand, because you do not have our ideographic writing. For Shitao, a painter is nothing more than a writer working with a brush and ink. In Chinese, the character for painter also means writer. I tell you this because having become adept at painting, it was natural that I turn to writing. I started working in a biology lab somewhat by accident, but when I did I was immediately fascinated by research. So I began studies in biology, and worked as an assistant. To make myself useful, I also started to write. I could have just as well chosen to paint what I saw in the laboratory to cheer up my colleagues, if the director had not convinced me to write."

"Are you the first to do this kind of work?"

"Yes, but I am part of a tradition. Fate had given me the same name as my country's first archivist. You perhaps know the misogyny embedded in Chinese culture. Writing has traditionally been considered a masculine activity. Ban Zhao lived in the century after Jesus Christ, during the Han dynasty. His brother Ban Gu held the position of the ruling dynasty's official scribe. He died quite young and his sister took his place and his name, for the father did not want the family to lose the honor of the position. So Ban Zhao became the first female writer in China and is said to have turned the Records of the Court into a veritable analytical history. She was also the author of *A Treatise on Women*, which made her famous. So there is such a thing as destiny, Dr. Verne."

"Thank you, Ban Zhao, for telling me about yourself," said Verne, with some ceremony.

He looked around briefly, then took a piece of paper on which he had copied Milner's message. He put it on the table and covered it with his hand.

"I guess you know that I have a message for you."

"From Dr. Milner."

"Yes, that's right."

She looked at the paper.

"As you might know, the message was for me, not you," Verne added.

Verne explained how he had recognized the mistakes in the symbolic transcription and decoded it working from this premise. He also told Ban Zhao he was now wanted by the Mafia and the FBBS, both of which were intent on learning what the message was.

Ban Zhao seemed a little surprised that he was wanted by the government, but that he was also being chased by the Mafia left her perplexed. Verne recounted what Engelhardt had told him about the NOX, and about Engelhardt's hope to come to a "business arrangement" with Socrates.

It was Ban Zhao's turn to surprise Verne.

"What you are saying fills me with joy. We have been experimenting at Beijing University with Sozo Kawakami's NOX — or its equivalent — for two years, and we, too, have perfected it. This is known by few. But I believe the government is letting us proceed. The Chinese position with regard to the implants is not as clear as it might seem. Perhaps a holdover of Buddhist skepticism."

"Yes, but . . . the Mafia is a criminal organization! Do you understand that?"

"I respect your idealism, but we are fighting a war, Dr. Verne. Whether NOXes become available through a criminal organization or through some other means makes little difference to us. I am persuaded that the implants have a negative effect on men, and therefore on women, and that this effect overshadows the question of the inhibition of sexual functions. It is psychological, or physiological, whichever you wish. Their most noble capacities are limited because of this — the creative capacities, for example — and that affects the ability to transgress taboos. Many of those in Confucius do not have an ASP."

"And in your laboratory?"

"Every male in the laboratory has a NOX. This has played a large role in changing the way the lab functions."

"They have sex?"

"They take certain precautions. But yes, they do have sexual relations."

There was a moment's pause, then Ban Zhao added, "I also am sexually active."

They remained silent for a while. Glorious sunlight was streaming through the windows.

"I think perhaps we should part," said Ban Zhao.

"Yes. I want to tell you that . . ."

"Tell me what, Dr. Verne?"

"I want you to know that you can count on me, Ban Zhao. That . . . Socrates can count on me."

"I was hoping for that answer," replied Ban Zhao.

They were both silent a moment.

She leaned toward him. "As soon as we have parted, go to the twenty-second floor, where our delegation has its office. There you should ask for Shen Xi. Will you remember?"

"Yes. Shen Xi."

"He will help you leave the U.N. We have said a great deal to each other, have we not?"

She put her hand on his.

"Good-bye, my friend. I think we will not see each other again, but I am happy we have had this time."

"Farewell, Ban Zhao."

Verne stared for a long time at the door through which Ban Zhao disappeared — with a final delicate wave of the hand.

Part III

Two months later

Chapter 19

1

During the latter half of March, President Elizabeth Hughes repeatedly gathered her entire cabinet together for emergency meetings relative to the massive demonstration being planned for April 23. The idea that she would have to witness a demonstration of tens of thousands of people in her capital, all denouncing her administration, was unacceptable.

After first learning about the "Second Appeal of the Boston Group," many of her closest advisers — among them Director Black — urged her to take full advantage of the broad powers accorded her by the Fuchs Amendment: "To suppress or outlaw organizations, publications, films, video programs, pertaining to the Spermatic Fever or Sacred Fire epidemic, for as long as that epidemic continues and until such time as a specific treatment is found and the disease is no longer a menace to national health and security."

Her advisers in the cabinet and on the National Security Council were as divided as she was on the issue. Tired of their vacillation, Hughes let herself be seduced by a proposal from the Secretary of the Navy, Admiral Bernadette Anderson, who, along with the Chairman of the Joint Chiefs of Staff, General Ibbetson, recommended she permit the Marines to be called in for the demonstration. The deployment of the armed forces would be a far more potent message than outright outlawing the demonstration. By allowing it to take place the Hughes Administration would thereby demonstrate its tolerance and sense of fair play to the entire country. Next year was an election year.

Admiral Anderson found an ally in Attorney General Taylor, who feared above all that were the demonstration banned, things could deteriorate. A well-run demonstration was infinitely better than a riot.

Howard Black, Vice President Knight, and the rest of the cabinet were of the opinion that it would be better simply to ban the demonstration, even if it meant sealing off access to the city for an entire week.

Allison Karter, director of the CIA, presented the argument President Hughes found the most convincing of all. She raised the point that outlawing the demonstration would signal victory for the Network and could shift the center of public opinion toward the left.

Denying permission involved considerable political risk, putting the president in opposition to one of the oldest of American traditions: the right of assembly.

On March 24, the White House spokesperson announced to the press that by personal decision of the President of the United States the Boston Group demonstration, slated to take place on April 23, would be permitted.

2

Clara was sitting on the floor, leaning her head against the bed. This time when she fell out of bed, her fall had been broken by the blanket she had spread out on the floor before going to sleep.

The lights were on twenty-four hours a day. Her cell was square, windowless, and covered entirely in tile — floor, walls, and ceiling. The blinding whiteness was not tempered by the two bands of blue, about six inches wide, that ran from floor to ceiling.

When she had first arrived — whenever that was — she had the feeling that she had walked into an immense gift box with two ribbons tied around it.

In a corner were the necessities. A toilet, a small sink, and a mirror in which she could see only part of her face. A shower was fastened to the wall, below which was a drain. The shower worked only when the green light was lit. Clara lived in abject fear that she would be asleep when the light went on, and that she would miss her five minutes of water. If she did, she would have to wait for the next time, and there was no predicting when that would be. As soon as the light came on, she ripped off her clothes — a blouse, skintight white plastic pants — and with indescribable relief ran under the water.

The camera pivoted on its axis to watch her bathe. There was no spot in the room where it could not find her. FBBS agents watched everything she did.

During the first days of her incarceration, she had waited for the lights to go out, though she was sure that they would watch her with infrared. But they stayed on night and day. She learned to pretend she was alone.

Clara got up and painfully slid onto the toilet seat. She looked at the clock above her bed — two blue needle-like hands affixed directly to the wall, no marks to indicate hours or minutes. Twenty to six. She didn't know if that meant morning or night. She had long ago lost all sense of time. All the clock told her was that time had passed.

She had not even been able to mark the walls with hatch marks, that classic jail-cell activity. There was no way of scratching the laminated tiles. And her jailers had of course refused to give her anything to write on or with.

Since being transferred from Los Angeles, she had had no news from the Network lawyer. Seeing her again was the only request she continued to make to Annabelle Weaver.

Her one source of distraction was the FBBS videos that would occasionally be displayed on a wall and then vanish. They were nearly all pure informational propaganda, but Clara waited impatiently for them. They had colors. The room was so devoid of color that Clara had managed to convince herself that the blue stripes were actually black.

The brilliant whiteness drained her. Only sometimes could she make out the faint outline of the door.

Food arrived every eight hours, day and night, through a slot at the bottom of the wall near the toilet. Each meal was exactly the same: cereal of some kind sweetened with sugar, a puree of artificial proteins containing necessary vitamins, and a glass of water. Then the hours would drag by, until she fell asleep exhausted on the bed.

She daydreamed nearly all the time. It was the only way to fight despair. She relived recent events or imagined other ones, made up stories and scenarios. Two people would sometimes appear in her daydreams and talk to her. One was Wes Marshall. Seeing him was always agony. She had failed him. She hadn't been able to bury his ashes in Laurel Canyon.

Paul Verne was the other.

She remembered nearly every minute of every day she had spent with him, seven in all, from the time they had met on the MID base until their parting at Sitt Hokkee's farm. She remembered everything he had said, or at least the tone of his voice when he said it; his voice was so near that sometimes she had to put her hands over her ears. Then the voice would move away. When it came back, she was overwhelmed with relief.

She tried to remember that first night in the ambulance, but all she retained of it was the strange sensation that her solitude was somehow now not as deep. A tissue of human connection had been created to bridge the gap that all Bios felt.

Something came to her from this man and followed her like her shadow. Stretched out on the white-tiled floor, one hand on her stomach, the other behind her shaved head, she knew whatever it was was touching the foundation of her existence.

"Amazing. Simply amazing. Can you increase the contrast?" Black asked the agent at the controls. "Try to get a close-up of her right hand. There, that's it. I want to know what it is doing."

"She's not doing anything too extraordinary," said Annabelle Weaver from behind. She laughed, delighted to see how much her boss appreciated her little discovery.

They were in the control room of the special wing of the District's federal prison facility Claudia Lombard had designed and built for FBBS use. Of the six screens, only the one of Clara Hasting's cell was on.

"There!" exclaimed Black, hardly concealing his excitement at the spectacle. "That position, the way she's lying on her back?"

"It's been going on for two weeks now. Everything is going on in her head."

"Some day, Weaver, we will be able to read those thoughts."

"Until then, take my word for it, Director. The signs are unmistakable. We can listen in if you want and you can hear for yourself. She's saying Verne's name. Yesterday she said his full name. When she does, the emotional and physical signs are as clear as day."

"If you are correct, Weaver, what you have discovered could be of the greatest importance. I am not exaggerating when I say it might even affect national security."

"I'm flattered, Director, but I don't understand."

"We just might have a solution to the problem I talked to you about."

"You mean the trafficking of — "

"This is not the moment."

"No — of course not."

"First, I need to be absolutely sure Clara Hastings has those feelings for Paul Verne."

"I assure you, Director, she does."

"Fine. This is what I want you to do." He brushed his hand over his tonsure. "Meet with Mr. Walton and devise a way of communicating this to the press. Listen carefully. Under *no* circumstances is there to be any mention of Paul Verne. Do you understand me?"

"The press?"

"And no mention whatsoever of Milner's letter. Nor of Hastings's part in delivering it."

"That simply isn't possible, Director."

"Socrates also must not come up. On the other hand, I do want the whole country to hear all about the Marshall brothers and the events following their death, all over again. All about Clara Hastings's failed attempt to get the ashes of — of — "

"Wesley. His brother's name was Calvin. Sir, have you considered the possibility people might sympathize with her? We couldn't control what — "

"Dig up even more details about her life. I want the public to be reminded again about her being the first Bio arrested for involvement in Network activities. Talk about her past, her adoption, her schooling, how she was recruited by the Network. That sort of thing."

"That could take time."

"Invent witnesses. We want people to become interested in her. Talk about her involvement with Wesley Marshall. That'll add a touch of romance."

"You want us to say she was in love with Wesley Marshall?" Annabelle was getting more and more confused.

"No, no. That might be held against her. This portrait of Hastings must arouse sympathy, even among the Uteros. Plenty of people are ambivalent about the Network. I want them to know all about this young Bio, this member of the Network, who risked her life to prevent Marshall's ashes from being scattered. You follow me?"

"Yes, Director. But I'm sorry, I can't do what you're asking unless you explain why."

"You will get explanations later."

"Director, the story may interest no one. What does anyone in this country care about two-month-old news?"

"We have to make them care. Quietly hire a lawyer to start a campaign among the press. She might contest the legality of her extradition to D.C., for example."

"Hastings has a lawyer."

"The Network lawyer? See that she disappears for a while."

"What do we do if Clara Hastings's cause becomes too popular?"

"Weaver, that is exactly what I want to happen. Thirty seconds ago you were wondering if anyone would care about her. Enough discussion. When the operation starts, I want you to have Hastings brought to my office. Wednesday at eight A.M. Clear it with Walton."

"That doesn't leave us much time."

"It should be enough. Do you still have her clothes?"

"They may be in Los Angeles."

"In that case, find her some. I want her looking as natural as possible."

"Should we take her out of the Special Wing?"

"We'll see. That could be another excellent cause for the new lawyer. I want to call this 'Operation Promised Land.' I like the sound of that," he said, wiping his fingers with a handkerchief. "Good-bye, Weaver. Keep up your excellent work."

"Damn that asshole," Annabelle muttered the minute he was out of the room.

"What?" said the agent at the controls.

"Mind your own business," hissed Annabelle. "Make sure you don't take your eye off your prisoner."

She slammed the door behind her.

3

Melissa Verne looked out the window. She could barely make out the houses in Marshall. Beneath the cloud-covered sky, the waters of Tomales Bay were covered with white foam.

She was sitting next to Margaret Brittain in Clayton Powys's living room at Laird's Landing. Around her were friends of Clayton's and Tim's, about twenty in all, seated in chairs or on the floor.

Aside from Tim, who was sculpting something out of a piece of bread, Melissa knew only a few of those present: Matthew Cregg, the plumber who had rolled the first joint of the day; Richard Church and his wife, Ruth, who as always was scowling; Isabelle Irkowitz, who hadn't taken her nose out of a book she was reading. There were others she recognized but didn't know the names of.

The entire west Marin Network committee was assembled at Laird's Landing, waiting for Clayton, who had gone to San Rafael to pick up the Network envoy arriving from Los Angeles. Tim had insisted Melissa keep her promise to Clayton and come to the meeting. He told her they needed her professional opinion about something.

Despite being overwhelmed with her new job as director of Reiss, Melissa agreed, on the condition that she could bring along Margaret Brittain. Tim had no objection.

Melissa and Margaret had become very close. Margaret had changed a great deal. She was less glossy and hard. She was letting her hair grow, and her makeup was applied with a lighter hand. She had also stopped wearing see-through blouses, favoring a loose-fitting black cashmere sweater.

Margaret had been an enormous help to Melissa. The lawyer had initially spent a great deal of time at the Reiss Institute assisting the new director, who she saw or talked to at least once a day.

Melissa had told Margaret she was selling the house to move into an apartment near the Institute. "Stupid idea," Margaret had said. She could imagine Melissa spending all her time in the laboratory and the director's office, devoting her life day and night to her colleagues, like Steve Jackson — who almost never talked to her anymore — or Doris Hathaway. But Melissa was adamant. Two days later, Margaret asked Melissa if she could move in with her at Inverness.

Now they were together all the time.

They avoided talking about Paul Verne.

The front door burst open and Clayton Powys strode in, gesticulating. He looked like a child expecting applause, and he was at least seventy.

"Look what I've brought!" Clayton exclaimed with infectious delight, pointing a finger behind him.

Everyone looked at the striking young woman behind him.

Dressed in black from head to toe, with a leather, waist-length jacket and balloon pants stuffed into heeled boots, she was tiny. Her black hair was brush-cut, her skin pale. She wore a crimson rose made of sparkling precious stones on her left breast.

She looked at the assembly and then stopped in front of Melissa, who was intimidated by the fierce intensity of her dark look.

"Let me introduce Diana," said Clayton, nearly crowing. "When she got off the bus at Green Bay she came right for me and asked if my name was Icarus. I said 'Yup.' Now I know how it feels to have your wings singed."

Everyone laughed.

Diana remained unperturbed. Melissa, who had not taken her eyes off her, thought that the goddess of the hunt was a good namesake.

"Please sit down," Melissa said to the newcomer, pointing to a spot between Margaret and her. "And don't mind my friend here. He makes no attempt to behave."

More laughter.

"I'm glad to be here," said Diana, sitting down.

Melissa noted the Mexican accent and the rose tattoo on her left cheek.

"You're Loca, aren't you?"

The young woman stared at her.

"How did you guess?"

"We have a friend in common. Kess Sherman."

At that moment Tim's voice broke in.

"Let's get started. Diana has been asked by the California group to meet with us. Clayton just explained to me that she was late because of a surprise FBBS security check at the airport. Before handing over the meeting to our new friend, I wanted to say a few words about why Melissa Verne and Margaret Brittain have joined us. Their presence does not mean they've committed to our cause. Melissa's here as a favor, because we need her thoughts. That's all. Let's listen to what Diana has to say."

He sat down, looking quite pleased with himself. Clayton straddled a chair nearby. Everyone was looking at Diana.

"I have two messages," she began. "In the name of the Resistance Committee of California, I remind you of the demonstration set for April twenty-third. This will be the first demonstration since the days of Stanhope Dillon. Since Fuchs, our fight has been underground and has taken various forms. The Network has been the major headache of the FBBS, but our successes have been too modest. We need a way to bring the fight into the second phase. This will begin with the crumbling of the present fascist regime and the reestablishment of democracy. We are beginning the second phase."

Her audience hung on her every syllable.

"The Boston Group is in possession of information that leads it to conclude that the time has come to push. That's what is behind this demonstration. One hundred and twenty political, philosophical, and religious organizations are going to be involved. The whole world will be watching to see if it succeeds. To avoid violence, organizers have been negotiating directly with the authorities. The President's decision to permit the demonstration is exactly what we had hoped. Now it's up to us."

She stopped.

Clayton raised his hand.

"It's been too long since we've had a march on D.C. It's a great idea, but what can I say? Diana, don't take me wrong, but you're much too serious. You remind me of the clowns who are already in power!"

"Clayton, you're out of line," came a voice from the back of the room. "What Diana has said is really important. What I think is — "

Suddenly everyone was talking. Diana simply waited, her expression unchanging. Melissa, watching her, thought here was someone who took life seriously.

"C'mon, you guys!" exclaimed Tim. "Diana is here especially to talk to us. I don't care what anyone thinks. We can talk after she's finished."

The babble died down.

Melissa thought the protest march was important and exciting. A march on Washington would tie them all to a tradition of protest that had been too long lost.

Diana began to speak again.

"The second message is that west Marin must offer a special contribution to the second phase of our fight. The Network needs a secret location where we can unload equipment that will help the cause."

"Contraband?" gasped Clayton in a melodramatic voice. "OK, now! This is getting somewhere!"

"Yes, that's right. Contraband. If anyone gets caught, it will mean prison or a work camp,"

"What kind of contraband?"

"Undetectable phony ASPs," replied Diana, measuring out every syllable. "They're called NOXes, Non-Operational ASPs. They'll be delivered sometime during the summer."

The announcement was met with general stupefaction.

Melissa understood why she'd been asked to come to the meeting. As a specialist in SF, she was supposed to ask Diana questions about the NOX.

She felt very uncomfortable. Just by being there she was compromising the Institute.

It was too late to think about leaving. The NOX could have far-reaching consequences. She needed to learn more about it.

4

Clara Hastings walked into Black's office. She took a step forward, then stopped, crossing her arms on her chest.

Black studied her in silence.

Weaver had tried very hard to humiliate the young woman. It had been a long time since he had seen a woman in a long dress. Only Asian women kept to that style. Yet the humiliation had not succeeded: Hastings wore the dress well.

"Sit down, please."

"I'd prefer not to."

"Suit yourself."

Clara had a hard time taking her eyes off the window and the view of the Capitol dome bathed in splendid spring sunlight.

Black started to rise out of his chair, but as soon as he did, he was seized by a sudden heaviness that forced him to grab the arm of it. It had been happening more and more frequently. Fred got up at six every morning without showing the slightest fatigue. Till now, Black had never really felt his age — and despite the protests of the president's bodyguard, he had insisted on making breakfast for him. It had been their first night together in a week. During the president's ten-day visit to Latin America, he had been crazy with impatience.

"Do you realize how interested the press has become in you?" said Black to Clara, moving to a table and pouring a glass of grapefruit Cocaid. Another bad habit he'd picked up from Fred.

"I'm sorry," he said, turning to Clara. "May I serve you some?"

"No." She was still standing ramrod straight.

"Aren't you curious what they're saying about you?"

"Not particularly."

"You'd be surprised," he said, picking up a newspaper from the coffee table, and reading the headlines. " 'Defense Lawyer Dewey Says Clara Hastings Held in Solitary Confinement for over a Month.' Here, it's in today's *Post*."

He offered the newspaper to Clara. She took it and scanned the account.

"Who is Art Dewey?" she asked. "I've never heard of him. The whole thing's a pack of lies."

"What? You don't know him? Why, let's open an investigation. No lawyer has the right to defend your interests without your cooperation."

"You enjoy yourself, don't you, Mr. Black? You know better than anyone in this city that the only person I've seen is that witch you call your assistant."

"You don't like Annabelle Weaver? She is a fascinating person. But about this Dewey. I thought you had met him in Los Angeles. Not so?"

"The name of my lawyer is Laurie Manheim. I have been asking to speak to her since I arrived here. Everything else is a setup."

"You're probably right. I wouldn't be surprised if the 'Group to Free Clara Hastings' didn't have some other goal in mind."

"What are you talking about?"

"You haven't heard of them either? That's odd. What have you and Annabelle Weaver been talking about? You knew she was the director of the FBBS?"

"That's not something I would boast about."

Clara handed the newspaper back to Black.

"This article has nothing to do with me. I was never a Network leader."

"That's what I wanted to talk to you about, Ms. Hastings. Everything started with the sudden appearance of this group to free you, about a week ago. You have become a subject of some concern to the government. Are you sure you don't want to sit down?"

Without replying, Clara sat on the edge of the chair. Black sat down in his chair, with some relief.

"What do you want from me?"

"I want you to denounce the activities of this group in public."

"Why would I do that?"

"Because they have done you an injustice. You have committed a crime."

"A crime? Don't make me laugh."

"But you have! My job is not to question a law that has been passed by a majority of Congress and ratified by the Supreme Court. My job is to enforce it."

"So do your job and leave me alone."

"Fine. It's just that I was thinking about your youth."

Clara rolled her eyes.

"I am quite serious, my dear Ms. Hastings. I admit that I find your involvement in the Network fascinating because of the circumstances of your birth. I think we can convince you that you have committed a mistake. Spending your life in a government work camp is a pointless waste. Don't you agree?"

"I do, as a matter of fact."

"You're right to. Ms. Hastings, the district attorney could argue there are extenuating circumstances in your case. You'd be in a camp for at most five years and then — free."

"Forget it."

"Don't be too hasty."

"May I ask you a question?"

"Please do."

"Can you tell me why I haven't met even once with District Attorney O'Neel? Not to mention that I've been asking to see Laurie Manheim for weeks. And now some stooge named Art Dewey, whom I've never heard of, suddenly comes out of nowhere and takes up my cause. Since I got to Washington on — "

"February eighth."

"And today is — "

"March twenty-sixth."

Clara's face tightened.

"That means I've spent almost two months in isolation."

"During which time an investigation was in progress. Anything involving the Sacred Fire epidemic and the Fuchs Amendment accords us full powers during a period of three months, renewable for another three months. That makes six months, during which we act as we see fit and, if we think it appropriate, to suspend your civil rights. As you know, bail was not authorized."

"I have nothing to do with SF."

"You're not going to tell me that the Network has nothing to do with SF! Come, come, Ms. Hastings!"

"The Network opposes antidemocratic methods undertaken by your government, period. For years you've been parading SF as a reason for *habeas corpus*. We both know it's nothing but abuse of power."

"Fighting that power is illegal."

"The Revolutionary War was illegal. The measures you've adopted in the name of the people are being used to beat them down. Fuchs makes a complete mockery of the Constitution. It's illegal both in spirit and word."

"A very large subject, Ms. Hastings. I would rather not take on the Constitution with you today, if you don't mind."

"You brought it up."

"How is that?"

"You just asked me to denounce the actions of the Group to Free Clara Hastings."

"That's correct, I did."

"In other words, you want me to deny the constitutional rights of a group of citizens — their right to free assembly and their right to freedom of speech."

"That's not illegal."

"You commit something illegal by asking me to say things and do things you would use to incriminate me."

"Very impressive, Ms. Hastings! I had no idea you were such an expert in law!"

"I'm not. This is going nowhere. I would rather be back in solitary."

Black smiled. The young woman was reacting exactly as he had hoped.

"As you wish. Do you want to know the names of the people involved in the Group to Free Clara Hastings?"

"I don't see what relevance — "

Black picked up a piece of paper on his desk and began to read the names slowly, as if he had a hard time sounding them out.

"Michael Klug ... David ... Hayes, Jane Shapiro ... Katheryn Finch ... Jesse Simon ... Paul Verne ... Bernadette — "

Black observed that Clara had gone white.

"Do you know Paul Verne?"

"You know I do. I don't understand your game, Mr. Black."

"I must confess I enjoy talking to you, Ms. Hastings. I like the way you think. Have you any idea why Verne is so interested in you?"

"Not really."

"It is strange, all the same, because — Did you know that he never went back to work at his Institute after your meeting?"

Clara swallowed hard, trying not to show any emotion.

"Where did he go?"

"We don't know. We lost track of him right after you were brought to justice. All we know is that he's somewhere on the East Coast. He must have benefactors. Possibly the Network."

"The Network? That's impossible."

"Why is that impossible?"

"Because — he has his work, his research. He's on the Biosociology Commission, he — "

"The letter of resignation he submitted to the Commission caused quite a stir. He seems to have given all that up, I'm telling you. Excuse me for saying so, Ms. Hastings, but you look very worried."

"He was a kind and gentle man. He helped me when I needed help. How do you expect me to feel?"

"What I would like to know is whether — in your opinion, of course — he stayed on the East Coast because of you."

"Because of me? You've had enough fun for today, Mr. Black. I want to go back to my cell."

Black sighed. "Very well. You have courage, Ms. Hastings. I have to give you that. Before having you taken back, allow me to ask just one more question."

"I just told you that — "

"If you answer, I will ask Director Weaver to transfer you to a low-security facility. You will be permitted to talk with your lawyer as well as with people from your liberation group. Now can I ask the question?"

"Go ahead."

"Why did you attempt to steal the ashes of Wesley Marshall?"

For the first time since she walked into the office, Clara smiled. It seemed to catch Black off guard.

"Do you really want to know?" she asked, with a hint of irony.

"I just told you I did."

"I suppose you will find it difficult to understand if I simply say that I did not want the remains of the man I considered my brother to be scattered."

"Your brother? You're a Bio. How can you consider him a brother?"

"I do, and that's all there is to it."

"You poor misguided girl. How can you talk about brotherhood to symbolize your connection to a . . . criminal?"

"You don't understand. Wes Marshall was my brother."

"You delude yourself."

"Delude myself?"

"Yes, Ms. Hastings. You would have had to have been born of woman to have the least idea of what you're talking about! Brotherhood is about as real for you as if you talked about — I don't know — motherhood!"

"You think you can draw upon some kind of superior knowledge of what family means because you were born of a woman. Isn't that so?"

"It seems natural."

"Do you have a brother?"

"No, as it happens I was a — "

"Have you made anyone your brother, or sister?"

"How can you be so naive? To say that someone is your brother or sister is to posit the existence of some biological bond — that of the mother. You have no idea what you're talking about."

"And I'm telling you, Wes Marshall was my *brother*. We didn't need your theory and we didn't need to be carried by the same woman to know that we were bound together. We came from the same family. And — since this is the way you seem to understand things — the certitude of that came from my *own* womb, because I have never known another's. You know what, Director Black? You're limited by the fact that you believe you know your biological connections. All I can say is I'm glad other Uteros don't feel that way. Wes didn't and — "

"And neither did Paul Verne."

"And neither did Paul Verne. Correct. Despite what you think, I believe that Bios may be the best judges of what is and what is not brotherhood or sisterhood, if only because they know when a man or a woman brings to them what they were born without."

"You talk about brotherhood and sisterhood as if they are things you discover in life."

"Yes, discovery is the right word."

Black was silent. For a fraction of a second, he had the impression that a voice inside him, a voice he had never heard before, was speaking to him.

338 /

Clara got up. Mechanically, Black rose as well.

The young woman began walking to the door.

"I'm going to have you transferred," Black said. "It will take a few days."

Clara faced the door, waiting for Larry Walton to escort her to the guard waiting outside.

When she was gone, Black walked over to the picture window. He felt a sharp pain in the pit of his stomach. Irritated, he once again dismissed the idea that he might be coming down with something. Only one thing counted now: he was sure he had found the solution to the Mafia problem. Promised Land was beginning to work.

Now, Dr. Verne, thought Black to himself as he watched the traffic along Pennsylvania Avenue, it is coming down to you.

5

Several days later Verne was smuggled into Canada, to a Mohawk Reservation, to meet with the legendary Peter Alexos.

Alexos's features and white hair reminded Verne of the figure of John the Baptist in Grunewald's *Retable*. The saint sits in deep conversation with St. Anthony, who is wearing his simple monk's habit. Alexos's eyes were creased in a way that gave the impression he was continuously on the verge of smiling.

Their talk took place before a fireplace. Alexos launched right into what was on his mind.

"I know that Milner's message was for you and that you figured it out. He felt that no one else would further the cause he lived for better than you, Verne. He couldn't be swayed from the belief that you were the only hope for Socrates in America."

"But there must be other members of American Socrates much better qualified than I am. I understand its purpose better, thanks to Ban Zhao, but I know nothing about the organization, its means of communication, its hierarchy. How can I represent it?"

"Because you're the only member," replied Alexos.

"I represent American Socrates?"

"Yes. There isn't any American Socrates, Verne. Confucius is an Asian organization, and Socrates is European. North America is behind. Nothing has happened here yet, or very little. The reason is simply that American science is more advanced. You were the one we were waiting for. That meeting you had with Ban Zhao was far more important than you realize."

They began to talk about the NOX. Alexos had found out about the thing after the disastrous meeting between Engelhardt and Sherman. He clearly had no scruples about working with the Waikiki Cartel, any more than Ban Zhao did. The National Council — which, outside of the members of Boston Group, consisted of Network leaders from every state — had given Alexos full powers to proceed with negotiations for NOX distribution.

A meeting had taken place between the Mafia and the Network on the Ojibway Reservation in Ontario. Verne was reacquainted with Engelhardt, who expressed his admiration at Verne's disappearing act in New York. Verne thought Engelhardt looked subdued, though his strange-looking eyes did twinkle when he asked Verne whether he had thought about a NOX implant. Sustained by the certainty that he was an outlaw, that the Reiss Institute, the Commission, and Melissa were now parts of a former life, and that he was now a member of the Network, he decided to rid himself of his ASP. It would help him launch the American Socrates.

He boarded Engelhardt's yacht when it was moored in the St. Lawrence Bay, near the Madeleine Islands.

Verne was impressed with the equipment on board the yacht. He asked that no anesthesia be used so that he could follow the procedure. The request was granted.

Lying on a table, his head shaved, he watched via a mirror hanging above his head the extraordinary speed and precision with which the robotic arm — guided by two technicians — worked. His fascination was stronger than his fear.

Thirty minutes later, the "roof spider" was gone.

The car rolled on through the night. Verne rubbed his eyes and looked at the moon blinking through the trees. He had to resist the impulse to lower the window to breathe in the odor of the forest, in case it made his head ache more, the only consequence of the procedure.

Hannibal was driving. Next to him, Melos was on the point of falling asleep. His head was nodding.

Verne had met them that same morning when he arrived at Kahnawake, the Mohawk reserve located on the south bank of the St. Lawrence, a few miles from Montreal. Melos had offered to help Ulysses — Verne's new code name — and Hannibal get back to the United States.

They had gone by boat across Alexandria Bay, on the eastern shore of Lake Ontario, where the St. Lawrence begins. Swollen by the melting snow, the river had not given them an easy passage, though Melos's expertise got them through.

Verne glanced at his watch and sighed. Ten after nine. They would be in Buffalo in an hour.

"How long are we going to be in Buffalo?" asked Hannibal.

"Why do you ask?"

"Because I need to see a friend during your meeting. I'll come back to get you at midnight."

"Fine."

Verne thought it was a little curious. Wherever they went, Hannibal always had to go and visit a friend. Probably Network business. Still, it made Verne feel a little nervous.

He shuddered but resisted the urge to take a pill. Since the procedure he had been having the strangest sensations. He had as yet noticed no difference in his genitals. Still, a vitality buoyed his moods, a new source of energy.

The lack of erections was due to all those years of sexual inhibition. He was discovering the thousands of ways fear of a discharge had affected his body. The side effects would probably last for some time. But what surprised him even more was a new capacity to make mental leaps. He would jump from subject to subject or abruptly burst out laughing. The hormonal rush was making him act like a teenager.

The Socrates Project was taking up all his time. Despite his exhaustion, he felt about his new life as one feels about a sudden release, or the arrival of spring. He would never have imagined that he would take such pleasure in meeting men and women in so many different settings.

He did feel an occasional twinge of guilt when he thought about Melissa, who had vanished from his life as if she had never been a part of it.

One day he might feel that he had lost someone precious, but right now, he was living as he wished. His heart was free to move anywhere it wanted. More than anything, he wanted to share his new joy with Clara.

The second time he had seen Engelhardt, he asked him to do anything he could for Clara. Initially Engelhardt made an obscene comment or two, but Verne had reacted with such violence that the Mafia capo did not raise the subject again, except to say that he would do what he could.

In the car, Verne felt a wave of panic. He found himself performing the old maneuvers to ward off a discharge — pressing his tongue against the roof of his mouth, bending over. Nothing happened. He began to breathe normally again.

Two weeks earlier, he had learned from Hannibal that Clara was being kept in isolation in a D.C. prison.

Verne had gone to Washington, and met with a *Washington Post* journalist, Alexia Pollock, a sympathizer if not a member of the Network, who had learned some things concerning Clara Hastings from a young lawyer named Art Dewey. Verne and Pollock went to see the lawyer, an impeccably dressed man of about thirty. They decided to form the Group to Free Clara Hastings, about which Pollock wrote for the *Post*. Forty-eight hours later, the whole country knew about her.

"Hannibal," Verne said. "When we're finished with things in Buffalo, I want to go to Washington."

"I'd have to make new arrangements."

"Can't we use the same contact as before?"

"Nope. He was picked up for alcohol trafficking."

"So we find another. Can we get as far as Baltimore?"

"I'll need to make a couple of calls."

"OK, do."

"Whatever you want. This is your show. What about our Native American brother?"

"He'll have to get back to Canada as best he can."

Verne lowered the window. The night air felt good. He couldn't help it. He would give anything to hold her again.

Chapter 20

1

The maple in Anacostia Park was in full leaf, just as it had been the first time Black met with Gabriel. But there was a distinct difference between then and now: Black realized how much physically weaker he was. Every step was painful and difficult. Betty Shrine had offered to go along, but he insisted in going alone. He did not want to deviate from the ordinary. The meeting was too important.

Leaning his full weight on a cane his father had used, Black made it to the tree. He caught his breath by leaning against the trunk and looked out across the city.

An indefinable rage flashed through him at the sight of the Capitol dome. An image came: he wanted to lift the Washington Monument like a sword and smash the eggshell of the Capitol.

The image vanished before his conscious mind took it in. His conscious mind was thinking what a fool the President was to allow the demonstration to proceed.

He sneered at her stupidity, then was wracked by a coughing fit that bent him over double. He hawked and spit, tears in his eyes; it took several minutes to catch his breath. As always, he was able to push away any worry about these symptoms. His condition was worsening with every passing day, but he adamantly refused to see a doctor. He almost never left his office anymore.

Fred didn't seem to have a free minute to come visit him — not since that night they had spent together after the President's return from South America. Black had tried to persuade him, threaten him, anything, but the young man steadfastly refused to come and spend even an hour with the director of the FBI. Black couldn't understand why. Few around Black dared to admit their boss's health was worrying them, and when anyone mentioned something to him, however harmless, he quickly put them in their place.

His mother seemed aware of nothing. All she thought about were the Sundays they would be together.

Even Larry Walton didn't attempt to talk about it. He watched the daily progress of the disease with quiet despair.

But today, Black wondered for the first time if the reason Fred was avoiding him was because he was sick. The idea so enraged Black that he struck the tree savagely with his cane and nearly fell over backward.

He heard footsteps behind him. Betty Shrine was approaching him at a full run.

"Director Black," she said, breathing hard, "a messenger from Gabriel just arrived. He said that at the last moment his boss was forced to bring someone else to this meeting."

"What do you mean 'someone else'?"

"That's what he said. Gabriel had no choice, at least that's what the messenger said."

"What is he offering, then?"

"It seems to be a take-it-or-leave-it proposition."

"Take *what* or leave *what?*"

"He comes with someone or he doesn't come. Shall we abort?"

"What good would that do? Let me think. Are they proposing to use the same path?"

"Yes, sir. Both will go through the metal detector. Several of our agents will monitor them. But, sir, if I might suggest. I don't like this last-minute change. Something's wrong. My advice — "

"I don't want to hear it, Betty. But thank you. I'll see them both. Did you notice anything else?"

"No, sir. Well, yes, I did. Gabriel's men were not wearing their hats this time."

"What?"

"I said that this time they were not wearing hats. Maybe it isn't important."

"It's very important. Tell Gabriel I will wait for him. Keep them in your sights."

Black shivered violently and wrapped his camel-hair coat around him a little tighter. He was feeling miserable. He would talk to Gabriel for a few minutes and then be taken home.

He saw two men climbing the path. Gabriel was walking ahead. He looked preoccupied. His usual assurance was gone.

The other man wore a dark suit and was almost as short as Gabriel, but he held himself very straight, as if trying to look taller. Black didn't recognize him. The agents taking photos were probably already researching his identity. If he was willing to expose himself this way, it was because he had nothing to fear.

The two men approached to within a few yards of Black. Gabriel avoided looking at him.

"How are you, Director?" he said with forced joviality. "You look tired. And thinner. Too much work, right?"

"I'm feeling fine, Engelhardt. Why don't you introduce your friend here, the one you have the effrontery to bring to this so-called confidential meeting. I propose that he — "

"Allow me to present Marcello Cavani," interrupted Engelhardt. "He's going to be taking over some of my duties."

Black felt himself swelling with rage.

"Engelhardt," he began, making a supreme effort to control himself, "it is absolutely out of the question that we talk with a third person present. This man is a stranger to me."

"I'm afraid there is no choice," said Marcello softly. "You were told a few minutes ago that I would be coming along. You could have refused then."

Black sensed immediately that this man was far more dangerous than Gabriel.

"Director, look, I'm sorry," Engelhardt chimed in. "Marcello is here on orders."

For perhaps the first time in his life, Black was unsure what to do next. Much more than the nervous twittering of his staff, his hesitation convinced him he really must be very ill.

Breaking with the Mafia was out of the question. Not before the elections.

There was a heavy silence. Black was fighting off nausea.

"You must understand that I need to take precautions," he began. "Engelhardt, are you quite sure your friend here will hold his tongue?"

"Director, how could you have even a second's doubt?"

"All right. This is what I came to tell you — Clara Hastings will be transferred to Horton Prison on April seventeenth."

"What time?"

"In the morning. You'll have to take it from there."

"We will."

"Let me remind you of our agreement. You have to tell me where she is each and every day."

"Agreed."

"Now, a question. Do you know where Verne is?"

"Yes."

"That is all I need to know."

Engelhardt glanced quickly in the direction of his companion, who had not moved an inch. Black could see that Engelhardt was nervous.

"Your agents have been a little heavy-handed with some of our people in St. Louis," Engelhardt said finally. "We hope this was an isolated instance."

"I'd need to know more about it. Alcohol was probably involved."

"That's not a reason. One of my godsons was wounded."

"I am sorry to hear that."

"Otherwise, we are satisfied. I have a message from Mr. Capecchi. He says he hopes very much you will continue to occupy the director's office at the Hoover building in two years."

"Tell him I am flattered, and give him my best."

Black understood he was being informed that the agreement between them would not be allowed to disintegrate after the elections.

"Director Black, my respects. I will use the usual procedure to contact you if I need to."

"As will I, Engelhardt."

"Director," said Cavani, turning away.

Black didn't respond.

He watched the two men walk away. He had a strong feeling he would not see Gabriel again.

2

At the Guest Quarters Hotel, where he had been staying incognito for a week, Verne read on the front page of the *Washington Post* that a van transferring prisoners to Horton Prison had been attacked. Three prisoners had disappeared, including Clara Hastings. It was assumed that this was the work of Network extremists.

Later, as he was walking near Dupont Circle, a cyclist nearly ran into him, deftly slipping him a piece of paper. That was how Verne learned that he was going to see Clara Hastings.

NATIONAL GALLERY, WEST WING, NORTHERN DOOR, APRIL 23. MUSEUM WILL BE CLOSED. 3 SHARP. THIRD DOOR FROM THE LEFT WILL BE OPENED. PASSWORD IS "SPINOZA." YOU WILL BE LED TO CH. NO SECOND CHANCE.

For two days, Verne continued to lead secret discussions with his professional colleagues from a research center in Bethesda to convince them to permit a "laboratory writer" to join their team. He patiently explained why and how it would assist them in their research and help them reevaluate their data.

The lab finally and reluctantly agreed to a trial run. Verne knew there would be interminable discussions, melodrama, and psychodrama, since what he was trying to convince these researchers to allow went against the grain of their habits and their training. It was necessary to swear everyone to secrecy until the day Project Socrates could go public, and this also made them nervous.

On the evening of April twenty-first, returning to his hotel, Verne wondered for the thousandth time what he would do when he was reunited with Clara. Should they run away? Where? Should he talk to Hannibal about it? Probably not. The fewer people involved the better.

They would just have to figure out what to do and where to go when the time came.

3

For several days, a bitter wind had been sweeping through the FBI offices. Everyone was having difficulty accepting the idea that this demonstration was actually going to take place.

Annabelle continued to think that Hughes had made the right choice and admired her acuity.

Two days before the demonstration, she was summoned to Director Black's home. On first entering the modest townhouse on Capitol Hill, she was struck by a strange, sweetish smell, the way the floor of a forest smells after a rain.

Black's mother was a stooped woman with blue-white hair and heavily made-up eyes. Annabelle smiled, amused by her vanity. The FBI director received Annabelle in the living room. He was sitting in a chair covered with wool blankets, even though the heat of the room was oppressive.

Black had aged several years. His skin was the color of clay. But it was his voice that spooked Annabelle the most; it carried the tones of an agony he had been living with — and denying with unparalleled ferocity.

Neither spoke for a while. Annabelle could see that Black was gathering his energy to talk. He had the solemnity of a sick person suddenly aware of how sick he was.

"As you can see, I am unwell," Black began in a shaky voice. "I need to make certain plans, since, at least temporarily, I will not be able to carry out the responsibilities entrusted in me by the President."

"I understand, Director."

"You are an intelligent person, Weaver. I have always thought that, despite your propensity to believe that the world would be perfect if WoMLiP held absolute power."

"I don't think that."

"Of course you do. But that's all right. I understand. What is important today is that men continue to wear ASPs. I assume you agree."

"How could I not?"

"Indeed. The demonstration will take place in two days. The President has not made the right decision, in my opinion. The NSC believes it is smarter than the rest of the world, and that everything will work out well. I predict disaster."

"Disaster, Director?"

"Yes. If I was not there to prevent it, the President would lose next year. Ah, I don't suppose you've heard about her intention to propose an amendment to the Constitution. To the Thirteenth Amendment, more precisely."

"The Thirteenth?"

"Yes, limiting a President's tenure to two terms. Hughes wants to run a third time. She sees herself as the new Roosevelt."

Black began a coughing fit of such violence that for a moment Annabelle wondered if he would emerge from it.

"You'll — pardon — me," he managed finally. "It's the bronchitis."

"Director, have you thought about — "

"You know what I'm going to ask of you, Weaver."

"Director, I was going to ask if you had seen a doctor."

A gleam of fury lit up in Black's eyes.

"Not you, too! I refuse to see those charlatans. I'll be better in a few days. If the President hadn't — She has asked me to find a replacement for a few days so that I could rest. I wonder if you knew that. Anyway, I thought of you."

"Me, Director?"

"You can handle it. Larry Walton will make sure that everything goes smoothly. You do what I tell you to do — you and Walton will be in constant touch. I need to present you to the President. Call her appointment secretary on Monday."

"Yes, sir."

"That isn't all. You're also going to take over the most pressing business of all. It involves — "

"Clara Hastings?"

"No, Weaver" — Black closed his eyes — "Hastings is the bait. The main course is Paul Verne."

Annabelle stared at him.

"Clara Hastings is being held by people I'm in touch with."

"You *know* where she is?"

"Not only do I know where she is, I know that in two days she will meet the resourceful Dr. Verne. Here in Washington. What do you say to that?"

"Do we pick them up?"

"That would be the biggest mistake of all. The important thing is not to lose track of them."

"I'm afraid I'm confused, Director."

Black was looking better. His excitement had put color back into his features.

"Because I want the whole country to know that the man who discovered Sacred Fire — discovered, nothing! *Invented* — has joined forces with the Network. I want everyone to know that while the entire country is courageously coping with the heavy hand of Fuchs, Verne is fooling around with a young fugitive Bio. Now do you get it?"

"You mean he doesn't have — "

"That is correct! He's wearing a NOX! Ha!"

"A NOX?"

"A false ASP!"

"But I had thought . . . you said that — That's terrible!"

"No, Weaver. It's really quite wonderful. Just imagine — instead of devoting his energy and abilities to finding a treatment or even a cure for SF, this former member of the Commission is harboring a criminal. With whom he is having sexual congress! And she's a Bio. Do you understand? The press is going to have a field day. We need to tape them together. We need incontrovertible proof. Imagine the repercussions of their trial. Their death sentence! The dispersion of the ashes! It will be a thing of beauty. I can just see the articles, Weaver! Famed scientist and discoverer of SF is debauching himself with a Network Bio. It will destroy the Network."

Black stopped, lost in self-admiration, then spoke again.

"Verne is going to lead us to the promised land. He is going to help us win the election, but, like Moses, he will not live to see us get there."

Black's cackle ended in another coughing fit.

Annabelle was just beginning to appreciate fully the Machiavellian beauty of the whole operation. The director of the FBI seemed to have thought of everything. He had known all along that the NOX was authentic, and that the Mafia and the Network were in collusion. And he was about to turn it all around.

Her admiration for him was mixed with fear. She had been little more than a cog in this man's diabolical scheme. Had he also planned Lombard's fate?

Leaving the room, she glanced back at the director. He was on the point of dozing off.

He would live, she thought. Somebody like him could never yield to a disease.

4

Since their creation this was the first time the Marine Corps had been called in to do a job that should have been done by the police, or the National Guard perhaps. No one could ever remember a time when the Marines patrolled the streets of Washington. The Joint Chiefs of Staff had argued strenuously that the Corps' prestige would accentuate the dissuasive role assigned to it in Operation Beaver, as it was being called.

Preparations for what would be essentially a military invasion had taken several days. During the entire week before April 23, Washington's citizens were treated to the sight of military personnel everywhere — officers and noncoms both, assiduously taking notes, pointing at maps, measuring distances, and identifying strategic locations. Demonstration organizers performed much the same preparations, glancing nervously at their military counterparts, who studiously ignored them.

On April 21, all government offices were closed at 2 P.M., by order of Federal and District authorities.

Thousands of bureaucrats were therefore able to join with all the other Washington residents already crowding East Potomac Park to watch the great theater of the landing of the Marines. They cheered lustily as the Marines marched by in full battle regalia slightly modified by crowd-control equipment.

At 4 P.M., all intersections, monuments, and public buildings were guarded by armored cars, tanks, and armored jeeps, while the air above was whipped constantly by the blades of hovering helicopters.

At 6 P.M., access roads to sensitive locations, principally the White

House, Capitol Hill, and the Federal Triangle, were blockaded. Only authorized personnel were permitted inside this perimeter.

Authorization to hold the demonstration had been made public on March 24, and had come as a complete surprise to the organizers. Many saw it as a sign that the government was at long last acknowledging the combined power of the groups — religious, charitable, philosophical, labor, and so forth — that had allied themselves with the Boston Group.

Nonetheless, the Network, considerably hardened by their dealings with the authorities, had expected opposition of the most insidious sort from the public powers: checkpoints, searches, intimidation. It was therefore caught off guard when, on April 9, a spokesman for the Secretary of Transportation requested that those who intended to travel to the District by individual vehicles display a decal of a beaver. The logo would be distributed by the government to facilitate the demonstrators' arrival in Washington and would permit them passage through the checkpoints. Why a beaver? Nature's engineer, explained a spokesperson. Also a builder of dams, responded many in the Network.

But officials were true to their word. Moreover, when they got to the outlying suburbs of the city, arriving demonstrators found signs with beavers on them, indicating the fastest routes to parking areas in Rock Creek, Potomac, or Anacostia.

This sudden show of tolerance on the part of the Hughes administration worried many protesters, who at first refused to display the logo. But given all the difficulties with traffic and parking their defiance created, most relented and affixed the beaver.

Friday afternoon and all day Saturday, supplementary trains arrived every ten minutes at Union Station. The airlines had increased the numbers of flights to the capital. Buses arrived by the hundreds, spewing out demonstrators. They gradually began to fill the entire area surrounding the expanse of the Mall and Constitution Gardens, in which the demonstration was to take place on Sunday, at 2 P.M.

The night before, taking advantage of the beautiful weather (though it was unseasonably cold), younger protesters — who had responded in huge numbers to the movement's appeal — spread out their sleeping bags in parks, grounds, and along the banks of the Potomac, and spent the night among the daffodils and budding trees.

That was how it was that on that night the population of the entire country went to bed with images, amplified through the media, of hundreds of thousands of American citizens converging on their nation's capital, in the hope their protest would bring about a meaningful change.

Chapter 21

1

Sergeant Charles Thurston was enjoying himself. From where he was standing, he could see a Clear Fighter laser tank stationed against the fence around the White House garden. Nearby, Firestorm trucks with machine-gun ports stood sentry at the intersection of Pennsylvania Avenue and 14th Street. The transport truck that had carried his squadron was parked a few feet away from the front of the Willard Hotel.

Since Costa Rica, where he had gone head to head against Mendez and others rallying to the Catho-Royalist Revolution, Thurston hadn't worn combat gear — except during maneuvers. His men called him Charlie Skinhead, just "Skin" for short, because of a wound he'd gotten six months earlier during an ambush near Puntarena. A piece of shrapnel had cleanly scalped the back of his head, right down the skull. After three months in a hospital in San Diego, where he'd had his missing piece of skull replaced by an acrylic patch covered with pinkish material, he had gone home to Afton, Minnesota, to recover.

During those six tedious weeks of convalescence, he had thought the boredom would push him over the edge. He was on the point of experimenting with every variety of Cocaid when finally he received orders to report to the Stafford Marine Base in Virginia as an instructor. Not long after, he found himself among the Marines being mobilized to guard the capital from the rising tide of invaders.

His mission had been made clear by Lieutenant Pfeiffer.

"They need to be impressed, Sergeant, and to do that you show them your hardware. That ought to keep them quiet."

Still, there was something else, Charlie thought, though what it was he could not quite tell. Months of training and two years in guerrilla warfare had taught him to take orders with a grain of salt. Orders could be as trustworthy as a quiet-looking coastline in Guanacaste or the smile of a native.

Since he had donned battle gear and strapped on his weapon, he had firmly decided to be ready for any eventuality.

"Hey, Skin. Our turn to patrol," came a voice behind him.

Charlie turned around and saw Shamal Davis running toward him.

"Slow down," drawled Charlie. "No one's balls goin' anywhere, no matter how hot they get." It was a matter of Marine tradition to brag about sex. But the Worshipers of the Sacred Fire knew that it was more than just talk. All the military branches were suffering a veritable epidemic of conversions to the new religion. Not Charlie Thurston. He wanted to become a prison guard at a place where all the "flamers" were locked up.

Charlie saw Susan Field's women's squad coming back from the Ellipse.

So it was their turn for patrol. Charlie adjusted his sunglasses and, followed by Davis, went back to the armored transport where his men were sitting.

"OK, let's move out!" he shouted.

His squad hopped out of the vehicle and fell into line.

"Hey, Skin! Should we put on the safety? Practice safe shootin'?" one asked.

"Stay cool. I'll tell you if we need to make any kind of move. Put safeties on and stay in formation. You'd mow down the whole patrol if you got spooked by your shadow."

The squad snickered.

Charlie began walking in the direction of the Ellipse, followed by his men. He glanced at his watch. It was 1100 hours. A beautiful day.

The *Washington Post* of Saturday, April 22, published an interview with Annabelle Weaver, newly appointed director of the FBBS, in which she explained that the entire FBI had been mobilized to recapture Clara Hastings.

Verne was sick with worry. He wondered if he had not made a mistake in founding the Group to Free Clara Hastings. Given the circumstances, all the media attention Clara was getting could pose a major problem.

The group's success went far beyond what anybody had thought possible. Every day the papers were filled with news — slanted in every way imaginable — about the odyssey of this extraordinary young woman. Letters-to-the-editor had arrived by the truckload.

"Excuse me, please."

Verne stepped aside to let an elderly woman get off the Metro at Federal Triangle.

The platform was oddly empty. Just above them were thousands upon thousands of people. They had probably misunderstood the signs posted everywhere by the Transit Authority, indicating that the stations wouldn't close on the twenty-third until 1 P.M. His watch read twenty past twelve.

Leaving his hotel, Verne had explained to Hannibal that he wanted to go out alone to visit a colleague and would see him later when he returned. He'd decided not to say anything about his meeting with Clara.

He felt guilty about lying to the man who had become his closest companion since that night at Bellevue. They had sequentially numbered tattoos on their shoulders. But he had no choice. Verne had taken all the money he could find — just over twenty-five thousand dollars — as well as some credit cards. He was ready.

Verne admired the Washington subway, with its colossal vaults in reinforced concrete, but he always had the feeling he was inside a giant ant farm. The muted light transformed passengers into supernatural shadows.

He got off at the Smithsonian, hopped on an escalator, and saw, far above him, a growing patch of blue sky.

When he emerged, he was stopped cold. The crowd was enormous, the noise deafening. A sea of humanity. He was instantly caught up by one current and realized too late that he wouldn't be able to change direction. His muscles tightened, his eyes fixed on the sky.

He ceased struggling, trying only to move toward the only point having any solidity in this maelstrom: the Washington Monument.

Despite the cries, the pushing and shoving, not to mention his fear of crowds, Verne started to relax. The mood was festive. People had been in isolation for too long. Finally they had a chance to assemble and give free rein to the simple joy of being alive.

Near him, a group of young people were singing hymns and neo-folk songs. There were groups carrying signs that read "Dallas Workers Hate Fuchs" and "Free Sex" and "Bury the ASP." Many were clumsy attempts at comedy: "President Hughes is Knocked Up"; "ASPs Bite"; "FBBS: Federal Bureau of Bullshit."

Verne found himself enjoying the scene.

The closer he got to the monument, the more the crowd got compacted. There were all races and creeds, old movements like the NAACP, AIM, NOW, Gray Panthers, even the revived SDS. And new ones — Arabic, Chicano, Japanese-American, Palestinian, Cuban.

There were the RUT, the neo-Hippie and Yippie groups, the Students Against Biological Predetermination. There were Mormons, Jehovah's Witnesses, Hasidic Jews, Pentecostals, Liberal Catholics, Reform Jews, Muslims of the Green Crescent, and the ACLU, which had argued against Fuchs in the Supreme Court and come within one vote of victory.

This surging mass of people was slowly coming to a standstill. Facing the monument, the crowd waited for the three minutes of silence that would symbolize their grief for the death of liberty. Afterward, they could chant their slogans and vent their frustrations.

Verne was glad to be a part of it all. He wanted to talk with people. He wanted to tell them all about Socrates. But he was beginning to panic at the idea that anything would prevent him from being at the National Gallery at three and started to elbow his way in the direction of the museum.

Suddenly, he heard his name. He turned. A dozen people were pointing at him. He had been recognized. Paul Verne, discoverer of Sacred Fire, former member of the Commission. They were not looking at him with hostility; it was more like curiosity.

The crowd began to thin; he began to breathe. His attention was drawn to a newspaper sticking out of the pocket of a demonstrator. The name *Engelhardt* was readable. He asked the man if he could glance at the headlines. It was the late edition of the *Washington Times*.

Next to the lead article about the demonstration was a headline: MAFIA LEADER MICHAEL ENGELHARDT GUNNED DOWN IN BROAD DAYLIGHT BY UNKNOWN ASSAILANT.

It was a terrible shock. Verne didn't grieve for the Mafia leader; he had lived by the sword. Verne was afraid Engelhardt's murder could mean his meeting with Clara wouldn't take place.

"Looks rather like an Oriental rug, doesn't it?" said Larry Walton.

Annabelle glanced at Black's secretary, who was standing next to her. His nose was glued to the craft's porthole.

"Now there's an image I never would have come up with," she replied.

Walton gave her a look of wounded reproach.

For the last hour they had been watching the city from the surveillance dirigible at the comfortable altitude of 500 feet. A dozen others were on board, but everyone besides Annabelle and Walton had a specific task to perform: the two pilots, the special agents using high-resolution glasses (one of them was reading the lips of a demonstrator), the photographers behind sophisticated telephoto lenses that, even from this height, could photograph a campaign button in such amazing detail they could tell you if the candidate had cavities.

The craft could stay aloft for several hours before it had to return to Stafford for fuel. Annabelle had chosen it as her command post to watch the demonstration. Since Walton had wanted to speak to her, she had asked him to join her.

They were standing at the rear of the flight deck, near a porthole that allowed them a clear view. The sound of the wind and whir of the engines — plus the tumult from below — meant they could talk without fear of being overheard.

"What's on your mind, Walton?" asked Annabelle, in a somewhat softer voice.

Black's secretary seemed to relax.

"I wanted to speak to you about Engelhardt's murder," he replied.

"Any idea why it happened?" asked Annabelle.

"Probably a settling of scores. No one would have dared do that without the consent of the Padrone."

Annabelle nodded, then looked down at the demonstration. The immense crowd filled nearly the entire space between Constitution Gardens and the Capitol. It was an impressive display.

The more she learned about the Mafia, the more she realized how sturdy the connections were between it and the Bureau. The days of the Committee for Public Health, which Sullivan had talked about on those tapes, were over. The legalization of cocaine production should have made the rupture with the mob definitive. Yet last night Black had made it very clear that those relations were still intact.

One explanation was that the Mafia had something on Black. Or on the President.

The thought sent a cold chill through Annabelle. If that were true, then Black's plan, "Promised Land" he was calling it, was at bottom a way of responding to Mafia blackmail. Everyone seemed to be preparing for the final battle. Engelhardt's murder was part of those preparations — somehow, he must have been compromising their position.

Everything hinged on the NOX business. If Promised Land was going to succeed, it would put an end to all that. If it didn't, the administration would fall, Annabelle with it.

Promised Land had to work.

"Engelhardt's death is no great loss," she said to Walton, who had not interrupted the silence. "However, I wonder what's going to happen to Promised Land. Wasn't Engelhardt supposed to tell us where and when we could catch Verne and Hastings in flagrante delicto?"

Walton didn't seem surprised that Annabelle knew about the contacts between Black and the mafioso.

"Nothing has changed," he explained, "except that now we have a new contact. Marcello Cavani. He's the right hand to the Padrone, Thomas Capecchi."

"How do we contact him?"

"He contacts us. It's in his interest as much as ours. All the more so since the Mafia doesn't seem to have grasped — not yet anyway — the true dimensions of Promised Land."

"You mean using the Verne scandal to combat the NOX?"

"Exactly."

"Ingenious. So, we sit tight."

"That's right."

Walton seemed hesitant to elaborate. Annabelle could tell there was something else he wanted to say. She decided to wait.

"Weaver," he said finally, "there is something else. I know the Director would kill me for saying this, but — "

"What is it?

"Well, it's just that I believe Director Black has — has Sacred Fire."

Annabelle had wanted to talk to Walton about Black's illness, but had somehow found it impossible to raise the question. Of course, she already knew. And she also knew how explosive that made the whole situation.

"Is the Director aware?" she asked abruptly.

"I can't say."

Annabelle noted how unhappy Walton looked.

"Weaver," he said finally, "if you're going to run Promised Land, I have to tell you something about the NOX."

"I think I know what you're going to say."

"You realize they *are* genuine?"

"Of course I realize that."

She wasn't going to tell him she had learned this only the night before.

"In a few months anybody will be able to get one," she added.

Annabelle knew now that Walton absolutely had to be her ally. She decided to prod further.

"Black is protecting the Mafia," she said in a neutral voice. "I wonder why."

Larry Walton smiled. Annabelle couldn't recall ever having seen him smile before.

"That is exactly what I wanted to talk to you about before you go to the White House. But I need some kind of assurance."

Annabelle waited for more. She knew Black's secretary was going to offer her a deal, and that meant he was committing treason against his boss. She felt exhilarated.

"Tell me what you're referring to, and maybe we can see about assurances."

"It has to do with President Gray's death. I can't tell you more until I — "

Annabelle stopped him short.

"All right, Walton, let's see what we can work out."

2

Melissa lowered her eyes. Never in her life had she seen so many people. For the last hour she had been walking behind Tim Lamar, known also as Herakles, whose bulk acted like an icebreaker for her. She was a little feverish and feeling strangely hollow. Noise from the crowd seemed distorted, as if people were walking on the other side of a pane of glass. Margaret Brittain was next to her.

Melissa wondered why she had come. She was sorry that she had not abandoned the idea. She should have reneged in her promise to Margaret. Caught up in the general enthusiasm of the meeting at Laird's Landing, she had agreed to join the demonstration.

Now that she was in Washington with Tim, Clayton, and the others, she could at any moment run into Paul. The possibility was becoming something of an obsession.

She glanced at Clayton, a step or two behind her. The poor man looked exhausted. Paradoxically, the noise and the music coming from farther away were worse than the noise near by. A group had formed around some Cherokees wearing traditional dress and chanting. Farther off, some African-Americans were singing spirituals and clapping to the rhythm. Behind her, she heard old Civil Rights songs, antiwar songs, Hare Krishna chanting.

Someone grabbed her arm. It was Loca, Diana.

"I'm OK," she said to the young woman, whose look held real concern. "Don't worry about me."

Everything was so confused.

Later, she recalled that she had been walking behind Tim, next to Margaret. Diana was walking with some women who wore the same rose tattoo on their cheeks.

"They call me Loca, the crazy one," Diana had replied when Melissa had asked her about the rose, at the end of the Laird's Landing meeting. "It's a mark of respect."

Melissa saw the Washington Monument and, for the first time since she'd been walking behind Tim, knew where she was.

A roar went through the crowd. Melissa looked up and saw a whirl of papers flying through the air, dropped by a helicopter passing overhead. People were rushing to pick them up.

Melissa felt her legs giving out. It was all she could do to resist sinking to the ground and letting the crowd trample her.

Kess Sherman moved away from the window. From his bed he had seen a sheet of paper fall into the hospital's inner courtyard. Then a second, followed by a third. He had gotten up and looked through the bars, but he saw nothing. Probably some patient on a floor above having fun.

This was the first day he'd walked without crutches.

He'd been in fine fettle since the beginning of the afternoon. Despite Dr. Cline's dire news the night before — that they'd be rid of him in three days — the sound coming from outside made him feel exultant. The noise of the crowd was a symphony.

"Hallelujah," he mumbled, walking back to the bed.

There was the sound of a lock opening. In came Hyatt, smiling as always.

"Mr. *Sherman!*" he said in a scolding voice, seeing him standing without the help of crutches, "you shouldn't be — "

"Mr. Hyatt, today is a grand and a glorious day. I want to give you a kiss."

"Mr. Sherman! Now be serious!"

"Mr. Hyatt, I warn you. Unless you let me kiss you I won't allow you to go to the demonstration."

With a boyish look of elation, Hyatt approached Sherman, who ceremoniously planted a loud kiss on his forehead.

"You should take a look at this," Hyatt said. He handed a piece of paper to Sherman. "Patients aren't supposed to know, but everybody on the staff is talking about it. Dropped out of a helicopter."

Sherman read the paper with growing amazement. It was a statement from the Secretary of the Army declaring he was opposed to the Fuchs Amendment. It had to be some kind of stunt. But even if it was, the fact someone would dare to pull it filled Sherman with elation.

"That's amazing," he said.

"That ought to shake things up in the services!"

"Mr. Hyatt, for this you get another kiss."

"Mr. Sherman, please." Hyatt's tone revealed how much he enjoyed taking care of Sherman. "Now be a good boy and use your crutches. The doctors are not going to be happy."

"Cline told me I would be leaving at the end of the week."

Hyatt looked at him with consternation. Sherman tried to comfort him.

"I'm afraid it's the truth, my friend. All good things come to an end. I have to pay for my crimes. So — "

Hyatt collapsed in a chair and burst into sobs.

Suddenly very serious, Sherman leaned down and took him in his arms. Hyatt sobbed quietly. Outside, the roar coming from the Mall grew louder and louder.

Sergeant Thurston speared a flyer with his bayonet and looked over at the demonstrators massing behind the metal barrier on the other side of the street. They were mostly young people, who had started to amuse themselves by shouting taunts and making obscene gestures at the Marines, who remained impassive.

Thurston had placed his men along the perimeter of the fence, at the spot where it forms a semicircle the length of Executive Avenue. The Marines stood several feet apart in ready position.

Charlie was aching to get his hands on just one of those protesting shitheads.

"Tell the men to keep their cool!" he cried to Bill Davis, thirty feet over on his right.

All it would take was one round from the Clear Fighter, sitting about a hundred yards off, to scare them half to death. He personally would have loved to send a round over their heads, just to watch them shit themselves.

Suddenly all the noise stopped. Everybody was looking at the Monument. It was eerie, this silence, alien. All of them looking at the Monument, and for no apparent reason. A wave of hate for the protesters swept over him.

Charlie tightened his hold on his P–26. He hadn't felt this kind of surge since Costa Rica.

Between Constitution Gardens and the Reflecting Pool, between Capitol Hill and the Tidal Basin, where the cherry trees were in glorious bloom, the crowd covered every inch.

Hundreds of thousands, all carried by the hope that democracy might return to the country that had invented it centuries earlier.

The image of this multicolored human expanse was transmitted around the world by television cameras hooked up to helicopters. Hundreds of millions of people around the planet saw Americans demanding their bodies back.

At precisely two o'clock, a silence began its way from the Monument outward, in all directions, extinguishing every chant, cry, song, conversation. There had been no starting signal. It had happened as planned, but also spontaneously, like a thought. Everybody straightened their shoulders, impressed by the gravity of the moment.

Their thoughts went to the people taken by disease.

Their thoughts also went to a simpler time, to a place preserved by nostalgia. Would they ever know a life without the constant threat of death? Would they know what it was like to drink from a river, or to make love simply because the spirit moved? All that life seemed to offer, the reason for being alive, seemed to have disappeared forever.

Innocence was lost when despair was born.

In those three minutes of silence, the crowd, as one, learned they would not have their freedom back unless they struggled to regain it.

Some pigeons, confused by the immobility and silence of this sea of people, began to swoop overhead.

First came a single cry, then three, then ten, and then it grew into a deafening roar. From the throats of hundreds of thousands:

"NO FUCHS! NO FUCHS!"

The words were less impressive than the sound. The power of that unified voice was everything — echoing in the universe from east to west, south to north, picked up and reborn again and again, growing into an infinite choir singing the chorus of the earth.

"Paul!"

Melissa dug her fingernails into Tim's arm.

"Melissa, what is it?"

"I saw Paul! Over there!"

"Positive?"

"Yes! And he saw me. He had on his corduroy jacket."

She must be losing her mind.

People around her had been yelling for several minutes. But she didn't join in. Chanting never changed anything.

She was also all too aware of the demagogy that could spring up if the government gave in to the pressure and repealed the Fuchs Amendment. The epidemic would sweep across the nation with such power that in ten years the whole population would be devastated.

And it was just as these thoughts were going through her mind that she had seen Paul. God only knows what shadows he had run after since January.

She leaned heavily on Tim's arm.

Around her everyone was still shouting and screaming. And laughing. The demonstration was turning into a celebration. Even Margaret looked as though she were having the time of her life.

"Tim, would you go see? I'm sure it was Paul."

"All right. Stay put," he said, turning. "Margaret!" he called.

Margaret heard and joined them.

"Melissa thought she saw Paul. I'm going to take a quick look," he told her. "Would you stay with Melissa?"

"Margaret, I swear it was him," said Melissa. "And he saw me."

Tim moved off in the direction in which she had pointed.

Despite the incredible noise of the crowd, Verne had distinctly heard someone call his name and had turned and seen Melissa, looking pale and tired, leaning on Tim Lamar's arm. His first impulse had been to run, and he did. Ignoring the remarks of people he had barged past, he headed east and reached 14th Street. Exhausted, he stopped before what looked like a gigantic metal ribbon reflecting the sunlight, then recognized that it was an immense Möbius strip by José de Rivera — *Infinity*.

He had run in the right direction. He was directly in front of the Natural History Museum. The National Gallery was only another three hundred yards away.

Verne left the Mall and hurried down Constitution Avenue. He got to the museum and sat down on a stone bench under a pine tree. Fifteen minutes to spare.

Melissa. He tried to convince himself that he had had no choice but to avoid her, that he couldn't risk being even a second late. He knew she would interpret it as cowardice on his part, and the thought made him wince.

But he would do what he had to in order to find Clara.

3

"Time to go."

Clara looked at the man who had opened the door to her room. She'd never seen him before. He was wearing a blue uniform with gold buttons, which she couldn't quite place. He couldn't look more different from the Japanese who had been guarding her in silence for the last few days.

Right after the abduction, she had been led up a steep stairway — she detected the unmistakable odor of cabbage — and was taken into a room in which the humidity was overpowering. They removed her blindfold. The room was lit by a single bulb.

Two men were sitting behind a table. Only the little one talked, the one with the odd-looking eyes. He introduced himself as a friend of Paul Verne's and told her that she would be staying with them for a few days. Then she would be reunited with him.

Though weak and confused, she had tried to ask some questions, but the man interrupted her. There was nothing more to be said.

They blindfolded her again and took her someplace in a car. Hands guided her down some steps, and then she was in this room.

She had had no difficulty getting used to her new captivity, which was infinitely preferable to the District prison. She could take showers without being watched and was given newspapers.

Still, she had no illusions. She'd been kidnapped, pure and simple, and after some money had changed hands — or some prisoner released — she would go back to prison. Telling her they were going to bring her to Paul was just a cruel joke to keep her happy. They must have known about her escape with Verne from the MID base.

She had followed the preparations for the April twenty-third demonstration with great excitement. She had also kept abreast of the campaign that had been organized by "her" liberation committee, whose activities had continued even after her disappearance.

Today they were coming to get her. She had little doubt she would be handed back over to Weaver.

And then she was being shown out the door by this man in blue.

"Will I come back here?" she asked him.

"I don't think so."

Clara put on the jacket they had given her. She was wearing corduroy pants and a turtleneck sweater. She put down the issue of the *Post* that contained the story of her exploits and followed the blue uniform into a little hallway.

He opened another door.

"I'm sorry, but the elevators aren't working today. There's been a short circuit somewhere. We'll have to go on foot."

"What's that noise?"

"That? The demonstration."

"How close to it are we?"

"Pretty close," replied the man.

"I didn't hear anything before."

"The room you were staying in is three levels below ground."

They reached the top of the stairs and the man opened another door.

Clara felt as if she had walked into a howling gale, so loud was the noise. Stunned, she followed her guide through still another door — and there she stood stock-still.

She was standing before a huge rotunda encircled by twenty or so Ionic columns in dark green marble, each sixty feet in height, supporting a dome that opened to a huge circular window. The walls were covered with light pink marble and the floor with dark flagstones. In the middle was a huge fountain in the shape of a giant bowl. A figure with wings on his feet was perched on top. But the noise was what was most extraordinary. Thousands of voices, distorted and amplified by the space inside this building, echoed off the pilasters and corners, the columns and balustrades, like lost souls in agony.

The demonstrators were just outside the wall of this building.

"Where are we?" she asked her guide, after a long pause.

"The National Gallery."

"What are we doing here?"

"You have a meeting" — the man looked at his watch — "in ten minutes."

"I'm supposed to meet someone?"

"That's what I was told."

"Where?"

"In the European Painting gallery. That way." He pointed. "At the other end of the hall is the Winter Garden. It'll be the room on your right."

The man indicated one of the two cavernous corridors that opened up on each side of the rotunda, forming an axis for the two wings of the museum.

"Are you sure?"

"Wait there. If there's a problem, we'll come and find you. I have to go now."

"Wait!" said Clara. The man turned.

"What?"

"I wanted to ask you something. What kind of uniform are you wearing?"

He smiled. "I'm a museum guard."

Clara walked down a hallway whose dimensions were as vast as the rotunda she had just left. Light streamed in through a skylight. On either side were exhibition rooms. The sound of the crowd was becoming more distant.

364 /

Clara got to the Winter Garden, a huge rectangular room filled with tropical plants and exotic smells. Instead of going right to the room the guard had indicated, she walked straight ahead, toward a round picture window.

She approached it slowly, fascinated. On the other side of the glass was an immense concrete terrace. The sight of all those people took her breath away.

She had seen almost no one for nearly three months, and she found herself looking hungrily at them. She wanted to call out, to tell them to come and get her so she could join in. It was an absurd idea. No one could see her. Even if they could, her cries would be soundless.

She watched for a few minutes, lost in wonder at the incredible sight before her.

Finally, she turned and walked back toward the European Paintings room.

The idea that she was going to meet Paul had simply not entered her mind. Rather, she had refused to let the idea in. If it were not true, the disappointment would be more than she could take. She had put every thought about him into abeyance. She was letting the moments carry her.

She walked into what was marked as room 72. A painting caught her attention, and she thought immediately that it must be a replica of — no, a *reply* to — the one she had seen in New York three months earlier.

It was another Manet — the same browns, the fierce contrasts, the freedoms. It depicted a man in profile wearing a matador outfit, lying on his back in the sand of a bullfighting arena, his head turned away from the observer. His right arm was folded and resting on his chest, fingertips on his abdomen, while in the foreground, his left arm was stretched out alongside his body, his hand still holding the top of a red cape. Near his head, Clara could just make out the handle of the sword he had dropped at the moment he had been struck down.

Despite the festive surroundings, there was nothing to be celebrated in this death. He had been killed brutally, coldly. All that remained were matter and a play of light.

Manet had painted the canvas in the same tones that he had used for *Young Woman in the Costume of an Espada*. The man wore the same dark suit — short jacket, knee breeches; and the same belt, white silk stockings, buckled shoes.

Clara recalled the excitement she'd felt when she saw the Manet painting at the Met. Here, now, she felt no joy. The corpse was the appropriate symbol: lifeless, useless. Human life reduced to mere outline.

Had Manet painted the young woman at the moment she was delivering the death blow? Clara remembered there had been something obscene about the way the sword peeked above the cape, which looked more like a dress than a cape. The painting was a drama about virility. A young woman triumphantly carrying the tattered remains of masculine glory. A man was lying dead at her feet, a man from whom she had stolen the suit of light, the illusions, the desire for power.

All that remained of that whole drama was death.

Images of the two Manet paintings intertwined in Clara's spirit in a vibrating spiral. From the moment she had arrived in New York to this moment, Clara had unknowingly woven together threads of connection. She had arrived at a turning point.

Now, and only now, did she understand she was going to see Paul Verne. She, a Bio, would carry his child.

When she heard him say her name, she found enough strength to tell him that she could not have waited for him much longer. Then she threw herself into his arms.

Tim Lamar looked everywhere for Verne. He was sure that Melissa had not been mistaken.

He had been waiting for this moment for weeks. Because of the Network, he knew more about Paul Verne's adventures than Melissa imagined. Like everyone else, he had heard of his resignation from the Commission, whose purpose he denounced.

But Tim knew that Verne was now actively working with the Network. An intellectual revolution was unfolding in the science world, comparable to what happened during the Age of Discovery and the nineteenth century. In this revolution artists, as much as scientists, would play their part. Tim collected driftwood spewed up by the tide, but his sculpture was a contributor to sea change.

That was why he had to find Verne. The urge to join Socrates stemmed from the same convictions that had driven him to devote his life to art. Combing Constitution Avenue, he spotted Verne, by incredible luck, a second before he went into the National Gallery.

He guessed Verne was meeting someone about Socrates.

He posted himself on a corner near the entrance, hoping Verne would come out the same door he went in.

A police vehicle turned slowly onto Executive Avenue and stopped in the middle of the street. Charlie Thurston watched it.

Just what we needed, he thought to himself.

He didn't like the police. They gave him a hard time every time he went into a bar.

Two uniforms got out of the vehicle. They looked sneeringly at the Marines, then headed straight toward some protesters who were screaming at the top of their lungs.

Carrying riot sticks, they walked up to the barricade and stared into the white of their eyes.

Those sons of bitches! If they're looking for a fight they'll find it, thought Charlie. But after swinging their sticks and spitting at the protesters, who backed away, they got back into their their vehicles, laughing.

"Hey, meathead!" one of them yelled back in Charlie's direction. "Good luck!"

The vehicle sped off honking and headed west.

Assholes, muttered Charlie.

The mood of the demonstrators changed. He saw one big guy wearing a denim jacket, drinking something.

Charlie decided to see what was going on, but too late. The can struck the fence, dousing him with alcohol. He had a flashback of a grenade being thrown into a transport truck. He lowered his weapon.

Seconds later, he and his men were being bombarded.

"Shamal!" Charlie shouted. "Get the Clear Fighter. Move it!"

Shamal took off at a run.

"Ready . . . arms!" shouted Charlie to his squad.

He assumed the firing position and put his finger on the trigger.

Just then there was some movement among the front ranks of the demonstrators. From out of the corner of his eye, he saw that his men were ready.

His attention was attracted by a group of four women, all wearing black leather — they looked like Chicanas. One of them was waving at him. Around them, people calmed. They seemed to be listening to her.

Charlie took aim at the Chicana.

More and more projectiles were landing around him. Some protesters had jumped over the barricade. A bottle struck him in the leg. Suddenly the Chicana was looking straight at Charlie. With a slow, theatrical gesture, she made the V for Victory salute.

Something snapped. In the seconds that followed, her head exploded, and her blood and bits of brain spread down her chest before Charlie had even heard his weapon go off. Her friends started to scream.

Some demonstrators were climbing over the barricade. The crowd was screaming, urging them on.

Charlie fired carefully, calmly. Every shot killed. That's how he was taught. No good soldier wasted ammunition.

He stopped firing when he heard the sound of the Clear Fighter. He had done his duty. Not a single demonstrator got within ten feet of the White House fence.

"Watch out!" cried Margaret. She was running, holding Melissa's hand.

They jumped and managed to avoid a woman who had fallen in front of her.

After the firing started, the panic was beyond belief. No one knew what was going on. When they heard the first shots, the two women had been sitting under some trees a few feet from the Ellipse, along with some of their friends from Point Reyes. After a moment of stupor, the crowd started to scream and run in the opposite direction. Melissa and Margaret lost their friends.

Running, stumbling, they managed to reach the corner of an enormous government building.

"Stop," groaned Melissa, trying to catch her breath. "What has happened?"

"How should I know?" panted Margaret.

"The Marines opened fire!" someone passing by shouted at them.

"Oh, God, it isn't possible," gasped Melissa.

"Melissa, come on. We've got to keep moving."

The two women began running again.

"The car isn't far!" yelled Margaret.

"People have been killed!" screamed some demonstrators running alongside them.

Melissa was hoping Paul wasn't among them.

"Paul!"

Verne jumped back. Instinctively, he threw a protective arm around Clara.

The two of them had just come through the door of the museum onto Constitution Avenue. They were still completely absorbed in each other. Verne immediately recognized the man running toward him.

"Tim! My God. What are you doing here?"

"Looking for you! What else? We'll talk about that later. We've got to get the hell out of here."

"What's happened?"

"The Marines opened fire. C'mon. I know the way."

"The Marines opened fire?"

Verne hesitated. How was he supposed to tell Tim that the woman with him was being hunted by every uniform in the country?

"Thanks, Tim. We can't." He nodded at Clara. "She — "

"Paul, I know everything. Stop arguing. Let's move!"

Verne looked at Clara. It was her choice.

"Let's go with him," she said. "We might have a chance."

"OK, Tim. We're right behind you," Verne said.

The big man's face melted into a grin.

"Happy to meet you!" he said, extending his hand to Clara. "I'm Herakles."

"I've heard of you, Herakles."

They started to run east, down Constitution.

Chapter 22

1

Annabelle Weaver looked at the pleasant Connecticut countryside. Two weeks had passed since the tragic events of April 23, during which over a hundred demonstrators were killed and thousands wounded.

The inquiry called for by the president, several hours after Congress had called for one, communicated its conclusions to the White House on May 6, twenty-four hours before they were made public.

The whole country held its breath. Competing and contradictory rumors circulated in the capital.

Alexia Pollock, the *Washington Post* journalist who had been instrumental in founding the Group to Free Clara Hastings, had done an exhaustive job of tracking down who had made the decision that the Marines should police the demonstration. Her article, which appeared a week after the events, had been a political bombshell, for it confirmed that decisions had been made at the highest level. The order had been approved personally by the president. A Congressional committee came to the same conclusions.

The mission taking Annabelle Weaver to Connecticut had also been directed by people at the highest levels. The very highest.

She had landed at Bradley International in Hartford on a commercial flight from Washington. It had been a beautiful morning. Now it was afternoon, and Annabelle, exhausted, was on her way back to the airport.

When she got back to Washington an official car would be waiting to take her directly to the White House. The president would receive her in the Oval Office, just as she had the day after the demonstration. Annabelle would tell her, in the modest tone she reserved for certain occasions, that her mission had been a complete success. She would refuse the reward that the president would doubtless offer her. Plenty of time for that later. Now that her career was officially linked to that of Elizabeth Hughes, complete circumspection was in order.

She had therefore firmly decided to support Attorney General Harris's proposal to nominate Patricia Johnson as director of the FBI. Pat was a pure product of the Establishment, and she was one of the Attorney General's oldest colleagues. Her nomination would be an overt gesture of reconciliation between the federal police and the Bureau, which in these difficult times for the Hughes Administration was not something to be sniffed at. Annabelle urged strenuously that Larry Walton be permitted to stay on in his position. As for her, she would be officially appointed head of the FBBS, just as Hughes had proposed. Walton would keep her informed about what was going on day-to-day at the FBI.

Actually, she had only one idea in mind: vacation. She had proposed to Mary Coleman, the secretary Larry Walton had sent her way — he had a wickedly sharp intuitive sense — that they spend a few days in Arizona. She had wanted for a very long time to climb down into the Grand Canyon. Strange that her name was Mary. One of those coincidences.

Annabelle was enjoying life. She was feeling secure, happy, satisfied with herself. The meeting she had just had with Thomas Capecchi had gone splendidly. She came away feeling that she had met the real power behind the organization, the capo of capos.

He had come in person to meet her in the huge living room on the first floor of Gordon Heights. He had proposed they take a turn in his garden.

She had found him perplexing, at first. The man plastered his head with grease, just like Al Capone, yet otherwise his appearance had absolutely nothing in common with that of a gangster. He was tall, had a slight paunch, incredibly long arms. Placid in appearance, he gave the impression of someone who never lost his temper. But he could also fix you with a look that froze the blood.

Capecchi had begun by asking Annabelle if she'd ever heard of Spinoza. Her response had disappointed him a little, but he gallantly took the trouble to explain that Spinoza was a Dutch philosopher on whose work he had just completed a book.

Then, with no attempt at a transition, he launched into the reason for Annabelle's visit to Gordon Heights.

"Are you a patriot, Ms. Weaver?"

"Uh, well, of course. More or less. Like everyone, I suppose," was her somewhat feeble reply.

"Now don't sell yourself short. Not everyone could do what you are doing — so successfully."

She'd jumped at that. Did "so successfully" mean he was in agreement?

"Listen to me carefully, Ms. Weaver. We agree to the proposal. My associates and I will break unilaterally with the Waikiki Cartel. We therefore agree to end the importation of the NOX into the American market. In return, we will be given control of the three companies that produce cocaine, and the various forms of Cocaid. That is what has been proposed, is it not?"

"Correct."

"The administration will therefore avert its gaze from the methods that we will use to achieve our ends."

"There will be — violence?"

"Ms. Weaver, we are not living in the past. To bring things to a successful conclusion, we have a great number of ways at our disposal, many of which are no different from those used in high finance. Indeed, Wall Street is one of the places we will act. But there are other places, too. What we are asking is that the administration not interfere. Do you understand?"

"Yes, I do, Mr. Capecchi."

"I must also tell you that the Waikiki agreement that bound us to the Yakuza pleased me not at all. Business is essentially what we are about, and I would prefer an arrangement that keeps everyone within their own borders. We are not against ASPs. They are a safeguard against undesirables. Don't you agree?"

They had returned to the house, where they were served tea. Annabelle chose that moment to thank the Padrone for so patriotically coming to the assistance of the Presidential Commission evaluating the events of April 23. She had just seen their report and its conclusions.

Thanks in part to Capecchi, the Commission had been able to establish that the Marines had acted in legitimate self-defense, had in fact helped to thwart an assassination attempt against the president herself. Only theoretical at the beginning of the investigation, the hypothesis had been considerably buttressed when the FBI discovered that among the dead was a young woman by the name of Loca, who had once been one of the leaders of an East Los Angeles gang of Chicanas called the Virginas.

Since Annabelle had had dealings with that gang, when it attempted to harbor Kess Sherman, she had been asked to describe in detail the events that led to the attack on their headquarters at her deposition before the Commission.

Loca was the first demonstrator Sergeant Charlie Thurston had neutralized, following continuous provocation. Three other former Virginas gang members were found among the dead.

This troubling fact had attracted the attention of the FBI — helped by several informants, who were encouraged by the Padrone to step forward — to the existence of a group of subversives taking advantage of the demonstration to attempt to assassinate the president. Guns and scaling equipment had been discovered on the bodies. The investigation established that the group from Los Angeles had been recruited from among several of the gangs flourishing in that city. It was patently clear that most maintained close ties with the Network.

The two soldiers who had dropped flyers out of a helicopter were discovered to be Sacred Fire Worshipers. Both were condemned to a hundred-plus years in a federal penitentiary.

"Liz now has everything she needs to save face," Capecchi had concluded. "And this is good for business. She took an enormous risk authorizing that demonstration. I wonder how anyone could have advised her to do it. Black was against it. By the way, will his death change anything?"

"Maybe. Maybe Engelhardt's death will also bring about a change," Annabelle had countered courageously.

The Padrone laughed.

"How did you know they were meeting regularly?"

"I have my sources."

"I see that Larry Walton has dealt you a winning card. I like that. The collaboration between Black and Engelhardt was good for both parties. But, at the point where we now find ourselves, I think the director acted honorably by doing away with himself."

A week earlier, a limousine had plunged into the Potomac. The bodies of FBI director Black and Fred Cooper, one of the president's personal bodyguards, were recovered. Some suggested that it was suicide, or murder made to look like an accident. Reports made public stated that no evidence had turned up to support either hypothesis.

"You may be right," said Annabelle vaguely.

She had seen the secret FBI report establishing suicide.

"I knew Black for a long time, Ms. Weaver." Capecchi paused, and then continued, "but now there will be no more deviousness. I will consider you as my personal contact. Do you accept?"

"I would say it is to our mutual benefit."

"There we are, then. You are an ambitious young woman, but that doesn't bother me a bit. On the contrary, I like it. Now I would like you to tell me how you are going to convince the president to give us the cocaine market."

Annabelle hesitated.

"I have told her that I was aware of the — how shall I say — circumstances surrounding the death of Nathan Gray," she said finally.

"You are referring to the plane accident."

"Yes."

"Who is your source?"

Annabelle said nothing.

"Larry Walton?"

Annabelle remained silent. Words were no longer necessary. Everything was in place now. What was left was to talk about Promised Land.

"Sir, I have one more thing to ask you."

"You are insatiable, Ms. Weaver!"

"We have lost track of Paul Verne and Clara Hastings. Do you know where we can find them?"

"Would you explain to me again why those two interest you so greatly?"

Annabelle smiled. Despite what she had told Larry Walton on the day of the demonstration, Don Capecchi was perfectly aware of the implications of Promised Land. All he wanted was to hear it now from the mouth of the director of the FBBS. In any case, now that the Mafia had given up commercial exploitation of the NOX, the danger it posed was diminished.

She told him about Black's plan to provoke a wave of public support for the reelection of Elizabeth Hughes.

Capecchi played the game, and said that he thought Black's plan an excellent one.

"Black had a keen political mind. That is clear. When the time is appropriate I will tell you where you can find Verne and Hastings."

Accompanying her to the door, he added: "It was thanks to our agreement with the Japanese that Dr. Verne was able to get himself outfitted with a NOX. That, as I understand it, is critical to the success of Promised Land, and to Liz's reelection. You see? Our relations were never interrupted. They just went over a few bumps, that's all. Unless they destroy each other, two powers such as ours are condemned to work together. Don't forget to remind Madame President of that, won't you, Ms. Weaver? Good-bye."

When Annabelle got back from her vacation, she planned to devote herself to the success of Promised Land. Robert Kane would become her assistant. Once they found out where it was they would plant cameras in their love nest. All she would have to do was wait for the day when she would have enough proof to nail them.

There would be a trial. National attention.

She could just imagine the headlines: DISCOVERER OF SF, LOVER OF A BIO

Or: PAUL VERNE SEXUALLY ACTIVE

Or: PAUL VERNE — NETWORK LOVER AND LEADER

It would be her finest hour.

2

Since morning Verne and Clara had been walking across Eldorado, in the Sierra Nevada, toward Lake Tahoe. They had a compass and a map.

Tim Lamar had left the night before for Point Reyes, having first promised to visit them next month at King's Beach, on the lake shore.

Verne, carrying the backpack, followed Clara while they climbed through a beech forest. They walked without speaking, exhilarated to be outdoors.

Verne was thinking about the past two weeks. The fact that Tim had been waiting for him at the National Gallery was still an incredible mystery. Perhaps it wasn't, actually. After all, Tim was an artist, a sculptor of the driftwood that washes up on shore. He found lost things.

The fugitives had left Washington in Tim's camper. The administration had decided to open the borders to the city after the shooting, so they were able to join in the general flight of demonstrators without incident. During the following days, because the public outcry against the "Washington massacre," as the tragic event was now being referred to, became increasingly hostile, even in the conservative press, the administration quietly ordered all border guards nationwide to ease crossing restrictions. Thus Tim and his clandestine passengers were able to reach San Francisco not only without incident but in record time.

Paul and Clara had been taken in by a Networker who lived in a Carpenter house at the top of a hill, deep in the forest outside Dogtown, near Bolinas.

Tim had almost immediately left for Canada with a message from Verne to Peter Alexos. Network friends would take it from Alberta to Montreal. The letter explained Verne's reasons for having to interrupt his mission, but assured Alexos that he would continue his work as soon as Clara was safe.

During the long days waiting for Tim to return, Verne had communicated relatively little with Clara. He had even avoided her. Idle for the first time in months, he was glad to have the time to catch up with life, he told her. She had replied enigmatically that after all they had been through they needed time to get to know each other.

Clara spent hours in the sun, reading. In the evening she would disappear into her room, leaving Paul to his thoughts. From time to time, worried that she might interpret his distance as a lack of interest in her, he came to her to talk of Socrates or some new research perspective. He avoided talking about himself or about her, or about what might happen to them.

Not once did either of them allude to Verne's new sexual capacities, now that he was wearing the NOX. The panic he had felt the first time he had awakened with an erection! He had lain there waiting for the first signs of an ASP discharge, until finally he realized there would be none. It was several days before he dared touch himself, his heart beating wildly, to verify that he indeed did have sensations.

When Tim returned, he told them that he had stopped at Forest Hill to see an old friend with a house on the shore of Lake Tahoe. It was an ideal location. The lake had the great advantage of being next to the California border with Nevada.

They left the next morning for Forest Hill and met with Tim's friend, a ranger named Baker. During the course of the evening, Baker told him that the twenty-five miles between Forest Hill and Tahoe was his favorite stretch of land in all the world. Paul and Clara leapt at the chance to cross the region by foot.

The sun had barely sunk behind the rocky peaks that towered over them in the darkening sky when the temperature began to drop, fast.

"We'll need to set up camp somewhere," said Verne, trying to conceal his anxiety.

"Over there," Clara said, pointing at a group of trees.

Without waiting for his reply, she set out on the path that led straight into a dense forest.

Verne wanted to tell her that it was too risky, that they might get lost. Clara seemed to know exactly where her feet were leading her.

"Here," she said, standing in a clearing encircled by birches whose silvery bark reflected the dying sunlight. "We'll spend the night here."

She took him by the hand and led him to a small grass-covered knoll.

It was a perfect spot. The knoll protected them from the wind coming out of the northwest. Verne took off his backpack and started to set up the tent Baker had lent them.

"Why don't we just sleep under the stars?" asked Clara.

"We'll get cold."

"No, we won't. All we have to do is put our two sleeping bags together and wrap the tent around us. Imagine how the constellations will look!"

Verne relented. He watched her take out the sleeping bags, unzip them, and place them next to each other. The only risk they ran was having to put up the tent in the middle of the night.

They decided not to build a fire, for fear of drawing attention. They ate quietly, listening to the sounds in the forest. It was a moonless night. The stars were spread across the sky.

Feeling self-conscious and awkward, Verne looked desperately for a way to bring up his new capacities. He couldn't.

The bed was ready.

"I'm going to turn in," Clara announced, yawning.

They took off their coats. Verne waited for Clara to get in, completely dressed, before joining her. He rolled the tent over their coats, then nestled himself deep to cover his shoulders.

Clara curled up in his arms with an impetuousness that paralyzed him. He realized that she had fallen asleep.

Lying on his back, enveloped in the heat produced by their bodies, he watched the stars with wide-open eyes.

Finally, his eyes began to close.

Verne was awake.

He had heard something.

He opened his eyes and turned his head, staring into the darkness. Maybe it was only an animal. Up till then there had been total silence. The air stung his face, yet his body was warm. Clara had been right.

Her back was to him; she was curled up in the fetal position.

He turned and wrapped his arms around her. Putting his hand gently on her thigh, he realized that Clara was naked.

How had she managed to undress without waking him? He was so surprised that he didn't at first notice his erection. When he did, he didn't dare move, knowing that if she was awake — was she awake? — Clara would feel him pressing against her.

After a moment, he held her tighter. She sighed and turned to him.

She was in his arms, her lips lost in his. He felt enveloped in an extraordinary calm. The fear, the anxiety, the impatience, had all disappeared. He was glorying in the certitude that nothing could prevent the inevitable.

Clara helped him take off his pants. He was laughing now, and so was she. It was all a comic and joyous battle against the confinement of clothing.

Finally he was naked (later he would find his shirt had been twisted over one shoulder). He guided Clara's hand, and with his own discovered her body. He had never known such complete abandon.

He knew she was ready. A new wave of strength swept over him and he moved inside her.

"Take everything," he said, when the moment came.

3

Clara and Paul moved into Baker's house, Rocky Roost, a labyrinth of giant hand-hewn beams and enormous boulders that jutted out over Lake Tahoe.

They talked and made love, endlessly, it seemed, happy to discover that between them there was no room for weariness.

Two months went by.

One morning at the beginning of summer, a boat landed at Rocky Roost. Herakles had come to get Verne. He was needed in Canada for an important meeting of the National Council.

While Paul was away, Tim kept Clara company and sculpted. He left as soon as Verne returned.

Then came the night Clara told Paul she was pregnant. They stayed awake all night, talking and thinking about the uniqueness of what they had created — a child born to a Bio and a Utero. Clara pointed out it wouldn't have maternal grandparents, but nothing could diminish their joy.

The summer passed. The FBBS seemed to have given up looking for them. The press no longer carried news about the Group to Free Clara Hastings. The media in all their forms were too engrossed in the presidential elections.

Paul and Clara would perhaps have spent peaceful months together, interrupted now and then by Verne's trips. In October, despite the risks, Verne decided to take Clara to San Francisco to see a friend who had once been a midwife, Dr. Marion Runcie. They traveled in the back of a state park vehicle. After some tests, Runcie told Clara that she was going to have a girl. On their return, they discovered that someone had broken into Rocky Roost. Nothing of value had been stolen, but it seemed an ill omen.

Worried that the FBBS might be involved, Herakles and Verne decided to take some precautions. They dug out a small cellar and connected it to an old mining tunnel that went down into the rock and emerged near the dock.

The work took a good month. Several people from the Network pitched in.

Winter came. After much debate, Clara decided she would have the baby at Rocky Roost. They would bring in Dr. Runcie. Verne also invited Sitt Hokkee and Mow to stay with them for a while.

Verne was delighted to see Sitt again. The plainsman was pleased to hear that Paul was no longer wearing a Pikkiemak, and that Clara was having a "natural" child.

Julia was born at three A.M. on February 29. By the time Dr. Runcie arrived, Mow had already wrapped the child and buried the placenta, as was Pawnee custom. Runcie was deeply disappointed at not having had one last chance to bring a child into the world.

The Hokkees left a month later.

In the spring, an elderly couple named Watson moved into a house a mile or so away from Rocky Roost. They tried several times to make neighborly contact with Paul and Clara, who were so terrified the new people would find out about the baby that they were almost rude. The Watsons finally gave up trying to be sociable.

In those moments when Socrates work gave him some respite, Verne studied German. The discovery of the language whose inflections he remembered from his childhood brought him great satisfaction.

The evening they decided to part from Julia — she would be hidden with some friends, before being officially adopted at the age of three — Paul remembered a line from a Paul Célan poem:

> Now what is joined,
> Appears, taking breath away

He wished time could have stopped on that moment.

Chapter 23

1

"That's unacceptable!" cried Annabelle.

She was furious. It took all her self-restraint not to order an immediate assault on Rocky Roost.

She had flown to Reno on the last TX flight of the evening and then hopped a helicopter for the Lake Tahoe region. So as not to attract attention, the helicopter had landed a few miles from the lake.

Kane appraised her about the electromagnetic problem they had had, how it was interfering with the cameras inside the house.

"Great. Just great," she muttered through clenched teeth. "When do they usually get back from their little boat ride?"

"Before nightfall, boss. Probably around five. The Watsons have been observing them every day and — "

"I know that," she said sharply, silencing Kane.

They were in the FBBS surveillance vehicle. The driver had pulled off so that they could see if the reception was any better from farther away. Annabelle wanted to be closer to the house.

"So what do we have? An hour? Where's John?"

"He's checking the equipment on foot. He thought a magnetic field might have created the static."

"I really couldn't give a shit what he thinks. He's had a whole month to get things ready. If we don't get a tape because of his bumbling — "

She sat down nervously in front of the monitors, which for the moment were blank.

Annabelle had reason to be exasperated. She had been waiting for over a year. A whole year, during which the Mafia had kept her in the dark about where Verne and Hastings were hiding out. The FBBS manhunt had come to naught.

In the first months, FBI director Johnson had confided to Annabelle her worries that Capecchi would fail to fulfill his part of the bargain.

Was this a tactic the Padrone was using to his advantage? Was he going to tell them where the two fugitives were, or did he want to wait until he had complete control over the cocaine market?

But Annabelle had never doubted Capecchi's word. There was no reason the Mafia would want to break with the Hughes administration, particularly not when it was getting what it wanted.

The first indications of what the Mafia was up to came to Annabelle's attention exactly two months after her meeting with the Padrone. Larry Walton, senior aide to Director Johnson, told Annabelle one day that the Justice Department had received secret instructions to permit the buyout of a company called CK International to go through, despite a complaint from the chairman of CK to the SEC that it would be a clear violation of the antitrust laws.

Sometime later, at a meeting with Marcello Cavino on a yacht anchored in Chesapeake Bay, Annabelle was told that the Padrone's silence about Verne and Hastings meant that the organization needed a guarantee.

Annabelle made only one request: that she be given the information in time. Otherwise Promised Land would not succeed. She said the latest date should be late May, six weeks before the Democratic Convention.

The CK business concluded successfully. On May 12, Annabelle got what she had been waiting for. A simple note informed her that Verne and Hastings were living in a mountain retreat called Rocky Roost, situated on the shore of Lake Tahoe, near King's Beach. Hastings had given birth to a child on February 29. Verne was frequently absent, probably attending meetings with the Network. The note was signed, "Cavani."

Annabelle had literally jumped with joy. A child! They had a child! It would be the media event of the century.

"*Kane? John,*" came a voice in the surveillance van. "*Do you read me?*"

"Yes, John," replied Kane, putting on his headset. "I read you. What have you got?"

"*It was a transformer at King's Beach. We should have it cleared up in ten minutes or so. The setup overtaxed the system.*"

"Roger."

"Does that mean the whole area is without electricity?" asked Annabelle.

"No, boss. John had to connect it directly. They had a backup plan ready."

"No more breakdowns. Is that understood?"

"I hear you, boss." .

"I'm holding you to that, Kane."

Annabelle was feeling incredibly tense. Confusion and uncertainty within the administration had been having a bad effect on the FBBS. It had been up and down ever since the April Episode. The number of terrorist attacks on AS checkpoints had risen. So had the number of prison riots.

Throughout it all, the president had remained remarkably calm, and Annabelle admired her for it. The last time she had met with her, a couple of days after getting the message from Cavani, Hughes had displayed unshakable confidence in the future.

The latest polls, conducted with utter secrecy, indicated there was one scenario by which she might lose the fall election. For the last several months, the polls had shown that there was a percentage of the population that shared some but not all of the Network's goals. This swing group had rejoined the Fuchs camp after a docudrama about the life of leisure Paul Verne and Clara Hastings were sharing together was shown repeatedly on TV. But the curve of support had peaked.

According to the polls, the percentage, which leveled off at about 8 percent, would climb to nearly 14 percent if the couple had a child — hypothetically — and go all the way up to 28 percent if they themselves, in person, were shown having sexual intercourse.

These surprising statistics would have considerable consequences. They proved that the president would win the election by a comfortable margin over conservative Democrat Roberto Wayne, the former singer. If the Democrats nominated Harry Calwell, the election would be very close.

Three independent polls were conducted and the evidence was clear: Senator Calwell, a moderate who wanted to make some adjustments in Fuchs, stood a chance of defeating the president if the Verne-Hastings intercourse was never aired. On the other hand, were there conclusive video footage, of the highest quality, he would lose by as much as four to five percentage points.

Verne's conjugal life had to hit the little screen.

"John's finished," said Kane.

Annabelle jumped.

"Sorry, you looked like you were so lost in thought, I cut off the sound."

"Hook it back up."

Kane fiddled with some dials.

"We're in luck. Verne's boat will be arriving in about ten minutes."

"Pass that on to all concerned. And tell the driver to move the van down as close to the house as he safely can. And Kane? This better work."

Kane swallowed, then mumbled some words into the microphone just as the van started to move.

2

She is climbing the wooden steps leading from the dock to the house.

She sees Paul ahead of her, carrying Julia in a blanket. The baby is fussing. Poor Julia! Ever since she was born she and Paul have had to keep her hidden. She never gets to go outside to smell the air or see the sky. Even at the eugenic centers, they know the importance of taking the babies out of enclosed spaces.

She glances behind her from time to time.

Paul was right. It was all becoming too much. They kept on spotting the Watsons every time they went out for a boat ride on the lake. Even out there, they didn't dare to bring Julia up from below.

But soon none of this would be a problem. Tomorrow Herakles would come to pick Julia up.

She sees Paul putting his hand on Julia's head. He is almost in the house.

Paul carrying my baby. The thought overwhelms her in its simple profundity.

My baby.

A sob rises in her throat, but there are no tears. She wants to strike out at something.

Paul opens the door and she follows. She smells the now-familiar odor of wood beams heated by the sun. She tries to relax a little.

They are in the kitchen. She hands Paul the bottle and asks him to feed Julia.

It has been two weeks since she stopped breast-feeding. She had no choice. For the last few days, she'd felt a tight pain in her chest. The first night, she'd gotten up to nurse Julia, and Paul came in. He watched them without saying a word. My two women, he said. This was the last time, he told her. Now she had to stop. Otherwise it would be worse. And of course he was right.

Today she is looking at them the way he had looked at them.

"She's got your appetite," says Paul.

/ 383

He turns toward her. He is smiling. She suddenly wants to hit him, to snatch Julia away. To run. If she could only just cry.

"Oh, who knows. My appetite, your intelligence . . . What will any of that matter in three years?"

"She's a wonderful little girl. The best thing that's happened to us. We should be grateful, Clara. Just think of all those millions of people who can't — "

"I do think of them, but it doesn't help. Let's go to bed," she adds, leaving the kitchen brusquely.

She does not understand why she is so angry with him.

"Let me change her," she says in a sharper tone than she'd intended.
"If you want to."

He hands the child to her.

She carefully washes Julia with liquid soap and cotton, then sprinkles on talcum power — she must remember to buy some cream — and, instead of a diaper, which are impossible to find in stores, she covers the child with a napkin.

Julia babbles happily, plays with the rattle that Tim gave her. She puts it in her mouth, which makes her drool.

She attaches the napkin with a Band-Aid, then puts Julia's pajamas on her and tucks her into bed.

She watches Paul kiss the child. The rage is disappearing as quickly as it appeared. Now she feels a wave of tenderness for Paul. She wants him to take her in his arms without being asked.

The weather is mild. Paul is on the balcony reading Kess Sherman's novel, which she gave him for his birthday. Tim managed to find it for her.

She is lying naked on the sheets, watching the red reflection of the setting sun in the mirror.

She examines her body. Her breasts are less sore, and the nipples are less pronounced. The bulge in her stomach has almost disappeared, but it doesn't look as it did before. She feels it more than she sees it.

She remembers her pregnancy. She would sit for hours in this room, watching, every day, as her belly grew. Time meant nothing. It might have gone on for months, or for years. Her only worries came when Paul was away for Socrates business. Both knew that at any time he might be picked up by the FBBS. They had planned for that. The Network would take her someplace safe, someplace she could have the baby.

Each time Paul came back there was the wonder of reunion. Each second was a victory over absence, over death. They made love and talked about Julia.

All across the United States, the Network passed the news that Paul Verne and Clara Hastings had had a baby girl. The first child born to a Bio. It was an important event, and Julia was an important symbol for the millions of people fighting to regain the freedom of their bodies. A message of congratulations got to them from the leaders of RUT. Even before her birth, Julia was a celebrity, a flag-carrier for a cause.

She was not entirely happy about that. Paul needed to explain to her over and over that they couldn't escape fate: Julia's birth was an event.

She doesn't care. She dreams of a future in which Julia can have a normal childhood. In truth, as she knows, there is no other child like Julia.

She remembers the first time she held Julia: her wonder at the nails, the hands that right away knew how to hold, the mouth that searched for the breast. Watching her feed, rolling her finger through the child's hair — she will remember these.

The decision to separate. There is no choice.

For her it will be like death.

She would cry but her eyes are dry. Paul is putting down Sherman's novel. He gets up and comes into the room.

"Don't turn on the light," she murmurs. "Come lie down next to me."

He takes her in his arms, holds her with all his might.

Then, finally, she can cry. She cries with all her soul. She covers Paul's face with tears. She feels his arousal against her, and takes hold of his sex. Take me, Paul. I need you so much.

He stops moving. She wants more. He rolls over on his back. She straddles him and guides him into her. She closes upon him. She hears herself groan. Oh, God.

"Ssshhh!" he hisses suddenly, grabbing her wrists.

"What? What is it? It must be Julia — "

"No. Listen."

A low purr is coming through the open window. A motor.

"A boat just landed at the dock. Get dressed. Hurry," he adds, pushing her almost violently.

Terrified, she dresses quickly — jeans, white shirt, sneakers. She runs down to Julia's room. Someone is knocking at the front door. Her heart is pounding. She picks Julia up and covers her with a blanket. Paul is talking with someone in the entranceway. His voice sounds normal. She goes to see, taking Julia with her.

/ 385

It's Tim. Thank God! But Paul is standing next to him, holding a weapon.

"Herakles! What are — "

The big man goes to her and kisses her swiftly on the mouth, leaving her momentarily voiceless.

"I just wanted to surprise you," he says jovially. "I thought I'd come spend a few days at Rocky Roost. Plenty of time for us to catch up."

A few days? Something is wrong. They were supposed to come for Julia tomorrow.

"Hey, Paul, don't you think this calls for a little something from your wine cellar? I could use a pick-me-up."

Paul lifts the trapdoor under the stairs and disappears. Tim turns to her, winks, and before she can do anything, takes Julia. She wants to say something, but stops. His wink. He is trying to warn her.

Just then Paul reappears halfway through the trapdoor.

"Come," he says firmly.

Tim heads toward him carrying Julia.

She follows them.

She trots to keep up, breathing hard.

Tim tells her that the FBBS have surrounded the house and that cameras are recording everything. She knows who is in charge of the operation: Annabelle Weaver. That woman saw her with Julia, saw her making love with Paul.

She is afraid.

She has trouble seeing Tim, who is carrying Julia in a blanket. Beams from the flashlight illuminate intermittently. She hears Paul's footsteps behind her. He urges her on every time she slows down.

The tunnel goes on and on.

Finally, there's light. Tim stops.

"Shit," he hisses. "They're using searchlights."

He hands the child to her, signals she is not to move, and moves cautiously toward the exit.

She holds her child against her breast. The baby fusses. Just so she doesn't start to cry. Paul comes up quietly and holds them both.

"I love you," he murmurs.

Julia whines a little.

"Is she hungry?" he asks.

"No, just fussing."

"Oh."

Please, God.

Tears are streaming down her cheeks. She hasn't stopped crying since Paul held her. A sob ripples through her. She feels Paul's hold tightening.

"We've got a slim chance," she hears someone say.

Tim has come back. She has trouble understanding what he's saying.

"The searchlights are all pointed at the house. The dock isn't lit. We'll have to run."

He is reaching out for Julia. No! She won't let him have her. She pulls back instinctively. At least she should hold the child if she has to die.

"Be reasonable," he tells her softly.

She feels Tim taking Julia from her. She lets her go. She wants to scream.

Her heart is a block of ice.

Herakles adjusts the blanket around the child, takes a deep breath, and sprints out of the cave.

"Run!" yells Paul.

She begins to run as fast as she can, faster than she knew she could.

Now she sees clearly. Tim is carrying Julia. Farther ahead, against the dock, is his boat. Forty feet beyond that is theirs.

She hears cries behind them. She tries to run even faster.

"They've seen us!" yells Paul. "I'll cover you!"

What did he say? Suddenly it is daylight. They've turned the searchlights on them.

She hears rifle bursts.

An explosion.

A cry.

Tim jumps with Julia into the boat. Julia is safe.

Where's Paul? She turns.

He is running toward her, bent over. Things hiss past, like large insects. She just has a few feet to go to reach Julia. Tim is yelling her name.

"Clara!"

Suddenly, she sees Paul stumble. She screams. She can't. She lifts her arm. He raises his head and yells at her. Thank God!

"Paul," she murmurs.

Something pushes her. Around her, darkness.

3

"I am a Bio. By creating this child, I have succeeded in taking hold of the shadow my life has been from birth just as it was about to disappear forever. It is as if I can finally read some message from out of the black night of my origins. I sometimes think about the people who lived in Pompeii and were engulfed in lava. Someone got the idea of pouring plaster into the molds formed by the hardened volcanic ash, so that he could create ghosts of them. I wonder what he thought when he first saw the expressions on the faces of these men, women, and children at the moment they were consumed in hot ash. Some had died in their sleep, others crying out in horror. The earth's fire suspended them in their last moment. Before the plaster, one slip and their traces would have turned to dust. That is what it was like for me. With Julia, I have found an essential part of myself, just when it was going to turn to dust.

"I do not think humanity will survive in Bios. Within two artificial generations, maybe three, all human traces transmitted by a mother's womb will have disappeared. Humanity won't be human any longer. It will be biological, but not human. Julia gave me my humanity. She brought me in from the outside. I carried her, but she gave birth to me. She brought life and she brought me to life.

"I carried all that in me with her, our daughter. It took form and become clear the more I felt alive in her. 'Take everything,' you told me, and now I know what you meant, even though you may not have known it yourself. You were letting me take life. And now you want to take her away from me?"

By a dim light — a flashlight wrapped in a handkerchief — Verne caresses Clara's face. They are on board the *Aleph*. She seems to be asleep. She has lost a great deal of blood, but he managed to stop the hemorrhaging and he knows she will live. The bullet struck her ribs. Had it gone a fraction of an inch to the right, she would have died.

Verne climbs to the deck. He nearly lost everything — Clara, Julia — and he knew it would be a long road before they would all be together again. His heart tightens.

He feels the boat's automatic steering system adjusting to the coordinates he has programmed in. They have to stay on course if they are going to make it to Skunk Island. There they will scuttle the boat, then spend the night in the cave he prepared with Herakles's help. That is where the Network will come for them. Thank heavens it was too dark for the FBBS helicopters to give chase. And that the *Aleph* was specially constructed to resist radar detection.

Verne enjoys the feel of the wind whipping past. He remembers what Clara said to him last night on the terrace, when they talked about separating from Julia. About Pompeii and those figures of shadow.

Hate has done far too much.

Time to change perspective, to think no longer that any form of life — even as small as a retrovirus — is an enemy to life. Human civilization, with all its magnificent forms of expression, is adding only a page to the history of Earth.

We must all learn how to remember, to imagine that the Sacred Fire retrovirus is something we have somehow forgotten. The path to explore is behind us. Joe Milner knew living with Sacred Fire meant recognizing its place among us. Refusing evil and choosing good.

There is our choice: remember life or become extinct.

"Turn to dust," Clara had said.

Sacred Fire is creation's revenge on a humanity that has forgotten it.

Verne knows it is time to trim the sails. In the night, the long silhouette of the shore stretches out ahead.

List of Principal Abbreviations

AD	ASP Discharge
AS	ASP Supervision
ASP	Anti-Sex Program
APU	Artificial Placentation Unit
CAE	Center for Applied Eugenics
FBBS	Federal Bureau of Biological Supervision
MID	Military Intelligence Division
MLP	Movement for Liberation from Pregnancy
NOX	Non-Operational ASP
NPACPH	National Political Action Committee for Public Health
RUT	Women for a Return to the Uterus
SF	Spermatic Fever, or Sacred Fire
SFV	Sacred Fire Virus
SH	Special Hospitals
WoMLiP	Women's Movement for Liberation from Pregnancy